SCANDALOUS

What Reviewers Say About Kris Bryant's Work

EF5, *Novella in* **Stranded Hearts**

"In *EF5* there is destruction and chaos but I adored it because I can't resist anything with a tornado in it. They fascinate me, and the way Alyssa and Emerson work together, even though Alyssa has no obligation to do so, means they have a life changing experience that only strengthens the instant attraction they shared."—*LESBIreviewed*

Home

"*Home* is a very sweet second-chance romance that will make you smile. It is an angst-less joy, perfect for a bad day."—*Hsinju's Lit Log*

Scent

"Oh. Kris Bryant. Once again you've given us a beautiful comfort read to help us escape all that 2020 has thrown at us. This series featuring the senses has been a pleasure to read. …I think what makes Bryant's books so readable is the way she builds the reader's interest in her mains before allowing them to interact. This is a sweet and happy sigh kind of read. Perfect for these chilly winter nights when you want to escape the world and step into a caramel infused world where HEAs really do come true."—*Late Night Lesbian Reads*

Lucky

"The characters—both main and secondary, including the furry ones—are wonderful (I loved coming across Piper and Shaylie from Falling), there's just the right amount of angst and the sexy scenes are really hot. It's Kris Bryant, you guys, no surprise there."—*Jude in the Stars*

"This book has everything you need for a sweet romance. The main characters are beautiful and easy to fall in love with, even with their little quirks and flaws. The settings (Vail and Denver, Colorado) are perfect for the story, and the romance itself is satisfying, with just enough angst to make the book interesting. …This is the perfect novel to read on a warm, lazy summer day, and I recommend it to all romance lovers."—*Rainbow Reflections*

Tinsel

"This story was the perfect length for this cute romance. What made this especially endearing were the relationships Jess has with her best friend, Mo, and her mother. You cannot go wrong by purchasing this cute little nugget. A really sweet romance with a cat playing cupid."—*Bookvark*

Against All Odds—*(co-authored with Maggie Cummings and M. Ullrich)*

"*Against All Odds* by Kris Bryant, Maggie Cummings and M. Ullrich is an emotional and captivating story about being able to face a tragedy head on and move on with your life, learning to appreciate the simple things we take for granted and finding love where you least expect it."—*Lesbian Review*

"I started reading the book trying to dissect the writing and ended up forgetting all about the fact that three people were involved in writing it because the story just grabbed me by the ears and dragged me along for the ride. ...[A] really great romantic suspense that manages both parts of the equation perfectly. This is a book you won't be able to put down."—*C-Spot Reviews*

"*Against All Odds* is equal parts thriller and romance, the balance between action and love, fast and slow pace makes this novel a very entertaining read."—*Lez Review Books*

Temptation

"This book has a great first line. I was hooked from the start. There was so much to like about this story, though. The interactions. The tension. The jealousy. I liked how Cassie falls for Brooke's son before she ever falls for Brooke. I love a good forbidden love story."—*Bookvark*

"This book is an emotional roller coaster that you're going to get swept away in. Let it happen...just bring the tissues and the vino and enjoy the ride."—*Les Rêveur*

"You can always count on Bryant to write endearing and layered characters, even in stories like this one, when most of the angst comes from the not-so-simple act of falling in love."—*Jude in the Stars*

"This book is a bag of kettle corn—sweet, savory and you won't stop until you finish it in one binge-worthy sitting. *Temptation* is a fun, fluffy and ultimately satisfying lesbian romance that hits all the right notes."—*To Be Read Book Reviews*

Falling

"This is a story you don't want to pass on. A fabulous read that you will have a hard time putting down. Maybe don't read it as you board your plane though. This is an easy 5 stars!"—*Romantic Reader Blog*

"This was a nice, romantic read. There is enough romantic tension to keep the plot moving, and I enjoyed the supporting characters' and their romance as much as the main plot."—*Kissing Backwards*

Listen

"[A] sweet romance with a touch of angst and lots of music."—*C-Spot Reviews*

"If you suffer from anxiety, know someone who suffers from anxiety, or want an insight to how it may impact on someone's daily life, I urge you to pick this book up. In fact, I urge all readers who enjoy a good lesbian romance to grab a copy."—*Love Bytes Reviews*

"If you're looking for a little bit of fluffy(ish), light romance in your life, give this one a listen. The characters' passion for music (and each other) is heartwarming, and I was rooting for them the entire book."—*Kissing Backwards*

"This is a contemporary romance that starts out as a slow-burn, but once the two main characters finally connect, it quickly becomes a very steamy novel."—*Rainbow Reflections*

Forget Me Not

"Told in the first person, from Grace's point of view, we are privy to Grace's inner musings and her vulnerabilities. ...Bryant crafts clever wording to infuse Grace with a sharp-witted personality, which clearly covers her insecurities. ...This story is filled with loving familial interactions, caring friends, romantic interludes and tantalizing sex scenes. The dialogue, both among the characters and within Grace's head, is refreshing, original, and sometimes comical. *Forget Me Not* is a fresh perspective on a romantic theme, and an entertaining read."—*Lambda Literary Review*

"[I]t just hits the right note all the way. ...[A] very good read if you are looking for a sweet romance."—*Lez Review Books*

Shameless—*Writing as Brit Ryder*

"[Kris Bryant] has a way of giving insight into the other main protagonist by using a few clever techniques and involving the secondary characters to add back-stories and extra pieces of important information. The pace of the book was excellent, it was never rushed but I was never bored or waiting for a chapter to finish...this epilogue made my heart swell to the point I almost lunged off the sofa to do a happy dance."—*Les Rêveur*

Not Guilty—*Writing as Brit Ryder*

"Exquisite! I loved this story! I have heard so many good things about it and it did not disappoint as it was so much more than

I expected. Kris Bryant, writing as her alter-ego was absolutely brilliant. The story is hot, passionate and filled with drama making a really exciting read. You can really feel the passion between Claire and Emery, that instant attraction between them was just perfect."—*LESBIreviewed*

"Kris Bryant, aka Brit Ryder, promised this story would be hot and she didn't lie! …I love that the author is Kris Bryant who, under that name, writes romance with a lot of emotions. As Brit Ryder, she lets chemistry take the lead and it's pretty amazing too."
—*Jude in the Stars*

Whirlwind Romance

"Ms. Bryant's descriptions were written with such passion and colorful detail that you could feel the tension and the excitement along with the characters…"—*Inked Rainbow Reviews*

Taste

"*Taste* is a student/teacher romance set in a culinary school. If the premise makes you wonder whether this book will make you want to eat something tasty, the answer is: yes."—*Lesbian Review*

Jolt—*Lambda Literary Award Finalist*

"[*Jolt*] is a magnificent love story. Two women hurt by their previous lovers and each in their own way trying to make sense out of life and times. When they meet at a gay and lesbian friendly summer camp, they both feel as if lightening has struck. This is so beautifully involving, I have already reread it twice. Amazing!"
—*Rainbow Book Reviews*

Touch

"The sexual chemistry in this book is off the hook. Kris Bryant writes my favorite sex scenes in lesbian romantic fiction."—*Les Rêveur*

Breakthrough

"It's hilariously funny, romantic and oh so sexy. ...But it is the romance between Kennedy and Brynn that stole my heart. The passion and emotion in the love scenes surpassed anything Kris Bryant has written before. I loved it."—*Kitty Kat's Book Review Blog*

"Kris Bryant has written several enjoyable contemporary romances, and *Breakthrough* is no exception. It's interesting and clearly well-researched, giving us information about Alaska and issues like poaching and conservation in a way that's engaging and never comes across as an info dump. She also delivers her best character work to date, going deeper with Kennedy and Brynn than we've seen in previous stories. If you're a fan of Kris Bryant, you won't want to miss this book, and if you're a fan of romance in general, you'll want to pick it up, too."—*Lambda Literary Review*

By the Author

Jolt

Whirlwind Romance

Just Say Yes

Taste

Forget-Me-Not

Shameless (writing as Brit Ryder)

Touch

Breakthrough

Against All Odds
(written with M. Ullrich and Maggie Cummings)

Listen

Falling

Tinsel

Temptation

Lucky

Home

Scent

Not Guilty (writing as Brit Ryder)

Always

Forever

EF5 (Stranded Hearts Novella Collection)

Serendipity

Catch

Cherish

Perfect

Dreamer

Gaze

Scandalous

SCANDALOUS

by
Kris Bryant

2025

SCANDALOUS

ISBN 13: 978-1-63679-874-5

THIS TRADE PAPERBACK ORIGINAL IS PUBLISHED BY
BOLD STROKES BOOKS, INC.
P.O. BOX 249
VALLEY FALLS, NY 12185

FIRST EDITION: NOVEMBER 2025

CREDITS
EDITORS: ASHLEY TILLMAN AND CINDY CRESAP
PRODUCTION DESIGN: SUSAN RAMUNDO
COVER DESIGN BY DEB B

Acknowledgments

This was a hard book for me to finish because too many things were happening at once, and life became overwhelming. I knew I was going to finish, I wanted to finish, but I needed more time. Trying to be creative when it feels like we're rolling back into the past is hard. Will our books still be available to our readers? Will I be able to find steady ground to build my stories?

The answer is yes. I love this book because so much of what I enjoy is on the page. A mini-animal rescue? Yes, please. Sign me up! It's the ultimate job for me. Helping animals survive and thrive would be ideal. That's the great thing about being a writer. If I can't have it, I can write about it. Thank you to Bold Strokes Books for giving me time to finish this at my own pace.

Shout-out to Stacy's cousins, Tristen and Leigh, for letting me get up close and personal with their mini-Highland rescues and learn about the ins and outs of farm life. Massive thank you to the real boss, Ashley, for pushing me to write a meatier story. It's been over ten years and our writer-editor duo is still going strong. All the love.

I will always be thankful and appreciative of the friendships I've made in this community. My lifelong nuggets, my writing buddies KB Draper and HS, my new friends, my old friends, and everyone who encourages me to continue to write. Deb's always given me space to create but stays close when I need her. That's a delicate balance that a lot of people don't understand so I am fortunate that she's in my life. And now I have baby Lincoln. And a car seat in my car. Who am I??

Most importantly, thank you to the readers for reading our books, dropping reviews, and encouraging other readers to give our books a try. You're the best. You make our dreams come true.

Dedication

To my Patreon family
because we are doing great things for animals

CHAPTER ONE

Just because you found it in the grass, doesn't mean it's yours." Amelia put her hands on her hips like a scolding mother would do with a petulant child in the throes of a tantrum. She huffed out a sigh and brushed the curly, reddish-brown hair out of Pippin's soulful eyes. She softened her stance and gave him a quick hug. He liked her hugs, and the moment she felt him relax against her, she grabbed the crushed juice box from his mouth victoriously. "Ha! Sucker." She held the slobbering mess over her head feeling dots of spittle spray her arms and instantly regretted the move. "Well, this is gross." She threw the litter in the bin outside his stall and held out a carrot for him to chew instead. "It was probably that little boy who screamed the entire tour yesterday."

Pippin stared at her while happily munching on his carrot. Either hearing her voice, or smelling the carrot, Patches, another red mini highland rescue with a unique, brown patch of long fur on her back, trotted into her side of the barn looking for treats. She lacked Pippin's curls and her horns were smaller, but she was just as precious.

Amelia held up an orange stalk and leaned over the railing that separated the males from the females when Patches got close. "Don't worry, sweet girl. I didn't forget about you." Patches snorted a thank you and left the barn with the treat firmly clamped in her muzzle. Snacks were a luxury as the grants and donations had thinned over the last six months. She wasn't on high alert yet but was getting close.

Amelia's shoulders sagged when the soft jingle of an incoming phone call filled her ears. She took a deep breath before she tapped her knuckle against her AirPod. "Mizzou Moos. This is Amelia. How may I help you?"

"Sis! What's up?"

Hearing her sister's voice was a nice surprise, but a flutter of panic tapped lightly against Amelia's heart. Whenever Zoey, her identical twin, called, it meant something big was happening. They texted regularly, but phone calls were scarce because Zoey worked in television and Amelia ran a miniature livestock sanctuary that had grown over the last three years. Their schedules were opposite. Zoey was on set until late in the evenings and Amelia was up before dawn getting breakfast ready for six mini cows, two mini donkeys, pygmy goats, babydoll sheep, chickens, and two faithful dogs who were dumped on the farm when they were puppies. There were a handful of cats who cleared the barn of mice and other rodents. Amelia always made sure they had a hearty kibble breakfast.

"Hey. Just hanging out with some cute gingers," Amelia said.

"Maybe one day you'll find one who doesn't snot all over your clothes or try to trip you," Zoey said. Amelia laughed at the memory of Mimsey, the smallest rescue mini highland cow, knocking down Zoey hard the last time she visited.

"Hollywood's softened you. You need another summer at the farm to toughen you up," Amelia said. It had been almost six months since she last saw Zoey. When they were little, they were inseparable. Even though they had their own rooms growing up, they slept in each other's beds up until college. When Zoey moved to Los Angeles after graduation to pursue her movie star dream, Amelia encouraged her and helped her pack. Her love for Zoey outweighed the selfishness of wanting her always by her side. "Are you calling because you're coming to visit?" Amelia heart wobbled and sank when she heard the slight hesitation and deep breath before her sister answered.

"I'm calling to tell you I have an audition for *Bounty Hunter 2* with Alec Montgomery."

"That's great news!" Amelia squealed with excitement. *Bounty Hunter* was last fall's blockbuster hit, and Alec Montgomery was the fastest rising star in Hollywood. "Oh, my God! Tell me everything."

"They are looking for somebody to play his sister who gets kidnapped."

"The sister? Why not the love interest?" Amelia asked.

"That's already been filled. But the sister is really a big part. She gets kidnapped, but it's a lot of on-screen time. I get to fight, go through emotional stuff, and fight some more. It's the opportunity I've been waiting for. I can finally show off my acting skills," Zoey said.

"Listen, *Thirteen Witches* shows off your acting skills, too. Don't sell yourself short. The episode where you got stuck in a time loop showcased your ability so well. You laughed, you cried, you got angry. You nailed it. I think that was the episode that made you a fan favorite." Pride, not jealousy, filled her heart whenever a neighbor stopped her in town to congratulate her on having such a talented sister. Zoey was living her dream.

"Oh, don't get me wrong. I owe the series everything. It's just nice to be recognized outside of it. I don't want to get stuck where the only acting job I get is as a witch," Zoey said.

"Stop it. You're amazing. You always have been." Amelia walked out of the barn and squinted as the hot, blazing sun momentarily blinded her. Summers in Missouri were miserable. She wanted to head inside the main house to cool off, but she still had to check on the two mini donkeys in the small barn. She acquired them last week from a rundown mine in New Mexico and was slowly introducing them to the goats. She wiped her hands on the rag hanging from her back pocket and tugged the brim of her Mizzou Moos ball cap lower on her forehead. "It's time the rest of the world knew. You're going to nail that audition."

Zoey had always been the center of attention since they were children. Maybe it was Zoey's brightness that made Amelia take a step back. She didn't want to take away something her sister desperately wanted. Zoey wanted all eyes on her, and Amelia wanted whatever her sister wanted.

"I'm glad you said that." Zoey dragged out her words and paused dramatically.

"Why?" Amelia's voice came out sharper than intended.

"Hear me out before you say anything, okay?"

Amelia placed her palm on the aging wooden door of the small barn and waited for Zoey to say what was on her mind. Out-of-the-blue calls from Zoey came with a price. She rolled her tense shoulders and nervously chipped away at the dull, cracking paint around the lock with her fingernail. "Okay. I'm listening."

"I know things are hard at the rescue. I know you're struggling, and I wish I could send more, but I know a way you can make thousands of dollars for just working a few hours," Zoey said.

"Whatever this is, it sounds shady and I'm not that kind of girl." She was half-joking. Amelia knew her sister wouldn't put her in danger, but when something sounded too good to be true, it probably was. But she was still intrigued. She needed money for hay, vitamins, salt licks, protein packs, medicine, and farm necessities. The tractor needed new tires and the barn needed a bigger junction box. Those were the pressing issues. While a lot of vendors reduced fees because of the good she was doing, all of it added up to more than what she had and she was starting to stress.

"You said you would hear me out," Zoey said.

Amelia nodded even though her sister couldn't see her. "You're right. Please continue with this very not shady idea. I'm all ears."

"You know I'm appearing at the HEXPO Conference next weekend in Vegas, right? Well, it also happens to be the same time I'm supposed to audition for the movie."

"That's bad luck," Amelia said. It wasn't sinking in.

"So, I need you—no, I'm asking you to please fill in for me at the con Thursday night and Friday until I'm done with my audition," Zoey said.

Amelia's mouth dropped open at her twin's audacity. They hadn't switched places to fool people since their senior year in high school. Need pushed its way through anger, disbelief, and a held back "hell, no." She needed the money. And it wasn't hard being her sister for a day. But their lives were so different. Amelia doubted she could pull it off like she could ten years ago.

"My anxiety just hit a ten. This isn't high school or us playing a joke on Mom and Dad. I can't pull it off today. We don't share the same world. I don't know your friends or even your coworkers."

"Sis, you know the show. You never miss it. You're the one who finds flaws when our writers don't," Zoey said.

"I don't know the actors. The minute I share space with them, they'll know." Amelia said.

"They're not going to know. We look the same, we sound the same, and you know all the gossip about everyone. We can go over every single cast member before the con. Just so you know, they stagger the actors so you won't be with the cast the entire time. I only need you to pose with a few fans for photos. Don't worry about talking to them. The con staff will shuffle them in for photos and immediately out. You won't have time to chat with them so it won't trip you up. According to the schedule, Friday morning there's a panel where you just show up, and in the afternoon, there's a photo shoot with four other actors with the cauldron and maybe a selfie station after that. And I'll be there Friday night and we can switch back."

"It sounds too complicated. What if somebody figures out I'm not you? We don't have the same hairstyle, wardrobe, or even voice. Listen to my voice. We don't even sound the same anymore," Amelia said.

"Your voice is higher because you're nervous. Come on, Amelia. We sound the same. You can always say you have allergies or you're getting over a cold. It'll be fine. You'll get my commission for being there and all the selfie money. You know I make a ton more working cons than I do on the show. For now, at least. I'm pretty sure the standard is forty dollars a photo. It adds up quickly, I promise," Zoey said.

Amelia knew Becks and her wife, Robbie, could run the farm for an extended weekend. Although she was nervous and didn't like crowds, getting away for a few days to be someone else sounded a little fun. She didn't want to cave quickly like she always did though. "I don't know. It sounds like stress I don't need."

"But think of the money. That'll help so much. And if I get the movie contract, I can donate more to Mizzou Moos. Plus, it'll mean more exposure for you. They'll want to know more about me and I can tell them about the rescue. People love people who save animals." Zoey was pushing all the right buttons.

"Walk me through exactly what I need to do hour by hour, day by day." Amelia winced when her sister squealed with delight.

"Fly here Wednesday so we can sync up and go over things. I can send you a ticket with my airline points. They have me flying to Vegas Thursday afternoon. There's a VIP dance party that starts at ten. Some of the crew will attend but it's not mandatory. Friday morning there's a kick-off panel. It's more for the writers but you'll have to at least be in attendance. Then the photo ops with fans. I should be there by six. You can fly home then or Saturday morning," Zoey said.

Amelia knew her staff could handle her being gone, but could she? She was right in that delicate state of introducing animals to one another and she didn't want a setback. And would Becks remember to never turn her back on Mimsey during feeding time or give Pippin extra love every morning? She would have to leave her truck for them to pick up the supplies, but then how would she get to the airport? It was a two-hour commute. There were so many things to plan and organize before she could fully commit, but for some reason, she said, "Yes."

"Great! I'll send you a ticket to fly here and you can use my ticket to get to Vegas," Zoey said.

"Look, I don't want to commit a felony so let's just book a flight under my name from there to Vegas. We'll just make sure it's the same flight in case they are expecting you at a certain time. Do you have enough points?" Amelia asked.

"Definitely. Okay, when can you get away?"

"Let me check with Becks and I'll get back to you. Nobody's going to know, are they? Like you're not telling anyone on the show what we're doing?"

"Absolutely not. We're the only ones," Zoey solemnly said.

"Isn't your agent going to know? I mean, you can't be in two places at once."

"Silvia says it's a bad idea, but she also knows it's the only way this is going to work. Don't even worry about her, though. Just send me a text so I can book your ticket. Thanks, sis. I really owe you for this."

Immediate regret and guilt replaced the excitement from thirty seconds ago. It was fun when they were kids and fooled everyone. The stakes weren't high. "Let's get through this without any issues. Then you can really owe me."

"I love you. Talk soon," Zoey said.

"I love you, too." Amelia disconnected the call and texted Becks to check her schedule. Once everything was cleared and a plan set in place, Amelia gave Zoey the green light hoping it wasn't going to be the biggest mistake of their lives.

❖

"I'm so glad you're here." Zoey hugged Amelia and pulled her into her apartment. "I'm sorry you had to take a Lyft. I'm going over the lines for the audition and didn't want to stop."

"Don't worry about it. You just stay focused on learning your lines. I didn't mind the ride at all. Beats driving in this traffic, that's for sure." Amelia dropped her bag on the beat-up leather recliner in the small living space. When Zoey said she moved, Amelia thought she meant to a bigger, nicer space. The only advantage this place had over the other one was that it was closer to the studio. "Do you need my help going over them?"

"Yes, but let's get you ready first," Zoey said. She circled Amelia like a drill sergeant inspecting her hair, her makeup, and how her clothes fit. Amelia preferred baggy and comfortable to chic and form-fitting. Zoey clucked her tongue and pulled at Amelia's shirt that was a size too big. "I can tell you're losing weight." She raised an eyebrow and continued to scrutinize Amelia. She looked at Amelia's wavy hair. "It's amazing how much the sun bleaches your hair. Don't you wear a hat?" Zoey asked.

"Sometimes the cows like to try to pull it off my head so not all the time." Amelia felt self-conscious in front of her sister and smoothed down her hair. "Why? Does it look terrible?"

Zoey pulled Amelia's hand away and gave it a reassuring squeeze. "Oh, my God, no. It looks amazing. I hate that the show makes me dye my hair dark. Apparently, it's more witchy. We can use temporary coloring that'll wash out in a week if that's okay. That way we don't have to permanently change anything about you."

"Except for hacking off a solid four inches," Amelia said. She wore it back every day so it didn't matter, but it was fun teasing her sister.

"Or you can just wear it up in a bun the whole time."

"Absolutely not. I'm just kidding. We need me to look like you as much as possible," Amelia said. This was really happening. She pressed her fist against her stomach to ease the guilt that burned inside. She was going to be her outgoing, famous sister for twenty-four hours. What if she forgot her manners and said something rude to a fan? Or worse, ignored one? Or two? Or all of them? Zoey cupped her chin and made her look at her.

"Are you overthinking this?" Zoey asked. Amelia nodded. "Don't. You're going to be better at me than I am," Zoey said.

Amelia rolled her eyes. "That's not even possible." The doorbell interrupted Amelia's new round of panic.

"I ordered pizza with lots of cheese and mushrooms. We can take this time to review the cast and crew. I can tell you if we're friends, frenemies, or enemies," Zoey said. She grabbed the pizza and pulled two plates from the cabinet. Amelia's stomach rumbled as the smell of burnt cheese and marinara sauce filled the room. She grabbed a piece and plopped down on the couch. Zoey sat beside her and pulled out her phone.

"Let's start with your friends. Who do you spend the most time with?" Amelia asked. She took a large bite and leaned closer to Zoey's phone.

"Rey, but she won't be there. Here's Olivia. She's nice and we're friendly, but we don't do much outside of the show." Zoey scrolled through more photos. "You know Dane. He's a beefcake and a massive flirt. Oh, and Dawn and I always joke about how cute Arman, the sound guy, is. She'll probably bring him up."

"What do you know about Arman?" Amelia asked.

"Not a damn thing other than he's hot and always winks at us," Zoey said.

"What about Chloe? I don't know much about her since she's so new." Amelia took a sip of her Coke. She thought about grabbing another piece of pizza but decided to wait until her stomach and her anxiety settled.

"Keep a wide berth. I don't trust her. She has bad vibes. She's the kind of person who's always looking for the next best thing, you know?" Zoey said.

They reviewed every single person who was going to be at the con until Amelia felt comfortable enough to move on.

"Come on. Let's raid my closet and gossip about the people I work with," Zoey said. She motioned for Amelia to follow her into her bedroom and opened the closet doors to reveal a wardrobe that made Amelia's jaw drop.

"Why do you have so many clothes?" Amelia thumbed through hangers of tops, pants, long elegant evening gowns, and short, flirty dresses. She pointed to the shoe rack that overflowed with strappy sandals and stilettos. "Please tell me you have ankle boots or flats?"

Zoey leaned against the doorframe. "You've been shuffling around in muck boots and Crocs far too long. It's time you remember how to walk in heels."

CHAPTER TWO

Lindsay Brooks hadn't slept in almost twenty-four hours. She stifled the yawn behind her notebook, refusing to sit down for fear that she'd fall asleep and miss Zoey Stark and Dane Fletcher's arrival at Caesar's Palace. She wanted to greet them, hand them their schedules, and head to her room to kick off her heels and slip into the marble Jacuzzi tub for a hot soak. Every minute they were late, she lost sixty seconds of relaxation before the conference unofficially began. In five hours, they were all highly encouraged to be at MGM's Thursday night VIP Party to kick off HEXPO. *Thirteen Witches* was growing in popularity, and this was shaping up to be their biggest event to date. Even though there were actors from four other television shows headlining the con, their show was the real draw of the event. She checked her watch and continued pacing the lobby glancing toward the entrance every few seconds. They should've been here by now. She checked the flights again even though she knew exactly when both landed. Their instructions were to come to the hotel immediately. This was a working gig. She wasn't sure if either of them needed security, but the conference strongly recommended it. Zoey was popular, and Dane received more fan mail than anyone else on the set. Of course, most of his fans were either teenage girls or grandmothers, but he didn't discriminate. He loved all attention.

"Lindsay, hey. Over here."

She turned to find Dane waving her over. "When did you get here?" She was perplexed and thumbed behind her at the lobby. There was no way he got past her. She was standing in the sweet spot where she could see all the entrances. "Is it just you?" She looked over his shoulder hoping to find Zoey whose flight landed before his.

"Just me. I came in on the casino side. Wait. Did you lose somebody already?" He threw his head back and laughed. "The con hasn't even started." His normally sexy voice grated on her nerves. It was probably the stress of corralling ten stars from the show who were coming in at all different times. She stared at him without cracking a smile until he held his hands up as though calling a truce. "Okay, okay. I'm sorry." He flashed her his famous smile. "What room did I get? Tell me you got me a suite?" She scoffed quietly and handed him a card holder and instructions for downloading an app for keyless entry.

He held it up with his forefinger and thumb. "Oh, fancy. A junior suite. Any other perks?" He looked at her expectantly.

"All your paperwork including your lanyard is in the packet. Wear it at all times," she said. She handed him the thick envelope. "Did you see Zoey at the airport? Her flight arrived before yours." Lindsay pulled up the flight tracker app to triple-check that it landed. Zoey getting abducted flashed in her mind, but she quickly pushed down the panic. Maybe she was getting souvenirs or freshening up in the platinum lounge before heading to Caesar's.

"No. I grabbed a cab as soon as I got off the plane," he said. She raised an eyebrow. "Well, after taking a few selfies. I mean, that's why I'm here, right?" He slid his sunglasses back on and confidently strolled away in the direction of the elevators. Lindsay suspected he was going to gamble or flirt and turned her attention back to the front doors. She breathed a sigh of relief when she saw Zoey slip into the lobby. Lindsay waved her over when they finally made eye contact.

"I was getting worried. Is everything okay?" Lindsay asked.

Zoey nodded and gave her a soft smile. Lindsay's brows furrowed for a moment. Normally, Zoey would give her a bear hug and thank her profoundly. Today Zoey shied away when Lindsay touched her forearm. Everything was definitely not okay, but Lindsay didn't press. She knew Zoey had recently broken up with her boyfriend so maybe she was late and quiet because they had another spat or she simply missed him. Lindsay couldn't understand that given that she found him to be a complete tool. When they broke up, Lindsay took great joy in taking his name off the all-access list. Now he wasn't allowed on set or at the studio.

"Okay, so here's your room information. And here are your passes and identification to get into the conference. I mean, just in case people don't recognize you." Lindsay watched Zoey look at the contents carefully. "Do you have any questions?"

"What's tonight again?" Zoey asked.

Lindsay leaned over Zoey's shoulder and pointed at the event on her personal schedule. "The VIP party. You and the cast will be roped off. It's just a chance to hang with the crowd but not really hang with them. It's not highlighted so you're not expected to be there, but it would be nice and the fans would love it if they saw you." Zoey smelled like fresh daisies and linen. Very different and very nice. Lindsay took a step back and forced a smile. What was happening? Her body was responding to being in the same space as Zoey and that had never happened before.

"But it's not mandatory, right?" Zoey asked.

Lindsay tilted her head and bit her bottom lip. "It's not. You can do whatever you want. Just make sure you're at the venue at nine tomorrow morning." She touched Zoey's arm. Yep. Still tiny tingles when her fingertips touched her skin. It was slightly unnerving. They worked long hours on the set together and the last thing Lindsay needed was a crush on one of the actors. "I'm going to head to my room. Let me know if you need anything. You know my number."

"What floor are you on?" Zoey asked.

"We're all in the tower. On the fourteenth floor," Lindsay said.

"Great. I'll follow you if you don't mind," Zoey said.

"Do you need any help with anything?" Lindsay asked.

"I just have one suitcase and this bag. I'm good. Thank you though," Zoey said.

Zoey always accepted help. Even if it was just carrying her backpack while she carried her purse. She was never rude about it, but she always said yes. "We're this way." Lindsay pointed to the casino floor. She leaned in closer so Zoey could hear her. "They do this so we'll be tempted to gamble to and from our rooms. There's no way around it."

"This is all so overwhelming. Thankfully, I don't gamble," Zoey said.

"Not anymore, you mean," Lindsay said. She glanced at Zoey and noticed the death grip she had on her suitcase handle and, how she clutched her bag closer to her chest. Maybe that night of gambling she'd cleaned up wasn't a fluke. What if Zoey actually had a problem?

"Uh, that's right. Not anymore," Zoey said. "Wow. This is quite the trek just to get to the elevators."

"You'll have to be careful with your time. It took me eight minutes to get from my room to the lobby. It's going to take longer now that it's almost the weekend," Lindsay said. She punched the button twice. "How has your time off been? Anything new and exciting?" Small talk was safe, and she knew Zoey was a talker.

"I've been fighting a head cold for the last week" She pointed to her face.

"That explains why your voice sounds a little different," Lindsay said. She held her hand in front of her for Zoey to enter the elevator first and swore Zoey blushed. They moved to the back as a large group of people pushed their way through, apologizing at their oversized luggage. A teenager about fourteen squealed.

"Oh, my God. Are you Zoey Stark? Mom, that's Zoey from *Thirteen Witches*."

Lindsay felt Zoey tense next to her. "I am."

"Can I get a selfie? Please?"

"Yes, of course."

The elevator stopped on eight and before the doors shut, the excited fan leaned close to Zoey for the selfie. "Thank you so much! I can't wait for the con to start. This is my second one." The teen bolted from the elevator and waved as the doors closed.

"Well, that was fun," Lindsay said. It never got old seeing how their show impacted people.

"It's a great show. I'm glad it's taking off," Zoey said.

"Same. I like knowing we have another season slated," Lindsay said. The elevator opened to their floor. "We're this way. I'm right next door to you." A panicky feeling crept into Lindsay's thoughts. "And Olivia is on the other side of you. Dane is down there." She motioned up and down the hall. "We have all the rooms from here to the very end. If you need anything, just knock or call," Lindsay said. Why was she being so weird right now? She'd worked with Zoey for the last two years.

"Okay, thank you. Do we meet here or down in the lobby for the VIP thing?" Zoey asked.

"The lobby is fine. Why don't you rest up and we'll see you later?"

Zoey nodded, gave her an awkward smile, and disappeared behind her door. Lindsay pushed her own door open, kicked off her very impractical high heels, and peeled off her blazer. As alluring as the bed was, the monstrous bathtub was too enticing to ignore. She turned the water on and kicked off the rest of her clothes. Vegas was too hot to wear this many layers and she vowed to keep her future outfits professional, but light. She unclipped her auburn hair and massaged her scalp with her fingertips while she waited for the tub to fill. The hot water sent chills across her skin when she stepped in it. When her body was fully submerged, she turned on the jets to massage her weary body. A Jacuzzi tub was on her list of must-haves when she finally bought her own place. She wanted to relax longer, but knew she needed a nap before tonight.

Vegas always destroyed her self-care routine. She didn't sleep enough, didn't stay hydrated, drank too much alcohol, and ate too much. Every trip, she tried to do better, and every trip, she failed. She dried off and slipped into bed without putting her pajamas on. There was something decadent about sleeping naked in the softest bamboo sheets she'd ever felt on her body.

As exhausted as she was, she couldn't stop thinking about Zoey. Why did Zoey seem not like herself today? And why did Lindsay have such a physical reaction to her? Was it because Zoey was single now? Zoey wasn't even queer so why did it matter now? Oh, God. Was she crushing on a straight woman? Lindsay had always found Zoey attractive but today seemed extra. Zoey's lips seemed a bit fuller than usual, and she wasn't wearing any lipstick. Did she get Botox injections? That needed to be approved and Lindsay didn't remember seeing an approval form circulate through Meador Entertainment. And Zoey had a nice golden tan which was unusual since the makeup team always had to put a layer of sunscreen on her face and arms, per her request, because she didn't want to wrinkle or get skin cancer.

Lindsay looked at the clock. If she fell asleep now, she'd get four solid hours she desperately needed. She wouldn't get back to the room until well after midnight and she had to be up and at the conference by eight. She set her alarm on her phone and willed her body to sleep. She tossed and turned restlessly before she did the one thing she knew would relax her body enough to fall asleep. She slipped her hand between her legs and gently rubbed her slit. When an image of Zoey popped into her head, she mentally pushed it aside and thought of the hottest queer movie star on screen instead. The actress was blond with long legs and piercing blue eyes. A bit femme for Lindsay's taste but thinking about her was building her up for the perfect release. She quickened her pace and moved her forefinger quickly back and forth over her clit. Nothing was pushing her over the edge though. She thought about the actress's hands touching her and her lips making a trail over her body, biting and sucking all her sensitive spots, but she couldn't finish even though she was right on the precipice of her orgasm. She teetered on that edge of wanting to finish but not wanting this feeling to end. She tensed her muscles and moved faster and harder and when her brain thrust a picture of Zoey in the elevator with their shoulders touching, Lindsay didn't shut it out. Instead, she pictured Zoey's mouth on her and came hard and fast. She sprawled and waited for her heartbeat and breathing to normalize. She fell asleep before the guilt could set in.

Chapter Three

I should've tried this dress on before I packed it," Amelia hissed at her sister over FaceTime.

"I love that dress. Here, show me. Put the phone on the dresser and stand back so I can see it," Zoey said. Amelia pulled at the plunging neckline trying to hide her cleavage as much as possible and took several steps back. "Stop it. You look hot. How are your boobs bigger than mine?"

"I like cheese. And bread. And carbs. That's why," she said.

"Pull your shoulders back. You're standing like you've never worn a dress or heels before. Speaking of which, when was the last time you wore a dress?" Zoey asked.

Amelia stuck her tongue out at her and pulled her shoulders back as directed. It only made her bustline even more visible and made her more uncomfortable. Why did she agree to do this? She fussed with the material until she was satisfied she was covered up enough. "Last year at Christina's wedding. I wore three-inch heels and hated every minute of wearing them."

"Then two-inch heels will feel like flats. You'll be fine. Just think of all the hay and protein packs you can buy with this gig," Zoey said.

"What should I do with my hair?" Amelia asked. She brought the phone into the bathroom and mimicked pulling it up, leaving it down, and then a hairdo that was half up and down. "I only have about a half an hour before I have to be in the lobby which means I really only have twenty minutes. What do you want me to do?"

"I want you to embrace being me. I want you to have fun and wave at fans and drink champagne and maybe even dance a little. Not that there's anything wrong with being you, but right now you're trying to be me and that's what I would do. Leave your hair down. It looks beautiful. And find some double stick tape. Ask Lindsay if you can't find any in the suitcase. She has everything," Zoey said.

"She's right next to me. We have communicating doors," Amelia said. She pulled the phone close to her face. "How's my makeup? I don't know if it's too much or not enough."

"Sis, you look great. Seriously. You're going to be just fine. Have a drink or two and then go back to the room. If you're not comfortable, then tell Lindsay you have a headache or you don't feel well. It's not mandatory," Zoey said.

"Zoey Stark most definitely would be at this party. Oh, did I tell you that I took my first selfie with a fan? In the elevator this afternoon." Amelia smirked at her. Zoey laughed, delighted.

"Being in the spotlight is pretty cool," Zoey said.

Amelia shrugged. "Maybe the perks are cool. You've always loved the attention. I was never one for it."

Zoey rolled her eyes. "Don't stress. Everything will be fine. Just remember that people are always watching even when you think they aren't. They will post on socials and tag you and the show. Try not to do anything embarrassing like tug on your boobs and accidentally flash the world."

"I should double my fee. Pay me more not to embarrass you." Amelia put her forefinger on her chin as though contemplating the increase even though she knew Zoey donated as much as she could to Mizzou Moos. Zoey wasn't making the kind of money most people assumed actors made on successful television shows. She knew Silvia was working out a fat contract with Meador Entertainment for the next season since Zoey was only slated for two. If Silvia didn't work some real magic and get Zoey the raise she deserved, Amelia was going to come unglued.

"Ha ha. Okay, I have to go but you're going to kill it. Send me a message if you need me for anything. You'll be fine. We've done this a billion times before," Zoey said.

"For fun and games. This is a whole different level," Amelia said. Doubt was blooming inside her head and weighing in her heart. "If this gets out…"

"Don't worry so much. You know me better than anyone else," Zoey said.

"Wait. Don't people already know you have a twin? I mean, haven't you talked to people about me? Like your co-workers? Hey, for Christmas I'm going back home to visit my twin."

"People don't talk like that. I say sister. I'm going to visit my sister. Although I should say my older sister," Zoey said.

"By two minutes." Amelia snorted. "Okay, break a leg tomorrow. I'm sure it'll be a late night for me. Let me know when you're getting in."

"I love you." Zoey normally exaggerated the words for fun, but this time she sounded sincere. The anxiety Amelia felt disappeared. Her sister needed her and she was going to suck it up and be the best Zoey she could be. As Amelia.

"I love you, too." Amelia disconnected the call and quickly spritzed her hair. The dress was still a problem so she dug around in the suitcase looking for the double-sided tape only to come up empty-handed. "Shit."

She unlatched the adjourning door and tapped lightly on Lindsay's door. She took a step back when she heard Lindsay unlock it. Amelia gasped with delight when it opened. This couldn't possibly be the same woman who handed her the convention schedule and walked her to her room earlier today. That woman was attractive but reserved. The woman standing in front of her was stunning. Amelia gave her an obvious up-and-down.

"You look amazing." Did Zoey say things like that? Probably something hipper. "That dress is hot." Lindsay was wearing a taupe, form-fitting dress that hit above the knee. The delicate spaghetti straps showed off an expanse of smooth, flawless skin. Toned calves and high heels made Amelia's heart flutter. She stumbled over her words. "I mean, I'm sorry, uh, I…" She took a deep breath. Round number two. "I'm hoping you have what I need." Fuck. That sounded suggestive. The wide-eyed look Lindsay shot her told her it sounded as bad as she thought. "I mean, I need your help."

Lindsay took a step back. "Of course. Come on in. What can I help you with?"

Amelia pointed to her boobs. "These keep trying to fall out and I thought maybe you had some tape or a solution?" Lindsay's eyes flickered everywhere but Amelia's cleavage.

"Um, sure. Hang tight. I have some in my travel bag," she said. Amelia watched her walk away and couldn't help but admire Lindsay's curves and toned legs. The dress complemented everything about her—the auburn hair, her fair skin, and her hourglass figure. Zoey had showed her a photo in their prep session, but the picture did not show how attractive Lindsay was. When she returned, it was Amelia's turn to look everywhere but at Lindsay.

"Here you go." Lindsay handed Amelia a roll of tape. Amelia felt an embarrassing heat blossom across her cheeks and neck at having to ask for help so soon. And about her boobs. "Is there any way you can help me with this?" she asked. Lindsay quirked her brows and blinked several times. "I'm just a klutz at doing it myself. I mean, if it makes you feel uncomfortable…" she trailed off. "It's okay. I got it." Amelia turned to head back to her room when she felt soft fingers stop her.

"I don't mind at all. Come here," Lindsay said. She waved Amelia to the floor lamp in the corner of the room. "We need good light." Amelia held her breath when she felt Lindsay's fingers brush the side of her left breast to slip tape under the material. "Where else do you want it?" she asked.

"Wherever you think. I don't want my boobs on social media," Amelia said.

"Then we should probably put a piece here and here," Lindsay said. Her fingers weren't touching Amelia's skin, but she could feel Lindsay's heat. Against her will and to her absolute mortification, chill bumps raced across her body. Lindsay didn't notice, or pretended not to, and remained focused on placing the tape where Amelia needed it most. "Have a seat on the bed. Let's make sure we got all the gaps firmly in place."

Amelia's skin was burning. Lindsay did nothing inappropriate, but something about Lindsay leaning over to fix her dress made Amelia lightheaded. What was happening?

"Go ahead and press the tape in place. I don't want to do anything uncomfortable. I mean, press too hard," Lindsay said.

Were they having a moment? Amelia looked at Lindsay and noticed her dilated pupils and slightly parted lips. Amelia kept eye contact and pushed her fingers against her cleavage. "Feels secure. Thank you." Amelia had to remind herself she was Zoey and slowly stood and walked back to her room. "I'll see you down there. Thanks again."

She pulled Lindsay's door shut and closed hers. Lindsay was with the show. *Get it together. Don't do anything to complicate Zoey's life.* She took a deep breath and headed back to the full-length mirror for a final look and to create space. Was Lindsay queer? She brushed off the thought. It didn't matter. She was here to work, not play. Besides, nothing could happen. After twisting in the mirror one last time to ensure her dress was secure, she grabbed her clutch and headed out.

Talking was pointless. She sat on the couch sandwiched between Dane and Olivia and slowly nursed a gin and tonic. The VIP section was a level above the dance floor right next to the speakers, which made communicating difficult. The base thumped in her chest and pounded her ears. She spent the last two hours waving to fans on the dance floor who yelled Zoey's name. How her sister enjoyed this blew Amelia's mind. She wondered when she could make an exit without upsetting the show people or whomever was paying attention.

Dane clapped his hands. "Let's dance," Dane said. He pointed at everyone on the couches. Amelia shook her head but he wasn't taking no for an answer. He gently pulled her and Olivia up from the couch and crooked his finger at everyone else who was paying attention. *What would Zoey do? What would Zoey do?* Amelia's shoulders sank. She would totally dance and have a fun time. At least she remembered to kick off her shoes first. She was thankful Dane brought the energy because she loosened up when more people joined their small dance group. Mindful of her dress, she shook her hips, threw her arms in the air, and jumped up and down with her group as they mimicked the jumping fans below. She was hot but laughing and surprisingly having a good time. She waved them off when she slipped out of the circle to grab a glass of cold water. She was afraid to sweat too much and lose the security of the tape.

"Looks like the dress is holding up," Lindsay said. She was sitting at the end of the bar drinking a cocktail completely unnoticed by Amelia.

"Why aren't you out there with us?" Amelia smiled at Lindsay not realizing she was leaning into her personal space.

Lindsay pointed at her dress.

Amelia scoffed and responded by pointing to hers. "Come on. You, of all people, know my wardrobe challenges." Amelia winked and immediately regretted it. She was having such a good time she forgot she was Zoey. "Can I get a water?" she asked the bartender.

"Are you having fun?" Lindsay asked.

"I am, but it's loud and honestly, I'm ready to go somewhere quiet, but I'm not sure when we can leave," Amelia said.

"You can leave whenever you want. I'm about ready to go myself," Lindsay said.

"Let me grab my shoes and we can share a cab if that's okay with you," Amelia said. At Lindsay's nod, she held her finger up and weaved her way back to the couch, waving off Dane's signals to rejoin them on the tiny dance floor. She grabbed her clutch and shoes and waved bye to the fans, telling herself the flutter in her stomach wasn't because she was going to be alone with Lindsay, but because she was finally able to leave. "Are you ready?" she asked.

"Yes. These shoes are killing me," Lindsay said.

"You should've taken them off like I did and joined us," Amelia said.

"The fans don't want to see me dance. They want to interact with you. All of you," she said.

"It's so dark in there how could anyone tell who was up there?"

Lindsay laughed. "Oh, they know. They know everything," she said.

"I'm just going to have to take your word. You missed out on an opportunity to let loose for a bit," Amelia said.

"It's been a really long day. I'm looking forward to my bed and six hours of uninterrupted sleep," Lindsay said.

"So, a quick drink at one of the bars is out of the question?" Amelia asked. *What was she doing?*

"As tempting as that sounds, I really need my sleep. Today was stressful and tomorrow's going to be at least twice as bad," Lindsay said.

Amelia lightly touched her forearm. "Why? The hard part was getting everyone here. You nailed that."

"You realize that ensuring everyone shows up when and where they are supposed to be is like herding cats. Especially in Vegas. I probably shouldn't have left them, but I have to remind myself that they are responsible adults and professionals. Most of the time they are reliable. I've only had a few mishaps." She looked pointedly at Amelia and Amelia knew somewhere along the way Zoey fucked up.

"Yeah, thankfully, that's in the past," Amelia said. She hoped that was a vague enough statement that covered whatever Zoey did.

When the cab dropped them off at Caesar's, Amelia frowned knowing their time together was coming to an end. She knew she wouldn't see Lindsay outside of the con after tonight. "Well, thank you for all your help today. I really appreciate it." She pulled out her key when the elevator stopped on their floor. Amelia was very aware that Lindsay had slowed down the closer they got to their rooms. They unlocked their doors at the same time.

"You look really beautiful in that dress," Lindsay said. She gave a small nod. "Have a good night."

Amelia knew Lindsay wasn't hitting on her, but it felt like there was a little tendril of smoke between them. She smiled at Lindsay and even though she knew nothing could happen, it was fun to imagine.

CHAPTER FOUR

Lindsay was in denial when her alarm beeped. How was it already six thirty? Didn't she just get to sleep? She rubbed her gritty eyes and grabbed her phone. Social media was alive with notifications from #HEXPO. Even though she pretended she was looking at each photo from the con, she really was looking for Zoey. There was something different about her. She was quieter, more reserved, and somehow prettier, if that was even possible. Maybe it was because she finally dumped her dirtbag boyfriend, Chase. She stopped scrolling and zoomed in on a photo of Zoey who was giving Dane space as he high-fived a fan down on the floor. She was lovely. The snooze alarm prompted her to put down her phone and get ready for the day. Today was going to be chaotic. Even though everyone had a schedule—one she personally made for each of them—they still hit her up with ridiculous questions. *Where do I need to be again? Where is Ballroom A? What time do I need to be there?* She got a message from Dane one time asking if he had to show up for the last day because he was only scheduled for a group panel. It turned out he wanted to leave early with his then girlfriend. This job really was babysitting the stars.

She was on the convention floor within the hour. The fans were already snaked around the velvet ropes anxious to see their favorite television stars. It made Lindsay smile. *Thirteen Witches* had something for everyone. Half the characters were queer and in supportive, positive relationships. It gave queer kids hope and

Lindsay was proud to be a part of it. She waved to the fans and slipped behind the black curtain. The first panel was a question-and-answer session with the writers and the actors. Four long tables were lined up on the main stage. Microphones were tested and taped down. Cords were carefully concealed under protective rubber strips so the cast wouldn't trip or disconnect sensitive electrical equipment. Cold water bottles were on the table, but Lindsay knew that most cast members would stumble in with to-go coffees. A lot of alcohol was consumed last night and there would be hangovers galore.

A woman with long black hair and short bangs approached her.

"Are you Lindsay Brooks?"

"I am. Can I help you?" Lindsay asked.

"I'm the conference liaison, Sparkle, she/her. Please let me know if you need anything at all. We're very excited to have HEXPO here in Vegas."

Sparkle. It didn't fit her at all. She wore all black clothing, had a chain around her waist, and wore a choker with the word *Enchanted* spelled out in small, metal spikes. Lindsay knew it was cosplay dress because one of their witches wore the same choker. "Sparkle, we're excited to be here. Thank you. I will do that. Is there anything you need from me?"

Sparkle quickly scrolled through her tablet. "Looks like I have everyone's schedule. Thank you for sending them to me. It's nice to meet somebody who's as organized as I am."

"It just makes sense, right? Too many things. I'm sure you are overwhelmed with everything going on this weekend," Lindsay said.

"I thrive on conferences." She gave a little fist pump and checked her watch. "We're going to open doors in fifteen minutes for VIP guests to find their seats and in twenty-five for general admission. What time is your crew arriving?"

Lindsay was fascinated with Sparkle's stiletto fingernails. They were filed to a long, sharp point and painted blue glitter. How was she able to scroll and type so quickly with nails so long? Were they real or press-ons? And why was she obsessing about this right now? "I told them to meet me by the side entrance ten minutes before the panel starts." The conference staggered kick-off panels so the four television shows represented wouldn't compete for audiences. Their show was first. Not by choice, but by random draw.

"Good plan," Sparkle said. She AirDropped her contact information and scurried off. Lindsay found her way to Ballroom D which was where the fans would line up to meet and take selfies with the stars. She put Dane and Zoey on opposite sides of the room since they were the biggest draws. It helped spread out the people and keep the flow moving. Lindsay stopped and looked at Zoey's banner. The photo showed a fun and flirty woman. Maybe Zoey was just a really good actor because that was not the woman from last night. This weekend was going to be interesting. She walked around the room ensuring all the banners were straight and everyone had signup sheets at their table. It was time to gather the troops.

"Good morning, *Thirteen Witches*," she said as she ushered the cast backstage. She immediately sought out Zoey who was wearing ripped jeans, a white T-shirt with the show's logo, and the leather jacket her character wore. It was her signature look. Her hair was down and her makeup dark. She was in character for sure. It made Lindsay smile. Hell, so much about her made her smile. "I'm happy to see everyone here and looking somewhat alive."

"I need coffee. Please tell me you have coffee." Dane whined.

"Nope, but there's water on the table. You all need to stay hydrated. Especially in Vegas," Lindsay said. She marched them down the back hall to the stage. "They'll announce you and when you get seated you can introduce yourselves," she said. They had done this so many times before that Lindsay was going through the motions. "Any questions?"

"Do we sit anywhere? Alphabetically? By character?" Zoey asked. She even raised her hand. It was adorable.

"I taped your names down so you wouldn't forget, but just sit in the same spot as last time," Lindsay said. She waved her off like it wasn't a big deal but it was concerning that Zoey didn't remember. "Okay, we still have a few minutes before we're introduced. I'll try to round up some coffee, but I can't promise anything." Dane made a celebratory noise and Lindsay tried hard not to roll her eyes.

Hi, Sparkle. It's Lindsay. Do you know where the cast can get coffee quickly? Is there a percolator backstage or some magical cauldron that has coffee for the crew? Lindsay was impressed when bubbles popped up immediately.

Sure. How many coffees do you want? We only have powdered creamer and sugar packets though.

"Hey, who wants a coffee?" Lindsay asked. She was quick to add, "it's crew coffee so keep that in mind." She counted hands and shot Sparkle off another text.

Eight cups please and just grab a handful of sugars and creamers. I'm sorry this is so last minute. This won't happen again.

No worries. I'll be there in five.

Thank you. "Okay, gang. We have coffee coming. Be sure to thank Sparkle when she gets here," Lindsay said. She pulled the curtains apart an inch to look at the crowd. Fewer than a dozen seats were available. She smiled when she saw the fans dressed in cosplay laughing with one another. Her pulse picked up knowing it was almost showtime.

Sparkle and another crew member slipped into their space and carefully handed out cups of hot coffee. "It's just Starbucks, but it should help nurse any hangovers you might have or wake you up. The early panel is always the hardest," she said.

"This is perfect, thank you." Lindsay grabbed the last cup and added a packet of sugar to cut the bitterness. Sparkle was right. It wasn't good. It tasted like it had been brewed through reused grounds, but thankfully nobody complained. She hissed out a breath and waited for HEXPO's appointee to welcome everyone to the conference and introduce the panel. She turned to the cast.

"Any last-minute questions?" The only face that didn't look hung over or bored was Zoey's. She looked nervous.

"Nope. Let's get this party started," Dane said. He put his hand in the middle of them until everyone stacked theirs on top of his. "Thirteen on three. Ready? One…two…three. Thirteen!"

Lindsay smiled as the fans on the other side of the curtain heard them and began clapping and yelling. She held Dane back until they were waved onto the stage. He fist-pumped, waved, and blew kisses to the crowd until everyone else had taken their seats.

"Whoop! Am I right?" he yelled into the microphone that he and one of the writers shared. The writer leaned back and winced at the noise before moving the microphone over to her.

The question-and-answer session went well. Dane answered a lot of the questions even though they weren't directed at him. The crowd loved it. Lindsay noticed Zoey taking pictures from the stage of the fans and the panel and expected they would be on social media sometime later. She was good at self-promoting. Almost nauseatingly so. When the panel was over, Lindsay motioned for them to return to her to review the schedule for the rest of the day. Photo ops started at one and ended at five. She was envious of the writers who were headed back to the hotel to get caught up on sleep. Lindsay was going to be on the floor until at least seven. There was a dinner with the VIP fans at seven in a private dining room to sit at tables with half the cast members tonight and half tomorrow night. Both nights sold out in minutes. The idea was to have each cast member rotate to every table after ten minutes of getting to know the fans. Zoey was scheduled for tomorrow's rotation.

"So, what happens now?" Zoey asked. She moved into Lindsay's space after everyone else scattered.

"What do you mean?" Lindsay asked. She double-checked her schedule and frowned. "I don't show anything until one. Did I miss something?" She briefly felt Zoey's hand on hers.

"No, I mean what am I supposed to do until one?" Zoey asked.

"Rest. Shop. The possibilities are endless. It's Vegas." Lindsay visualized Zoey being swarmed by fans. "Do you want a bodyguard?"

"Are you offering yourself?" she asked.

Lindsay wasn't sure if the slight smile perched on Zoey's lips was because she was flirting or she was nervous. Lindsay swallowed hard. "Sadly, no. I'm going to be here all day so I can't rescue you. You're on your own. I mean, unless you want security with you."

"Well, a stranger doesn't sound like a lot of fun," Zoey said.

She pouted her lips for a few seconds and Lindsay wondered what it would feel like press her lips against Zoey's full mouth. Lindsay sighed. "Not a lot of fun, but safe." She watched as Zoey slipped off her leather jacket and bent down to retrieve her backpack. The T-shirt exposed a small patch of bare skin and Lindsay bit her lip recalling how soft Zoey felt against her fingertips when she helped tape her dress into place last night.

"Is there a restroom or safe space where I can change out of this? I brought other clothes and can wear sunglasses and a ball cap to do Vegas-y things," Zoey said.

"There's a dressing area you can use. And you can leave your bag with me. I'll make sure you get it this afternoon," Lindsay said.

Zoey's eyes lit up. "That would save me a trip back to the hotel. Thanks, Lindsay."

"Follow me." Lindsay was very aware of Zoey right beside her. Their arms brushed several times even though there was room on either side of them to move away.

"I'm sorry your day is so busy," Zoey said.

"It's my job and I love what I do," Lindsay said.

"What exactly is your job title? I feel like Jill-of-all-Trades or *Thirteen Witches* Ambassador, but I could be wrong." Zoey winked playfully.

For the first time, Lindsay was embarrassed about her title because it didn't really give people the full scope of her job. "Technically, I'm a production assistant, but I feel like production ambassador is a stronger title. Remind me to bring it up before next season starts."

"Well, I'm impressed. You seem to know everything and I'm positive you know the schedule by heart."

Zoey's compliment brought a rush of heat to Lindsay's cheeks and made her smile. She shrugged it off as though she was just doing her job, but it was more than that. *Thirteen Witches* was her life. She wanted to be a producer of her own show, but this was a massive stepping stone, and she wasn't going to jeopardize it for nothing or nobody. She consciously took a step away from Zoey. The last thing she needed was to get fired for inappropriately fraternizing with the cast. That was a no-no in any job. She stopped at a curtained area Sparkle had pointed out earlier. "Here's where you can change." She pulled back the heavy material to the side and checked the space before motioning Zoey inside. "And consider taking me up on the security detail."

Zoey pointed to her bag. "If you can recognize me after I change, then I'll agree to your idea of a bodyguard. But if not, then set me loose in Vegas."

"Deal. I'll wait here." She stood firmly in place and gave Zoey a dismissive nod. Zoey grabbed her bag, shot Lindsay a devilish smile, and disappeared behind the curtain. As tired and stressed as she was, Lindsay felt a bubble of excitement float through her veins. It wasn't as though Zoey wore provocative clothing, but she was comfortable wearing plunging necklines and midriff-baring shirts. It was nice to fantasize for a few minutes. What she wasn't expecting was for Zoey to throw back the curtain and walk out wearing overalls, a plain white T-shirt, and dusty cowboy boots. Her hair was covered by a ball cap with a Mizzou Moos logo, and big sunglasses covered most of her face.

"Well, what do you think?" Zoey did a small spin and put her hands on her hips.

Lindsay's jaw dropped. "Who are you right now?" Her gaze traveled up and down Zoey's outfit in disbelief. "You are definitely unrecognizable." She tapped the brim of Zoey's cap. "Who are the Mizzou Moos?"

"It's my sister's rescue farm," she said.

"Did I know you had a sister?" Lindsay asked. She knew at one time but forgot.

"I do. She lives in Missouri where I'm from," Zoey said.

"She rescues cows?" Lindsay assumed cows didn't need rescuing. They ate grass and eventually ended up at the butcher. She never gave cows a second thought.

"You know those little mini highland cows with the fur? People buy them thinking they are pets, not realizing they are livestock. They get bored with them because they aren't cuddly or easily trainable so the cows have to be rehomed." Zoey pressed her lips together as though she said too much. "Anyway, what time do I need to be back here?"

"Did you forget your schedule, too?" Lindsay asked. She pulled up her phone to see when the photos were scheduled even though she knew the times by heart.

"I know they start at one, but what time do you want us to show up?" Zoey asked.

"Maybe fifteen minutes early. We'll meet at the same place. Just be sure to have your pass with you so they will let you in. I doubt they'll recognize you dressed like that." Lindsay stumbled over her words. It was very different for Zoey and once again, threw Lindsay for a loop.

"Let me know if you need anything. Coffee, tea, lunch. I'll bring it back," Zoey said.

"Thanks, but I have a meeting at noon and I'll grab something there," Lindsay said.

"Thanks again for all your help. I appreciate it." Zoey turned on her booted heel and marched down the hall. Lindsay watched her until she was out of sight. What was going on with her?

CHAPTER FIVE

Quick heads up in case you get a message from Lindsay. I kinda fucked up. But not bad. I'm wearing a Mizzou Moos cap and she asked me about it. I told her my sister ran a rescue in Missouri. What are the chances she googles it? Amelia turned the volume up on her phone so she could hear the ding of her sister's message back. Today was Zoey's big audition. Amelia was unsure how long it was going to last but wanted to prep her just in case. Zoey shared a few random texts last night with Amelia from the cast. Obviously, they couldn't exchange phones but agreed to forward messages. She quickly looked at her phone when she heard the ding.

Lindsay's too busy to worry about Mizzou Moos. You're fine. Gotta go.

Amelia dropped seven heart emojis. *Break a leg! Call me when you're done.* Her heart fluttered again as she thought about Zoey's stress level. She put her phone back in her pocket and walked to the Bellagio. Vegas blocks were a lot longer than Lincolnville, Missouri blocks and she was slightly overwhelmed with the people, the traffic, and the heat. She welcomed the cool air of the casino and sat at a slot machine in a low populated area.

"Something to drink?" A scantily clad waitress swooped into Amelia's personal space startling her.

"No, thank you," she said, but eyed the water bottle perched on the waitress's tray. "Actually, how much for a water?" The waitress handed it to her.

"On the house. Good luck." She beelined it away from Amelia looking for a customer who was going to tip. Amelia downed the small, six-ounce bottle in one gulp.

She considered gambling but decided to walk around the casino instead. She enjoyed the peace she found in the botanical gardens and grabbed a fifteen-dollar sandwich from the walk-up deli counter near a cluster of restaurants with fancy names and chefs she didn't know. Vegas was not her place. It was too flashy and loud. She checked her watch and still had an hour to kill before she was expected back. She picked a random slot machine and fed it a twenty-dollar bill, betting the minimum. Money went fast in Vegas and she had only allocated fifty dollars for gambling. She studied the game, read the rules on the menu screen, and played it down until she only had a few bets left. When the machine shrilled loudly and lights flashed, Amelia looked at the slot trying to figure out what was happening. Did she get a bonus spin? Did she win?

An older woman with short, spiky hair and a cigarette clasped between her fingers moved to sit right next to Amelia. She clapped awkwardly and blew out a plume of smoke while congratulating her. "Oh, my God! That's so great."

Amelia pointed at the slot. "I'm not sure what's going on here."

"Honey, you won the progressive. I was playing on that machine all morning. Lucky you."

The progressive total said seven thousand, one hundred and thirteen dollars. No way did that just happen. "I just won this?" Amelia asked.

"If you don't want it, I'll be more than happy to take it off your hands." The woman's lips were pinched in a thin line and her smile was forced.

"Oh, I can definitely use this if this is what I really won." She was in denial until two casino employees congratulated her, asked her for her identification, and if she wanted any taxes taken out. "So, I really did win this? That's incredible." She thought of the food and supplies she could buy with the five thousand dollars after taxes. She signed the paperwork, refused having her photo taken, grabbed her cashier's check, and got out of there. She wasn't late, but the paperwork took time and she was cutting it close to when she was supposed to be back at the conference. The last thing she needed was Lindsay to be upset with her. Or Zoey. She pulled her Mizzou Moos cap lower on her head and made her way backstage to the dressing area.

"I wasn't getting worried. Not yet," Lindsay said. She looked at her watch and stood when Amelia slipped into the room.

"Yeah, that took a bit longer than what I thought," Amelia said.

Lindsay's brow furrowed. "What do you mean? Did something happen?"

Amelia was always bad at keeping her emotions in check. How her twin ended up an actress blew her mind. She leaned her hip against the vanity realizing how small the area really was and how sweet Lindsay smelled. "Nothing really. I won a jackpot and I had to fill out a bunch of paperwork that took forever."

"I thought you didn't gamble anymore?" Lindsay looked pointedly at Amelia.

Amelia clasped her hands together and nodded knowing full well she never should've said anything about gambling or winning. This was the second time Lindsay mentioned something about Zoey and a possible gambling problem. She was going to have to bring it up with Zoey after the con. Amelia was playing a role and instead of keeping to herself and sticking to the script, she was sharing too much. "I was killing time. I didn't expect to win."

"There are a million things to do in Vegas besides gamble," Lindsay said. She held her hands up in a surrendering motion. "Sorry. That's not my business. Congratulations on your win."

Rather than argue, Amelia nodded and picked up her bag. "Should I change here or go somewhere else?"

"Oh, I was going to leave. Let me just gather up my things. I'll see you out there," Lindsay said. She smiled, but it wasn't a warm, genuine smile. It was the kind that a grocery store clerk doled out to every customer. It deflated Amelia and knocked her off her winning high. Lindsay assumed she was Zoey who maybe had a gambling problem. Lindsay had no idea the struggles Amelia had and even though she wanted to explain things, she knew she couldn't. She waited until Lindsay pulled the curtain back before she switched back into her conference clothes. She fixed her makeup and gave herself a pep talk before having to slip into Zoey's life again. The first hour was taking photos with three other witches around a cauldron and the second hour was selfies. Then she was free. She would switch with Zoey later tonight and catch the first flight back to Kansas City. She moved closer to the mirror to inspect her makeup and fluffed her hair. She stared at herself critically. Was she really fooling people? *Don't overthink it, Amelia.* One deep breath and she stepped out of the makeshift dressing room and into character. She threw her shoulders back and marched to the designated waiting area Lindsay showed her before. She could hear the excited fans behind the blue curtains. Tiny beads of perspiration annoyingly dotted her hairline. She fanned herself with a paper schedule hoping she didn't look as nervous as she felt. "Where would you like us to stand?" Amelia asked anyone who was within earshot.

"Anywhere along the marks behind the cauldron, but don't feel nervous if the fans ask you to stand in front of it in weird poses. It's just like any other conference and you're a pro," Lindsay said.

There was an underlying bite to her words. Why did it feel like Lindsay was upset with her? Before she had a chance to obsess, Sparkle, the woman who fluttered around the entire conference wearing a thin headset and clutching a tablet, announced they were opening the curtains in two minutes. Amelia closed her eyes and focused on her breathing. She thought about Zoey's personality and how excitedly she embraced life. Zoey didn't stress. Zoey loved attention. Amelia shook out her arms and waited next to Olivia until the first fan was issued into the space that looked exactly like the television set.

"You good?" Olivia asked. She clutched Amelia's hand with excitement and support. Amelia nodded.

"Of course. Just didn't get enough sleep last night. Vegas. Am I right?" Amelia almost rolled her eyes at her own words. It was a stupid thing to say, but Olivia laughed.

"Yeah, we all stayed up too late last night. What happened to you? Did you and Lindsay go somewhere fun?" Olivia asked.

Amelia was quick to correct her. "Nope. I went up to my room but got bored so headed down to the casino floor." That was a lie, but nobody cared. "What time did you drag it in?"

"Not until four." Olivia pinched her cheeks to bring color to them and smacked her lips together. "How's my lip gloss?"

"Stunning," Amelia said. Olivia had nice lips. She was a beautiful woman, but Amelia wasn't attracted to her. She cast a quick glance at Lindsay who stood beside the photographer instructing her on whatever the plan was for the photo shoots. Everyone working the show was dressed in black. Lindsay wore a black skirt and a sleeveless black shell. Her hair was pulled back in a clip with the bulk of it falling over one shoulder. She chewed on her bottom lip while pointing something out on the screen. Amelia didn't stop staring until Olivia nudged her with her shoulder.

"Happy smiles everyone," Olivia said.

Amelia put her hand on her chest hating the flutter of her heart under her fingertips. It was disturbingly thrilling. This was her first interaction with a lot of fans. Fans who would be able to call her out as a fake. People who would know that she didn't have the same scar on her hairline that Zoey did or how one of her bottom teeth was slightly crooked and why she didn't smile as broadly as her sister.

"Olivia, why don't you stand on one end and Zoey you stand on the other? Dawn and Chloe can stand between you. Unless the fans have other ideas. Let's start there," Lindsay suggested.

Amelia moved as directed. The only thing she remembered about Dawn or Chloe was that Zoey said they gave her weird vibes and for Amelia to keep her distance. That ramped up her anxiety.

She was perfectly fine standing next to Olivia. Pressure squeezed her chest and she took several shallow breaths to keep the panic attack from making an appearance. She forced a big smile on her face as she shook hands and hugged the first two fans who eagerly popped into the room.

"We just love your show so much." They posed for about ten seconds before the coordinator thanked them and motioned for the fans to leave through curtains on the other side of the room. People rotated in and out, several a minute, before Lindsay officially closed the curtains after one hour.

Amelia's jaw hurt from smiling so hard. "That wasn't so bad," Amelia said. She shook out her arms and kicked out her legs. She was riding a high she'd never experienced before. It was now easier to understand why Zoey loved it so much. The euphoria of being stanned was incredible, but also overwhelming.

"You have about ten minutes before the selfie stations start. Grab something to drink, go to the bathroom, make some calls," Lindsay said. Their eyes met briefly before Lindsay's gaze flickered away.

Amelia pulled her phone from her back pocket and frowned when she didn't see any messages from Zoey. Either she was still in her audition or was headed to the airport. Out of the corner or her eye, she saw Lindsay making her way over to her. Did she do something wrong? Was she supposed to be somewhere else?

"Are you okay?" Lindsay asked.

Amelia softened her facial expression. Lindsay must've seen the concern on her face. "I'm good." She waved her phone back and forth in her hand. "Just checking messages. How was your lunch?"

Lindsay shrugged. "About what I expected. We reviewed the conference schedule and checked to see if we need to make any changes. Thankfully, all our people are here. Some of the other shows are struggling. A few actors are sick so they are trying to get fill-ins but a lot of actors are on vacation or doing other projects. It's kind of a mess."

Amelia knew all too well about other projects. "On this side of things, it seems flawless so good job to you and everyone else behind the scenes." She rubbed her hand nervously on her jeans and told herself to stop acting nervous.

"Thanks." Lindsay checked the schedule. "Looks like you're on for only one more hour then you're free. Any plans with the crew?"

Amelia knew *Thirteen Witches* wanted their people to hang in groups or pairs for safety reasons. "I'll probably head back to the room. Maybe order room service."

"That doesn't sound like you. I figured you and Olivia would hang out. You don't have anything until noon tomorrow," she said.

"She'll be at the VIP dinner with some of the other actors." Amelia couldn't remember who was going to be there, only that she didn't have to be. "If you don't have to be there either do you want to grab dinner later?" Amelia wasn't listening to her own advice. She just told herself to stay professional and stay away from Lindsay, but here she was, asking for more alone time with her to stoke whatever spark smoldered between them.

Lindsay quickly studied her tablet. Amelia wanted to backpedal and make excuses for Lindsay, but she knew Zoey would stand there, maybe inspect her nails, until Lindsay gave her an answer.

"I mean, I guess so. Maybe," Lindsay said.

It stung and Amelia couldn't help but react. "If you have something better to do, that's fine. I can figure out something. There are so many restaurants in this hotel and in ours. It's okay." She took a step back, shoved her hands in her pockets, and turned on her heel. She followed the cast to the selfie room and slipped behind the curtains until she found Zoey's table. The line was already twenty people deep. A thin, wisp of a man slid in front of Amelia causing her to take a small step back. He was dressed in conference black and wore a thin headset like Sparkle.

"Hi, I'm Cole. I'll be collecting the cash and moving the line. Shout out if you need me to take the photo. We'll rotate the people in as they leave. Any questions?"

Amelia swallowed hard. "I need a water, please." She looked at the room buzzing with people and excitement. She and Dane had the longest lines. "How many people are signed up for selfies?"

"You're sold out. Hopefully, we can get this done in an hour."

"Hopefully?"

"We time it out and if it runs over, it'll only be a few minutes," he said. A cold water was delivered in record time. Amelia felt her phone buzz in her pocket and turned around before the first fan was waved over.

Don't get upset but I won't be there tonight, but I'll be there first thing tomorrow. Long story.

Amelia's stomach fell at Zoey's message. She didn't want to get stuck here. She wanted to get back to her own life and go shopping with the money she won so that Pippin had the medicine he needed for his eye and she could get the leak in the barn fixed.

Ok. I'll call you when I'm done here. She tamped down her quick anger at her sister. *I'm glad it's going well for you.* She put her phone on silent and smiled when the first person in line draped her arm around Amelia's shoulder for her forty-dollar selfie.

Chapter Six

L indsay was confused. What was Zoey's sudden interest in her? On set, she was always polite, but she never got the "let's be friends" vibe from her. And this new feeling? This was something different. It was private and gave her a hopeful thrill. Zoey had only dated men that she knew of so where did this sudden interest come from? Maybe she was reading the signs wrong. Yes, she definitely was reading the signs wrong. Lack of sleep and proper food was clouding her judgement. And Zoey was probably trying to keep her mind off her recent breakup. She needed a friend.

"First round of selfies is done. Looks like everyone is headed to the panels," Cole said. He handed Lindsay the tablet with everyone's numbers and a lockbox of cash.

She craned her neck to look around him. "Is the room clear?" she asked.

"There are a few stragglers. We're ready to lock up though. Maybe you can clear them out?" he asked.

Lindsay nodded and stepped around him before pushing her way through the semi-closed door. She walked to Zoey with purpose and stopped short of running into her. Zoey was talking to a super fan of the show—someone Lindsay recognized from cons' past.

"Excuse me, but Zoey, you're needed in the back. Also, I'm sorry to interrupt, but we're locking up the room. It's so good to see you here, Kyler." Lindsay turned and pointed to the door where Cole waited patiently to clear the room. "Sadly, we have to leave and I need to steal Zoey from you."

"This is my favorite conference ever. Thanks for taking time to chat, Zoey." Kyler gave Zoey one last hug before breaking into a soft jog toward Cole.

"It's impressive you remembered their name," Zoey said.

"How could I not? Kyler's podcast really helped get the word out about *Thirteen Witches* and HEXPO." Lindsay pointed to another door. "We're going to leave this way. I need to drop this off at the desk, but let's talk about dinner. You didn't give me enough time to work through my answer. I was trying to figure out what time I could get away. The answer is yes." She tried not to smile.

"Oh. Okay, well that's great. You probably have a better idea of good restaurants here so if you have some suggestions, I'm all for it. If you leave it up to me, I'll pick some place terrible," Zoey said.

Lindsay watched Zoey absently play with the zipper on her leather jacket. She picked up on Zoey's nervousness and placed her hand gently on Zoey's forearm. "I have an idea. Why don't you go back to your room and relax for a bit. It's hard being on all the time. Let me finish up here and I'll knock on your door at seven." She knew there were plenty of restaurants that would love to give them a table if she dropped Zoey's or the show's name.

"What's the dress code?" she asked.

"As sexy and bad ass as you look in character, let's do something with heels," Lindsay said. She gasped and covered her mouth. "I mean sexy like—well, you know. You're character oozes sex." A nervous laugh bubbled up and she tried covering it off with a small cough.

"Sounds great. I'll see you later," Zoey said.

Lindsay couldn't get away fast enough. Did she really just call Zoey sexy? She handed the lockbox to hotel security and checked the schedule. Her only obligation was to ensure everyone got to the VIP dinner and then she was free. She already knew what she was going to wear tonight. The flirty, floral dress she'd brought just in case. It was sexy, showed a hint of cleavage, but wasn't overtly promiscuous. Plus, she could wear it to a five-star James Beard restaurant or to eat chili dogs from a food truck off the strip. That was the great thing about Vegas. Nobody cared. But she cared. Probably more than she should.

Her phone rang and she immediately sobered up. Her boss, Roger Pitts, only called her to get intel or complain. It was always a crap shoot with him. She learned to answer his questions directly and knock out all small talk.

"Hello, Mr. Pitts. What can I do for you?"

"I'm checking on the conference. Is everything going well?" His loud, gruff voice grated on her stressed nerves.

"Yes, sir. Like clockwork," she said. She didn't elaborate and he didn't ask.

"Good, good, fine. Let me know if something happens. You know we can't afford any mishaps. You remember what happened in Minneapolis, right?" he asked.

She covered her face with her palm and tried hard not to groan. Minneapolis was a shitshow. Two actors from a now canceled television show got really drunk, dared each other to strip, and their naked, glittered bodies were splashed all over the internet the next day. "Nobody will ever forget Minneapolis," she said even though she tried hard to tuck it deep into her memory bank. "This conference will go smoothly. Everyone is here. Dane's been warned." Nobody wanted to lose their job after the show just signed for third and fourth seasons, not before their contracts had been signed. Even Dane.

"Thanks for taking care of things. Talk soon."

Lindsay appreciated that he at least thanked her even if he was curt. She scrolled on her phone until she found who she was looking for. "Hello, Sparkle. It's Lindsay from *Thirteen Witches*."

"Hey. Are you having a good con so far?"

"Everything is great. Thank you for asking."

"Is there something you need? Coffee? Help with the cast?" Sparkle asked.

Lindsay didn't hesitate. "I need a restaurant for tonight. Party of two. At seven-thirty. Do you have anything?"

"Romantic or not?" Sparkle asked.

Lindsay stumbled over her answer. "Not necessarily. Just nice and maybe not so flashy or loud."

"I've got just the place. Whose name should I place the reservation under?"

She counted to three and chickened out. She backed away from the door. Why was this so hard? She smoothed down her dress and checked her reflection. She looked hot and knew it, but her confidence wavered whenever she got close to the door. She gasped slightly when she heard a knock coming from Zoey's door.

"Lindsay? Hello? Are you there?"

Oh, for fuck's sake. Grow up, Lindsay. She's just a woman. She pulled the door open and greeted Zoey. "I was just about ready to knock." She took a moment to appreciate the vision in front of her. Zoey's sapphire blue dress, how beautiful she looked in it, and the way her hair flowed like silk around her shoulders. "You look lovely."

Zoey shot her a sexy smile. "Why, thank you. You look amazing, too. I'm looking forward to a nice, relaxing dinner."

"Then let's get going. I have a car waiting," Lindsay said. They could've taken a cab, but she decided she wanted a night of pampering. There was so much prep leading up to the con, that she convinced herself she deserved it. Deep down she knew she was doing it for Zoey. Zoey was used to nicer things. It just made sense.

"I could get used to this," Zoey said.

Lindsay held back a snort. Zoey's Instagram was full of the finer things. Not in a snobbish way, but in a I can't believe this is happening to me way. Zoey was always gracious about her success. It was one of the things Lindsay admired in her. So many actors had moved on from their television show to the big screen without looking back. So many actors didn't even know Lindsay's name. She was just a face in a sea of a production team on a show. Zoey not only knew her name, but was really making her feel seen at this conference.

"It's nice. I like having a driver more though. Driving to the studio every day is a bit much."

"How long is your commute?" Zoey asked.

Lindsay quirked her head. They lived five minutes apart. "About the same as yours."

Zoey gave a nervous laugh. "Well, you know traffic changes every minute and you get there before me."

"Very true." During production, Lindsay was on the set at five a.m. "Enough about work. We're going to Fennel's Restaurant. Have you heard about it?" She clasped her hands together when Zoey shook her head. "It's supposed to be wonderful. I'm the most excited about dessert. Is that bad?" She stifled a shiver when she felt Zoey's warm hand close over hers.

"We don't eat enough dessert. Let's spoil ourselves," Zoey said. She slowly moved her hand away. The chill bumps were still on Lindsay's skin. They weren't having a moment, but there was a definite shift. Lindsay wished the drive lasted longer. They were in front of the restaurant and their cute, little moment had sadly come to an end.

The maître d' greeted them warmly. Lindsay smiled at the flicker of recognition in his eyes when he noticed Zoey before he carefully composed himself and led them to their table informing them their waiter would be there momentarily.

"This is nice. Thank you for making the reservations," Zoey said.

"I called in a favor. Besides, your name carries weight. They were more than happy to accommodate us." Lindsay, a self-proclaimed sommelier, made several suggestions as she reviewed the wine list.

"Whatever you recommend. I trust you," Zoey said. Her voice was throaty and so low that Lindsay had to lean forward to hear her.

"Then let's have the '22 Caymus Cabernet." Lindsay closed the menu, ordered the wine, and listened attentively to the waiter who was rattling off the specials. Even though her eyes were on him, she could tell Zoey's eyes were on her. It was unnerving and exciting. She ordered the salmon and Zoey ordered the filet, medium.

"So, Zoey Stark, why did you decide to become an actor? What was the draw?" Lindsay gently swirled the burgundy liquid in the glass. It was one of her favorites. It was pricier than she would normally allow herself but the occasion warranted it. Zoey seemed to follow her movements, swirling and sipping moments after she did.

"I've always liked attention and honestly, it's fun to play somebody else even if it's only for a little bit. We grew up in front of the television. I would watch a scene that touched me. Whether it made me laugh or cry. I would recreate the scene for my parents. Sometimes I'd even drag my sister into a scene," Zoey said.

It was obvious that Zoey was very fond of her family. Lindsay noticed her body relaxed when she spoke of them and her lips spread into the most genuine smile. "How does your family feel about your success? They must be so proud of you and your accomplishments at such a young age," Lindsay said.

Zoey stiffened slightly and Lindsay leaned back a fraction. "My sister is proud of me. We lost our parents about six years ago. My father died in a farming accident and my mother died six months later of complications from pneumonia," she said.

Lindsay covered her heart with her hands. "Oh, my God. Zoey. I'm so sorry. I didn't know," she said.

"Thank you. It happened a long time ago." Zoey folded her napkin across her lap. She fiddled with her silverware, avoiding eye contact with Lindsay. After about five seconds, she composed herself and met Lindsay's eyes. "I'm okay. My sister and I are very close and we have a lot of family friends we grew up with back home in Missouri. Our grandparents are still alive, but they live elsewhere."

"Do you get to visit with them? I know the last two years for you have been very busy." Lindsay couldn't remember seeing any of Zoey's family on the set.

"I try to visit my sister a few times a year. Around the holidays and during the summer. As much as I love this lifestyle, it's nice to disconnect from it," Zoey said. Her smile returned.

"Where in Missouri?" Lindsay asked.

"Just a few miles north of Columbia, Missouri. Tiny town called Lincolnville. Smack-dab in the middle of the state. What about you? Are you a California girl or did you run to Hollywood to follow your dreams, too?"

"Outside San Francisco." Lindsay tilted her glass at Zoey. "I moved to get a show of my own."

"Well, that's exciting. How long have you been in the business? How did you get your start? Tell me everything." Zoey linked her fingers together, propped her elbows on the table, and rested her chin on her hands signaling she was completely invested in Lindsay's story.

Lindsay waved her hand at Zoey. "Like you, I came here to follow my dreams. I always wanted to produce. Directors have the vision, but the producers? They have the power. They make the important decisions." Lindsay shrugged, but she meant every word she was about to say. "I like to control things."

Zoey's brows shot up. "Interesting. I guess I never knew the depths of your duties," she said.

Lindsay giggled. "Oh no, that's not what I do now. I'm just a lowly PA. I fetch coffee and organize our people at conferences. But one day, I'll make it happen."

"I believe you do more than that, but I also believe you will make it happen for yourself," Zoey said.

Lindsay blushed because she felt Zoey's words. She waved her off though as if it wasn't a big deal even though it was everything to hear somebody else support her dreams. "Thank you for the vote of confidence. This business is all about who you know and the opportunities that are in your path."

"I wholeheartedly believe that," Zoey said. She lifted her glass. "Here's to making dreams come true."

Lindsay clinked her glass against Zoey's. "I'll drink to that." She took a sip, her eyes never leaving Zoey's. She put her glass on the table and gently twisted the stem back and forth. "So, tell me why you dumped Chase. If you want. No pressure."

Zoey coughed, almost choking on her sip of wine. "We had different views about my career," she said. She said it with such conviction that Lindsay knew without a doubt that Zoey was done with him.

"That's tough. I'm sorry. I know breakups are hard," she said.

"My heart isn't broken. He was just somebody I spent time with." Zoey shrugged and took another sip of wine. "What about you? I know your schedule is bonkers. Is it hard to maintain a relationship?" she asked.

Lindsay shrugged. "It's hard. I'm single now, but my career is very important to me. This is a selfish thing to say, but I don't have time for a relationship."

Zoey nodded as though she understood. "I completely understand. I'm taking a break. I was with Chase for what? Ten months? No thank you. Although he was my longest relationship since high school."

"That surprises me. My longest was when I first moved here. To be fair, it was probably more one-sided. I didn't want to be alone and she was very outgoing and knew a lot of people. Not that I'm proud, but I might have used her toward the end. I simply don't have the time for anyone," Lindsay said. In that little blip of a conversation, she made it crystal clear she wasn't in a relationship and not looking for one. But hookups were completely different. What was the saying? What happened in Vegas, stayed in Vegas? Zoey's eyebrows lifted in surprise and Lindsay wasn't sure if it was because she said she was queer or that she admitted to using somebody. Zoey already knew she was queer, right? She shrugged. "Good news though. I still talk to her. She's married with a baby. Sometimes, it doesn't matter how wonderful a person is, the timing is just off."

"I get it. A relationship isn't necessary, but a no-strings attached night of fun just to blow off steam is perfect. I think that's what I'm going to do for the foreseeable future," Zoey said.

Lindsay's body tingled and throbbed at the thought of a casual night of passion with Zoey. "That's been my life for the last five or six months." She gauged Zoey's reaction and was pleased to find a small smile perched on her full lips. Were they flirting? She took a sip of her wine and stared at her. Everything about Zoey screamed she was interested. She was leaning forward, her pupils were dilated, and her mouth was slightly open. Maybe there was something there. Mr. Pitts popped in her head at the most inopportune moments like right now. No viral videos of misbehaving crew members, no damage repair, just a perfect conference. She sighed and leaned back.

"What's wrong?" Zoey asked.

Lindsay shook her head. "Nothing. I was just thinking about a phone conversation I had with the boss earlier today."

"Oh? Was it good? Bad?"

"He warned me that this conference had to go without a hitch," Lindsay said.

"What does that mean?" Zoey asked.

"That means no scandals," Lindsay said.

"Well, that sounds boring." Zoey finished her glass of wine. "And I don't like boring. How about we live it up for a few hours? Who's going to know?" Zoey looked around the room. "Nobody even cares that we are here. Let's go to the bar, have a few martinis and see what happens."

Lindsay felt like a thousand shooting stars streaked through her veins. What exactly did Zoey have in mind?

CHAPTER SEVEN

What in the living hell am I doing right now? Amelia asked herself. The pull that Lindsay had over her was strong. She was a moth and Lindsay was a hot flame. Amelia fluttered around her getting pulled in with any attention Lindsay gave her and pushing back when it got too hot. Right now, she was on fire and she wasn't moving. The gravity between them was too strong. Lindsay had grabbed the check when it arrived telling her the show would take care of the bill. While Lindsay was preoccupied with signing the check, Amelia studied her. Her hair looked like copper in the soft glow of the candles and her mouth held a hint of provocativeness that Amelia took as flirting. She wondered if Lindsay was obsessing about the rest of the night like she was. Since Lindsay had just confessed she was interested in casual sex, Amelia's walls had shifted. In her mind, she knew to stay far away, but she was weak and missed the attention of a beautiful woman.

"Are you ready?" Lindsay asked.

Amelia sat up straight and looked away hoping that Lindsay didn't see the unguarded look while she was staring. She grabbed her clutch. "Definitely."

"We can hit the bar near the entrance. It looks inviting." Lindsay pointed off to the side where it appeared to be quieter than the dining room. And darker.

"Sounds great. I could use a martini before bed," Amelia said. Lindsay looked at her watch and frowned.

"It's barely nine. You can't possibly want to go to bed this early? I mean, we're in Vegas on a Friday night," she said.

"No. I have to push until at least ten," Amelia joked. She walked ahead of Lindsay and paused at the entrance of the bar not sure where to go and not expecting Lindsay to stumble against her. Her body felt every single curve Lindsay pressed against it. The side of her breast, the curve of her waist. She bit back a moan at the contact.

"Oh! I'm so sorry." Lindsay steadied herself by holding onto Amelia's elbow. Amelia could only smile. Her throat, now the Sahara Desert, couldn't make a sound. She tried swallowing but failed. It was as if she'd forgotten how to act around beautiful women. Perhaps spending all the time on the farm and not around other people had made her more socially awkward than she realized. "Just the two of us," Lindsay said to the hostess. She pointed to a small table near the back. "And if that's available, we'd love it."

The woman smiled, grabbed two drink menus, and asked them to follow her.

Amelia was very aware of Lindsay in her personal space and how their knees brushed as they got comfortable in their chairs. "This is cozy," Amelia said. She felt heat rise and settle in her cheeks as Lindsay leaned closer and pointed to something on the menu.

"I think this is my favorite place in Vegas so far. Are you still up for a martini?" She leafed through the menu slowly. "The espresso martini sounds delicious," Lindsay said. She smacked her lips together and made a noise that wasn't supposed to be sexy but it made Amelia's pulse quicken.

"Let's do it," Amelia said.

The first cocktail went fast. They kept the conversation light. Amelia avoided everything about relationships. She encouraged Lindsay to talk about her family and her pets. It was hard not to jump in with stories about Mizzou Moos. Lindsay grew up with Halloween cats—one orange and one black. Amelia had two gray and three black cats at the farm but couldn't share. Playing the role was harder than she expected. After the second martini, Amelia relaxed her shoulders and quit shaking her foot. It warmed her blood and, without warning, she blurted out what she'd been thinking for the last forty-five minutes.

"So, wait. Let's go back to what we were discussing at dinner. You had a girlfriend." She could hear herself say the words, but didn't believe she said them out loud.

"You heard that." Lindsay quirked her eyebrow. "Yes, I had a girlfriend. A few. And I've had a few boyfriends." She shrugged and winked. "More to choose from."

Amelia laughed nervously. "I get it. It makes sense." She paused and thought about her words. "Do you have a preference?" What she really wanted to ask was about Lindsay's type. And if she fit that mold.

Lindsay sat back in her chair and crossed her arms. For a moment, Amelia thought she'd gone too far. That she had crossed the line with her question. Before she had a chance to backpedal and mentally smack herself for being rude, Lindsay leaned across the table and touched her hand. "It really depends on the person. I've always believed in being open." It was the way Lindsay looked at her. Not as a new friend, or a colleague, but as somebody who was interested in her. Amelia reached for her glass and frowned when it was empty. "Would you like another?" Lindsay asked.

Amelia shook her head. It was time to be responsible and get back to her room. She received a text during dinner that Zoey was working hard getting to Vegas but the last plane out was having a mechanical issue. She said worst-case scenario, she would drive to HEXPO, but Amelia told her under no circumstances was she to get behind the wheel and drive for over five hours. Her sister just had the longest day of her life. They needed to stick to the script. "I think we should probably go. Busy day tomorrow."

Lindsay's smile disappeared when she pressed her full lips together and nodded. "You're right. Come on. I'll call our car," she said.

"We can just take a cab. It'll be quicker," Amelia said. She signaled for the waitress to bring the check and paid for it under protest from Lindsay. "It's only fair. You picked up dinner." Amelia disguised her reaction at the two-hundred-dollar amount, plus tip. Even though she won a jackpot earlier, for a moment, she panicked. That was more than she wanted to put on her credit card. Vegas was too expensive. It was time to go back home.

"Well, thank you," Lindsay said.

"It was fun. I'm glad we did this," Amelia said. She was torn between wanting more time with Lindsay and ending the night cold. By the time they reached the hotel, Amelia's anxiety had wedged itself between her shoulder blades and she wasn't sure if she should recommend another night cap or part ways.

"Are you going up to your room or hanging out down here?" Lindsay asked. She moved closer as the noise from the casino cut through their conversation.

Amelia pointed up. A part of her wanted Lindsay to say she was done for the night, too. A large part. "I think I've had enough for one day. I'm ready to relax, especially after those martinis."

Lindsay wrinkled her nose playfully. "Those were stronger than normal. I'm surprised I'm not wobbling all over." She stumbled and put her hand on Amelia's arm to steady herself. She snorted and covered her mouth. "Okay, see? I need to go upstairs, too." She didn't let Amelia's arm go and Amelia didn't shake her off. She enjoyed Lindsay's warmth until the elevator arrived. Amelia's heart sagged when they reached their floor and found herself moving closer to Lindsay as they walked the hallway to their rooms. "Thanks again for tonight. It was nice getting to know you better," Lindsay said.

"It was a great way to decompress," Amelia said. She stalled outside her door. The energy that swirled between them felt hesitant but crackled with what ifs. What if Amelia brushed a small kiss across Lindsay's lips? What if Lindsay accepted it and kissed her back? What if she pushed her away? Worse, what if she accepted it? She couldn't do that to Zoey. She blew out her breath and unlocked the door. "Have a nice night. Get some sleep, okay?" The way Lindsay looked at her was intoxicating. It was hard to walk away from feeling this good about this night.

Lindsay nodded. "Good night."

She disappeared behind her door and Amelia knew she wouldn't see her again. Zoey would be here early in the morning, they would switch back, and Amelia would go home. She kicked off her shoes and slipped out of her dress. Down to a bra and panties, she flopped on the bed and looked up at the ceiling.

"Why did I do this to myself? Why did I do this to my sister?" Amelia groaned. "Zoey's going to kill me." A knock on the adjoining door startled and thrilled her. She froze and scrambled looking for clothes when she heard Lindsay's voice.

"Zoey? Are you awake?"

"Yes, hang on. I'll be right there." Amelia grabbed a pair of boxers and a T-shirt she accidentally threw on backward before grabbing the doorknob and opening it with more excitement than she should have. "Hi." Realizing she was standing there in her ratty pajamas with a giant grin on her face, she took a step back and curbed her enthusiasm. Her face fell and she put her hand up near her neck in alarm when she looked in Lindsay's eyes. "Is everything okay?" Lindsay leaned against the doorframe and slowly nodded.

"I don't know what I'm doing here," she said. Her low voice sent a shiver across Amelia's skin. Lindsay looked softer. Unguarded. Amelia knew exactly what Lindsay was doing. She took a step closer even though her brain had the word "no" on repeat. *Don't do it. Don't touch her. No. Don't screw it up for your family. No.*

"I know what you're doing here," Amelia said. She ran her finger across Lindsay's smooth cheek and across her jawline. She briefly closed her eyes when she felt Lindsay lean into her touch. She gave herself ten seconds. Ten seconds to enjoy a beautiful woman she had no business leading on. She gently pulled Lindsay closer and when their lips touched, Amelia forgot about everything. She forgot the rules, pushed aside reason, and submerged herself into feelings she hadn't felt in a very long time. Passion exploded in her chest and flooded her senses as their kiss deepened. Lindsay's mouth was hot and needy against hers. She felt Lindsay's hands slide down her back and squeeze her hips.

"Zoey," Lindsay whispered.

Her sister's name brought her back to reality faster than she wanted. She pulled away quickly and stumbled back until she hit the bed. She held up her hand when Lindsay moved closer.

"No, wait. Lindsay, I can't. I'm so sorry."

"What? I don't understand," she said.

Amelia distanced herself more. "I think you are wonderful and beautiful, but this can't happen. Too much is at stake." *Holy shit, how was she going to explain this to her sister? Hey, I made out with your production assistant. Hope that isn't awkward for you.*

"It doesn't make sense. I was picking up vibes. Was I wrong? Did that kiss just now not mean anything to you? Oh, God. Was I an experiment?" Lindsay backed away. Amelia moved toward her.

"Absolutely not. I shouldn't have led you on. I'm so sorry, Lindsay," she said.

Lindsay turned and walked back into her room. Amelia followed but stopped in the doorway. "I think you are such a beautiful woman, inside and out. This is just the worst timing for me. It's my fault." She ran her fingers down Lindsay's arm and held her hand. "Please forgive me." Regret settled in her stomach when Lindsay pulled away.

"I'm going to go. Thank you for…" she paused and nervously crossed her arms over her chest. It took several seconds for her to make eye contact with Amelia, but when she did, Amelia saw the fire. She didn't blame Lindsay for being upset. "Thank you for tonight. I'll see you tomorrow." Lindsay closed the door and Amelia's heart sank when she heard the click of the lock from the other side. She wanted to knock on the door and beg for forgiveness, but she couldn't.

"Fuck."

❖

"You're kidding me right now." Amelia jumped up from the uncomfortable sofa in the hotel room and started pacing. "I'm not ready to be you. I'm all packed up and in disguise ready to head to the airport and now I have to go do a panel because you won't be here on time?"

"I'm really sorry. I know this has been horrible, but I can't help rolling fog. I'm boarding now and should be on site by eleven thirty. Where do I need to be? Send me instructions. We can swap clothes then and get caught up. I'll see you soon," Zoey said.

Amelia tapped her phone against her forehead. How was she going to handle being face-to-face with Lindsay after last night's debacle? She groaned and angrily pulled up the itinerary. Zoey was supposed to be on a panel in an hour. How was she going to get into character and be at the panel by then? She yanked open the closet and pulled out a red shirt, dark jeans, and the leather jacket. She had to change and put her makeup on in twenty minutes. Yesterday it took half an hour just for the makeup. Amelia leaned closer to the mirror and groaned at the dark half-moons under her eyes. This was ridiculous. She did the best she could, grabbed everything she needed for Zoey to have a smooth transition, and raced to the elevator. By the time she got to the conference, her anxiety was a solid ten. She wasn't late, but she wasn't early. She slipped into the group backstage five minutes before the panel started.

"Cutting it close, huh?" Dane elbowed her playfully.

The laughter that bubbled up in her throat sounded foreign and a solid octave higher than her voice. "Well, you know me. Better late than never." Amelia figured that sounded like something Zoey would say. Her eyes darted around the space looking for Lindsay, but she didn't see her. Maybe she was supervising another panel. She relaxed a bit and shook out her hands. The panel was different practices on different shows. She and Dane were on it with two actors from *Potions* and two from *Consecrated Ground*.

Thankfully, she watched *Potions* but *Consecrated Ground* was a new show streaming on a service she didn't subscribe to.

She looked at her watch when it buzzed. Her sister had landed and was headed to the event. Amelia gave the message a thumbs-up and followed Dane onto the stage. The next fifty minutes were going to feel like a lifetime. She just hoped she wouldn't fuck it up.

❖

I'm here. Where do I meet you? Amelia almost cried when she got off stage and read Zoey's message. She gave her directions to the curtained rooms set aside for cast members and headed there hoping it would be empty. "Zoey, are you in here?" Zoey peeked her head out from behind a rack of clothes and ran to Amelia for a hug. "I can't tell you how happy I am to see you." Amelia wiped away her tears. The relief she felt was overwhelming.

"Glad I finally made it, too. Hurry. Give me your clothes," Zoey said. They quickly traded outfits. "Tell me everything."

Amelia bit her lip knowing she had to tell Zoey. "Don't get mad, okay?"

Zoey eyed her warily. "What did you do?"

Amelia sighed. "I kissed Lindsay last night."

"What! Why on earth would you do that? Amelia! Oh, my God. I can't tell you how much this complicates things for me." She threw her hands up in frustration. "You only had to be me for thirty-six hours."

"I know, I know. I didn't want it to happen. It just did. We went to dinner and there were sparks and she looked at me with those beautiful lips and I couldn't help it. But I stopped it before it got out of control."

Zoey grabbed the makeup bag from Amelia and used the small vanity to darken her makeup. "Well, that's going to be uncomfortable."

Amelia twisted her own anger at herself outwardly. "I mean, it sucks but also I did you a favor. Don't forget that part."

"Fine," Zoey said. She slipped on the leather jacket and brushed out her hair like Amelia had it styled. "How did she take the news? What am I up against?"

"She wasn't happy. She's probably going to be very cold toward you. I'm really sorry. It shouldn't have happened. I hadn't felt that way in a long time and it took me by surprise."

Zoey held her hands. "Look, I get it. I'm sorry I didn't get back in time. This wouldn't have happened if my audition hadn't run over, or we hadn't had bad weather." She sighed and pulled Amelia in her arms. "But on the bright side, I'm one of three contenders for the job."

"That's great! I'm so happy for you. I really hope you get it." Amelia tamped down her sadness. "Now your next panel is in ten minutes, then you have photos. Other than Lindsay, nothing else noteworthy happened. You read all my texts with things fans said. You should be able to slip back into your life as you."

"I like Lindsay. I'll be sure to be cordial and not dismissive. Don't worry. Now go home. Tell everyone I said hello and that I miss them." She pulled Amelia into another tight hug. "I love you so much for helping me. Let me know when you get home." Zoey released Amelia and slipped through the curtains back into her world. Amelia grabbed her backpack, threw her hair up under her hat, slipped on her sunglasses, and headed to the taxi line. She wanted to put as much space between her and Vegas as possible. *Good riddance.* But deep down, she didn't hate that she met a beautiful woman. She hated that she had to lie to her. She was never going to play Zoey again, ever.

Chapter Eight

*O*nly *one more day. I just need to make it through one more day.* Lindsay sat at the hotel bar nursing a gin and tonic and her tender ego. Zoey turned her down. Worse. She hit on a cast member and got turned down. How stupid was she? If that got out, she would lose her job in a heartbeat.

"Can I get you another?" A bartender swooped in front of her with a dazzling smile and perfectly coiffed hair. He had a face that Hollywood would love. Lindsay wanted to know his story and would probably ask after at least one more drink.

"Sure. Why not?" She polished off her glass and slapped it down on the bar. Alcohol numbed her idiocy. Today, Zoey was a completely different person. She was distant but cool. She avoided eye contact and quickly put space between them when they shared it. To say Lindsay was uncomfortable was an understatement. At least she had time before she had to be on set with the cast after the con. HEXPO was their only obligation until the new season started filming in six weeks. That gave her time to stamp out any flicker of a flame she felt for Zoey and maybe have a few dates under her belt. The dating apps were a last resort, but Lindsay was desperate to erase Zoey's wicked kiss that had burned itself into her brain. It was all-consuming.

"Here you go. If you put a dollar in that slot machine right now, this is free." The bartender pointed to the drink he still had in his hand. "Once I put it down, it's full price and a pretty girl like you shouldn't have to pay for drinks."

For fuck's sake. Why did men always say the wrong things? "I'm good, thanks." She placed a twenty on the bar and scrolled on her phone. Should she send Zoey a message? Nope. Bad idea. Zoey made it crystal clear nothing could happen. She was getting out of a relationship and wasn't interested. Was she even queer? She kissed her like she was, but there was no mention of a previous girlfriend and nothing queer on her socials. Not that Lindsay stalked her, but she did a relatively deep dive just to see. Her account only went back to the start of her Hollywood career. Several posts from commercials, a pilot about a college life show that never took off, and photos on the set of *Thirteen Witches*. Lindsay wondered if Zoey had changed her name when she got to Hollywood and had a second account for family. A lot of actors did that. Lindsay sighed and put her phone down. If Zoey wanted her to know her personal account, she would've given it to her.

"Why aren't you celebrating with your crew?" Sparkle leaned on the bar next to Lindsay. It took ten seconds for Lindsay to recognize her.

"Oh, hey. They're doing their own thing. They like to blow off steam and I don't want to be around them when they do," Lindsay said. She was tired of babysitting them. They were adults. She side-eyed Sparkle as she took another sip. The gin was kicking in and she felt her smile grow and her inhibitions slip away. "You look different." Sparkle looked down at her jeans, T-shirt, and Dr. Martens. Her hair was loose and her body and wardrobe void of any metal.

"You're used to my con outfit. I like to fit in with whatever conference is going on. People are more comfortable and trust you when you look like them," she said.

"That's brilliant. Does that mean you're from here or do you fly in for certain events?" Lindsay asked.

"Born and raised in Vegas," she said.

"How did you get into this business?" Lindsay pointed to the bartender. "Can we get her a drink?"

"You don't mind?" Sparkle sat next to her.

"Nope. I welcome the company." Lindsay realized she meant it. She was tired of having her guard up around the people she worked with. "What's next for you?"

"Star Trek. I need to get my Vulcan ears ready."

"Seriously?"

Sparkle laughed. "It's the truth. It starts Wednesday. I get a few days of downtime and then it's going to be brutal."

Lindsay noticed Sparkle had moved into her personal space. Her full lips were parted and her eyes slightly hooded. The signs were unmistakable, but she paused because she was wrong before. Very recently, in fact. When Sparkle playfully touched her hand, things got interesting.

"Then you're going to need that drink," Lindsay said. Sparkle was easy to talk to and, out of costume, attractive with bright blue eyes and a welcoming smile. "Unless you haven't eaten."

"I'm starving," Sparkle said. She gave Lindsay a look that made it seem like it was more than just food she was hungry for. Oh, things definitely got more interesting.

"Since you're a local, I thought you'd have suggestions," Lindsay said.

"I know a few restaurants off the strip. Are you up for an adventure?" Sparkle asked.

Lindsay drained her glass and hissed out a breath. "Absolutely."

"Let's go then. I know the perfect place."

She followed Sparkle out to the parking garage. *Was she really getting into a stranger's car without anyone knowing where she was?* She opened the passenger side of Sparkle's Camaro and slipped inside. "This is a nice car."

"It's a gas guzzler but I believe in spoiling myself."

"There's nothing wrong with that." Lindsay adjusted her seat belt and nodded to Sparkle indicating she was ready to roll. She needed to decompress and what better way than a Saturday night in Vegas?

❖

Technically, it wasn't a one-night stand and Lindsay didn't think she was sneaking out even though that's exactly what she was doing. She tiptoed around the bedroom picking up hastily discarded clothes, pausing every time Sparkle moved or made a sound. She found a notepad in the kitchen and scribbled a message thanking Sparkle for the night and how she would see her later at the con. She ordered a Lyft and slipped out of Sparkle's apartment when the driver was one minute away.

It was dawn. The city had slowed a bit, but there was still a lot of traffic on the strip. Lindsay sat back wondering if it was worth it to try to get more sleep. She and Sparkle drifted off about three hours ago after two rounds of satisfying sex. It wasn't mind-blowing, but it was exactly what she needed. The first time was frenzied as they both sought release, but the second time was softer, gentler, borderline boring. Lindsay hated that it didn't make her feel anything more than just okay. Nights like this only disguised the underlying reminder that she was alone.

She shrugged off the uncomfortable feeling that crept in and pulled out her phone. Again, she found pictures of HEXPO and again she searched for Zoey. This time, Zoey was front and center in photos with fans and even the VIP dinner. She sighed and slid her phone back into her purse. Only a few more hours until she could get back to her life and not be constantly reminded of Zoey. She thanked the driver when he dropped her off and made her way up to her room. Exhaustion pushed through the adrenaline rush of the evening, and she dropped onto her bed without even taking her clothes off.

When her phone rang before her alarm went off, she hit the button on the side to silence it. She was off the clock, and it was still too early to field calls. There were only two events before the end of the con. Whoever was calling could wait. When her phone rang again, she sat up immediately. The name Roger Pitts flashed on the screen. Something was wrong. She cleared her throat before answering.

"This is Lindsay." Her voice sounded hoarse and felt like sandpaper. She fucking hated how dry the desert was. She fumbled for her water bottle that was somewhere on the nightstand.

"Can you tell me what in the hell is going on with Zoey Stark? Aren't you still in Vegas?"

Panic spread through her body followed quickly with an iciness that flooded her veins. What in the hell was he talking about? How could he know that she had kissed Zoey? "What do you mean? Of course I'm still in Vegas. The con isn't over yet." Everything was fine a few hours ago. Lindsay looked at her watch to confirm. She had only been asleep for two hours. Her mouth felt fuzzy and her arms heavy.

"Pull up TMZ. Now," he said.

Lindsay almost dropped her phone in her haste to put it on speaker and pull up the website. Her fingers shook as she scrolled. It was a picture of Zoey and somebody who looked exactly like her exchanging clothes. The title read, "Seeing Double?" What the hell was this? She shook her head. "Sir, I don't know anything about this. Let me look into it and get back to you."

"See that you do. You're there to prevent this very thing from happening. I expect a call soon. I have Meador Entertainment breathing down my neck," he said.

As soon as he disconnected the call, Lindsay read the article. "What? What!" It didn't make sense. Or did it? She threw on her robe and knocked on Zoey's door. "Zoey? Are you in there?" She didn't even try to be quiet. She pressed her ear to the door but couldn't hear anything. Either Zoey was a heavy sleeper, or she wasn't in her room.

Her stomach dropped at the thought of Zoey not in her room and all the reasons why. Lindsay picked up her phone and texted her. She stared at the screen wishing for three dots, but nothing.

She flipped back to the article and zoomed in on the picture. The likeness was uncanny. She couldn't tell them apart. Her mouth dropped when she finally put it together. Zoey had an identical twin and that twin had stepped in for Zoey at the con. Twenty bucks said the twin was queer. She needed answers. For herself and for her boss. She called Zoey again only to get sent straight to voice mail. Where the hell was she? Even though it was early for everyone, she shot off messages to the cast. Somebody had to know where Zoey was.

Her first message back was from Olivia.

Ugh. No. It's early.

The second one, from Dane, carried the same tone. *No. Am I late?*

Lindsay couldn't help but roll her eyes. *No, I'm trying to find Zoey. You're not on until the final panel at noon.* She googled *Thirteen Witches* and felt her heart sink with every headline she read. She flipped over to social media where the show was getting trashed. *Check your forty-dollar selfies. Was it with Zoey or her doppelgänger? Did* Thirteen Witches *cast a spell on their fans? I want my money back.* Lindsay felt her heart flutter. She took several deep breaths. This was terrible. She didn't know how to combat this kind of scandal or get ahead of it. Their first panel was in an hour. For sure people would talk and ask questions and she didn't know how to answer them.

She thought about leaving immediately to find Zoey, but after late night and early morning sex, decided a five-minute shower was a necessity, regardless that Mr. Pitts wanted her to drop everything to get answers. She dried off, slipped on workout clothes, and texted Zoey one more time before she raced downstairs to try to find her.

Where are you? We need to talk as soon as possible. That was direct and to the point. Surely Zoey understood how serious this was. She looked up when she heard a small, low knock on the connecting door. She counted to three before she opened it.

"What's going on? Was that your twin? Did this really happen? Start talking so I can figure out how to clean up this fucking mess." She was shaking, but her voice was firm.

Zoey held her hand up. "I know. I've been on the phone with my agent. I know I fucked up. I got here during yesterday's panel. I was at an audition and my sister filled in for me. I was supposed to switch out with her Friday night, but things happened, and she stayed until yesterday morning."

Lindsay threw her hands in the air. "Figuring this sort of thing out is literally my job. You should've come to me first." She starting pacing. "You disappointed your cast, your fans, and your boss." She had to think. How could she swing this? What would make this okay? She chewed her bottom lip and thought of possible angles. Zoey was sick and didn't want to disappoint her fans. *No, that wouldn't work because whatever audition she had would catch them in that lie.* "Wait. What audition?"

"Does it matter at this point?"

Lindsay put her hands on her hips and stared at Zoey. She and her twin really were identical, but she noticed a few differences like the small mole by Zoey's ear and how Zoey stood straighter with more confidence than her twin. Fuck. She didn't even know who she kissed the other night. "What's her name?"

Zoey sat on the edge of the bed and dropped her head in her hands. "Amelia. She didn't want to do this but I begged her."

It occurred to Lindsay that as angry as she was about the pressure of this moment, her career wasn't on the line as much as Zoey's was. She took a moment to refocus her energy. As stupid as this was, she needed to find a way for Zoey to save her job. What was the best solution for everyone?

"What did your agent say about this?" she asked.

Zoey seemed defeated. "She didn't say anything. She just told me to sit tight. She's currently calling the studio I auditioned for to gauge their reaction."

If the studio was anything like Meador, they might not be so forgiving. Lindsay needed to get a handle on the HEXPO reaction before Zoey's entire career disappeared. Maybe they could just tell the truth. Her fans would be hurt but the diehards would want her to succeed.

"I think what we need to do is just tell the truth. Your fans will understand. We can refund the money from the selfies from Friday and offer up a discount or free merch. Maybe if we spin like it isn't a big deal, the fans will take it lightly."

Zoey looked hopefully at Lindsay. "You think so? I mean, I'll do whatever it takes. Maybe we can offer a free T-shirt to everyone who shows us the pic of them with Amelia. I'll pay for whatever. I mean, not that I'm expecting *Thirteen Witches* to pay." She fell back on the bed and groaned. "I really fucked up, didn't I?"

CHAPTER NINE

B eing home was nice, safe, but lonely. Vegas opened up a door that Amelia had nailed shut and now she couldn't close it. Thoughts of Lindsay's soft lips and even softer body flooded her mind incessantly. It was ridiculous. She barely knew Lindsay. They shared one kiss. Granted, it was a very passionate kiss and their bodies were pressed against one another in a way that signaled more could happen, but Amelia had to shut it down to protect her sister. Family first.

She sat on the fence and watched Patches scratch her horns on the side of the barn. Everything at home was the same. She hadn't been missed. Today's tours were over. Amelia was pleased at the amount of donations, but happiness couldn't find footing in the swirling, sticky mess of self-pity. She was feeling sorry for herself. Lindsay was perfect. When was she going to meet somebody else like her? She was stuck in the middle of Missouri, in a small town, with an even smaller pool of queer people. She was getting too old for the college women in Columbia. She would have to drive to either Kansas City or St. Louis to find anyone outside of the handful of lesbians who showed up for every queer happy hour or MeetUp monthly potluck dinner in Columbia. She jumped and turned when Becks whistled at her.

"Hey, Zoey's trying to reach you. Where's your phone?" Becks yelled from the other side of the pasture. She waved her phone in case Amelia didn't hear her. Amelia checked her pockets and frowned. Where did she put it? She shrugged at Becks and hopped off the fence to retrace her steps. She went to the barn, checked the feeders, and finally found it on one of the workbenches from when she grabbed a hammer and nails to fix a sign near the rescue's entrance. She had fourteen missed calls from Zoey. Sweat broke out on her forehead. She felt cold and nauseous. Her hands shook as her mind played out every scenario of why Zoey would call so many times. She was hurt, needed help, something bad happened. Or, she got the movie part. Either way, her sister had news. She punched Zoey's name on her phone and waited anxiously.

"There you are! Oh, my God. I have so many things to tell you." Zoey's voice was filled with dread and Amelia's heart sank.

"What happened?" she asked, afraid to know but dying for the answer.

"Have you looked at social media today?" Zoey asked.

"No. I had two tours this morning. I just finished taking care of the Highlands. What happened?"

"They know," Zoey said.

Her words made Amelia's blood go cold. "What do you mean they know? Who knows?"

"Everyone. Somebody was backstage when we were behind the curtains exchanging clothes and they got a super clear photo of us. TMZ put out an article. It's everywhere."

Amelia felt her knees go weak. She found a bucket and flipped it over before sitting. She rubbed her hand across her face and sighed. "Oh, no. Are you okay?" She didn't think about how this would affect her. She was only concerned about Zoey. "Did you get into trouble?"

"Lindsay's doing damage control at the con and Silvia's trying to save my career. We decided to tell the truth and most HEXPO people were understanding. I offered free signed stuff, anything I could find like mugs and T-shirts, in exchange for a selfie retake."

"If I need to come back, I will. Anything to help." Amelia pushed thoughts of seeing Lindsay again to the back of her mind.

Right now, she wanted to help her sister. Zoey had worked too hard to get to where she was to lose it all now. "How did your boss take it?" Amelia asked.

"Not well. He was already an asshole before the con. I'm dreading that conversation when we get back to LA. We have a meeting Monday morning. I think they're going to fire me. The show just got two more seasons and I don't even have a contract yet." Amelia heard the defeat in Zoey's voice. "Honestly, my future doesn't sound great for *Thirteen Witches*. Not to mention the movie."

"Well, hopefully Silvia calls soon. They were so excited about your audition, right?" Amelia asked.

"They were, but I'm sure they don't want to hire a problematic actor," Zoey said.

"You're not problematic." Amelia paused for the right words. "You're inventive and if they can't see that, well then you're better off." Her voice trailed off knowing her words weren't encouraging. She thought quickly. "Hey, there have been tons of other actors who have done far worse than something as minor as switching places and they are still getting jobs."

"They've all been men," Zoey said.

She wasn't wrong. Amelia couldn't think of a single actress off the top of her head who survived a scandal. But this really wasn't a terrible one. "You're too good, Zoey. People know this. You're gaining popularity. Hell, people swarmed me because they thought I was you. This will blow over. And if you think about it, what we did wasn't terrible. It's not like you cheated on somebody or stole money from orphans."

"I know you don't understand this, but people are always looking for juicy gossip. Yes, I'm worried about what people will say about me, but also I'm worried about you."

Amelia frowned. "What do you mean? Nobody knows who I am."

"Oh, they'll find you if they haven't already. Just be ready for reporters in case this blows up even bigger. Lindsay told me to let you know right away. If anybody shows up at the rescue trying to get information, tell them no comment and tell them to leave immediately. Then call the cops. As a matter of fact, tell Sam what's going on so he knows what he's up against," she said. Their friend from high school, Sam Bowman, was the sheriff of the Boone County Sheriff's Department.

"Really?" She was excited about Lindsay mentioning her. She shook her head, silently scolding herself for not focusing on what was important.

Zoey misread her excitement. "Definitely call Sam. Give him a heads up."

"Are you sure? What if we're blowing this out of proportion? I mean, we're in Lincolnville, Missouri." Amelia hoped she sounded convincing.

"It's such a small world right now and I don't want people to get pissed and take it out on you and the rescue. I don't want to take any chances. You know Sam well. Just ask him to be discreet. As a matter of fact, he'll probably get a kick out of it."

Sam wasn't immune to their switching games. He'd seen it in action more than once growing up. "Okay, I'll call him and I'll be on the lookout." Amelia wanted to ask about Lindsay and what she said about her exactly, but Zoey was on a whole different level of stress and it seemed like an inopportune time. She was also curious about the gambling jabs. Why did Lindsay bring it up twice? She took a deep breath. It was definitely not the time. She'd wait. "Keep me posted. I'll let you know if anything happens here." Amelia disconnected the call worried about her sister's career and wondering about Lindsay's reaction to the truth.

"Did you get ahold of Zoey? Is everything okay?" Becks trotted over to Amelia with a worried look in her eyes. Amelia wasn't thrilled about having to confess but had to since Becks was the first one to answer the phone.

"Zoey's fine but we kind of screwed up," Amelia said. She pointed to the house. "Let's grab teas and I'll tell you all about it."

"Oh, shit. This sounds ominous." Becks quickly fell into step beside her. "Is it bad? Really, really bad or just kind of meh, things are fine and this is just a minor inconvenience?"

Amelia shrugged. "It could go either way." She held the door open for Becks and followed her through the foyer into the kitchen. She grabbed two glasses from the cabinet and filled them with ice cubes.

"I'm not going to push you, but right now I'm dying inside and I want to scream 'tell me' but I'll wait until you're ready," Becks said.

Amelia poured the tea and slid one glass in front of Becks. "As you know, I went to Vegas to see Zoey."

"Nothing wrong with that, right?" Becks's eyebrows raised in alarm. Her wedding ring clinked repetitively as she nervously tapped the side of the glass.

"Remember how Zoey and I used to switch places growing up just for fun to mess with everyone?"

"Oh, no," Becks said. She covered her mouth with her hand and stared wide-eyed at Amelia.

Amelia pressed her lips together and nodded. "So Zoey had a movie audition and asked me to fill in on a few panels and selfies at HEXPO so she could be in two places at once."

Becks groaned. "Tell me you didn't. Well, I know you did but what happened?"

Amelia wondered how much she should divulge about her Vegas trip. She decided to stick to the swap story only and leave Lindsay out of it completely. The less Becks knew, the fewer questions she would ask. Besides, the scandal wasn't about Lindsay at all. It was great that Becks had a wonderful, healthy relationship, but Becks was always pushing for Amelia to find her forever girl.

"Let's start off by saying I was only supposed to do a thing on Friday morning and some photos during the afternoon. That's it. That was all. Everything snowballed from there. She had a late dinner with the movie producer and the red-eye had mechanical issues. She ended up getting to Vegas late Saturday morning after a fog delay."

"So, that means you had to do more, right? And then what happened?" Becks started chewing on her thumbnail. Her anxiety was ramping up Amelia's.

"We almost got away with it."

"Oh, shit." She put her hands over her chest. "How did you get caught and who did it?"

Amelia pulled out her phone and pulled up the TMZ article Zoey had told her about. She quickly looked at it. The photo was really clear. Resigned, Amelia showed Becks the article. She was too scared to google and find more. "This was the outlet that broke it, but apparently, it's everywhere. Zoey called to let me know that we might get reporters calling and if they do, just tell them no comment and hang up."

"Do I have to be nice about it?" Becks asked.

"Sadly, yes. I don't want to jeopardize Zoey's career any more than we already have. I feel so bad. After all this, she doesn't know if she's getting the movie deal. Hell, she might not even have a job. After the con, she has a meeting with the higher-ups about the show." She wrung her hands nervously. "I don't know how to fix this."

"It's not up to you. It sounds like this is going to be a rough ride for everyone, but I'll do and say whatever you want me to," Becks said.

"Thanks. Also, we're supposed to call Sam," Amelia said.

Becks stood. "Do we have to hire security? Do we have the money for it? Wait. Why would they come here?"

"To say mean things? To get my side of the story? I don't know. Zoey didn't explain. We just have to be ready for anything," Amelia said.

"I wonder if people will sign up for tours just to try to ambush us," Becks said.

"I'm more worried about people in town," Amelia said. What if she lost the donations from the grocery store or the extra hay her neighbors dropped off during harvest because they hated that the Roberts sisters pulled the wool over the world's eyes?

"We will figure out something if they do. Look, we've always landed on our feet." Becks put her hands on Amelia's shoulders and gave a quick squeeze. "The town has always rallied around Mizzou Moos. It brings them business and everyone knows that."

"Let's hope they stay loyal if this scandal reaches town," Amelia said.

She and Becks hugged before breaking to finish chores. The animals needed care whether Amelia's world was imploding or not. She shot off a text to Zoey telling her Becks knew and they were on alert and ready for anything. It was the first time she was scared to be on the farm by herself. For a moment, she thought about asking Becks and Robbie to stay the night but brushed off the panic. Zoey was on a successful show, but she wasn't a household name. Not yet. She crossed her fingers and wished that some good came from duping people this weekend.

CHAPTER TEN

Anger flushed Lindsay's cheeks and caused her to grit her teeth, but she stayed outwardly calm as she sat in front of Roger and continued taking the verbal blows about what happened at HEXPO over the weekend.

"You had one job, Ms. Brooks: Make sure the conference went off without a hitch," Roger said. He looked down his nose at her. "And you blew it."

Lindsay was past the point of being pissed. She leaned forward and looked him dead in the eye. "First of all, I'm not a babysitter. Keeping the cast in check isn't my job. Every single actor on the show is an adult and capable of making their own choices. I ensured they showed up where they needed to be and on time. That part I nailed."

"Then how did you miss that Zoey Stark wasn't Zoey Stark?" His sharp voice boomed in the small space between them.

She raised hers, too. "Everyone thought they were the same. Not a single cast member questioned it either." His face grew red and tiny sweat beads popped up on his forehead and upper lip. There was no circulation in his office and the stench of his onion breath and cheap cologne almost made her gag. She had never seen him so worked up before. Meador Entertainment must have pressured him for answers, but she had none. Deep down she was just as mad at getting duped as he was, but for very different reasons. "I don't know what you want from me, Roger. I was just as shocked as you were. I thought we handled it well at the conference. Zoey paid for every piece of merchandise and retook selfies. Not a single fan left there unhappy. The only people who are making a big deal of this are you and the press. This isn't any different than Dane in New York, or the cast of *Worlds Apart* and what they did in Minneapolis." No one talked about Minneapolis. Lindsay was hesitant to bring it up. Roger leaned back in his chair.

"Just so you're aware, we aren't renewing Zoey Stark's contract. We've decided to send her character on a quest that she's not going to make it back from."

Lindsay's jaw dropped. "Because of what happened? That's not fair." She stood. "Why can't the show lean into this and use it to their advantage? Let's ask Zoey's sister to be on the show. We could have a few episodes of a spell that goes wrong and Zoey splits into two people like a good side and an evil side. Just have her sister on a few episodes. The press will love it." She kept talking for fear that he would shut her down. The more she talked, the more his face pinched with disdain.

He held his hand up at her. "It's already been done. You should focus more on your job and less on what the writers are doing."

Lindsay didn't like his words. "I have a longer list of worse things that have happened within these walls and in this studio. This so-called-scandal is tame."

Roger pointed his meaty finger at her. "Is that a threat, Ms. Brooks? Because I don't like it when people threaten or blackmail me."

Lindsay blew out a breath. This conversation had escalated beyond what she expected. "No, that's not what I mean. Other actors have survived greater scandals and Meador has stood behind them. Why Zoey? Because she's a woman? If you fire her now, this show will tank. She's a fan favorite and has elevated the show in ways you can't understand. Those ratings are because of her. If she goes, the viewership goes."

"I have faith that Dane will continue to carry the show. And we're hiring a new witch. She's going to fill the void that Zoey will leave behind." He held his hands up. "It's already done."

Lindsay stood. "What are you talking about? It's been less than a week." She hated how fast Hollywood moved. Nobody stood by anyone anymore. Cancel culture raged through the town like wildfire and she was sick of it.

"Sit down, Ms. Brooks."

She pointed back at him. "I will not be talked to like a child. Part of my job is to protect the actors and that's what I'm doing. For you to let Zoey go because of a blip of a scandal is absurd. It's a mistake." She felt her chest rise and fall and hated how her clothes felt tight. It was stifling. "Honestly, I don't want to work for a company who doesn't protect their employees." She pulled at her lanyard that held her identification, a token of her career at Meador Entertainment, and tossed it on his desk. "I quit. This isn't what I signed up for. Congratulations. You just sank this show, Mr. Pitts."

She grabbed her bag and stormed out of his office not caring who heard or saw their exchange. It felt exhilarating. And scary. There went the dream of getting her own show any time soon. Or maybe people would applaud her for doing the right thing. It was time to update her resume and pray that he didn't blackball her. A two-week notice wasn't necessary because honestly, she didn't care. They didn't give Zoey a two-week notice so fuck them. Did Zoey even know? She grabbed a banker's box from the supply room and headed to her office. Roger was already there, standing in her doorway with his arms crossed and a pissed off look.

"Let's talk about this," he said. She stared at him until he moved to the side.

Lindsay kept her cool and walked stiffly by him, careful to keep her emotions in check. "There's really nothing to talk about. You don't support your employees and I don't want to work for you."

"You have a non-compete with Meador Entertainment. If you walk now, you can't do anything in this industry for six months. You can guarantee that I'm going to make sure it sticks," he said.

Lindsay snorted. "You might want to check with your lawyers. Non-competes are illegal in California." She took great comfort in recognizing his discomfort. He had nothing to hold her. She packed up her things as he watched.

"You don't want to do this. You might get a reputation for being difficult to work with," he said.

Lindsay stopped and stared at him. "Is that a threat? Did you just threaten me again?"

He held up his arms. "Let's just take a step back. Why don't I get management together and we have a sit-down." He checked his watch. "I'm sure I can get people rounded up in an hour. Would you be willing to wait around so that we can have a civil conversation about what's happening?"

"Did you already fire Zoey Stark?"

He moved his fingers back and forth across the back of Lindsay's guest chair and looked everywhere but at her. He nodded. "We've sent her the paperwork."

"Why? Seriously. Why?"

"She was under a contractual obligation to be at HEXPO for three days and only showed up for one and a half. She had her twin sister fill in for her while she basically interviewed for another job. She lied to us and her fans."

Lindsay waved him off. "Oh, please. So many other actors have side gigs during time off. I'm sure Zoey was aware of the schedule and what she could and couldn't commit to." Lindsay wasn't sure of that. Since *Bounty Hunter* was such a hit, she was sure they wanted to start filming right away which would mean there would be scheduling conflicts. She continued gathering her personal items. "I know for a fact that Dane's voice-over in Pixar's *Stop Time* was done when *Thirteen Witches* was filming. And knowing how Meador obviously supports the men in the industry, I'm sure he got special privileges."

"That's not true. He asked us and we worked with his schedule."

Lindsay stopped rummaging through her desk and put her hands on her hips. "Did you give Zoey the same courtesy?"

"Dane's commitment was to us, not Pixar. When their schedule bled into ours, he asked permission," he said.

Lindsay slowed when she finished emptying the last drawer. "I don't like how this went down. I don't expect you to support me or my career. I've worked with you long enough to know that you'll do everything you can, just out of pure spite, to make my life miserable in Hollywood." She squared her shoulders and picked up her surprisingly heavy box of personal belongings and walked to the doorway where he loomed. "Best of luck to you and the show. I'll see myself out."

She brushed past him and marched down the hall, ignoring wide-eyed stares and whispers from interns. The first angry tear didn't fall until she was safely in her car, tucked under the seat belt, ready to drive out. The rest dropped in a heated mess as she cried out her anger. She sniffled and put her car in drive. Figuring out the next step was hard but at least she still had her integrity, which was more than she could say about Roger Pitts or Meador Entertainment.

❖

"Thanks for calling me back," Lindsay said. She had ignored call after call as her resignation spread through Hollywood but couldn't answer her phone fast enough when Zoey's name flashed across the screen.

"What's happening?" Zoey asked. For a moment, Lindsay panicked and thought maybe Zoey didn't get her walking papers. "Please tell me you didn't quit because they fired me."

Lindsay's anxiety lessened its grip. Zoey knew. "They suck. I don't want to be on a show that's going to tank after letting their top star go. And I don't want to work for a company that doesn't protect its employees," Lindsay said. "I'm not worried. We'll both end up on our feet," she said with more conviction than she felt. "Did you hear back from your manager about the audition?"

"It's between me and another actress but I don't know what's going to happen. Alec pushed for me. I'm just waiting for the call. If I get it, filming starts soon. Good news, now I won't have to ask for time off or have them adjust their schedule for me."

"What will you do in the meantime?" Lindsay asked, wondering the same of herself.

"I'm on my way to my sister's. Instead of dying down, more photos have surfaced of Amelia in Vegas with terrible headlines so I want to be there to help any way I can. Losing the HEXPO money has put a strain on Mizzou Moos so I'm going to see what I can do. I hate that all this is my fault."

It was the first time Lindsay didn't tense when Zoey brought up Amelia. She was hesitant to even mention her. The name sounded foreign when she rolled it around in her mouth. "Is Amelia not doing well? I mean, is the rescue not doing well?"

"It's just hard to maintain when the only income is from tours and the generosity of the town. Amelia's working on an online shop of merch like T-shirts and mugs. She's just getting started and she's not great at it so I'm going to help."

Lindsay's mind was whirling with ideas for Mizzou Moos. Not only was it a catchy name, but their story was heartbreaking and heartfelt at the same time. She couldn't help but google it when Zoey confessed after their picture was plastered all over the internet. And she knew the name because Amelia was wearing a ball cap with the logo stitched on it when she slipped into— herself. When she was just being herself. Lindsay still felt foolish about it all, but if she looked at it logically, Amelia was only trying to help her sister. She pushed Lindsay away because she didn't want to complicate things. But no way was she going to talk about Amelia to Zoey. She wanted to scrub that kiss from her memory, but then she wouldn't have that rush of heat to her lips and the throbbing heartbeat in her clit when she thought about Amelia pressed against her for several glorious seconds. "I know she was happy about winning that jackpot." Lindsay rolled her eyes. She didn't last five seconds without talking about Amelia. Now that she knew why it was so important, she felt a prick of guilt at giving Amelia a hard time about gambling.

"That will help for a bit. Anyway, that's my problem. Listen. Thank you for all you've done for me over the last two seasons and trying to help me not get swept away with this scandal. If there's anything you need from me, please let me know. I owe you."

"You don't owe me at all," Lindsay said. She wanted to offer her help, but also she needed to figure out her life first before trying to help others. Zoey indicated she would be fine, but Amelia? Did their little stunt risk donations? And why did she care about Amelia's fate? They had one kiss. She tilted her head as she thought back to all the times they were together. It was brave of Amelia to walk into a foreign space and act like a movie star. Being front and center wasn't in her blood like it was for Zoey. That was a brave thing to do. Lindsay also knew firsthand how hard it was to say no to Zoey. "Let me think of a few things that maybe you can do while you are waiting for the call. I'll reach out in a bit."

"Thanks, Lindsay."

Lindsay plopped down on the couch with her phone and started thinking of ways Zoey and Amelia could generate more money and interest for their rescue. The town obviously knew of the twins. What was their take on the whole swapping lives thing? Were they used to it? She pulled up a random social media site and scrolled through messages and videos. An idea formed in her head and she typed in Mizzou Moos on all social media platforms. Only one had a site and the last post was from last year. She sat up. What if they did a blast on social media? Strike while the iron was hot. She sent Zoey a text. *I have an idea. Are you up for company?*

I'm already on my way to the airport. What's up?

Lindsay thought long and hard about her response. *Since I have a lot of free time on my hands, I'd thought I'd visit the farm and give you all suggestions. From a marketing standpoint, if you're interested.* That was too much. It was too much, wasn't it? She smacked her forehead and told herself to calm down.

I know you have a lot going on right now. You don't have to help us, but if you want to, that's great. We have plenty of rooms at the farm. You can stay with us. Amelia won't mind.

Lindsay snorted. Like hell she was going to stay there. She didn't even know why she was doing this in the first place. *Thanks. We can talk about that when I get there. It probably won't be until tomorrow.*

Great. See you then.

She put her phone down and sighed. What was she thinking? It was in her best interest to walk away from this situation and never look back. Even though she told herself it was just to help a colleague out, deep down she knew she wanted to see Amelia face-to-face again. She needed to find out if their connection was real, or if she was pretending with her as well.

CHAPTER ELEVEN

"Why are you being weird?" Amelia smacked her sister's hand away when Zoey reached out to smooth down her hair.

"I'm just trying to make you look presentable," Zoey said.

Amelia dodged Zoey's hand again. "Who cares what I look like? We don't have any tours today and I still have to feed the animals. They certainly don't care what I look like." She pulled her hair back into a ponytail and tucked it under a ball cap. The dark color hadn't completely washed out even though she had washed her hair eight times in five days. She stopped and put her hands on her hips. "What's going on?"

Zoey held up her hands. "Nothing's going on. I just hate that you look more and more like Mrs. Haley down the street. You're too young and too pretty to not care."

She felt the sting of her sister's words but pretended they didn't bother her. "Mrs. Haley's nice. Leave her alone."

"Yes, she's very nice and she was comforting when we lost our parents, but she could use a spa day and a decent haircut that she didn't give herself," Zoey said.

"You've never been mean like this before." Amelia stared her down while she slipped on her muck boots. "And she goes to Judy's Salon in town. I've seen her there."

Zoey threw up her arms. "And I rest my case." She shooed her out. "Hurry up. I'll fix lunch. Then we can talk about a plan."

Amelia frowned. The scandal wasn't going away. She purposely stayed out of town and let Becks pick up supplies. They had several calls about the infamous body switch and people questioning where the donations were going, and by the end of day Wednesday, she was glad all calls went straight to voice mail. "Give me twenty or so minutes."

It was another hot day and storms were expected within the hour. Amelia needed to get all the animals to safety before they hit. She grabbed a few apples hoping to lure the mini Highlands into the big barn first. Patches, Pumpkin, and Mimsey were their own little cow gang. Just the smell of the freshly cut pieces of any fruit had them trotting over to Amelia. She coaxed them into their stalls and rubbed their muzzles affectionately. Pippin and Gus jogged into their side of the barn once they realized treats were being handed out. She closed the gates and whistled for Henry, the last of the minis. He was on the other side of the pasture grazing on high grass. He wasn't as attentive as the others so Amelia slowly walked over to him, careful not to spook him.

"Come on, buddy. Let's get back to the barn." She cut off a piece of apple to entice him. He obliged and lumbered over to her. She stayed clear of his horns and coaxed him with another slice. She sweet-talked him all the way back to the barn. Once he was safely through the gate, she fed him the rest of the apple.

On her way to the chicken coup, Amelia noticed a sedan she didn't recognize in the driveway by the house. Both Zoey and Becks were inside so whoever it was, they'd been buzzed in. The gate was locked on days tours weren't scheduled. Amelia grabbed a bucket for feed and locked up the chickens. She secured the tarps and headed to the small barn. The donkeys and goats were already locked up. She checked the time. Half an hour had passed. She hustled back to the house happy that all animals were safe and put up before the weather turned.

"Sorry, I'm late. Do I have time to wash up?" Amelia kicked off her boots in the mud room and hung her cap on a hook. She wiped the sweat off her brow with her T-shirt's neckline and walked into the kitchen, forgetting the car by the house and unaware that somebody might be watching her. "I smell like hay and sweaty donkey."

Amelia froze when she saw the one woman she never expected to see again. Lindsay Brooks sat cross-legged at the kitchen table with her forearm resting casually next to a glass of iced tea. Amelia looked back and forth from Zoey to Lindsay and settled on Becks whose chair scraped against the hardwood floor as she stood in haste.

"Well, I need to go and be anywhere but here. Lindsay, it was nice to meet you. Call me if you need me." Becks pointed at the small building that housed Mizzou Moos office and their fledgling storefront. "I have some paperwork that I don't need to be doing right now."

Mortified, Amelia tugged her T-shirt down, quickly patted her hair, and tightened her ponytail. This was a worst-case scenario and she was beyond embarrassed. "What are you doing here?" Well, that sounded rude. She shook her head. "Not to be rude, but what are you doing here?" That was just as bad. Was Lindsay there for her? And was she as dusty and dirty as she felt? "Before anyone talks, I need to shower." How many times had she wiped cow slobber on her jeans? She didn't dare look down. Her eyes locked on Zoey's who wrinkled her nose and nodded.

"We'll be here." Zoey dismissed her quickly.

Amelia flashed Lindsay a quick, awkward smile that felt more like a snarl, and bolted up the stairs. *Holy shit, holy shit! What was she doing here?* Amelia started the shower and ripped off her clothes. She scrubbed quickly, hoping the sandalwood and jasmine soap would rid her skin of the farm smells. Zoey was right. She was turning into Mrs. Haley. She dried off and tried on outfits until she settled on a clean pair of jeans, a black V-neck T-shirt, and black sandals. She towel-dried her hair, put on light makeup and was downstairs in thirty minutes. She spent a solid minute psyching herself up to stroll into the kitchen like nothing happened. "Hello, Lindsay." Amelia sat at the table with them and tried to seem normal. "Welcome to Mizzou Moos." Who says that? Out of the corner of her eye, she saw Zoey slowly shake her head.

"Lindsay's here because she offered to help get more exposure for Mizzou Moos. It's kind of her thing. She knows we've been struggling for donations and the scandal isn't going to make people donate more. We were looking at the website while you were getting ready and she has some really good ideas on how to improve it," Zoey said.

Amelia knew she wasn't great at updating the website, but she didn't need everyone's opinion. "How can you be here? Isn't your job in California?" Amelia finally looked Lindsay in the eyes. Her heart fluttered and she dropped her gaze immediately down to Lindsay's lips. It was hard to stay focused.

"You mean because I don't have a twin? Simple. I quit."

"You what?" Amelia asked. She almost reached out to grab Lindsay's hand but stopped herself just in time. "But that's your dream job."

Lindsay shrugged. "It was a stepping stone. I'll find something. I'm not worried about me."

"She's worried about us. Both of us," Zoey said.

Amelia looked at Zoey in alarm. "Why? Did you hear back from your agent about the movie?" She already knew they fired her from *Thirteen Witches.*

"Nothing yet," Zoey said. She sounded slightly stressed. She handed Amelia her phone. "We can't shake this. The media is like a dog with a bone. They want me, you, and Mizzou Moos canceled. It's so ridiculous."

Amelia read the screen of Zoey's phone. The headline "Farm or Front?" made the blood in Amelia's body turn cold. She swallowed hard and skimmed the article that accused them of gambling away donations and living it up in Vegas. Her blood heated up. "These are hateful people. Why do they even care about a little farm animal sanctuary in Missouri?" She handed Zoey's phone to Lindsay. Their fingers briefly touched and Amelia felt electricity but chalked it up to the storm that started kicking up dust around the house. It was in the air, not between them.

"They're trying to find an angle even though Zoey already explained what happened when she was at the con. These journalists want everyone who has donated to Mizzou Moos to feel like they've been duped. The world needs another scandal, but until then, you're it," Lindsay said.

Amelia scowled. "But Zoey paid everyone back."

"Only because she was found out," Lindsay said. Amelia shot Lindsay a look. Lindsay held up her hands defensively. "I'm on your side. That's why I'm here." She leaned forward and cracked her knuckles. "I've been doing this for years. This isn't a bad scandal, but it's unique."

"You should listen, Amelia. Lindsay has great ideas on how to reach a larger audience," Zoey said. The excitement Amelia saw in her sister's eyes made her wary. Usually, when Zoey got this excited about something, bad things happened. Like HEXPO. "I know what you're thinking, but there are no drawbacks to her plan."

Amelia sat back in her chair and crossed her arms. "What is it? What am I missing here?" She looked at them. "Well?"

Zoey looked at Lindsay and nodded. "Tell her everything you told me." Zoey couldn't contain her excitement. "Before Lindsay starts explaining things, just know that I think it's a great idea. You're going to have to keep an open mind and maybe do things you're not quite comfortable doing."

"Again?" Amelia asked dryly.

"Really. This is safe. It'll be fun and hopefully will only help Mizzou Moos," Lindsay said.

Lindsay leaned forward and Amelia held her breath. God, she was exquisite. Her eyes were bright but guarded and Amelia felt herself getting lost in them. Again. She looked down at her hands to break the connection. "Hit me."

Lindsay stood. "Okay, so there are several social media outlets you can utilize. Think about when you're scrolling on different social media sites and you see videos like Reels on Instagram. Those content creators have millions of followers and they get a lot of money from their content." She pointed out the window. "You have animals. Super cute miniature animals that everyone wants to see. I think if you started making one-to-three-minute videos of everything about Mizzou Moos, you can get a following and the more followers the more money."

"I don't know anything about—" Amelia started.

Zoey interrupted. "That's why Lindsay is here. This is her wheelhouse. She knows how to set things up and get us started. I thought it would be fun for both of us to do videos together. I mean let's lean into the twin thing. I have a decent amount of followers." Zoey's shoulders slumped a bit. "I lost several, but I still have enough to get us a running start."

"I like Zoey's idea of leaning into the scandal. We could do playful videos of both of you with the animals," Lindsay said.

"Ooh, we can talk about Mimsey and how she's out for my blood," Zoey said.

Amelia was starting to warm up to the idea but hated that she was going to have to be in videos. She wasn't a natural in front of the camera like Zoey. "Mimsey's pretty cute. And Pippin has the most adorable curls that hang down in his eyes." She felt light in her heart just thinking about her animals. "Both are big hits during the tours."

"And we can promote tours and show people what they can expect. But mostly, we can show the good that Mizzou Moos does," Lindsay said.

Thunder cracked overhead and Amelia saw Lindsay wince. She wanted to squeeze her hand assuredly, but physical contact was out of the question. "If we lose power, we have a generator out back. This will be over in about half an hour, tops. And it's not a bad one," Amelia said. Lightning lit up the dark sky illuminating the dark, angry clouds. "We'll be fine."

Zoey grabbed a notepad and started taking notes. "What should our first video be? Should we do one of those trending videos like where we dance? Maybe I can start the dance and you can pop out behind me."

"No," Amelia and Lindsay said in unison.

"Why not?"

Amelia answered first. "Because it's about the rescue and not about us."

Lindsay agreed. "We can do something cutesy like you're suggesting, but people love animals and that's how you're going to hook them at first. But we do want to have a few videos about you being twins. I mean, that's why this is happening." She pointed outside. "When did you say this is supposed to end? And why is it so dark outside? Should we be worried?"

Amelia walked over to the window and watched the rain angrily pelt the glass. She looked at the weather app on her phone. "No tornadoes. Just strong storms. It should clear up by late afternoon. We can give you a tour then. Where are you staying while you are here?" Amelia asked. She tried to sound aloof and nonchalant. When Lindsay and Zoey shared a look, her stomach dropped. She knew before anyone answered.

"Sis, she's staying with us," Zoey said. She stood and excused herself. "I think you two have a lot to talk about so while we have downtime, I'm going to answer some emails and disappear."

Awkward silence filled the space between them. Amelia pulled back a chair opposite Lindsay and sat knowing this talk was inevitable. "Zoey's right. What we did to you and to everyone was wrong."

"Zoey explained that you only did it to help her," Lindsay said.

True, but there was more going on here and they both knew it. Were they just going to pretend that incredible kiss didn't happen? Amelia stared into Lindsay's eyes looking for any sign of weakness or encouragement. She bit her bottom lip and weighed the pros and cons of pushing the conversation past this politeness.

"I'm sorry you were duped, but I'm not sorry about what happened between us," Amelia said.

She wanted to pace the room and throw her hands up and release the stress and uncomfortable feeling that pressed against her ribs. She wanted to tell Lindsay how that kiss was everything to her, but she stayed in the chair waiting for a reaction. Any reaction besides silence. Every second felt like an hour. How many times had she blinked? Was she blinking too fast? Why wasn't Lindsay saying anything? It was so frustrating.

"I mean, I don't expect you to say anything." Except she did. "I just wanted to apologize. It wasn't fair to you and it put you in a really weird space."

Lindsay seemed to have pulled away a bit. "It was a very strange weekend. Lots of highs and lows. You and I had a nice night though. When the photo was released, it played with my head, but I understand why you did it. There are no hard feelings."

If Amelia hadn't been watching her so intently, she would've missed the slight downward pull of the corners of her mouth for a fraction of a moment when she said it. She hated that there were, in fact, hard feelings, but didn't want to push Lindsay.

"But you quit your job and now instead of looking for a new one, you're here helping us. Why? Not that I'm not appreciative, because I am," Amelia said. She linked her fingers together to keep from shredding the paper napkin in front of her on the table.

"Honestly? I needed to step away from Hollywood for a bit. I knew Zoey was coming here and I invited myself. I've always liked Zoey and when she mentioned she was coming here to help you, I followed suit." Lindsay took a sip of her tea.

A bolt of lightning struck near the house and she shrank in her seat. Even Amelia winced but waved it off like it wasn't a big deal. Her heart was beating fast as she worried about the minis.

"I think what you're doing here is great. I know a lot about marketing and I think I can help you," Lindsay said.

Lindsay obviously wasn't going to talk about the kiss, but did that mean flirting was off the table? Was she interested in her? Maybe Amelia would sprinkle in a hair flip or try harder with her makeup. Laugh louder at her jokes. How did people flirt and why was she so bad at it?

"I really love what you're doing here, Amelia. And I want to help. Besides, it keeps my mind off trying to find a job. I've sent my resume out and now it's a waiting game. I might as well kill time doing something I love," she said.

"If we haven't told you yet, thank you for doing this. I appreciate the help. I know keeping up with the socials is important and it really is a good idea," Amelia said. She tried to sound grateful even though her heart ached. The kiss obviously didn't occupy Lindsay's thoughts as much as it did Amelia's. "It looks like it's starting to let up. Hopefully, we can get out soon."

"I think I can do a lot of good here," Lindsay said.

Amelia made herself smile. She hated when talking things out made things worse. That wasn't supposed to happen. "I think so, too. Where shall we start?"

CHAPTER TWELVE

It was an adorable place that needed a good polishing. Amelia's two-story house had a wraparound porch with rocking chairs and hummingbird feeders on every side. The white paint was peeling near the gable and one side of the porch sagged near the front steps, but Lindsay felt the love here. Amelia and Zoey were obviously proud of this place.

It took three wrong turns and sketchy directions from a gas station attendant who was far more interested in his comic book than helping a sweaty damsel in distress for Lindsay to find the place. At the top of her list was better directions on the website and more physical signs. The tour of the sanctuary only ramped up Lindsay's excitement of things they could do to promote Mizzou Moos.

"This is Pippin and he's the best boy. He loves muzzle rubs and apples," Amelia said. She brushed his curly hair back from his eyes and fed him a slice of apple. He nudged her again until she laughed and fed him another slice. It was wonderful to see Amelia shine. Lindsay walked with Zoey as though they both were experiencing the tour for the first time.

"How long has Mizzou Moos been operating?" Lindsay asked.

"About five years. We had to sell off a lot of land to pay for taxes and other things," Amelia said. She brushed her hands on her jeans and moved to the next stall. "Looks like Patches is out enjoying the cooler weather. You'll have to meet her later."

Cooler weather? Lindsay was sweating in places she didn't want to think about. How did people and animals survive without air conditioning? "We could do an introduction video of each of the animals being cute and post it to Mizzou Moos's socials, once we set them up, then Zoey and I can repost and get people to follow and repost across all platforms." Lindsay pulled out her phone. "I'm going to take random videos and you both can decide what you're okay with. We won't post anything that isn't one hundred percent approved by both of you."

"Let's all take videos and we can decide which ones to use over dinner," Zoey said.

"Amelia, you could get some really good videos being up close and personal," Lindsay said. She swallowed when Amelia looked at her.

There was a lot to unpack between them, but for some reason, Lindsay had chickened out. Amelia sat across from her a few short hours ago and opened the line of communication. She gave her a spotlight and rolled out the red carpet and what did Lindsay do? She waved her off. She pretended it didn't matter. That the kiss was just a random kiss. In the back of her mind and somewhere in the corner of her heart, Lindsay knew she traveled almost two thousand miles to get clarity. Maybe it wasn't today, but soon. Today was a lot. Plus, she still felt guilty about Sparkle. She was no stranger to casual sex but she felt bad that she'd slept with Sparkle when she was hung up on Amelia.

"It doesn't hurt that they are super cute and have great personalities," Amelia said.

Seeing the twins together, Lindsay could tell them apart. The differences were subtle, but Lindsay noticed. Amelia's lips seemed fuller than Zoey's. She had a sprinkle of freckles across the bridge of her nose whereas Zoey's skin was flawless.

Amelia nodded. "Let's see if they're going to cooperate." She hopped the fence, pulled out her phone, and hit record as she moved closer to Pippin. Lindsay melted at how playful Amelia's laugh was and loved that it echoed in the barn. Pippin stuck his tongue out and followed Amelia around the stall trying to taste the phone or her or whatever cows did. It was such a genuine interaction, and she tried hard not to think of it as a marketing opportunity. Amelia was so lively here. It was as if she and Zoey switched again. Zoey was more reserved and obviously didn't like getting dirty or too close to the animals, whereas Amelia was right at home. Literally.

"Oh, that's good," Lindsay said. She caught herself staring too long at Amelia and flipped into marketing mode. She took videos of the entrance to the barn, cats sleeping on bales of hay, and a dog, whom Zoey referred to as the Mizzou Moos greeter, who wagged his tail and waited for friendly pats on the head.

"We have the best doggos," Zoey said. She squatted and rubbed Tigger's belly.

"Aren't you afraid they'll run off or get stolen? He's a beautiful dog." Lindsay wasn't a dog person, but she was genuinely concerned for their safety.

"You're such a city girl. They wouldn't leave. They stay close to the house and always alert Amelia if somebody is coming. I like that they are here," Zoey said.

"Do you worry about your sister being up here all alone?" Lindsay asked.

Zoey nodded. "She's a single woman but she knows how to protect herself. And Becks and her wife, Robbie, aren't too far away. We know our neighbors and crime is minimal out in the country."

Every single scary movie set in a remote location rushed to the front of Lindsay's mind. *The Strangers*, *The Hills Have Eyes*, *Friday the 13th*, *Jeepers Creepers*. She couldn't believe Amelia was the only one here. "This blows my mind. I'm nervous walking from my apartment to my car."

"You and I live in a big city. Amelia grew up here. It's hard for people to get up to the house without the dogs or even the security cameras catching them." Zoey pulled out her phone and showed her a view of six different cameras strategically placed around the rescue. "The app notifies us if anything larger than a dog is on the property. It's also a good way to see if any of the animals get out of their pens."

Lindsay shuddered. She was too afraid to be out in the country by herself. She shook her head. "Nope. Can't do it. I wouldn't sleep well."

"There's also the house alarm. And nothing chases burglars away faster than a Rottweiler mix. You haven't met Wally yet, but his eyes are on you, trust me," Zoey said.

Lindsay looked around in alarm and took a step closer to Zoey. "Where is he?"

She laughed and whistled. Wally galloped toward them, then barely stopped short of knocking them over. After a brief introduction and Zoey telling Wally that Lindsay was safe, Lindsay petted him softly. "It's so nice to meet you, big guy. Please be my friend."

"He's fine. You're in the club," Zoey said. She pointed over to the small barn. "How about I introduce you to the cutest mini donkeys you've ever seen in your life?"

"You have mini donkeys? How big are they?" Lindsay asked.

Zoey held her hand at mid-thigh. "This tall. They're still new and skittish, so we'll have to be careful." She turned to Amelia. "Hey, Amelia. We're going to go see the donkeys." Amelia waved and continued playing with Pippin.

It was hard not to stay and watch her, but Lindsay had to stay on task. Work first and then maybe a late-night chat later after Zoey went to bed if Amelia was up for it. She spent the next hour taking videos of the donkeys, the dogs, the cows in the pasture, and the entire rescue through fresh eyes. She took videos until her phone buzzed with only ten percent battery left. She waved her phone at Zoey. "I'm out of juice."

Zoey checked the time. "Let's go inside and cool off. Amelia might be used to this weather, but I'm melting."

Lindsay clutched Zoey's arm. "I know, right? I thought I was being a baby."

"Let's grab some iced teas and I'll start the grill," Zoey said.

"Should we tell Amelia?" Lindsay asked.

"She'll be in soon enough. We can go over the videos we took in the meantime." Zoey motioned for Lindsay to follow her into the house even though Lindsay wanted to find Amelia and start the line of communication.

"Sounds great." Lindsay slipped inside the cool house and sighed in relief. She washed her hands and gratefully accepted the tea from Zoey.

"If you want to sit at the table, there's a charger by you so you can plug in your phone. I'm excited for your videos and see what your vision is for Mizzou Moos. Here's my phone. See if you like any of the videos I took," Zoey said.

Lindsay scrolled through Zoey's videos. They were okay. Nothing really popped but she nodded and smiled since Zoey wanted her approval. "You have some good shots we can use."

Zoey did a little fist pump. "Great! Maybe I got into the wrong profession."

"You definitely need to be in front of the camera," Lindsay said. Realizing that it might be taken in the wrong context, Lindsay quickly added, "Not that you couldn't direct, but you're so good at acting."

"Tell my agent that."

"You still haven't heard?" Lindsay asked.

"Nope. She's as anxious as I am. She left a message this morning, but we haven't heard back."

Lindsay squeezed Zoey's hand. "I'm sure they'll call you soon. It's only been a week. The movie industry is slower than television. Hang in there. Something will happen soon."

Amelia opened the door and saw them holding hands. Her puzzled look made Lindsay slowly pull away from Zoey. Great. That was all she needed.

"Did you get some good footage?" Amelia asked.

"I'm going through Zoey's phone now. I can't wait to see your videos." Lindsay focused her attention back to the phone in her hand.

"Sis, show Lindsay your videos. I'm going to make dinner. Lindsay, do you have any food allergies or food you don't like?"

"No restrictions. Whatever you put in front of me, I'll eat it." She cleared her throat when Amelia sat next to her.

"Then steak and salad it is. Lindsay, how do you like yours cooked?"

"Medium is fine, thank you. Are you sure I can't do anything? Cut up vegetables or something?" Being shoulder-to-shoulder with Amelia was unnerving.

"No, thanks. You just look over videos and help us find something we can use," Zoey said.

Lindsay gave Amelia a small smile. They were sitting close enough to where Lindsay could make out perspiration beaded on Amelia's hairline and how it curled the hair at her temples.

"If I smell like cow slobber, I'm sorry," Amelia said.

Lindsay shook her head. "You're fine." Amelia smelled like fresh rain and sweet pollen. Or maybe that was honey. Whatever the combination was, she smelled nice. She handed Amelia Zoey's phone and looked through Amelia's videos. "These are really great. It's like you were in my head seeing exactly what I wanted. Can I send the videos to my phone?" Then she would have Amelia's phone number and vice versa. Not that she would use it for anything but videos. This was a work trip. Or maybe she should just AirDrop them and not have Amelia's number. That sounded safer.

"Sure. Whatever you need," Amelia said.

"Great." Lindsay selected twenty videos and AirDropped them to her phone. The transfer took some time, but she started watching as soon as they came in. She was so wrapped up in the project that she forgot everything until a dinner plate was carefully placed in her line of vision. "Oh, my gosh. I'm so sorry. I didn't mean to lose myself." She put her phone down and accepted a glass of red wine from Amelia. "Thank you." The muscles in her stomach clenched when Amelia's fingers gently brushed hers as she transferred the glass. Their eye contact lasted more than just a casual glance. Lindsay felt a stirring and was sure Amelia did, too.

Zoey interrupted what Lindsay thought was a genuine moment and sat across from them. "Do you think we have enough for several videos? Did anything really stand out?"

Lindsay pulled her focus away from Amelia and back to the project. "Definitely. I'm going to work on piecing together a couple of videos tonight. Maybe at the same time, you can open accounts across all platforms and then tomorrow we can post a few videos. We don't want to overdo it, but I want to have several ready to go."

"Amelia and I can do that while you do your thing," Zoey said.

"Sounds like a plan." Lindsay said. She wasn't sure how long she was going to stay. It would go a lot faster if Amelia agreed to do twin videos with Zoey. Hopefully, she would agree after the first couple of videos dropped and the number of followers grew.

"Oh, my God! It's Silvia." Zoey grabbed her phone and raced into the other room to answer it. Amelia quickly followed leaving Lindsay alone in the kitchen. She calmly cut her steak and waited knowing full well she'd know the moment Zoey got off the phone. Less than thirty seconds later, both Zoey and Amelia shouted and whooped. Lindsay smiled, took a bite of her perfectly grilled steak, and waited for them to officially tell her the good news.

"I got the part!" Zoey danced into the kitchen shaking her hips and lifting her hands high above her head as though she just scored a touchdown.

"She got the part!" Amelia wasn't as animated as Zoey, but her excitement was still evident. As was pride for her sister. Amelia was beaming.

Lindsay jumped up and high-fived Zoey. "Awesome!"

"They didn't even care about what happened at HEXPO."

"Not at all?" Amelia asked.

"Not after I told them that I paid everyone back. You were right, Amelia. They thought the switch was very inventive but told Silvia they could've rescheduled me," Zoey said. She rolled her eyes. "But that doesn't matter. I got the part!" They sat back down at the table, all three too excited to eat. "There's a catch though."

"What?" Amelia's voice held a note of hesitancy.

"I need to be at the studio Monday morning. I'll be gone for at least three months. I have to be on location. In South America. Which means we'll have to record as many videos as we can in a short time," she said.

"First of all, that's exciting. You worked hard to get here. And I know you love to travel. I'm so happy for you. Secondly, we cannot do three months' worth of videos in three days. That's impossible. There's way too much for me to learn," Amelia said.

Lindsay cleared her voice for attention. It worked. "I could stay longer if that's okay with everyone." Even though she told herself it was for the success of Mizzou Moos, she knew ultimately it meant alone time with Amelia.

CHAPTER THIRTEEN

Everyone is looking at us," Amelia mumbled under her breath as they marched into the grocery store. Zoey clutched a crumpled up flyer she ripped off the telephone pole outside the market. They had had enough. The chatter on Ring was out of control. The townspeople were questioning if donations were really being used to help the rescue. Several pointed out the twin swapping was cute when they were young but using it to dupe people out of money was criminal. It was infuriating.

"I want them to. I want to be out in the open so that people can ask us questions instead of whispering behind our backs," Zoey said.

Amelia thought it was a waste of time because small towns ran on gossip and fake smiles. Talking wasn't going to help because people loved fueling scandals. The whole reason they drove to town was because Zoey opened a letter from the Missouri Rescue Organization thinking it was just their annual grant notification, but it was the exact opposite. The organization thought Mizzou Moos's staff's behavior was counter to their mission statement and were pulling their funding.

"I'm tired of the lies. These people have known us our whole lives and they are making stuff up online just to get attention. I'm done," Zoey said. It was reasons like this very thing that Amelia was happy that she wasn't on the socials, but she wisely kept that to herself. Zoey was on a tear.

"Zoey and Amelia Roberts. It's so nice to see you girls out and about. I figured you'd be hiding after what happened in Vegas." Eloise Gardner, noted town gossip, slithered up in front of them, preventing them from taking more than two steps into the store.

Amelia hissed out a slow breath. They had no choice but to stop and engage. Eloise ran the pottery store where people could paint premade bowls, cups, plates, and drink wine. If somebody wanted gossip, they dropped in to see her. She was a wealth of hearsay.

"It was fun when you were little, but now it looks like you're paying the price. That last stunt you pulled is making people notice." She tsked and slowly shook her head.

Mary Teeter scooted up right next to Eloise, her arms crossed and a disapproving frown pinching the corners of her thin mouth. "So many people think you conned people out of thousands of dollars. Not us, of course. But people." Mary was Eloise's best friend and Amelia's nosy neighbor.

Less than a week after they buried their mother, the twins were approached by the Teeters about selling their land. They acted like they were doing the twins a favor, but the lowball offer was insulting. Every time there was an issue and Mizzou Moos needed to borrow a tractor or a wagon to haul hay, Bob or Mary worked in an offer for the land during the conversation. Amelia always politely turned them down. Asking them for help was always a last resort, which was frustrating because they were Amelia's closest neighbors and they had a ton of land with a lot of equipment. Thankfully, most of her other neighbors were helpful.

When Amelia had to sell several acres to pay taxes and have money for the upkeep, Bob and Mary came through with a fair offer, but not until Robbie negotiated the deal. Sadly, they wanted more land and if things didn't improve, the Teeters might get their wish. Amelia felt her anger rise at the unjust situation and shoved her hands into her pockets so they wouldn't see her fists and know how easily they got to her. She stayed quiet and let Zoey take control of the conversation. Amelia could tell her sister's laugh was fake and forced.

"Oh, Mrs. Teeter, that was nothing. Just me and Amelia doing what we always do. And Mrs. Gardner, you know how the media likes to blow things out of proportion."

Mary tilted her nose up. "Hmm. Sounds like you upset quite a few people with your antics." She riffled through her purse and pulled out a flyer just like Zoey clutched in her hand. "Have you ladies seen this?" Her voice fluctuated as though she was giving them fresh, juicy gossip. Amelia rolled her eyes at Mary's audacity.

Zoey waved her off like it was no big deal. "It's amazing what people will say and do once you're famous. That scandal happened days ago. It's already blown over in Hollywood."

Eloise quirked an eyebrow as though she didn't believe Zoey. "Oh, really?" She pursed her lips and looked down at them.

"My fans got all the photos they wanted." She pointed to herself. "Of me, not Amelia. And they got free swag from the con. It was a win-win situation." She linked arms with Amelia. "Amelia helped me out of a bind and my true fans understood that. She's the best sister."

Amelia forced a smile and decided to change the subject. She didn't want to give these women the opportunity to continue. "I love that Zoey is back in town for a few days. Eloise, is Kevin around? I wasn't sure when he was getting out, but it would be kind of fun to catch up. Is he home yet?" It was a total dick move, but Amelia wasn't in the mood to play nice. They'd gone to school with her son Kevin. He was a nice guy, but he had a serious drinking problem. Mrs. Teeter only made it worse by filling her shop and their house with cases of wine. Kevin was currently serving six months in the Jefferson City Correctional Center for driving under the influence. It was his third offense.

Eloise huffed and stared at them. Amelia hoped her face didn't show anything other than kindness. She knew Zoey wasn't struggling as much as she was.

"He will be home in August," she said.

Zoey sighed. "Oh, that's too bad. I start filming my new movie next week so I'll be leaving in a few days." She touched Eloise's hand briefly. "Please tell him we're thinking about him and maybe next time I'm in town we can all have dinner." Amelia stopped the incoming eye roll. Zoey could charm anybody anywhere.

"Are you really telling us your underhanded plan worked?" Mary asked. She scoffed and looked around as if expecting anyone within earshot to rally with her against them.

Amelia gritted her teeth but kept her cool. Her words came out sharper than she intended. "Call it what you want, but Zoey got the part and the fans got what they wanted," she said.

"Let these ladies do their shopping, Mary," Eloise said. She moved out of the way but put her hand on Zoey's forearm before they could make a fast getaway. "I will let Kevin know. You girls have a good day. It's good to see you, Zoey. I'm glad you're keeping your chin up. We all know that scandal wasn't anything but hogwash," she said.

"No reason to have my chin down but thank you anyway. Now you take care, Mrs. Gardner." Zoey linked her arm with Amelia's and walked away.

"You're so good at schmoozing," Amelia said. She grabbed a basket from the stack and returned to Zoey's side.

"Me? You're the one who brought up Kevin," Zoey said.

Amelia scoffed. "I just find it a little annoying that she's judging us. It's not like we put anyone in danger with our stunt. Besides, you dragged me into town. Did you actually expect me to be nice?"

"We're here out in public because we're going to make sure everyone in town knows this didn't break us. That we didn't do anything wrong. Well, not super wrong," Zoey said.

"Super wrong? Nice," Amelia said. They didn't get far into the store before Zoey was approached by young fans wanting photos. Nobody looked at them with disdain. Amelia stood back when people asked Zoey to take photos and when adults started asking about the Vegas switch, Amelia moved closer to Zoey.

"I had to be in two places at once and I put my sister in a bad spot. It wasn't fair for me to ask her to do it, but she loves me and has always had my back." She pointed to somebody in the small crowd. "Is that you, Peter Watkins? Remember when Amelia and I swapped places at debate club so she could interview for college?"

"You were terrible. What were we debating? Global warming? You stood in front of everyone and talked about nothing for five minutes," Peter said.

"And you know what? Amelia's interview with the college went well, she got the scholarship, and nobody got hurt," Zoey said.

"Hey, if you can get away with it, then good for you," Peter said.

"Obviously, it doesn't always work," Zoey said dryly. "That's what happened in Vegas. Of course, we've learned our lesson now."

"Did you get the part?" somebody in the crowd asked.

"I got the movie role, but I will no longer be on *Thirteen Witches*," Zoey said.

The ten or so people that gathered around them all groaned. Amelia heard "No way," and "that's crap."

Zoey held up her hands. "It's okay. My dream has always been to be in a movie so things are looking up." She high-fived some of the crowd. "We're going to finish our shopping but please come by Mizzou Moos and meet our latest additions. We now have miniature donkeys. They are super cute. Also check us out online. We're creating fun content across social media." Zoey waved to the small cluster of people. Amelia grabbed her arm and pulled her down a different aisle to finish their shopping and made their way to checkout.

"You're so good at this," Amelia said.

Zoey shrugged. "I have faith that people will talk and get the word out. I'm going to try to get as many people out to the farm as I can. I hate that our government funding is getting pulled because of my stupid idea." She checked her phone. "Let's hit a few more stores and get back to Moos."

Amelia slowed her pace and waited until people weren't in earshot. "Don't be mad at me, but I need to talk to you about something."

Zoey looked at her in alarm. "What? Is everything okay?"

Amelia nodded. "Everything's fine. I'm just curious about something Lindsay said to me in Vegas and I wasn't sure when to bring it up."

"Okay. What's up?"

"She mentioned a few things about you gambling and I want to make sure you're okay and there isn't a problem." Amelia blew out a quick breath. "When I won the jackpot, she scolded me and said 'I thought you weren't gambling anymore' and then made another comment later. What was that all about?"

Zoey held up her hand. "It's not a problem. One terrible night, some of the cast and crew of *Thirteen Witches* went to a casino to celebrate something. I don't even remember for what, but I spent too much money and drank too much wine. Chase tagged along and contributed to some very unflattering photos. Lindsay did a great job of cleaning the whole thing up."

"Oh, my God. How much did you lose?"

Zoey shook her head. "An amount I'm not proud of. I promise you I don't have an addiction. My only problem was falling for a gym rat who was using me to meet other actors and for a fat paycheck that didn't really exist. When Lindsay made it disappear, I swore to her that I was never going to gamble again. And I haven't."

"Well, that makes sense. And I'm glad he's gone. I never liked him. Thanks for telling me."

"You know you can talk to me about anything any time you want." Zoey threw her arm around Amelia's shoulder. "And if I'm ever in real trouble, you'll be the first one I turn to."

"Thanks, sis." A giant wave of relief washed over Amelia and a lightness she hadn't felt in days filled her heart. Her sister was fine.

Zoey's phone dinged. She grabbed it out of her back pocket and smiled. "Yeah! Lindsay has three videos she wants to show us."

Amelia felt her heart skip a beat at hearing Lindsay's name. "That's exciting."

Zoey briefly cringed. "Look, I'm sorry I didn't tell you Lindsay was coming. I thought you'd see each other and things would be gloriously gay and happy. I expected fireworks and unicorns dancing around," Zoey said.

Amelia nudged her with her elbow. "I'm still trying to pick up her vibe. Whatever happens, I'm glad she's helping us," Amelia said. She scanned the few items and pulled out her debit card to pay.

"The vibe is really good, trust me. If she wasn't into you a little bit, she wouldn't be here. Yes, she's great at what she does and she dabbles in the social media sites for *Thirteen Witches*, but she and I are not that close."

Amelia frowned. "What do you mean?"

"I know her and we've shared space, but she's not here for me. She's here for you," Zoey said.

That stupid flutter hit her in the chest again. "That's not true." Amelia wouldn't allow herself to believe it. When they talked earlier about Vegas, Lindsay just glazed over the conversation. "Why though? She's Hollywood. I'm just a farm girl living in small town America." Zoey turned her so they were face-to-face.

"Listen to me. You are more than just a farm girl. You have the biggest heart out of anyone I know. You're smart, brave, obviously sexy and beautiful, and you deserve the chance at something with somebody who is equally as special." Zoey held her hands. "I'm sorry you have to hear this, but it's all true."

She wasn't used to the attention on her. "Thanks, but in case there's a sliver of truth, you need to make yourself scarce tonight after dinner. Not that I don't want to spend every single minute with you, but I'd like to see what could happen when Lindsay and I are alone."

Zoey smacked her forehead. "I'm an idiot. I just kept rambling last night. Why didn't you stop me?"

Amelia put her arm around Zoey's shoulders and walked with her over to the truck. "Because I don't see you enough as it is."

"Come on. Let's hit the feed store and then hit the coffee shack next to it. Maybe I'll do a livestream of us buying pellets or petting baby chickens," Zoey said.

"I'll hold the camera," Amelia said.

"You need to be in the shot. This could be our first video or live stream together. We'll make it sweet and fun. No talk of scandal or anything heavy," Zoey said. She pulled out her phone and waved it back and worth at Amelia. "Come on. Let's do it."

Amelia blew out a breath. "Fine. But only when I'm ready."

Zoey did a small victory dance before she pulled open the car door. "You got it, sis."

"This video is playful and fun and shows the world what exactly Mizzou Moos is. I think you'll like it." Lindsay turned her laptop around so Amelia and Zoey could see the final project. It was ninety seconds long and a sweet introduction to Mizzou Moos. It ended with Zoey and Amelia popping into view and waving at the camera. They weren't dressed alike and didn't lean into their twinness like Amelia expected. For that she was thankful. Amelia gritted her teeth but didn't say anything. She was always going to be critical of herself.

Zoey clapped with delight. "This is amazing, Lindsay. I love it."

"It's really good," Amelia said. She had to admit that it turned out better than she expected.

"If everyone approves, let's blast it," Lindsay said. She waited for their approval. "This will go great after the livestream you did at Oakley's Feed. The baby chicks were a nice touch."

"We've been petting the chicks since we were little girls. It was always a treat when we went into town," Amelia said. She didn't want Lindsay to think they just did it for the followers.

"I didn't mean anything by it," Lindsay said. She played it again. "Your livestream got a lot of attention. It's the first time you've been on camera since Vegas. Most of the comments were good, but there were some shitty people saying shitty things. That's to be expected. When we post, we can turn comments off, or we can just delete the bad ones if necessary. Or you can address them. The choice is yours," she said.

"I think it's up to Amelia. She's going to have to maintain the accounts. What do you think?" Zoey asked.

Amelia blinked and stumbled over her words. "Uh, well. I mean, somebody's going to have to show me how to do everything." She leaned back in the chair and crossed her arms. She was trying not to shut down. Running a rescue was hard work. Adding another responsibility was overwhelming. She liked the concept of it, but didn't want another thing on her plate.

"Becks will for sure help. She and Robbie are always taking videos of the babies," Zoey said.

"The second and third videos are ready if you want to approve them as well." Lindsay pulled up the second video. It was only about the mini highland cows. Amelia was in the video introducing each cow. Amelia couldn't help but smile. Lindsay really captured the love she had for the rescue and for each mini cow.

"I need somebody to explain to me how we make money by posting videos. I didn't know this was a thing," Amelia said.

"Your videos will be on a creator fund platform so every time somebody watches the video, you'll get paid," Lindsay said.

"How much are we talking about?" Amelia asked.

"It's going to take time, but enough to help feed the animals if it takes off," Zoey said. She pointed to the laptop. "What's the third video?"

"Take a look." Lindsay hit play. It was a video entering the rescue, the drive up to the main barn, a panoramic shot of the property, and all the animals saying hello. The dogs wagged their tails, the cats stretched and pawed the camera, and Pippin stuck his tongue out. It showed a quirky and fun trip for people who wanted to see and pet miniature animals. Amelia wanted to point out that it was an educational experience, too, but they could save that for future videos.

"Let's launch them, share, and then go out to dinner," Zoey said. "That way we won't obsess about number of views the whole night."

"Let's do it," Amelia said with conviction. The sooner they left, the sooner they would return and maybe she and Lindsay could finally have the chat that had been hanging in the air between them.

Chapter Fourteen

L indsay couldn't sleep. She wasn't used to the deep, repetitive belching noise of bullfrogs and the annoying shrill of the cicadas could fuck off already. They were two new sounds the twins identified for her earlier and now she couldn't hear anything else. She missed the low hums of the late-night city traffic. Country life was overrated and kind of scary. She threw off the covers and crept down the stairs, careful not to wake anyone. It was still hot. She poured a glass of cold water and stepped outside hoping to feel a breeze against her warm skin. She smiled when she heard soft moos and snorts coming from the barn.

"Can't sleep?"

Lindsay shrieked. "You scared me." Amelia was sitting in a rocking chair about three feet away. "What are you doing up?"

"I couldn't sleep either," Amelia said. She pointed to the rocking chair next to her. "Have a seat."

Very aware she was clad in only boxers and a thin T-shirt, Lindsay sat at the edge of the chair. Being this close to Amelia was unnerving. "Will I really see shooting stars from here? Because that would be amazing," Lindsay asked. She sat down but kept her gaze focused up. The twins had promised shooting stars were common, but she wasn't sure she believed them.

"Definitely. With the lights off, you'll see so many constellations. If you're into that," Amelia said.

"My mom is really into it. She always brought us to the planetarium when we were little," Lindsay said.

She and Amelia didn't get a chance to talk after dinner. On their way home, they helped a teenager who had run his car off the road. It took some time for his parents and the tow truck to show up so by the time they got home, it was late. Amelia looked tired, so Lindsay decided to call it a night and maybe try to carve out some alone time with Amelia tomorrow. Technically, it was tomorrow and they were alone.

"I think we should talk more about Vegas. The other night I should've said more. It was a big deal to me and the whole thing hurt my feelings." The night offered a veil of privacy. Any emotions that crossed Lindsay's face were hidden.

"I'm so sorry. We never meant to hurt anyone. I didn't want to, but I'm always going to help Zoey when she needs it. Just know that even though I was playing a role, I was also being myself. I should've made you understand that my feelings were real," Amelia said.

Lindsay slid back in the chair and relaxed her body even though her stomach quivered. She wanted to just brush it off and tell her it wasn't a big deal, but it was. Lindsay wasn't used to putting herself out there and she sure as hell wasn't used to being rejected. That wasn't the bad part. It was the duping. Why didn't Amelia explain things to her that night or even last night? Before she had time to get out what she wanted to say, Amelia continued.

"I had a really nice time with you and I shouldn't have. I was there playing Zoey and it was wrong for me to even lead you on. It put everyone in a bad spot. I can't imagine what went through your mind thinking I was Zoey the whole time. I was just supposed to go in, play her for twenty-four hours, and then go home. I wasn't supposed to get close to you and for that I'm sorry," Amelia said.

Did Amelia regret the kiss? Did Lindsay read the situation wrong? "So, you regret it?" Lindsay asked.

"I regret putting you and Zoey in that position. That couldn't have been easy after I left. You wanted answers and she probably avoided you like the plague."

That wasn't the answer Lindsay wanted. She wanted to know if the kiss meant anything, but she knew that if she asked, it would put a strain on the reason she was here. And she really believed in the rescue. "It was awkward. Zoey avoided me whenever we shared space."

Amelia's soft laugh made Lindsay smile. "Well, just know that she chewed my ass out for that. Zoey doesn't get mad at me often, but she really got pissed. I don't blame her."

"You did a good job playing your sister. Now, it's obvious to me, but before, not so much," Lindsay said.

"Oh, what's different about us?" Amelia asked.

This was the time to be honest, but Lindsay was nervous and stupidly toned it down. "You're more tan. Zoey is always very insistent on sunscreen when we film outdoors."

"Yeah, I should use it more. I'm sure I'll regret it in twenty years," Amelia said.

"Or ten."

Amelia playfully groaned. "You, too?"

Lindsay shrugged. "Science isn't wrong. And the sun here feels like it's five inches from your body. Why is it so hot here? People think California is so hot and sunny, but holy crap. They need to come here. It's terrible."

Amelia nodded. "It really is. The humidity makes it unbearable."

"Do you have a pond or a lake or a pool here to cool off?" Lindsay asked. She fanned herself with her fingers even though it did nothing to conjure up a breeze.

"The big cows have a pond. I'll probably dig a tiny one for the Highlands. Sadly, I do not have one of my own," Amelia said. She shook her head. "I mean, the big cows would share but I'm not interested in swimming in a place they've been."

"I don't blame you at all. Wait. Can cows swim? Turns out, I know nothing about them," Lindsay said. She refrained from making a steak comment because she wasn't sure if Amelia would find it tasteless. Or tasty. Stop, she chided herself.

"They can. The pond isn't very deep though. We end up adding water to it every year. It's amazing how expensive water is," Amelia said.

Lindsay slipped into work mode. She needed to ensure her plan worked so that they could get a steady flow of money coming into Mizzou Moos. Tours were nice, but Amelia admitted to her that the number of tours had dropped this week. They weren't sure if it was because of summer vacations or that the locals were upset by the scandal. "You don't happen to have your phone with you, do you? I forgot to check our numbers when we got home."

"It's three in the morning," Amelia said dryly.

Lindsay pointed. "Right. Sorry. Sometimes it's hard to turn it off."

The small stretch of silence that followed was enough of a break for Amelia to change the subject. "Let's talk about you. What happens now? Do you have anything lined up?" Amelia asked.

Lindsay hated that the conversation got derailed. She wanted to get back to their night in Vegas and the kiss they shared, but she was also excited about the success of their videos. Timing was everything in both instances. She really didn't want to talk about her career. "I've told a few people I'm available." She left out the part about Roger possibly saying terrible things about her. Amelia didn't need that stress on top of the financial burden. "I'm not worried though. Something will happen." Lindsay was extremely thankful for her small nest egg. Plus, if things got bad, she could sublet her apartment to somebody at the studio.

"I'm glad you aren't worried. I'm sure a great opportunity will come up," Amelia said.

Lindsay watched Amelia brush her fingers through her hair and tuck it behind her ears. "This is a nice break. I'm not worried at all."

"Good. Okay, I guess I should get back to bed. Those cute snoring donkeys are going to be screaming for breakfast in a few short hours," Amelia said.

Lindsay's stomach dropped. Since when did she shy away from hard-hitting topics? There was something about Amelia that made her back down. Maybe it was how vulnerable Amelia made her feel or how perfect that kiss was. She simply nodded and followed her into the house. "Well, I hope you get to sleep." She stood at the bottom of the stairs waiting for something, anything to happen.

"I hope you sleep, too. See you later," Amelia said.

She could've reached out and stopped Amelia or asked her to please stay and talk more about what happened last weekend, but what else was there to talk about? It was a nice kiss. The only thing left was if they should continue kissing or not.

She mustered a weak smile and climbed the stairs behind Amelia. She said good night one last time before closing her bedroom door. Slipping into the cool sheets felt nice, but she was still heated thinking about Amelia's lips. That was one thing she didn't tell Amelia. She had nicer lips than Zoey.

Lindsay woke up to excited voices downstairs. She should've jumped up to find out what all the squealing was about, but she was tired. It took her over an hour to fall asleep. Her body felt heavy. She rolled over and shoved a pillow over her head to drown out the noise. It almost worked. She drifted off but jumped when somebody knocked on her door.

"Lindsay! Lindsay! Are you up? Look at social media." Zoey was on the other side of the door rapping her knuckles repeatedly. Lindsay lifted her head and fumbled for her phone. Where did she put it? She slid her hand along the mattress until her fingers brushed the aluminum case.

"Okay. Please stop knocking," she said.

"I'm coming in. Cover yourself," Zoey said. She opened the door five seconds later and sat on the edge of Lindsay's bed. "Look. We have over ten thousand likes and a ton of shares."

Lindsay brushed the sleep from her eyes and tried hard to focus on what Zoey was saying. "That's great. Hopefully, people are watching the full video. That's what gives you the money."

"How do we find that out?" Zoey pulled up the account.

"Use the app's calculator. Right now, it's probably too soon to get an accurate number. We need more videos. The more we post, the more followers we get."

"Looks like we're going to be making videos today, sis," Zoey said.

Lindsay was mortified. She had been unaware that Amelia was somewhere behind Zoey. This was not how she wanted Amelia to see her. Her hair was a tangled mess and her breath probably smelled worse than the donkeys' stall. Her T-shirt had risen and was showing more skin than a bathing suit and, well, she felt exposed. Amelia must have noticed her discomfort.

"Hey, let's give her time to wake up. Coffee's on. We'll see you downstairs," Amelia said. She dragged Zoey away and shut the door, but not before she gave Lindsay a look that made Lindsay's stomach tumble. Once they shut the door, Lindsay jumped out of bed, sprinted to the bathroom, and was downstairs, fully clothed with fresh breath and brushed hair in twenty minutes.

"Sorry I slept in," she said. She sat at the table and opened her laptop.

"It's barely nine. You're not late. I'm sorry Zoey woke you up." Amelia slid a cup of coffee in front of her. "I'm making French toast if you're interested."

Lindsay wasn't a breakfast eater, but if a beautiful woman wanted to cook her breakfast, she wasn't going to say no. "That sounds great. Thank you." She looked around. "Where's Zoey?"

"She's on the phone working out the details of where she needs to be and when. She might need some additional vaccines. She'll be back soon," Amelia said.

"No worries." Lindsay wanted to say something about last night, but Amelia was busy cooking. She diverted her attention to Mizzou Moos social media accounts. The first account had thousands of likes and hundreds of comments. Most of the comments were nice. The really nasty ones were easy to delete. "I'm dropping another video. I think we should strike while the iron is hot." Lindsay had it set up so they only had to upload one video and it would share to all platforms. She knew neither of the twins had the time to upload each one every time.

"Okay, I'm all set." Zoey walked back into the room. "Did I miss anything?"

"I just told Amelia that I'm posting another video. How does everyone's day look to record more content?" she asked.

"We have tours starting at eleven so we might be able to record for a bit before they start," Amelia said.

Lindsay pointed at Zoey. "Do you do the tours, too? Or hide out?"

"Oh, they're here to see animals, not me," she said.

Amelia put a plate of French toast, a plate of bacon, and maple syrup on the table. "They would love to see both of us. Maybe visitors would be willing to sign release forms and be in the videos today. It might give off a feel of authenticity and tell the viewers yes, we do have tours, and yes we do need money to keep this place afloat."

"I like the way you think," Lindsay said. She winked at Amelia as she reached for a piece of bacon and was rewarded with a nice pink flush. Maybe if she would have pushed the conversation last night, this morning would have a different vibe.

The rest of breakfast was mostly Zoey reading comments out loud and either rolling her eyes or smiling happily. "This is turning out better than I expected. Maybe a scandal isn't the worst thing to happen."

"You say that now. Those are mostly your fans. Today is the first day I'm doing tours. Who knows who's going to show up. Maybe it'll be fine or maybe it'll be tons of reporters," Amelia said.

Lindsay could tell Amelia was nervous. She hadn't felt the wrath of a scandal yet like she and Zoey had. At least Zoey had a blockbuster movie to keep her employed. Lindsay had nothing. And yet here she was, in the middle of the country, trying to help somebody she barely knew all because of a kiss. The energy between them was undeniable, and yet they talked about the weather and how many vitamin pellets was too many for the mini donkeys.

"Just text me and I'll handle it," Zoey said.

Lindsay liked how protective the sisters were of one another. She wanted to tell Amelia that she, too, could intervene if necessary. She knew enough about handling delicate situations, but she was sure everyone knew it already. "Same."

Amelia excused herself to change into work clothes leaving her and Zoey alone at the table. Zoey leaned closer.

"Have you talked to her yet?" Zoey asked. Her voice was low so it didn't carry beyond the kitchen. Lindsay stiffened.

"What do you mean?" She knew exactly what Zoey meant but tried to play it off.

"Oh, stop. I know you're here for her." Zoey held up her hand to stop Lindsay from defending herself. "I love that you're showing us very important things that will definitely help Mizzou Moos, but I want you and Amelia to talk it out. Whatever it is. Every time I walk into a room the tiny hairs on my arms stand straight up because of the electricity between the two of you. Stop wasting time. Ignite that fire."

"It's not like that," Lindsay said. But wasn't it? Didn't it feel like the energy twirled them closer together whenever they shared space? Zoey gave her a look. Lindsay's shoulders slumped. "We talked about it the other night. But that was it. Once we get Mizzou Moos up and running on social media, then maybe we can talk about it more."

"You either go for it or you don't. You're either into her or you're not." Zoey leaned forward and whispered, "But I think you're into her. And I know she's into you. My sister isn't the kind who makes the first move so if you want something to happen, you should go for it."

The memory of last night pushed its way to the forefront of her mind. They were alone. It was dark and peaceful. "Sadly, I'm also not really one to make the first move either."

"Who kissed who first in Vegas?" Zoey asked.

Lindsay honestly didn't know. They gravitated toward one another. Nobody made the first move. They were suddenly, wonderfully, passionately in each other's arms. Was it one kiss or several? Did it last ten seconds or ten minutes? She didn't have a clue. "It just kind of happened."

Zoey smiled and leaned back in the chair. "Oh, yeah. Those are the best kind."

Amelia strolled into the room wearing a fitted red polo shirt with a Mizzou Moos logo and jeans. Her hair was braided back away from her face to show off her large, expressive eyes. A small smile shifted from one side of her mouth to the other until it finally landed as a smirk. "I figured we could get started shooting videos now if you all are up for it." She stepped into her steel-toed cowboy boots and grabbed her Stetson hat to complete the farm girl look. "This is normally what I wear when I'm giving tours."

Lindsay blew out a breath. Who knew a farm girl could be so sexy? "It's a good look."

"Hell, she grew up in overalls. Most of the time she's in those. This is a treat," Zoey said. Lindsay caught the stern look Amelia shot Zoey and pressed her lips together to keep from smiling.

"I have to look the part," Amelia said.

Lindsay couldn't remember a time when Amelia looked bad. "I'll grab my phone and we can start shooting. Zoey? Do you want to be a part of this?"

"I feel like now would be the perfect time to twin," Zoey said.

Chapter Fifteen

"Mizzou Moos. Thank you for calling. Would you like to schedule a tour today?" Amelia didn't answer the phone a lot, but Becks was running late.

"I'm trying to reach Zoey. Is she available?"

Amelia was taken aback by the question. It was the first time she fielded a call for Zoey. Becks and Robbie answered the business phone and hadn't mentioned anyone calling for her sister, but they likely shielded her since the scandal broke. It was unnerving. "She is not. Is there anything I can help you with?" Amelia's entire body tensed as she waited for the person with the gentle southern voice on the other end to answer.

"I'm just trying to get in touch with her," he said.

"I can take a message and relay it," Amelia said. No way was she going to. Zoey had enough things to stress about.

"That's okay. I'll see her later."

Amelia frowned when the caller quickly disconnected the call before she could answer. She scrolled to find the name or number of the person but the only information she found was private caller and no phone number.

"What's going on? You look worried," Lindsay asked.

"Nothing. Just another weird phone call," Amelia said. Lindsay didn't need to know about the details about the call either.

She quickly put the business phone down when Zoey entered the kitchen. There was no reason to alarm her. Zoey was getting

KRIS BRYANT

ready to leave the country and the last thing she needed was to worry about another fan looking to make contact.

"Are we twinning in our videos today?" Amelia put her hands on her hips.

"I figured we might as well. And since this is the official outfit of Mizzou Moos, I thought I'd wear it. That way we can do some twinning videos." Zoey looked down at clothes. "The shirt is a little big on me. Your boobs must've stretched it."

Amelia pulled the brim of her hat down so that Lindsay couldn't see her cheeks engulfed in flames. "I'm sure we have an extra small in the office," she murmured.

Zoey gasped and busted out laughing. "Whatever. Let's get started. Oh, wait. I need my hat. Do you know where it is?"

"Try the office. I think Becks stored it there," Amelia said. She watched Zoey retreat as long as she could before it got weird and turned her attention back to Lindsay. "What do you have in mind for today?" She didn't like that Lindsay was wearing sunglasses but couldn't blame her. She smiled when Lindsay took them off.

"Zoey had some good ideas that might push you out of your comfort zone," Lindsay said.

"Oh, we're way beyond that, don't you think?" Amelia said with a bit more bite than she intended. All of this was her own fault. Lindsay opened and closed her mouth. "I'm sorry. None of this is your fault. You're here helping us and I'm being an asshole because I'm mad that we're in the mess in the first place."

"It's okay. I understand. Do you want to carve out some time later. Just us?" Lindsay asked.

The way she barely bit her lip after she asked the question made Amelia swallow hard. "Definitely." She dropped her gaze down to Lindsay's lips remembering how demanding they were. Kissing her was tempting, but Amelia wasn't sure where they stood until she looked back into Lindsay's deep blue eyes and saw a pure, unguarded look that it made her knees weak.

"All right. Let's do this." Zoey slapped her hat on her head and pointed to the sign over the barn completely unaware of the

• 148 •

moment Amelia was having with Lindsay. "How about you film Amelia introducing the viewer to Moos and then I pop out behind her and say something cutesy and clever and we do that all around the farm. Like we go see Pippin and Amelia leans against the fence, you record from the side, and then I lean forward and say something cutesy and clever and so on. Does that make sense?"

"Are we going for humor then? Not sincere?" Amelia asked. She wasn't sure what the right approach was. Did they go for laughs or for serious content?

"Humor," Zoey and Lindsay said in unison.

Amelia shrugged. "Whatever you think. Both of you are in television. Maybe instead of Zoey popping out, Lindsay can just move the camera around. I think jumping out is kind of corny—like a used car salesman."

"That's a valid point," Lindsay said.

They had taken several videos, most of them boring, but only one that made them laugh until they cried. Pippin, who was fast becoming the star of the Mizzou Moos videos, managed to stick his tongue out and lick both Amelia and Zoey as though directed to do it. Both ran off in opposite directions yelling his name. It was hilarious. Lindsay had dropped to her knees from laughing so hard.

"Oh, my God. That's priceless. He's your moneymaker," she said.

Zoey stumbled over to Lindsay holding her stomach. "Please tell me you got the shot."

Lindsay nodded. "I can't wait to see it inside. It's too bright out here."

Amelia wiped her tears with the back of her hand. "I hate that I have to go greet our guests and that I have no time to wash his slobber off." She used the bandana from her back pocket and wiped her face the best she could. "I think he got my nose."

Lindsay laughed again. "He certainly did. Do you mind if I keep taking videos of him while you do your tour?"

"Feel free. He's in a good mood. I think he knows we're filming him," Amelia said. She hated leaving now but was glad

Lindsay got good videos. Everyone agreed to continue to shoot videos and meet up after tours.

"Stay out of the sun," Amelia said more to Lindsay, but Zoey answered.

"We will. I don't want skin cancer or to look like I'm eighty when I'm thirty," Zoey said.

"Love you." Amelia waved without turning around.

"Ditto."

She smiled. It was always nice when Zoey was around. She was going to miss her when she went on location.

"This is one of my favorite stops along the tour." Amelia was hyper aware of every man on each tour. The person who called earlier made it clear that he would see Zoey today and this was the last tour of the day. Maybe he was just bluffing. They hadn't had a single issue all day. "Three years ago, we rescued six pygmy goats from a petting zoo in Arkansas who all had significant health issues. Thanks to generous donations from you all, we were able to get them the healthcare they needed and now they are thriving." Amelia opened the first door to the pen and ushered the small group inside. "Here's the fun part. Everyone gets to bottle feed the babies. But only if you feel comfortable being around them. I'm going to warn you. They have terrible manners. They will nibble on your clothes, try to climb into your lap, and will most likely leave milky drool stains on your clothes."

"So, you're saying one hundred percent of our donations go into Mizzou Moos?" a guy toward the back of the group asked.

Amelia couldn't tell if the man was picking a fight or here to support them. He didn't sound soft-spoken like the man on the phone, but something about the way he asked the question seemed off.

A part of her wanted to let Becks run the tours today, but after the strange phone call earlier, Amelia decided to engage more—a decision she was regretting. Becks had warmed up the tour with a walk-through and Amelia stepped in to take them into the barn to feed baby goats.

"Yes. Every penny from the tours and any additional donations go into a fund that helps pay for upkeep of Mizzou Moos, medicines for the animals, and special food. Running a sanctuary is a lot different than a zoo. We work hard on getting the animals healthy, physically and mentally. Trust isn't easy. The babies were born here so they are used to being around humans, but a lot of the adult goats are wary and skittish around us even though we've been working with them for years." Amelia hoped that the lengthy explanation was enough to appease the guy and move the tour forward. She smiled sweetly at him hoping Zoey's attempt at being charming would work. No such luck.

"Is it true that you and your sister duped a lot of people into giving your rescue money?" The man looked around and nodded to the group. "Yep. It was all over the internet. You can look on your phones now. Just type in Mizzou Moos scandal."

Amelia froze before the angry heat took over. With as much calmness as she could muster, she answered him. "Nobody was swindled out of money. I filled in for my sister for one day at a conference so she could go to a movie audition." She shrugged nonchalantly for effect.

"Sounds like duping to me. I'd be mad if I paid a ton of money to attend a fan show to meet a star and ended up paying a lot of money to get my picture taken with an impersonator," he said. When he had everyone's attention, he kept going. "Are you really using the tour's money to help these animals or are you spending it on expensive trips to gamble in Vegas and exotic boots?" He pointed down to her bull hide boots. The boots were a gift from Zoey when she got her first paycheck from *Thirteen Witches*.

She was losing ground and the crowd. This guy could fuck right off. "The Vegas trip had nothing to do with Mizzou Moos. Everyone at the conference got their money back and received free merch."

"I heard a lot of people are pulling their funding from Mizzou Moos. Like big grants." There was no way this asshole could know as much as he did without digging deep.

Amelia was flustered but kept her cool. "The money is for the animals. Nothing has changed here. That's our mission statement and I stand by it." She adjusted her hat and stared at the man. He smirked and flipped the page on a small notebook he was scribbling in. "Are you with the press? If so, no comment. If you're here for the tour like the rest of these nice people, let's go feed some baby goats. It'll help ease the obvious stress in your life." Amelia noticed a few people had taken out their phones but put them away when she mentioned feeding the baby goats. She handed everyone a baby bottle from a bucket that Becks had filled before the tour started.

The goats knew they were going to be fed so chaos won over the jerk. She handed him a bottle which he immediately rejected. Amelia smiled and focused on the people who wanted to be there. She recited the spiel she knew from heart about how the goats came to be at Mizzou Moos. The children in the group asked fun questions and she loved watching them wrestle bottles from aggressive babies.

It wasn't until she was almost done with the tour that she spotted Lindsay. She had worked her way into the crowd and was recording Amelia. Amelia's anxiety pinged at an uncomfortable ten. It was one thing knowing Lindsay was recording her and another when she didn't. Suddenly, her words sounded clunkier, her voice sounded higher, and sweat was gathering under the brim of her hat. Great. Her hair was going to be wrecked. She opened the gate and ensured it was latched before walking the group back to the parking lot.

"Are there any more questions? If not, feel free to check out our gift and souvenir shop on your way out. Take home your own baby goat, the stuffed animal version that won't spill milk everywhere. We're running a special on them. Thank you for visiting Mizzou Moos and please tell your friends to stop by." Amelia waved to everyone and headed back to the barn to lock it up and ensure there weren't any stragglers. She wasn't alone. The man in the Cardinals hat who tried to stir up shit walked quietly out from the shadows.

"You got me back there," he said. His gait was slow, but with purpose. Everything about him screamed danger. "I'm a reporter. I figure if this story is juicy enough that your sister lost her job, then there has to be more. I'm here to get your side since you were obviously part of it," he said.

Her heart jackhammered. She clutched the front of her shirt and stood still. The most frightening thing was that he came out of nowhere when her guard was down. It was the first time she felt unsafe on her property. He put his hands up but still walked toward her.

"I'm not here to scare you. I just want the truth."

She cleared her throat and moved closer to the gate that corralled the goats. Earlier, she left a shovel leaning up against it and planned on using that as a weapon if necessary. "I told you. No comment. You're going to have to leave now. The tour's over."

"You don't want to be rude. I might say something unfavorable in my article about Mizzou Moos and I'm sure you and your sister don't need any more negative press," he said, emphasizing the word more.

Amelia repeated herself. "No comment. Now please leave before I call the sheriff to throw you off my property."

He tilted his head and shrugged. "I'm going to get this story one way or another."

"Well, it's not going to be from me so go be creative elsewhere." She said it with conviction she didn't feel.

Zoey flung open the door and walked over to Amelia. "What's going on here?" She stretched out her hand. "Hi, I'm Zoey Stark. And you are?" she asked.

The man shook her hand. "Brian Jones. I'm a journalist from St. Louis. People are talking in town about how you are misusing the funds here at Mizzou Moos. I know you've lost funding and I want your side of the story."

Zoey pointed to the camera above their heads. "Well, Brian Jones from St. Louis. You're trespassing and we have no comment. You need to leave immediately. Lots of cameras here, Mr. Jones, if that's even your name." She put her arm around Amelia's shoulders. "We even have a camera in the parking lot so we'll know if you leave or not. We'll watch you though. Just in case the long, straight driveway isn't easy enough for you to follow."

Having Zoey by her side gave Amelia strength. "I have the sheriff on speed dial. We're friends. So, if you don't leave now, I'm going to have him come up here and literally throw you out."

"Like I said, if you talk to me and I get you on record, I can tell your side of the story. I can tell your rescue is hurting. How long before you can't pay the mortgage and have to send these animals off to other farms because you can't afford them? Your careless scandal made a lot of people nervous," Brian said.

Zoey got close to him and pointed. "It's like you heard nothing we said." She pointed again to the camera above them. "You went about this the wrong way. I don't trust you. You are not welcome here. And if you write anything unfavorable, we'll release this tape where you are clearly threatening us."

"Thanks for showing me all the cameras." He barked out a harsh laugh, turned on his heel, and left the barn. Amelia and Zoey followed him out. Amelia locked up the barn while Zoey made sure he left.

"What's going on?" Concern etched the corners of Lindsay's eyes as she walked over to Amelia. Lindsay in a power suit was hot. Lindsay in an evening dress was sexy as hell. But jeans and a white shirt with the sleeves rolled up? And ankle boots with a square toe that looked like cowboy boots? Amelia couldn't stop smiling. This woman could wear anything. And with her hair back in a braid, she looked like she belonged at Mizzou Moos.

Amelia tried to relax. She waved her hand as though it was no big deal when her body was still on high alert. "Did you see that tall guy in the crowd?" Her voice came out higher than normal. She cleared her throat. "He was wearing a red Cardinals hat."

When Lindsay nodded, Amelia continued. "Well, he says he's a reporter and he threatened us. He demanded an interview and said if we didn't talk to him then he would make shit up."

"What? He can't do that," she said.

"The good news is that we have video of him saying all of this," Amelia said. Lindsay slid her hand into hers. Her body reacted so quickly, shifting gears from a low cautious rumble to high speed.

"Does he know about the cameras? Hopefully that'll deter him," she said.

What Amelia thought was a gesture of support was now them just holding hands. She didn't know how to do this without acting awkward. Thankfully, Zoey returned.

"Well, he's gone. I jotted down his license plate just in case the camera in the parking lot didn't get a clear picture," Zoey said. Amelia saw her eyes drop down to their hands and lift her eyebrow. She ignored it and kept her focus on the reporter. "I hate that you're going to be here alone. South America is a lot farther away than Southern California."

"I'm not worried," Amelia said. She one hundred percent was worried. The last thing she wanted, though, was her sister to stress about a creeper. "I have Becks, the neighbors, my guns, all the animals, and Sam."

"And me," Lindsay said. "You have me for as long as you need me."

Amelia smiled when Lindsay squeezed her hand and frowned when she dropped it. "You're welcome here for as long as you want. We really appreciate your help. God knows I wouldn't know how to get started. I mean, I still don't know the steps, but I'm going to take really good notes."

"We can practice tonight. I think I got some pretty good shots today. I'll splice something together and you can upload and do the caption and hashtags," Lindsay said.

"I'm not afraid of a challenge," Amelia said. She didn't mean that to sound suggestive but wasn't embarrassed she said it either.

Being close to Lindsay sounded great. The reporter threw her off, but she didn't want it to ruin her night. "I'll lock up and meet everyone up at the house. Sound good?"

"I'll get started on dinner," Zoey said.

"Can I tag along?" Lindsay asked Amelia.

"Of course. It's boring work, but I'd love the company."

"I'd feel safer if Lindsay went with you," Zoey said. She pointed to the house. "I'm going to go before I stir up too much attention." She looked at Amelia. "Let Becks shoo people out. We have work to do."

"Becks is in charge," Amelia said. She couldn't help that she loved the rescues and wanted to talk about them to anyone who would listen. It was the one thing she was confident about. Mizzou Moos and all the animals inside its gates.

"That's right. And tell Becks she's invited for dinner and if she whines about having to go home, Robbie's invited, too. I'm making enough food for an army. And it will be ready in an hour or so," Zoey said.

They watched Zoey march up the stairs and into the house. "Does she always cook a lot of food?" Lindsay asked.

"She cooks when she's nervous. And she's nervous about everything right now but she's trying to play it off," Amelia said. She was nervous, too. Not only did she have to worry about the reporter, but she was going to be alone with Lindsay after Zoey left to be on location.

"I love how you protect one another," Lindsay said.

"Are you close with your siblings?" Amelia asked. She held open the door to the store and waited for Lindsay to enter. A few people were inside looking at the T-shirts and mugs. Amelia smiled politely at them and nodded at Becks who busied herself by straightening the highland cow stuffies on the shelf nearby so she wouldn't be hovering at the register.

"Not nearly as close are you two are, but then I'm not a twin," Lindsay said.

Amelia smiled fondly. "It's fun." And ninety-nine percent of the time it was. Except when they got caught. Like right now. What they were going through now wasn't fun. "Do you think we should do a video explaining what happened in Vegas? I mean, Zoey already got fired and signed a movie deal so it won't hurt her, right?"

"I'm sure this will always be around for her, but right now I'm worried about how it will affect you. If your videos take off like I think they will, then more people are going to google Mizzou Moos. I want them to see only the good. Maybe we can record an explanation video but not post it unless things take a turn," Lindsay said.

Amelia nodded. "Okay. It sounds like we have a lot to do before Zoey leaves."

"Are you okay with me staying here for a bit after she's gone?"

Amelia looked for anything on Lindsay face that showed discomfort but found only vulnerability. Her eyes were welcoming and her body language was open. Not that Amelia was an expert, but it seemed as though they were getting close to being in the same space they were in Vegas and she was thrilled at the possibilities of what could happen. "You can stay as long as you want. I think you being here is going to be good for me. I mean, for us." She blushed and stammered out, "For all of us at Mizzou Moos." She cringed as Lindsay threw back her head and laughed.

CHAPTER SIXTEEN

B y the end of the night, Mizzou Moos had a total of nine videos uploaded across all social media platforms. Zoey and Lindsay had shared them on their own personal accounts and Lindsay was pleased with the growing number of followers. She was right. Nobody could resist a cute animal video, and the one of Pippin licking both Zoey and Amelia went viral. Tomorrow she would help Amelia with the website and create a webstore better than what was there now. There were several on-demand printing merchandise websites that would send them payouts every month so inventory wasn't an issue except for what Amelia wanted to stock in the store at the rescue. But they needed cash flow to make that happen.

Zoey stood up and stretched. "It's after midnight. I have a long day tomorrow." She hugged Amelia and Lindsay good night. "Don't stay up too late. Somebody has to drive me to the airport at eleven."

"That would be me," Amelia said.

Lindsay closed her laptop. "You're right. We should call it a night." Amelia shot her a quick look that suggested she should wait a minute before retiring. "But I'll finish my drink first." She held up her beer and smiled.

"I'll stay with you. I still have a sip left." Amelia held up her glass of wine. Zoey smiled at them and disappeared. They sat at the table and waited until the creaks from the upstairs bedroom stopped and Zoey was presumably in bed.

"Do you want to go for a walk? There's a nice breeze and we can see all the stars," Amelia said.

"Will there be big, giant country bugs?" Lindsay asked.

Amelia nodded. "Without a doubt."

Lindsay wrinkled her nose. "I know this sounds bad, but I don't want to go to bed smelling like insect repellent." What Amelia didn't know was that Lindsay took great effort tonight to look casual by styling her hair in a way that wasn't too obvious, but still chic. She'd also applied a lotion with hints of vanilla and sandalwood. The last thing she wanted was to cover that up with a strong, medicinal scent of citrusy chemicals.

"We can wear clips. That way the repellent isn't on our skin." Amelia pulled out two belt clips from the closet, inserted new refills, and handed Lindsay one to attach to her waistband. Lindsay frowned at the bulkiness of it. "And yes, it's necessary. You'll thank me later."

She clipped it on her jeans like Amelia showed her, grabbed the flashlight Amelia offered, and followed Amelia out into the dark night. She fell in step beside her as they walked on the gravel path, past the barns, and turned into one of the fields.

"I'm so surprised at how loud it is in the country," Lindsay said.

"It's just different. To me it's peaceful. It's home." Amelia shined the flashlight in front of them to avoid stepping in any holes or ruts left behind from the animals or the tractor.

"I get the peace of this place. And the animals are very sweet. I can tell you love them very much," Lindsay said.

"When both our parents died in the same year, we thought we were going to lose this farm. I was a hot mess. This is where I belong. I couldn't imagine having to rehome all the animals again. We had to take drastic measures," Amelia said.

"Like what?" Lindsay asked. Having spent so much time here, she knew Amelia would do everything possible to keep the farm.

"We sold a hefty chunk of the land just to stay afloat. It's amazing how many people want to take advantage of people who've fallen on hard times."

"People don't always have the best intentions. Or maybe they thought they were helping you out by offering to buy you out," Lindsay said. Her voice inflicted a note of skepticism.

"Yeah, no. It was terrible. Commercial real estate people approached us like sharks and wanted to buy all the land for well below market value. We even had neighbors try to cheat us. We were just kids. We had a lot of people telling us a lot of different things."

"Did you have a family lawyer who helped you with things?" Lindsay asked.

"No. We didn't have a family lawyer. My parents always thought they would grow old together so they hadn't made any arrangements. After my dad died, my mom got a few things in order, but we still had to scramble."

"I'm sorry. What happened to your family was terrible. You had to make big decisions when you were so young." Lindsay couldn't imagine a life without her parents even though now she wasn't as close with them as she should be.

"Everything happened at once. There was a push not too long ago for farmers around here to drill for oil, which turned out to be nothing. And then some companies wanted the farms to lease the land to install solar panels, but there was a lot of pushback from the community. We were confused and overwhelmed to say the least." Amelia stopped to sip her drink and take a breath.

"I'm sorry that people tried to take advantage of you. It looks like you made a good decision, though. You still have Mizzou Moos and you're still saving animals."

"It's been hard but rewarding. Zoey finding work in Hollywood was the best thing that happened to us. She gives as much as she can to Mizzou Moos. I wish I could do more. You coming here to help us try to raise money a new way is a blessing," Amelia said.

Lindsay heard the emotion in Amelia's voice and touched her arm. "Stay on top of the socials and I promise you'll make money for the rescue. There are so many influencers who make money and don't deserve it. This place deserves it and people will know that. You've seen how it can happen. Eventually, you'll be able to collaborate with other influencers or even with companies who sell animal supplements or whatever and you can make money that way, too."

The moon was bright enough that Lindsay could tell Amelia was biting her bottom lip in doubt. "Don't do that."

"Do what?" Amelia asked.

Did she really say that out loud? "Doubt yourself. You're going to be fine," Lindsay said. God, she hoped she was right. She would hate to get Amelia's hopes up and then have them crash and burn because her ideas failed. She stopped walking. Amelia stopped, too.

"I hope so. We're almost at rock bottom. I have a few cows left that we can sell to get us through the winter, but I have no idea what to do after that," Amelia said. She brushed away a tear. "I don't want Zoey to always have to chip in and save us. She deserves to keep the money she makes. Even though she didn't make a ton on the show, she always added extra to the bank."

Lindsay felt bad for judging Zoey, not knowing how much she invested in the farm. "You two have the biggest hearts out of anyone I've ever known. Zoey's going to be okay and so is Mizzou Moos. Now, let's focus on the night and you can tell me farm things and what you do for fun in the summer out here." Lindsay tried to lighten the mood. She wanted the evening to go a different way. She smiled when she heard Amelia chuckle.

"Well, I'm old now so I hang out with my friends, the animals. But know that farm teens are bored and they get into trouble very easily."

Lindsay snorted. "All teens are bad because they're bored."

Amelia faked gasped and put her hand on her chest. "You probably never did a bad thing in your life."

"I think we all go through something as we try to figure out who we are. Especially as we stumble into adulthood," Lindsay said.

"I want to show you what we did when we weren't being bad or when we sneaked out." Amelia held Lindsay's hand and walked her through a field over to a hay bale. "We're going to climb this and look at the stars."

"These sure are a lot bigger up close." She tried to figure out a toe hold or what to grab but struggled, especially in the dark. "How do I get up here?"

"Put your knee in the middle. There's a soft spot. Then reach up and find the net on top and try to pull yourself up. I'll go on the other side and help," Amelia said. She was on top of the bale in ten seconds and reached her hand out to help.

"How did you get up there so fast?" Lindsay graciously accepted Amelia's hand. It was nice to feel her touch again. They were alone, in the dark, and a chill of excitement tickled its way up her body. She shivered, not because she was cold, but because she knew what was going to happen.

"Years of experience." Amelia peeled off her flannel shirt and placed it on the bale behind them. "Now we lie back and make wishes on shooting stars."

"I can do that." She scooted down until she got comfortable and looked up at the thousands of twinkling lights. "This is so beautiful. There are so many."

"This is my therapy. I come out here when I need clarity," Amelia said.

Lindsay pointed. "Look! A shooting star! Your sky is on fire!" Amelia followed Lindsay's finger then gently held her hand.

"Make a wish," she said. Lindsay tried to do that but couldn't focus on anything other than Amelia's fingers interlocked with hers. It was such a smooth and natural move that the wish was forgotten. All she could think about was Amelia's body pressed next to hers and their hands resting against their thighs. "Did you make a wish?"

Lindsay turned her head. The moon was a sliver in the sky but gave enough of a glow that she could see Amelia's face. "You distracted me."

"I distracted you? How did I do that?" she asked.

Lindsay gently squeezed Amelia's hand. "You touched me."

Amelia looked at her. "That's okay, right?"

Lindsay licked her lips and looked at Amelia's hoping she'd pick up on the clue that it was more than okay. Touching was okay and kissing was definitely on the table. She nodded.

Amelia released Lindsay's hand and leaned up on her elbow. "Want to know what I wished for?"

Lindsay rested her fingertip on Amelia's full lips. "If you tell me, it won't come true." She felt Amelia's lips press against her finger. She was tired of waiting. She was a grown woman who wanted to be kissed. With as much passion as before. Only this time she knew who was kissing her. "I hope you wished for anything but a kiss." She wasn't disappointed.

Amelia moved closer and slipped her leg between Lindsay's. If Amelia's warm body wasn't partially on top of hers, she would've floated away in the night. A kaleidoscope of emotions exploded once Amelia's lips brushed hers. Elation, passion, desperation, satisfaction, and delight. She wound her fingers in Amelia's hair and deepened the kiss. She didn't mind the straw poking the back of her arms or how hard the hay bale was. She only cared that after days of sharing space, they finally reconnected. Amelia broke the kiss first.

"My wish came true," Amelia said.

Lindsay's heart pinged in her chest. It was way too early for love, but the feeling was a combination of lust and fondness. She needed to be wanted and Amelia made her feel special. "Time alone?" she asked.

Amelia nodded. "Something like that."

Lindsay wrapped her arms around Amelia's neck. "Thank you for sharing your country paradise with me. It's beautiful out here."

"It's beautiful right here." Amelia looked into Lindsay's eyes.

Lindsay lifted her head and captured Amelia's lips again. She ran her hands down Amelia's back and slipped them under her tank to touch her warm, soft skin. Amelia shifted her weight so more of her body was on top of Lindsay.

"You're missing all the shooting stars," Lindsay said.

"Everything I could wish for is right here," Amelia said.

Lindsay wanted to lighten the moment and say that Amelia probably said that to all the girls she brought up here but deep down she knew Amelia didn't share it with a lot of people. Rather than saying anything to break the moment, she lost herself in another passionate kiss. Amelia rolled her hips and Lindsay lifted hers. They both moaned at the contact. Amelia in charge was hot and not what Lindsay was expecting but wholeheartedly accepted.

"Is this okay?" Amelia whispered.

"It's perfect." Lindsay caught her breath and grimaced.

Amelia leaned up. "What happened?"

"I'm getting poked." Lindsay bit back a grin. "Ow. There's a really sharp piece of hay digging into the back of my thigh." She felt around and tried to pull it out but it wouldn't budge.

Amelia sat up. "I should've brought a blanket but I didn't want to be presumptuous." She looked at her phone. "How about we go back to the house? It's getting late and I need to get up early."

Lindsay sighed. "You're probably right. I really like this place though. Can we come back again?" Lindsay asked. Amelia climbed off the hay bale and reached for Lindsay. With Amelia's help, Lindsay slid down the front of the hay bale right into her arms.

Amelia nodded. "Next time we'll bring a blanket and a bottle of wine."

"It's a date," Lindsay said. They held hands as they walked back to the house. Lindsay saw another shooting star and stole several kisses. By the time they got to the front porch, she was tempted to invite Amelia back to her room, but St. Louis was a long drive and it would be morning soon. She kissed Amelia softly outside her bedroom door. "Thank you. I had a wonderful night."

"Thanks for coming out to help us. It means so much to me," Amelia said.

Lindsay almost teared up at the sincerity in Amelia's voice. "We're going to do good things for Mizzou Moos. I promise you that."

CHAPTER SEVENTEEN

Amelia hugged her sister tighter than normal. She knew Zoey would do an incredible job, but that didn't mean she wouldn't miss her. Amelia released her. Both were ugly crying. This was going to be the longest and farthest they were ever apart.

"Be careful and don't go anywhere alone," Amelia said.

"I'll be careful, I promise. I'll text every day. And if you need me to do any videos, I will. Just let me know," Zoey said. A honk behind them made them hurry up their goodbyes. Zoey turned and held her hands up. "All right. All right. Geez."

Amelia pulled Zoey's suitcase out. "What time do you leave LA?" Amelia asked.

"Tonight at seven. That gives me enough time to pack a bigger bag or two and lock up any valuables. That way Marshall won't be tempted to rifle through my things," Zoey said. Amelia was surprised she agreed to sublet her apartment to Olivia's nephew. Maybe they were closer friends than she thought they were. Or maybe Zoey didn't care as long as he didn't burn the place down and the rent was covered.

"Keep me posted. I love you," Amelia said. She hugged Zoey again. The car behind them honked again and she knew, without a doubt, that Zoey was flipping them off.

"I love you, too. Have fun with Lindsay. Let loose," Zoey said. She slipped on her sunglasses, grabbed her suitcase, and disappeared behind the automatic doors.

Amelia waved apologetically at the impatient driver behind her and jogged back to the driver's side of her truck. She slipped into traffic and made her way back to I-70 West, back to Mizzou Moos, and back to Lindsay. What a weird and fascinating day yesterday was. The man in the Cardinals hat scared the living shit out of her and reminded her to always be aware of her surroundings, they had one of their first videos go viral, and she and Lindsay made out under the stars.

She set cruise control to seventy miles-per-hour, anxious to get back. Today was a slow day. Maybe she could talk Lindsay into an evening horseback ride. Becks had a stable of horses and beautiful land. They could take the ATVs over after tours and last feedings unless Lindsay wanted to work on videos. She had to admit, making videos was fun. It kept her mind off the bills and she got to hang around with a beautiful woman with fair skin, red hair, and full, demanding lips. She smiled thinking about last night. The last person she made out with on a hay bale was her first girlfriend and that was twelve years ago. It was a lot more romantic in her head. The stars were amazing, but the bale was smaller than she remembered and a lot harder. She had to come up with something different, but just as special.

She pulled up to Mizzou Moos right when another tour was starting. Amelia grimaced at the thinning group. Becks gave her a nod and motioned for them to move toward the big barn. Robbie was running the store, and their seventeen-year-old nephew, Mason, was walking on the property in case there were any stragglers. He worked part-time after school, but since the story broke, he'd been hanging around more at their request. He was over six feet, a solid two hundred pounds, and had a full beard. Even though he was still a teenager, he could be very intimidating.

"Miss Amelia, how are you today?" Mason opened her door when she parked.

"I'm glad you're here, Mason. I'm good." Amelia grabbed her bag and locked her truck.

"I heard some dude was here yesterday who shouldn't have been. I'm going to stick around until weight training starts at three," he said.

"Thank you. I really appreciate it. Help yourself to anything in the kitchen if you get thirsty or hungry," she said.

"Aunt Robbie said another guy in the first tour this morning was talking shit—uh, crap about Miss Zoey and what happened in Vegas."

"What? How come she didn't call me?"

"Oops. Maybe I wasn't supposed to tell you." He chewed on his lower lip and toed the gravel.

"Did she tell you what happened?"

He shrugged. "He thought Aunt Robbie was just someone taking the tour and started bad-mouthing Miss Zoey and how ya'll were gambling away the money in Vegas. But don't worry, she shut him down. And I made sure he left right away."

"Thanks for letting me know and thanks for taking care of it."

"You're welcome," he said.

He tipped his hat and sauntered off to check the barns. He was such a great kid. Young man, she corrected herself. She was torn between wanting to hear more about the guy and running up the steps to find Lindsay. Before she had a chance to decide, Lindsay greeted her at the screen door. The stranger was forgotten.

"I'm sure it was hard to say bye to Zoey, but I'm glad you're back," Lindsay said.

How did she look so refreshed and happy? First thing this morning, Zoey was at the table with a fresh pot of coffee when Amelia and Lindsay dragged their tired bodies into the kitchen. It was a nice surprise.

"Thanks. It was hard, but this is such a great opportunity for her. She promised to check in a lot so that'll help me. I'll bet her hours will be more wild than when she was on the *Thirteen Witches* set." Saying the name of the show made Amelia frown. She was still pissed that they fired Zoey, but it ended up being a better move for her sister. She would make more money and in less time. Not to mention get a thousand times more exposure. "What have you been up to?"

"I put together another video for your approval," Lindsay said. She pointed to the cars in the parking lot. "But we can look at it after tours."

"I have a few minutes. I can watch it now." Amelia looked down at her shorts and T-shirt. "I need to change into work clothes first. The donkeys like to chew on shorts. The hem is at the perfect level for them to reach through the gate and start pulling."

"Oh, I think that would be kind of a cute video." Lindsay shrugged and offered a toothy smile.

"As long as Tater doesn't rip my clothes, we could probably film something cute," Amelia said. She held up her bag. "Let me put my stuff down and let's give Becks enough time to get the tour through the small barn where he is."

"It might be a good idea to wear a Mizzou Moos T-shirt. That way we're pushing your logo and the name as much as we can," Lindsay said.

Amelia smiled when Lindsay grabbed her hand and pulled her inside the house. Lindsay kissed her after the door closed and Amelia moaned. It was amazing how their relationship had changed so quickly and so smoothly.

"I've been thinking about your mouth all morning," Lindsay said.

An indescribable feeling bubbled up in Amelia's chest at Lindsay's words. It made her feel light and happy. Any stress she had floated away when she looked into Lindsay's big, blue eyes. "Oh, yeah? What if I told you I have been thinking about yours as well?" It was true, but it had been a while since Amelia had a healthy relationship with a woman and wasn't sure if openly admitting it was okay.

Lindsay moved so that their bodies touched and kissed her again. "Then I would say great minds think alike."

Amelia wrapped her arms around Lindsay's waist and held her close. One kiss wasn't going to cut it until the end of the day.

She needed more. She sucked Lindsay's lower lip into her mouth and ran her tongue over it slowly until Lindsay opened her mouth demanding more. Amelia slipped her tongue inside Lindsay's mouth, deepening their kiss. She felt Lindsay's hands on her hips, the pressure of her fingers sending little sparks of pleasure down Amelia's spine. Amelia ended the kiss first. Too many people could walk in and now wasn't the time.

She rested her forehead against Lindsay's and touched her cheek. "This will keep. I'll be back in a flash." With a final, swift kiss, she turned and bounced up the stairs to her room with renewed energy.

She found a yellow T-shirt with Mizzou Moos printed across the front, quickly brushed her hair, and touched up her makeup. She smiled at herself in the mirror. When was the last time she cared how she looked on the farm?

"Okay, what's the plan?" Amelia asked. She was very aware that Lindsay gave her a complete look over when she entered the room.

"If the tour is out of the small barn, let's see if the donkeys really like to chew on clothing or not," Lindsay said.

"Watch my luck and they'll be sweet," Amelia said. They quickly crossed the gravel parking lot, careful to avoid most guests. She didn't want a repeat of being confronted again.

"Let's just see what happens," Lindsay said.

Amelia caught her breath when Lindsay looked at her. She knew, without a doubt, that something incredible was going to happen tonight. A thousand butterflies danced under her skin as she moved next to Lindsay and listened to her direction for the short video. She felt happy and carefree even though she was still very much in the middle of a scandal.

Lindsay held her phone in front of her and hit record. "Tell us everything you want people to know about donkeys. What they eat, what their personalities are like, do they get along with other animals?"

As if on cue, Tater brayed and tugged on her shorts with his velvety lips. Amelia couldn't help but laugh and stroke his soft muzzle. "Three weeks ago, Tater was scared of everyone and hid in the corner of the barn. He was malnourished and it took several days for the vet to get close enough to assess him. He's not the weight we want him to be, but he's getting there." Amelia gave him a slice of apple which he loudly munched in her ear and demanded more by pulling at her clothes again. "He's not shy and he's probably going to win more hearts than Pippin," Amelia said.

Lindsay gave her a thumbs up and stopped recording. "Can you record close ups and fun angles?"

"Absolutely not. I think you need to get in here and experience this for yourself," Amelia said.

Lindsay wrinkled her nose. "He's cute and all, but kind of smelly."

Amelia shrugged. "Farm life. Earthy, animally, and definitely smelly. But it's good for you. There's really no better experience."

"Honestly, being here has been great for my mental health. Getting away from the stress of the job, of my life, has been a game changer," Lindsay said.

"If you think living in the country is great for your mental health, wait until you have animals who depend on you. They are just wonderful creatures. You probably know that already since you had cats." Amelia opened the gate and motioned for Lindsay to enter. "Get in here and meet Tater and Tot. Tot is still a little shy, but Tater wants to be your best friend."

"Hello, boys," Lindsay said. She looked at Amelia. "They're boys, right?" At Amelia's nod, she turned her attention back to them. "Oh, why is one limping?"

"Tater is the one with the limp. He had a rough life before he came here. He's fine now, but he'll always have a limp," Amelia said. She pointed to the feeder behind Lindsay. "Grab some hay and hold out your hand. "

Lindsay held out a handful from the feeder and nervously giggled when Tater heartily chomped at it. "What if he bites me?"

"He won't. Well, if he does, it's not on purpose," Amelia said. She pulled out her phone and videotaped Lindsay feeding both

Tater and Tot up close. She hopped the fence and got videos of the pygmy goats bouncing off tree stumps and rocks on their side of the barn. Who knew she would have this much fun sharing her life with the rest of the world?

"I think we have enough for several videos, and I could really use a shower," Lindsay said.

"Okay. I need to work at the store for the rest of the day. Robbie has an appointment so find me there if you need me," Amelia said. They left at the same time, for safety, and parted at the barn's entrance.

Amelia entered the shop and waited until the last customer was out before asking Robbie about the unwanted guest. "Do we know anything about him?"

Robbie shook her head. "I couldn't tell if he was a Zoey fan or just wanted to stir shit up. It was very confusing, but we got him out of here. What a jerk."

"I don't know what to do anymore. Zoey and I talked to people in town, we addressed the bullshit on Ring, and Mizzou Moos is still getting shit on. It doesn't make sense. Why would people who have been here and see what we do want us to fail?" Amelia asked.

Robbie gave her a hug. "Sometimes people are just assholes. Speaking of, Wilbur Bauer wants you to call him today."

Amelia frowned. "The accountant in town? Why? Oh, tell me some rich aunt I never knew we had died and left us a zillion dollars."

"I didn't ask," she said. "I left his number by the phone."

Amelia picked up the business phone and called Wilbur. She dealt with him when their parents died but had switched her business to a queer-friendly accountant Becks and Robbie recommended as soon as she could. "Hello, Mr. Bauer. This is Amelia Roberts. I'm returning your call."

"Amelia, how are you? How's Zoey?" He didn't give her a chance to answer. "Thanks for calling me back. Do you have a minute to talk?"

She heard the creaking of his chair and the rustling of papers and could almost picture his slight frame with thinning hair sitting behind a giant oak desk. He was almost sixty-five but acted and sounded much older. He was known around town for wearing brown three-piece suits and Bugs Bunny ties. Amelia remembered he told her father that people trusted him because he dressed well and kids liked him because he had fun ties. "Yes, I have a few minutes."

"I've known your family for years," he started, but paused for her to agree with him.

"Yep, you worked with my parents and grandparents. What can I do for you?" she asked.

"I remember when you little ladies were born. You were the first twins this town had seen in years. Anyway, I called because there's been a lot of talk around town. I couldn't live with myself if I didn't at least honor the memory of your parents by offering my services during this difficult time."

What the hell? "What do you mean, difficult time?" she asked.

"Don't get upset, sweetie. I'm here to help you. It seems you are mismanaging donations and I want to step in and help until you can get back on track. Pro bono, of course. That's what your parents would want me to do," he said.

Amelia gritted her teeth until her jaw popped. She could hear his heavy breathing through the phone as he waited for her answer. She took a deep breath. He was being brutally inappropriate, and he didn't even know it. She wanted to correct him, but she knew he meant well even if it was condescending. "Now, Mr. Bauer, that's a very kind offer, but I think we're doing fine. I appreciate your concern and I'll reach out if I change my mind. Thank you for the offer. Have a nice day." She hung up before she gave him the opportunity to respond. She scowled at the phone.

"What was that about?" Robbie asked.

"Just Wilbur doing Wilbur things. Not important." Amelia changed the topic. "How's business today?"

"Meh, could be better. How's Hollywood?" Robbie pointed at the house, referring to Lindsay.

Amelia smacked her forehead. "I need to introduce you two. I'm sorry I haven't brought her by. That's rude."

"Becks has nothing but good things to say about her. She's very pretty," Robbie said.

"I wanted to ask if we could come over and go for a horseback ride. Maybe the four of us could go on one of the trails this week," Amelia said.

"How about tomorrow night? We can barbecue and then go for a ride or vice versa. Or you both can go on a romantic sunset ride. How does she feel about horses? Has she been on one before?"

"I don't know. I mentioned that I wanted to go for a ride and she didn't say no. I think she likes it here." Amelia waited for Robbie to gather her purse and drink before she slipped in behind the counter.

"I like what she's doing for the place. The videos are wonderful. And I make sure everyone who comes in scans the QR code for all the socials when they buy something." Robbie pointed to the large, laminated poster that had all Mizzou Moos's socials listed.

"I love that. Have a lot of people scanned it?"

"Almost every person who comes into the store. It was Lindsay's idea," Robbie said.

Amelia crossed her fingers. "Lindsay thinks we can make money this way and with everything slowing down and the sanctuary losing grants, we need all the help we can get." She only knew they needed a lot of people to view all their videos.

"Who's working on new merchandise?" Robbie asked.

"Zoey reached out to an artist friend. Pippin's going to be the face of Mizzou Moos. I opened up an account on Print Press so whenever we get the new logo finalized, we can upload the design and people can print it on anything. T-shirts, mugs, phone cases, notepads, even temporary tattoos. We'll have some stock here, too."

"Are you going to have a store on the socials?" Robbie asked.

Amelia nodded. She didn't know what that entailed but Lindsay strongly suggested it. "For sure. Lindsay said people want product fast. Print Press will produce and ship so we're going to have the store link in our social bios."

Robbie grabbed the doorknob and slipped on her sunglasses before pushing it open. She looked back at Amelia. "I think all of this is going to blow up. In a good way. I'll see you tomorrow night. Have fun and good luck with Ms. Hollywood."

Amelia could feel her blood heat up at the thought of being alone with Lindsay again. "Thanks." She shuffled paperwork until she heard the door close. She loved Robbie, but she was Becks's opposite. Robbie wanted every single detail, whereas Becks just nodded and gave Amelia privacy.

When the last car left the parking lot, Amelia hit the remote to lock the gate. She fed the animals for the last time and made it up to the house by six.

"Hi. I'm just finishing up two videos. As much as we love Pippin, I really think Tater's going to win hearts, too. Do you think Zoey's artist friend can do a logo with him, too? Or maybe a logo with several different rescue animals? Pippin, Tater, and one of the goats? What's the black one with the white head called?" Lindsay asked.

She was in work mode and it was sexy as hell. Amelia wanted to sit with her and absorb her energy and steal several kisses from her soft lips, but she had to clean up first. "Oliver Patrick."

"Oliver Patrick? Really? That's a terrible name for a goat," Lindsay said.

Amelia shrugged. "He came to us with that name. I can't change it now. He answers to it." When Lindsay motioned her over again, Amelia waved her off. "I need to shower. I smell like the barn. Give me fifteen minutes." She took the stairs two at a time, removing her clothes as she climbed. She wanted to be downstairs sitting next to Lindsay as soon as possible.

After her quick shower, she checked her email and smiled when Zoey had forwarded artwork from her friend. The new logo was perfect. Whoever he was, he captured Pippin's playfulness perfectly. She couldn't wait to get downstairs to show Lindsay. She sent her sister an email approving the design and asked her when they could start using it.

"I think we got our new logo. Check it out." Amelia handed Lindsay her phone when she walked into the kitchen and accepted Lindsay's laptop to check out the new video. It was adorable. Tater was both onery and lovable and chewed on Amelia's shorts as she told his story. It made his terrible backstory bearable because the viewer knew upfront that he was good and healthy. "With videos like these, Mizzou Moos will be on the map in no time." Amelia paused. "We're not overdoing it, are we? Like shoving our rescue down people's throats?"

Lindsay shook her head. "No. The algorithm will hit accounts differently. If they are interested, they'll go directly to the main account and look through all the videos. That's exactly what we want."

"What do you think about the logo?" Amelia asked.

"It's great. Pippin's perfect. Do we have permission to use it?" Lindsay asked.

Amelia checked her email and gave Lindsay a thumbs-up. "Zoey sent the signed release from her artist friend. We're good to go."

"Let's pop a pizza in the oven and get the logo on the website. If you want, we can get merch lined up now everywhere. We can also place our first order for the store here," Lindsay said.

Amelia sighed. That meant spending money she didn't have. She wanted one night where she didn't have to think about the rescue. She was excited that they were moving forward by leaps and bounds for Mizzou Moos, but what she really wanted was to put the rescue on the back burner and explore the other burning need between her and Lindsay instead.

CHAPTER EIGHTEEN

Lindsay woke up next to a soft body and an annoying crick in her neck. She was in Amelia's living room, lying on the couch wondering what time they fell asleep and why they were on the couch. The early morning light filtered in through the partially closed blinds. It was peaceful here, and as much as she liked waking up next to Amelia, she had to move. She slipped out from Amelia's arms and stretched. It was almost six in the morning. They'd been up most of the night working on the website. Amelia was a quick learner. She was afraid of doing something wrong, but once she got comfortable, she was able to make changes quickly. She even posted two videos. It was exhausting work, but Lindsay knew it would pay off.

Amelia stirred on the couch. "What time is it?" she grumbled.

Not a morning person. Lindsay smiled. "Almost six. What time do you have to get up?"

Amelia groaned and sat up. "Now. What time did we fall asleep? Like an hour ago?"

"About three hours ago, but just think about how much we accomplished," Lindsay said. She watched as Amelia stood and stretched. "I know that doesn't mean a lot now and you're going to feel like a zombie all day today, but we did a lot." She pointed at Amelia. "You did most of the work. Now you know how to piece together a video and add music."

Amelia snorted. "Barely. I did one with heavy tutelage."

Lindsay softened. "You'll get there. Come on. Let's get ready for the day. You have hungry babies out there and I have emails I need to answer."

"Anything job related?" Amelia asked.

Lindsay wasn't sure if it was a serious inquiry, but Barkley Swan wanted to Zoom about a possible upcoming position. They were a relatively new firm in Hollywood, but had produced cooking shows and two home improvement reality shows that were prime time popular. "Yes. They aren't deciding for a while, but I'm going to Zoom with them later today."

"That sounds great. I'll try to keep the kids quiet," Amelia joked. Lindsay noticed Amelia's smile faltered but she kept her chin up and excused herself to get ready for the day.

"It'll be fine. I'll take the call upstairs in my room. Now go take care of the animals before they start revolting." She winked at Amelia to lighten the mood. Once Amelia pulled the door shut, Lindsay climbed the stairs and closed the door to her room for extra privacy. She massaged her neck and pulled up Mizzou Moos's socials. They had a lot more followers since last night. Now that she was here and believed in the rescue, she felt comfortable asking her influential friends to share. There was still the whole scandal thing and she would ask them to share only if they felt comfortable.

By the time Lindsay was showered and dressed, Amelia was already out feeding the animals. Two cars were parked by the office. Lindsay decided it was time to introduce herself to Robbie since they were invited over to their house tonight for dinner and a horseback ride. Lindsay hadn't been on a horse since she was a kid. She opened the door slowly and peeked in. "Hello?"

"Good morning. Come on in." Becks waved her into the store.

"I saw two cars and figured you were both here and thought I should pop in and properly introduce myself." She turned to Robbie. "Hi, Robbie. I'm Lindsay. It's nice to meet you." Robbie shook her hand.

"It's so nice to finally meet you. I've heard nothing but great things. Thank you for coming here and helping us out."

Robbie sounded so sincere that Lindsay almost got choked up. She knew things were bad here but didn't realize everyone felt it. "I certainly hope it helps."

"So, you worked with Zoey on *Thirteen Witches,* right?" Robbie asked.

"Yes. I was on the production side of things," Lindsay said.

"But you're so good at marketing. Was that part of your job or your background?" Robbie asked.

"Excuse my wife for being extremely nosy. What she means is welcome to Mizzou Moos. If there's anything you need, please let us know," Becks said.

Lindsay laughed. "It's totally fine. I love marketing. It's nice to start from scratch because anything we do will boost. Did Amelia show you the new logo?" Lindsay didn't wait for them to answer. She pulled up the email Amelia forwarded to her and showed them. The changes weren't live on the website yet. They wanted Zoey's approval on the site before they hit the button.

"I love it! Oh, look, it's Pippin with the curly hair hanging in his eyes," Robbie said.

"We worked on merchandise on the website. We also put in a small shipment to stock here in the store," Lindsay said.

"I just hope things turn around here. These girls deserve a break," Becks said.

"Have you always known them?" Lindsay asked. Becks and Robbie were at least ten years older than the twins so she knew they didn't go to school together.

"I babysat them. We've always lived next to each other," Becks said.

"I'm sure you have stories then." Lindsay smiled.

"The kind we'll share over barbecue and beers. What's your favorite beer?" Becks asked.

"Why don't you let me bring the beer?" Lindsay asked.

"Because you're our guest and we invited you," Robbie said.

"Any sort of darker ale. But whatever you have chilling is perfectly fine. I'm not picky at all," Lindsay said.

"Perfect then. Tours are light today so I think you'll get done early. Are you making more videos? How many do you have up now? A dozen? Or more?" Robbie asked.

"The rule is to not post more than three or four a day when you're just getting started. Once we get a larger following, we'll slow it down to one or two a day. It really depends on Amelia and Zoey and what they want to do." It felt weird talking about a future that she wasn't in. "It's always good to strike while the iron's hot even if it's bad."

"How has the reception been?" Becks asked.

She probably knew, but Lindsay humored her anyway. "Most of it's been positive. Probably ninety percent." She lowered her voice as though Amelia could hear her even though they were the only ones in the store. "I've been weeding out the nasty ones. Amelia's starting to get more comfortable in front of the camera. I'd like to get her to the point where she can address certain comments. Or maybe Zoey can from location. People do it all the time. If it's necessary. Right now, it hasn't been too bad. But you've had a few people that weren't here for the right reasons."

"One of the guys said he was a reporter, but I doubt that. I need to call Sam to see if he's had a chance to look into him. Last I heard, Sam said there was no record of him on any of the websites for any of the St. Louis papers, but he still needed to check into freelance journalists. I sent the video of him threatening the girls. I'll give him a call in a bit," Becks said.

"Thank you." Lindsay was concerned for their safety and realized she didn't know how many employees worked at Mizzou Moos. "Is it just you two and Mason here? Does Amelia have any other help?"

"She has part-time help during harvest and she hires local kids when fall festivals begin. We're it for full-time help," Becks said.

"It's about neighbors helping neighbors. Her grandparents moved a long time ago, but their friends always stop by and check on Amelia. I'm surprised she hasn't had more people check in," Robbie said.

"We've had a few. Since Amelia's been locking the gate, most people can't just pop in after hours. If you cut across the field, we're right behind the house. You can see our house lights when it's dark outside," Becks said.

"Good to know. Okay, well I just wanted to introduce myself. I need to get back to emails. It was nice to meet you, Robbie. I'll see you both tonight," Lindsay said. She was looking forward to spending time with them. They were different from the couples she hung out with in Hollywood. They seemed so down-to-earth and genuine.

She went up to her room and started answering the emails that had stacked up over the last week and a half. A lot of people were curious about her departure from Meador Entertainment. Several wanted to know if she was looking for a job and several were just nosy about why she quit. She wasn't going to burn any bridges so she answered each email cordially, respectfully, and kept her reasons vague. When it was time for her Zoom, she found the quietest place and joined the meeting.

"Hello, Ms. Brooks. I'm Simon Barkley from Barkley Swan. I've invited Sarah Dutton, producer, to join us. Thank you for agreeing to meet today," he said. He had a gentle face with expressive eyes. She could make out light stubble across his chin and upper lip. His slightly disheveled look gave the appearance of a college professor or a middle school science teacher, not the owner of a multi-million-dollar production company.

"Thank you for the invite. Please call me Lindsay," she said. She wasn't nervous. She had nothing to lose and everything to gain. It was worth listening to whatever they had to offer.

"Let's get the hard stuff out of the way first. We're aware you walked away from Meador. Is that something you want to talk about or no?" Simon asked.

"I don't mind telling my side of the story. I didn't like the way Meador handled the Zoey Stark situation at HEXPO. I didn't think they should've fired her over it." She probably shouldn't have said that, but it's what she felt. "I've seen them protect actors over far worse situations."

"I understand everything worked out for Zoey," Simon said.

"Thankfully," she said.

"What are you doing now?" Sarah asked.

"I'm working on a marketing plan for an animal sanctuary. I'm getting them set up on all the socials, revamping their webpage, creating a webstore. I'm going back to my roots for this project," Lindsay said.

"Is that something you'd like to do or is production your real dream?" Simon asked. Before Lindsay could answer, he kept feeding her information. "You've been on two television shows. *Thirteen Witches* and a *Semper Fi or Die.* Which one gave you the most experience?"

"Definitely *Thirteen Witches.* I had more freedom on set and learned a lot," Lindsay said.

"What was your favorite part of the experience?" he asked.

The question surprised her. She thought she was going to say it was being the person who kept things smooth between the actors and the studio, but that's not what she said. "As much as I enjoyed working with the actors, I really enjoyed pitching ideas for episodes. I was allowed to be more creative on *Thirteen Witches* than I was on *Semper Fi or Die.*" Some of the actors were borderline unbearable, but others like Zoey and Olivia were very nice.

"We're a much smaller company than Meador Entertainment which means the job would entail a lot more hats. We need somebody who knows union laws and is in from start to finish. It's a lot of hours, hard work, but we also offer profit-sharing so the harder you work, the more you get paid. The better the show, the more you get paid. Our shows have been well-received and we're growing faster than we can keep up. We need help and we need it fast."

"That sounds like an exciting opportunity." That was a lot to digest. Yes, Lindsay needed a job, but she wasn't done with

Mizzou Moos. Was Simon expecting her to drop everything? Was this an actual job offer?

"You were given quite the opportunity at Meador. A lot of people in the industry would've given anything for your job, yet you were quick to throw it away," Simon said.

Lindsay tried not to stiffen at his words. It was an irrational decision, a moment of reacting to the misogyny she often felt in the business. "Too many times I saw Meador protect the men in this industry. Cover up their indiscretions, make their problems go away, but the second something happened with their biggest star, who happened to be a woman, they fired her."

Sarah nodded at Lindsay. "I respect that."

"We don't like any scandals, regardless of gender," Simon said.

"Part of my job was to minimize them. Get ahead of them. With the Zoey Stark incident, we offered retakes and free merch to everyone affected by her actions. I was satisfied with how it was handled, but Meador was not," Lindsay said. She was careful not to call it a scandal.

"I appreciate that. Do you have any questions for us?"

"I'm curious about the culture at Barkley Swan. What is your company philosophy? What keeps your employees interested?" she asked. She didn't want to experience the same pitfalls she did with Meador and it was better to find out now than after paperwork was signed.

"We're focused on success, but not at the expense of our employees. We value their input and ensure everyone gets the help they need whether it's an assistant, a therapist, or even a weekend getaway to regroup," Simon said.

"I'm glad you place a lot of emphasis on mental health. A lot of employers don't." It sounded too good to be true. Lindsay was cautious.

"I'm going to send over an email with the job responsibilities. Please review it and feel free to email me any questions or concerns you might have. We're beginning the interviewing process but just know that you are at the top of our list," Sarah said.

"Thank you for reaching out and I look forward to future talks." Lindsay disconnected the video feed and sat back in the chair. She was torn between being excited about a massive opportunity in the profession she always wanted, and helping Mizzou Moos get started. Working on such a worthy cause filled her heart like nothing she'd ever experienced before, but it wasn't her future, it was Amelia's. She had no idea if it was going to be lucrative or a bust and she made a promise that she would stick around until something happened. She closed her computer and headed downstairs, feeling more confused with every step she took. What would happen if they offered her the job? When would they want her to start?

She pulled a glass from the cupboard and poured a lemonade. It wasn't as if she was snooping, but it was hard to miss the letter peeking out from under a partially folded newspaper. It was the newspaper that caught her eye first. Who still got the newspaper delivered? Amused by the teasing headline of the secret star at this year's state fair, she picked it up only to be more intrigued by the letter underneath. It was from the Midwest Farm Association announcing they were pulling their funding due to cutbacks, and they wished Mizzou Moos best of luck.

As though it burned her fingers, Lindsay quickly put the letter back on the table and folded the paper the way she found it. Son of a bitch. Amelia acted as though nothing was wrong when everything was crashing down. With Amelia still working tours, Lindsay went back upstairs, got her laptop, and started an email campaign that she knew would cost her a lot of favors. She wasn't sure she had a lot of pull left, but it was worth a try.

Chapter Nineteen

The four-wheelers were twelve years old, presents from their parents when they turned sixteen, but Amelia had taken such good care of them that they looked and ran like they were new. Amelia gave Lindsay a crash course on how to use the clutch and gears and handed her a helmet.

"Why don't we just walk? I can see their house from here." Lindsay pointed to the small, pointed roof off in the distance.

Amelia smiled. "You wanted a taste of farm life. This is what we do. Plus, we'll get there in record time. That way we can eat and have a nice sunset ride around their trail." It was a great way to get there and get home fast. They could've driven in the truck, but where was the fun in that?

"I feel weird not bringing anything. Are you sure we shouldn't bring like a six-pack or a bottle of wine?" Lindsay asked.

"Becks and Robbie will get mad if you show up with anything so it's better to let them fuss," Amelia said.

"Okay, so I'm going to be nosy and ask a very personal question and you don't have to answer," Lindsay said. Amelia guessed what Lindsay was going to ask. Most people wondered about Becks and Robbie's finances. They weren't wealthy, but they didn't have to work an eight-to-five job to pay the bills. "I'm trying to figure out how they can work here, run their farm, and..." she trailed off waiting for Amelia to step in.

"They rent their land to farmers who grow crops. Becks inherited the property from her grandparents. She was never going to leave Missouri. She met Robbie at MU, they got married, have been here ever since," Amelia said.

"What crops do they grow around here?"

"Mostly soybeans and corn. And if the town ever approves solar panels, most of the farms around here will have giant solar panels in the fields to harvest energy along with their soybeans and corn," Amelia said.

"That sounds like a win-win situation. Why wouldn't they get approval?"

"The town thinks that panels are eyesores and will lower property value in an already plummeting economy," Amelia said.

"How do you feel about it?" Lindsay asked.

There were pros and cons. Amelia had to fight for every dollar for the rescue. If she had the area, she would agree to it, but her acreage was so small that energy companies overlooked her and approached the surrounding farms instead. Only three farms voted for solar panels: Becks and Robbie, the Logans, and the Teeters.

"If they want to pay millions of dollars to cleanly harvest energy, I'm all for that. I don't know long term effects, but Robbie has done her homework. It could be worth millions. They just need hard numbers and facts to share with the town." That was probably more of an info dump than Lindsay wanted, but it had been the talk of the town for years. "Sadly, Lincolnville isn't progressive. They'd rather lose an entire town on weak principles than watch only a few families flourish. I think unless everyone stands to gain, they'll just keep voting it down."

"That's unreasonable. We have solar panels everywhere in California. They aren't pretty, but they're functional. You all could gain so much by having them." She waved off Amelia. "What I really want to know is how they met. They seem so happy and in love. I'm glad they are in your life."

"They are wonderful and just being around them is so relaxing and peaceful. That's hard to come by. But you'll have to ask them the story. It's better directly from them." It was a fairy tale, and she knew Lindsay was going love every word of it. "Are you ready?"

Lindsay pointed to the handles. "Clutch, shift, brakes. Got it." She tapped the helmet. "Do I have to wear this? I just styled my hair."

Amelia leaned closer and brushed her lips over Lindsay's. "And you look beautiful, but I'm going to say one word that's going to make you put the helmet on immediately. Are you ready?"

"What? Accident? Rollover?" Lindsay smirked. "I'm not a daredevil so I'm not even worried about that."

Amelia lifted her brow. "Bugs."

Linsday quickly put on the helmet and lowered her visor. "Noted."

"Close your mouth, too. Just in case." Amelia winked playfully and jumped on her four-wheeler. She instructed the dogs to guard the place and motioned for Lindsay to follow her through the field behind the house. Even though Amelia only had fifty acres of land left, it was her little slice of heaven. It was close enough to town in case of an emergency, close enough for people to visit even if they were just passing through, close enough to the interstate, but far enough away for people to forget about their problems while they learned about farm animals, bottle fed baby goats, and learned livestock had personalities.

Amelia had different dreams when she was growing up, but sometimes life and death got in the way. She wanted to be a veterinarian but had to quit school after her father's death and help run the farm. Her mother needed help, and after her mother died, they were in a bad spot. They didn't have a working knowledge of the business. Selling off a hundred acres to pay off debts left them with fifty acres for a small herd of livestock and Mizzou Moos which, before the scandal, was barely staying afloat. People and corporations were pulling their funding, fewer tours were scheduled, bills were piling up. But right now, none of that mattered. Tonight, she was on a date with a beautiful woman, riding four-wheelers out to her friends' house to have a good time. Those problems could wait until tomorrow.

She slowed so Lindsay could catch up. She pointed and made the okay symbol. Lindsay nodded and returned the gesture. The ride was less than ten minutes, but it always made her happy. Amelia quickly opened and closed the gate between their properties. They slowed down the closer they got to Beckses' driveway and parked by the barn. Amelia smiled watching Lindsay carefully remove her helmet and run her fingers through her hair.

"How do I look?" Lindsay asked. She straightened her lightweight pants and removed the borrowed flannel shirt.

"You look good in my clothes," Amelia said.

"Ha. No, seriously. How do I look? And why am I even nervous?" she asked.

"Robbie calls you Hollywood, just so you know," Amelia teased her. She hung the shirt on the handlebar and pulled Lindsay close. "And you look amazing."

Lindsay laughed. "Hollywood. Hmm. I don't know if I like that or not."

"It's said fondly. Only because she doesn't know anything about you," Amelia said. She held Lindsay's hand as they made their way to the backyard where music and delicious smells wafted in summer air.

"Whatever they are grilling, it smells delicious," Lindsay said.

Robbie greeted them with cold beers and a warm smile. "I trust the ride was uneventful."

"The cows stayed clear," Amelia said.

Robbie turned to Lindsay. "Now did you ever think you'd hear that sentence in your life and that it would make sense?" Lindsay shook her head and laughed. "Neither did I and yet here we are."

"Oh, how much my life has changed the last several weeks," Lindsay said.

Amelia wasn't sure how to take it. Lindsay's words sounded harmless but her expression made her pause. Was she regretting her decision? And how long was she going to stay? She didn't talk much about the Zoom conversation and Amelia didn't press. Maybe no news was good news. But she wasn't sure if it was good news for her or for Lindsay. Time to get out of her head. "What's on the grill?"

"Robbie made chicken and mushroom kebabs. It's the only way she can get me to eat vegetables. And some other stuff," Becks said.

"Some other stuff" ended up being potato salad, garden salad, watermelon, roasted corn, honeydew, and a pineapple upside down cake.

"You always go overboard," Amelia said. She plucked a piece of watermelon from the table and bit into the fruit. "But I'm not complaining." She quickly held the rind away and reached for a napkin as the juice ran down her arm. "If it wasn't for your leftovers, I'd never eat."

"This is true statement. Amelia's notorious for forgetting meals," Becks said.

"With delicious food like this, why would you miss it?" Lindsay asked.

"Everything tastes better when somebody else prepares it," Amelia said. It wasn't as though she didn't like to cook. She just didn't like to cook for one person. It was a waste. She ate well when Zoey visited, but most of the time, she ate a quick sandwich or a bowl of cereal for dinner while streaming something on Netflix.

"I agree with Amelia. It's hard to prepare food for one person. That's why I DoorDash," Lindsay said.

Robbie choked on her beer and then snorted. She covered her mouth and apologized. "Well, that wasn't very ladylike. It's just that DoorDash doesn't come out here. Nothing comes out here. Sometimes we can get Mason to pick up grocery orders, but that's only if we tip him well." She linked her arm with Lindsay and whisked her over to their picnic table. "Come have a seat. Let's get to know you better."

"How are things going?" Becks asked.

"It depends on what you mean. We've made and posted several videos now but I don't know how it's going to help us. We lost funding from our two biggest donors and tours are down, but—" Amelia stopped when Becks held up her hand.

"That's not what I mean and you know it. This isn't a work dinner. This is a fun dinner. I'm talking about Lindsay. How are things going between you and her?" she asked.

A warm flush tingled Amelia's skin and she couldn't help but smile recalling their passionate kisses and soft touches. "It's going really well."

Becks took a step closer and made an inquiring face. "Oh? Like well well or just well?"

Amelia pressed her lips together. How much did she want them to know? "Hmm. Right now just well, but ask me tomorrow. It might be well well by then." Becks squeezed her arms and did a silent, celebratory scream where Robbie and Lindsay couldn't see them. She was never this animated. Amelia couldn't help but laugh. "Stop. I'm trying to keep my cool and you're not helping."

Becks took a step back, reached for her beer and turned her attention back to the grill but not before dropping an exaggerated wink at Amelia. "Well, these are about done." She yelled louder so Robbie and Lindsay could hear. "Grab a plate. Things are ready here."

They would've chatted longer over dinner, but Amelia promised Lindsay a horseback ride and they had about an hour before the sun set. Becks helped them saddle two mild mannered horses and recommended the short one-mile path just in case Lindsay hated it. She handed Amelia the reins of Arrow, her favorite horse, and left her to straddle him.

"Horses are a lot wider in person than most people think." Becks brought a small step stool over to Lindsay to help her get on Nola's back. "Just grab the pommel and pull yourself over like Amelia did." Once Lindsay got settled, Becks gave her a crash course on horseback riding and ended with, "They know their way back home so if you drop the reins, they'll just come back. Have fun."

Amelia slowed Arrow down until he was next to Nola. "How are you doing? Are you okay?"

"I'm swaying a lot," Lindsay said.

"Oh, yes. The sway. If you lean the opposite way he steps, then you won't be jostled as much," Amelia explained.

"Becks was right. Either Nola is a chonky horse, or they are wider than you think they are. I'm probably going to feel this ride for days," Lindsay said. She adjusted her body, sat up straighter on the saddle, and held the reins like Amelia held hers. "I think I'm getting this down."

"You're a natural."

"It's very beautiful here. I understand why Becks stayed and why Robbie didn't need any convincing."

"I always love hearing their story. It becomes more romantic every time I hear it," Amelia said.

"They are very sweet friends. I'm glad they are in your life. They seem more like family," Lindsay said.

"We do the holidays together. I don't think Robbie's family approves of her being queer so we're her family."

"I love that. Sometimes our family is the people we choose."

"Tell me about your family. I suddenly realize I don't know a lot about you. We've been so focused on me and Moos, that I've selfishly taken all the time for me," Amelia said.

"You know everything about me. I work a lot. I don't play a lot," Lindsay said.

"Tell me things like your favorite show. What was the one that made you go to Hollywood? What's your favorite food? Favorite color? What's your favorite thing to wear on a lazy Sunday morning? What are you afraid of? What makes you happy?"

"Whoa. That's a lot. Let me see. I can't possibly narrow down a favorite show or the one that made me race to Hollywood because all of them did. Cheeseburger, green, I like to sleep in on Sundays so I'm in my pajamas most of the day, I like fall, I hate bugs because I'm afraid of them, and music makes me happy," Lindsay said. She grabbed the pommel when Nola stumbled a bit and smiled when she steadied herself. "Also, I do like your stars. They make me happy."

Amelia's chest felt tight. She held Lindsay's gaze, and the look that passed between them seared her. Tonight just got way more interesting. Suddenly the need to get back to Mizzou Moos was pressing. She wasn't going to push though. She had a feeling Lindsay was worth the wait.

"Was that already a mile? That was quick." Lindsay pointed as the roof of the barn breached the horizon.

"It's a quick trail and not everyone is a natural on horseback. A lot of people are scared of horses," Amelia said.

Lindsay patted Nola's neck. "Who would be scared of this sweet, gentle giant?" Amelia smiled inwardly because she knew Lindsay was about thirty minutes ago. "Hey, I know there's a lot going on and we've been busy making videos and working on the stores and websites, but I really am having fun with you and your friends. I think we both needed tonight. Thank you for the break," Lindsay said.

"You didn't have to uproot your life for me and Zoey, but you did and whatever happens, thank you." The way the warm glow of the setting sunlight fell softly on Lindsay's skin and highlighted the copper in her hair made Amelia's knees weak and her stomach clench. She was breathtaking.

"It's a nice change. And I've learned so much about a different industry. It's helping me, too," Lindsay said.

Amelia didn't want to pry, but she also needed to know. Should she invest more of herself, or leave it surface level? "How did your talk go today? Was it more of an interview?" She was pleased that her voice sounded normal.

"It turned out to be kind of an interview. It's for a company that's just getting started. It would mean a lot of freedom but a lot of responsibilities and a lot of long hours," Lindsay said.

The heat that flooded Amelia's body five seconds ago turned icy. "But that's kind of what you're looking for, right? A fresh start from the ground up?" Again, a silent pat on the back for being chill.

"It's sounds right up my alley but so many things have to happen first," Lindsay said.

"When do you think you'll know?" Amelia didn't want to push but wanted to know how much time they had.

"I have time," Lindsay said.

It was all Amelia needed to know. She helped Lindsay off Nola, careful to keep her hands in respectable places but very aware of her curves. Before Amelia could steal a kiss or press her body against Lindsay's, Becks greeted them. "Go ahead inside. I'll take care of the horses. Robbie's brewed fresh coffee and has a thousand more questions for Lindsay."

Amelia narrowed her eyes at Becks for ruining their private moment. "Thanks, friend," Amelia said. Becks smiled sweetly and led the horses away.

"What kind of questions has she been asking you?" Amelia asked.

"She's very curious about my job and my background. Apparently, Robbie went to college as a screenwriter. Well, first journalism, then she switched to playwright, then screenwriter," Lindsay said. Amelia knew that, but it was fun to see Lindsay's excitement.

"Did she tell you how they met on campus?" Amelia asked.

"No. We didn't get that far, but that's next. They seem like such a great couple. How long have they been together?" Lindsay asked.

"Twenty years." Amelia opened the side door for Lindsay and welcomed the cool air. "This feels wonderful."

"Welcome back, you two. Just so you know, they're forecasting pop-up storms. I wasn't sure if you saw any lightning, but you might think about beating them, or sticking around until they're done," Robbie said. She pointed to the carafe. "I have fresh coffee and we still have dessert. We can make a night of it."

Lindsay answered for them. "We should probably go because I have several videos I want to finish and I want to make some changes to the accounts." She held Robbie's hand. "But just know I had a great time tonight and I hope we can do this again soon."

"It was our pleasure. Be careful going home. We'll bring the cake over tomorrow," Robbie said.

Becks met them in the driveway. "I was going to tell you it was starting to thunder. Let us know when you get home." She pointed at Amelia. "Go slow."

Amelia was sure she meant with the four-wheelers, but she wasn't a hundred percent. "Will do." She got Lindsay's bike started and climbed on hers. Lights on, thumbs up, and they were off. Amelia went slow knowing that even though the headlights were bright, driving through a field in the dark was still hard. The cows hadn't moved much so they were able to get by without incident. Amelia jumped off the bike to open the gate and felt the first drops of rain hit her skin. She waved Lindsay through and motioned for her to keep going, but by the time they reached the garage, they were soaked.

"Head for the mud room. We have towels there," Amelia said. It didn't make sense to run since they were drenched, but they did anyway. She handed Lindsay a towel to wipe off her face and arms. Lindsay's teeth were chattering. "If you give me your wet clothes, I can throw them in the washer." When Lindsay was down to just her bra and panties, Amelia wrapped her in a large towel and rubbed her hands up and down her back trying to warm her with friction. "Go upstairs and slip into warm clothes. I don't recommend showering since it's storming." Lindsay nodded and padded out of the room. Amelia kicked off her boots, peeled off her wet clothes including her bra and panties. She covered herself with a towel and put the clothes in the washer. Everything could wait until the morning. She liked getting caught in the rain. It heightened her senses. And seeing Lindsay stripped down to her bra and panties amplified her sense of smell. Lindsay's hair smelled fresh and florally like peonies blossoming in the sun and her skin felt smooth and almost too delicate to touch. Amelia's heart pounded furiously in her chest and her fingers shook with the need to pull Lindsay close. Knowing that Lindsay was cold and miserable, she sent her upstairs to warm up and put space between them, but Amelia knew their night was far from over.

CHAPTER TWENTY

The irony of wearing a *Thirteen Witches* sweatshirt didn't escape Lindsay, but she was cold and her wardrobe was limited. Zoey had given her the sweatshirt earlier in the week. It was snug, but very much appreciated. She was anxious to find Amelia. It was time to explore what has happening between them. She reached for the door handle and pulled her hand back when a knock on the other side startled her.

"Lindsay? Are you awake?"

She stood frozen for several seconds. Why was she hesitating? This was exactly what she wanted. She opened the door. "Hi." Amelia was wearing shorts and a tank top that showed off toned arms and equally impressive legs. Lindsay was staring and didn't even try to hide it. "How are you not freezing?"

"I'll adjust the thermostat. I run hot." Amelia blushed at the innuendo. Lindsay smiled at how innocent Amelia was at times.

"You don't have to change it for me. I'll just have a nice cup of hot tea," she said.

Amelia took a step toward Lindsay. "Or we could find another way to keep you warm."

It was everything Lindsay wanted to hear. She knew it was hard for Amelia to make the first move and this was her chance. "I just got into these clothes and now you want me out of them?" She ran her fingertips down Amelia's arm and gently held her hand. "I think that sounds like a great idea." She pulled Amelia close, ran her hands up Amelia's arms and linked her fingers behind Amelia's neck. She was right. Her body radiated so much heat that Lindsay regretted the layers of clothes she just wrapped herself in. When they finally kissed and Amelia gently slipped her tongue inside Lindsay's mouth, Lindsay knew everything would change tonight. A shift was happening, and she tried not to read too much into it. This wasn't permanent. This couldn't be permanent. Lindsay knew she was avoiding her problems by throwing herself into Mizzou Moos. By doing so, she was leading Amelia on. That hurt her heart, but she selfishly wanted this night. She broke away from Amelia's warm embrace only to peel off the tight sweatshirt she slipped into a few minutes ago. Their kiss ignited her blood and her clothes felt heavy. The longer she had them on, the quicker they would catch fire.

"Are you sure about this?" Amelia asked.

Lindsay saw such intensity when she looked in Amelia's eyes that she couldn't even form a simple one-syllable word. She swallowed hard and nodded. Amelia's lips were on hers in a flash. Everything happened so quickly. She was back in her room, Amelia's hands were pulling at her clothes, and she was desperately tugging on Amelia's tank top. She floated onto the bed with Amelia nestled between her legs. Why did she put on so many clothes? Her leggings were twisting around her calves and her tank had bunched up under her breasts. She broke the kiss.

"I'm so uncomfortable. Can we take off my clothes?" Lindsay asked. She smiled at Amelia's determination but dropped her smile when Amelia flipped her on the bed to pull off her leggings. She hissed out a breath when she felt Amelia's lips nip at the back of her calves and sensitive thighs. She clutched the sheets in her fists when Amelia's tongue swirled across her ass and her teeth scraped the small of her back. "That feels amazing." She sighed when Amelia's naked body pressed against her back. Her full breasts and taut nipples pushed into Lindsay's skin, now flushed with desire.

"I've been wanting this for so long," Amelia whispered before softly biting Lindsay's earlobe.

Lindsay lifted her hips when she felt Amelia's mouth drop to her neck and gently suck on the sensitive skin. She reached back and held Amelia's hip against hers. She missed Amelia's lips on hers, but something about Amelia taking control right now was decadent. She dropped her hand when she felt Amelia's hand slip between their bodies. She spread her legs and unabashedly lifted herself up to her knees. She was wet and borderline desperate to feel Amelia inside her. When Lindsay let herself go, especially during sex, everything else drifted away. The rain pelting the windows was replaced by her rapid heartbeat. The sweat between their slick bodies smelled like sandalwood soap and the fresh scent of earthy rain.

Amelia's damp hair surrounded her face making her breath labored but Lindsay didn't want to move. She sighed with disappointment when Amelia's sinewy, sexy body shifted off hers but was rewarded with long, strong fingers stroking her pussy. She moved her hips trying to push herself down on Amelia's fingers to get her to fuck her, but Amelia pulled away and held Lindsay's hips firmly in place. Lindsay looked back at her. Even though it was raining, there was still enough light filtering in from the hallway.

"Why are you teasing me?" Lindsay asked.

Amelia smiled and flipped Lindsay so she was on her back. It was the first time Amelia was seeing her naked and for a split second she thought about covering up, but Amelia's eyes sparkled with appreciation, and she licked her lips unconsciously. It was the best compliment.

"I want to stretch our first time out as long as I can," Amelia said.

It was romantic and it made Lindsay pause. Not everyone wanted to orgasm right away. She was so used to fast and hard, that she forgot about what it was like to date somebody and take their time. Amelia wasn't like people she dated before.

She took a deep breath and sighed. "You're right. I'm sorry I'm rushing. We have all night."

Lindsay put her hand on her chest as though keeping it there would keep her heart from escaping. It was alarming how fast it was beating. She took deep, slow breaths and pulled Amelia to her for a kiss. A soft gentle kiss to let her know that it meant something to her as well. The problem wasn't that she didn't care, it was that their passion ignited even when the kiss was a soft brush. They just kissed perfectly. There wasn't a learning curve. Maybe having sex would douse the fire and kissing wouldn't mean as much as it did right here right now.

"You have such a beautiful mouth." Lindsay touched Amelia's lips and smiled when Amelia held her fingertips there and kissed them. "I've always thought that." She was rewarded with another kiss, only this one lasted longer, was deeper, and tasted sweeter because it came with words that melted Lindsay's heart.

Lindsay wanted to smile, tried to smile to lighten the mood, but the seriousness of this moment was too much and the smile she tried to force disappeared into the darkness. No more words, no more playing, she thought. She would convey all her feelings through touch. All the things she couldn't, no, wouldn't say to Amelia, would happen right now. In the darkness of night, through the tenderness of touch, and in the safety of one another's arms.

Lindsay turned on her side so they faced one another and ran her fingertips over Amelia's neck, over her breasts, down her stomach, and back up again. She felt empowered when Amelia's body quivered and chill bumps followed her touch. She reminded herself to go slow and did the same path until the bumps faded and Amelia's skin acclimated to her touch. She shifted lower so her hand could touch Amelia's hip and stroke her slit. She watched Amelia's face when her fingers touched her clit and ran up and down the swollen folds of her pussy. Amelia's mouth dropped open and her breath caught. She bit her bottom lip and held back a soft moan. Lindsay couldn't remember the last time she stopped and watched her lover become aroused. It was intoxicating. Amelia spread her legs giving her more access and Lindsay circled the wet, soft opening several times before slowing entering Amelia. She arched her back and blew out a sharp breath.

SCANDALOUS

"Yes," Amelia said. Her voice was a soft whisper, but to Lindsay it felt like the word echoed loudly in the space between them.

She felt weak with need and rested her forehead against Amelia's for a moment before kissing her again. She moved slowly and tried not to moan at how deliciously tight Amelia was and how her moans fueled Lindsay's need to give her as much pleasure as she could. When she added a second finger, Amelia fell back on the bed and adjusted her hips so they were closer to Lindsay's hand. Even though Amelia was wet enough, Lindsay withdrew her fingers, sucked on them to wet them even more, and slipped them back inside Amelia. This time she was at a different angle. This time she had better control. She licked her lips, tasting Amelia's tangy essence, and started moving slowly. Amelia rocked her hips against Lindsay's hand and wrapped her arms around her shoulders. Their lips brushed with every thrust. It was sexier than kissing. It felt more intimate.

Lindsay knew this was more than just sex. As much as she tried to deny it, this was making love. This was an exchange of trust, vulnerability. Maybe they weren't at a place where they were going to say it to each other. Maybe that day would never happen, but Lindsay felt it. It twirled between their bodies like a spinning top tapping on her chest, skipping around not knowing how long it would turn or when it would simply stop. She had to stay in the moment and not think about the future.

"Don't stop. Don't ever stop," Amelia whispered.

Feeling Amelia's pussy clench around her fingers and her legs quiver knowing she was responsible for giving her pleasure escalated the need to continue. She didn't want to stop. She slowed down only to build her up again knowing that when Amelia came, it was going to be incredible.

"I promise this time I won't stop, but I want to taste you," Lindsay said. She kissed her way down Amelia's body and spread her legs apart before running her tongue over Amelia's swollen lips and sensitive clit. She would have to be careful since Amelia was already close. She slipped her fingers inside and rested her tongue against her smooth clit, careful not to apply pressure yet. Amelia would let her know when she was ready. She moved her fingers in and out slowly at first, then faster. When Amelia cried out, Lindsay sucked her clit until Amelia had enough.

"I can't anymore. My body...I..." she said.

Lindsay stroked Amelia's thighs, kissed her stomach, and grabbed the covers before snuggling up next to her. Weird because she didn't consider herself a snuggler, but Amelia's arms around her gave her a feeling of peace. This time she didn't accidentally fall asleep or try to sneak out or make an excuse to leave. Instead, she threaded her fingers with Amelia's and rested her head on Amelia's shoulder. She didn't want to talk. She wanted to stay like this, under the covers, and listen to the rain that had slowed to a gentle sprinkle. Her eyelids closed several times and even though she didn't think she was tired, she fell asleep in Amelia's embrace.

Lindsay winced at the bright stream of sunlight that fell across her face. What time was it? She cracked an eye open and looked at her phone. It was just after six. It seemed brighter this morning. She frowned at the empty spot beside her and tried hard to ignore the emptiness that settled somewhere behind her ribs. It was a foreign feeling and she didn't like it. She knew Amelia was taking care of the animals, but it wasn't the way she wanted to wake up this morning. She showered quickly and slipped into fresh clothes. She pulled out her phone and looked at Mizzou Moos's account. Another video had blown up. She did a little fist pump. Everything was going according to plan.

"I think you have the best smile."

Lindsay froze when she heard Amelia's voice. She didn't hear the door open and seeing Amelia standing in the doorway with her hair braided over her shoulder wearing tight jeans, boots, and a Mizzou Moos T-shirt made last night's activities rush back to flood her senses. She could almost taste Amelia, feel the softness of her skin, smell the rain in her hair, and hear her moans. Lindsay closed her eyes for a fraction of a second to focus.

"That's sweet of you to say." She closed the distance between them and kissed Amelia softly. "I missed you this morning. You should've woken me up."

Amelia played with Lindsay's hair. "You looked so peaceful that I didn't want to wake you. I know you haven't been sleeping a lot lately."

Small jolts of happiness pinged her body. She was tired, exhausted really, but the adrenaline rush of hours of sex with Amelia kept her body humming. "I was lonely." Lindsay pouted playfully and moved into Amelia's embrace. It was nice how perfectly she fit in Amelia's arms and how the wall between them was gone. This was the intimacy she missed. This was the closeness she craved.

"Next time, I'll wake you before I leave," Amelia said.

Lindsay closed her eyes when she felt Amelia's soft lips press against her forehead. "Thank you. How were the animals?"

"I was ten minutes late. You would've thought I hadn't fed them in days, but they are good." Amelia slipped out of Lindsay's embrace to grab a mug from the cupboard. "What are you doing? Checking our videos?"

"Yes, and I'm excited because another video went viral. Guess which one?" Lindsay asked. She sat in the chair and handed Amelia her phone after Amelia added milk and sugar to her coffee.

"This one? Wow. I'm surprised," Amelia said.

"I told you. Animals are wonderful, but a good, heartfelt story is what people need right now." She put her hand over Amelia's. "This is why I want to add a tip jar," Lindsay suggested.

Amelia immediately frowned. "It feels like begging."

"It's not. I promise. A lot of creators have tip jars. You'd be surprised what people will donate to. Haven't you seen people drive around with their Venmo accounts written on the windows of their cars? Like I'm getting married or I lost my job or buy me a coffee?" Lindsay asked.

"No, I haven't."

Lindsay smiled for a moment forgetting that the population of Lincolnville was only two thousand twenty-four. "Not even in Columbia?" Amelia shook her head. Lindsay assumed Amelia didn't pay attention. "Well, they do. And people give them money. Depending on whatever they want the money for, they can get hundreds or even thousands of dollars," she said. Amelia frowned and kept her eyes on her coffee cup. "This is strictly for Mizzou Moos and we'll be very specific about where the money is going. We can say we need two thousand dollars for medicine, a thousand for new harnesses and leads. I promise, it's a very acceptable way for people to donate."

"Let me think about it a little longer. Is that okay?" Amelia asked.

"That sounds fair," Lindsay said. She put her hand on Amelia's thigh and kissed her softly. Her lips were still sensitive from last night but that didn't stop her from deepening the kiss. They had unfinished business and Lindsay's body was tingling.

"I suddenly don't like that you're dressed," Amelia said. She slipped her fingers under Lindsay's T-shirt and brushed her fingertips along the soft skin below her bra.

"Do we have time before the first tour?" Lindsay peeked around Amelia to look at the clock on the wall. "It starts in twenty-two minutes."

Amelia's fingers pressed into Lindsay's hips. "I think that's plenty of time, but you tell me."

"Definitely," Lindsay said.

The determined look in Amelia's eyes made Lindsay swallow hard. She visualized several ways Amelia could pleasure her in twenty minutes. Wasting no time, Lindsay grabbed Amelia's hand and raced up the stairs. She ripped her T-shirt off and tugged Amelia's jeans down.

"This wasn't how I pictured my day starting," Amelia said.

Lindsay stopped. "I'm so sorry. I just thought since we both fell asleep last night before we were done, that you'd be okay with us picking right back up."

Amelia pulled Lindsay flush against her. "I meant that in the best way possible. The tour can wait if I'm late." She gently pushed Lindsay back on the bed and straddled her.

Lindsay loved how the sun shined into the room and cut across Amelia's lean body. She ran her fingers over Amelia's muscular abdomen and tight stomach. It amazed her how running a farm kept her in better shape than anyone back in California who went to the gym weekly. "You're so beautiful. So soft and hard. I don't know if twenty-two minutes is enough time for us."

"Nineteen minutes," Amelia said.

Challenge accepted, Lindsay thought. She gasped when Amelia slid her body down until she was on the side of the bed, on her knees, between Lindsay's spread legs. Lindsay shivered when she felt Amelia's fingertips graze over the soft lace of her panties and moaned when Amelia's palm pressed against her warm, swollen pussy. Amelia placed small kisses up one thigh and down the other. Lindsay greedily lifted her hips when Amelia hooked her thumbs into the waistband of Lindsay's panties to pull them down and toss them over her shoulder. Knowing they were pressed for time amplified the need to please. Lindsay gasped when Amelia's tongue touched her slit. Her body was tense and vibrated with need. Lindsay wanted to enjoy this moment, but time and instant gratification were pushing her to climax fast and hard. She could take her time later tonight when they weren't rushed with responsibilities.

"I'm not going to last." Lindsay's voice was hoarse and breathy.

"I don't want you to. I want you to let go," Amelia said.

Lindsay's eyelids fluttered shut when she felt Amelia slip two fingers inside. She arched her back and pressed her hips into the mattress. When Amelia quickened her pace, Lindsay grabbed the sheets tightly and anchored her heels into the side rail of the bed frame. It only took five long, slow licks over her clit before she exploded. Passion overtook Lindsay's body and waves of pleasure shook her like an earthquake followed by smaller, less intense, but equally exciting aftershocks. If this was fast sex with Amelia, she was more than excited to explore a long night of nothing but sex for hours.

"Wow. I'm so sorry I fell asleep last night and didn't get the chance to find out how beautiful you are when you come," Amelia said.

Lindsay gave a tiny, tight laugh that quivered as she continued to ride out the wave of pleasure. She reached down to brush her fingertips across her clit to intensify the aftershocks.

"Apparently, I stopped too soon." Amelia pushed her hand away and ran her tongue up and down Lindsay's pussy. She flattened her tongue across Lindsay's clit and pulsated soft pressure until Lindsay's entire body stiffened and she came again. "Fuck," Amelia whispered several times.

"Anytime, anywhere," Lindsay said. She meant it. Everything about Amelia was amazing. She looked at the clock. Ten minutes had passed. "Except right now because you have to get ready for a tour even though I think you should call in sick and stay in bed with me." She tried standing but fell back onto the bed and laughed breathlessly. "My knees are shaking. Give me a quick minute." She sank on the mattress to catch her breath while Amelia scooped up her hastily discarded clothes. Amelia placed the clothes next to Lindsay on the mattress, stood between her legs, and hugged her. So many emotions danced on her heart and she was afraid if Amelia looked deep into her eyes, she would know. She tried her best to guard her feelings and project a strong, playful voice.

"Okay, cowgirl, you have five minutes before the first tour starts. I'll work on social media and you work on getting more donations out of your group," Lindsay said. She smiled when she felt Amelia's lips on her forehead. Even though sex only complicated things in the long run because this relationship wasn't sustainable, Lindsay wasn't going to say no to pleasure this fantastic.

CHAPTER TWENTY-ONE

Amelia slapped her Stetson on her head and leaned her arms over the wooden fence. Tater and Tot were playing with a large rubber ball. It was more like Tot was playing keep-away from Tater, but they seemed to be in good spirits. Their corral was heavily shaded by a row of elm trees that had survived straight-line winds, killer bugs, poisonous fungi, and the time Zoey sliced three tree trunks with the tractor blade during a dare when she was ten years old. Amelia pulled out her phone and recorded them. She knew Lindsay would love it. Her phone buzzed. She smiled when her sister's named popped up on her screen.

"Hey! How's it going?" Amelia asked.

"It's going great. It's so much different than being on the *Thirteen Witches* set. Everybody gets along. We do things as a group. It's wonderful," Zoey said.

"That sounds amazing. Are you on break right now? Have you filmed any scenes? How does it all work?" Amelia had tons of questions but was afraid they would be rushed off the phone like before when Zoey was doing television.

"They don't film in order, but yes, I've done a few scenes. I was calling to check in with you. How are things there? How's Lindsay? How's business? Any more flyers or crap on Ring?" Zoey asked.

The last thing Amelia wanted to do was make her sister worry. A couple of people kept calling Mizzou Moos and asking for Zoey.

The guy with the southern accent had called multiple times and there was a woman who called consistently as well. The only thing they could do was block unknown and private callers, but they still managed to get through a few times generating numbers from an app. Thankfully, there hadn't been any more incidents during tours.

"Things are good. Lindsay's great. Several videos have gone viral."

"I know. I think that's great. Did Sam ever get back to you about that guy?" Zoey asked.

"They haven't figured out who he is but they don't think the guy is a reporter. Or if he is, he's not from any news outlet around here," Amelia said.

"That doesn't make any sense. If he was from TMZ or any of the gossip papers, he'd have published something by now," Zoey said.

"Maybe we scared him off?" It was probably wishful thinking, but maybe he just realized they were more trouble than it was worth. "Oh, and guess who offered to take care of our donations and finances pro bono because he thinks we are making bad decisions?"

Zoey groaned. "Ugh. You're going to say Wilbur, aren't you?"

"Yep, creepy Wilbur. I'm sure he's just hearing what people are saying in town. Maybe he saw those stupid flyers or read about us in Neighborhood Notes," Amelia said. Lincolnville had a small website where people could post things for sale or discuss farm business. Someone put their Hollywood scandal photo and a few others that had surfaced including the one of Amelia getting a hand pay in Vegas on the site and the comments were terrible. People hid behind fake usernames and dropped cruel comments.

"Fuck them. Let's get back to Lindsay. Tell me why things are great. I want details and leave nothing out," Zoey said.

"Why don't we save the best for last? Let's talk about what we're working on first." Amelia looked around in case anyone was within earshot.

"Okay, fine. Okay, tell me everything else," Zoey said.

Amelia told Zoey everything that Lindsay was pushing. "We're adding a tip jar to the YouTube channel and she wants to add a GoFundMe link to fix the barn. She said there's no such thing as bad press. She wants to pin the video of us explaining our mission here."

"She's right. Our subscribers and followers are growing every day across all platforms. According to Lindsay and Google, YouTube pays the best right now. We're coming up to the first month so you should have an idea of how much money we're earning," Zoey said.

"You don't think the tip jar thing is too much?" Amelia needed Zoey's validation to confirm it was the right choice. It felt too much like begging.

"No way. The idea of a tip jar is brilliant."

"Lindsay explained that so many people have them for online things like concerts or question-and-answer sessions. It sounds okay, but what am I doing? I'm not offering anything special," Amelia said.

"You're giving the world cute animal videos. You're saving animals. I think that's way better than concerts or other things. And the GoFundMe sounds like a good idea. Lindsay's smart. Let's talk about her. What else is going on between you two?" Zoey asked.

Even though the temperature was in the nineties and the humidity was terrible, Amelia felt her cheeks heat up thinking about last night and the few stolen moments they had today. "Well, we had dinner last night with Becks and Robbie."

"That's great. I miss them, but I want to know about you and Lindsay. Have you done more than kiss? Are you sleeping in the same bed yet?" Zoey asked.

Amelia groaned. "You sound like a dude right now. But also, yes, we are." Amelia winced as Zoey celebrated on the other end.

"Woohoo! I knew it. I knew it was going to happen. Tell me everything," she said.

"Uh, no. We had sex and that's all you need to know," Amelia said. She had to make tonight special since last night they fell asleep quickly and Amelia didn't get the chance to do everything she wanted to with Lindsay.

"So now what?" Zoey asked.

"What do you mean?" The question came out sharper than she intended. "I mean, I don't understand the question." She did, but she didn't want to think about it. It meant dealing with the future and that wasn't something she was ready to face.

"Have you talked about what happens next? Like down the line for you?"

"Come on. You and I both know there really isn't a future. I think our story is a happy for now. My life is here and hers is in California." Amelia tried to make her voice sound cheery, but she wasn't fooling either one of them.

Zoey wisely sidestepped. "Have you done the date up in the barn yet? Because that's always a home run, too."

"Did you just do an exaggerated wink? Because it sounded like it," Amelia said.

"I did and you know I'm right. Make it happen," Zoey said.

Amelia already planned it, but she didn't want Zoey to know that she was as invested in her relationship with Lindsay as Zoey was.

"Okay, tell me about the cast. How's Alec? Is he nice? Mean? What about Gracie Shaw? I bet she's horrible. She looks like she's difficult to work with. Her resting bitch face is terrible," Amelia said. She didn't know anything about those actors which was completely unlike her. She was so invested in Zoey's career and knew all about the cast members before Zoey even signed up on *Thirteen Witches,* but the scandal had put Mizzou Moos front and center and she didn't have time to study *Bounty Hunter 2.*

"They both are surprisingly nice. I know it's only been a short time, but I feel like I'm part of a family. Low budget versus endless money makes a huge difference," Zoey said.

"That makes me so happy. It sounds like you're having nice time and people respect you as an actor. Why haven't you sent any photos?" Amelia asked.

"I will. But don't share them. I need to find out what I can share on the socials."

Amelia huffed. "Oh, please. I can barely remember to post daily on our socials. I can't even think about yours, too. I just want to see what it's like for you. Regardless of everything else, I'm so proud of you. This movie is a steppingstone. You'll be the lead before you're thirty."

"Oh, hell. This movie won't even launch until I'm thirty. It takes forever to produce, shoot, edit, promote, and release. Hopefully, by then, I'll have a few more movies started. Or at least the opportunity to test for them," Zoey said.

"That only you will test for." Amelia emphasized the word you. "I will never play Zoey Stark again. Ever. In the history of ever. Lesson learned the hard way." She shook her head thinking back to the last month of her life and how much it had changed all because she pretended to be Zoey Stark.

"I get it. And trust me, I'll never ask. Well, not about something as important as a job. I mean, we can still mess with our friends and family, right?" Zoey asked.

"I don't know. I'm pretty gun-shy after this. And you should be, too," Amelia said. They talked for another ten minutes before saying goodbye. Her heart felt both lighter and heavier after the conversation.

Lindsay slid next to Amelia and leaned her head on Amelia's shoulder. It felt nice. "Okay, everything is set up. I've uploaded the video of you explaining why Mizzou Moos came into existence and you now have a tip jar and a GoFundMe link."

"Thank you. For everything. I just got off the phone with Zoey. It sounds like everything is going well for her," Amelia said.

Lindsay slid her arm around Amelia's waist. "That's great. I'm so happy to hear. Movie sets can go either way so I'm glad it's going well for Zoey."

"Do you know anything about the actors or producers she's working with?" Amelia asked.

"Not really. Did she say anything about them?" Lindsay asked.

"Just that she's having the best time, but it's also the honeymoon stage. She was like that with *Thirteen Witches* and look what happened," Amelia said.

"Sadly, that's the business."

"Well, that sucks. What do you know about Alec Montgomery and Gracie Shaw? Zoey seems to like them, but I'm a bit more cautious."

"Both are nice. Alec is like Zoey because he just got out of a relationship, too, and Gracie is happily married with a small child. They have good reputations and they have good chemistry on screen. But then again, Alec has good chemistry with everyone. He's just one of those actors," Lindsay said.

"I wonder if I can go see her." Amelia grabbed high-fiber straw and added it to Tater and Tot's feeding basket.

"I think that would be great if you could. I'm sure Becks and Robbie can handle things here," Lindsay said.

"Not while all this crap is happening. I'll wait a bit. I'll want to wait until we can afford to shut down tours for a week. I don't know if we can do that though." Amelia wanted to invite Lindsay, but that was too much like a relationship, not their situationship.

"I think you should go. You don't get a lot of free time and don't tell me Vegas because that didn't count," Lindsay said.

Amelia didn't want to have this conversation now. It was fine having it with Zoey, but it was uncomfortable having it with Lindsay. It didn't include her and that stung. It was more important to focus on right now. She pulled Lindsay close. "I have an idea. Let's have a real date night tonight. Just us. No plans before or after so we're not pressed for time."

Lindsay's smile took her breath away. "I think that sounds lovely. What did you have in mind?"

"It's too hot for a picnic but maybe a movie. Which means I'm going to have to disappear for a bit as I get things set up." Amelia brushed the hair from Lindsay's face with her fingers and tried hard not to look at her with anything more than fondness. "I think we both deserve a break. You've been working hard and I've been stressed about everything." There was so much that Lindsay didn't know. If Amelia didn't get money trickling in somehow, she and Zoey were going to have to sell the rest of the cattle and maybe even the land behind Mizzou Moos. Bob Teeter called regularly under the guise of checking up on her, but he always managed to throw out the idea of buying the land if they needed to sell. It was just a matter of time before other circling land vultures smelled blood and tried to squeeze them out. Too many people around them lost their farms because they couldn't afford the land loans because they borrowed against them during drought years and never caught up. This wasn't Lindsay's problem. It was hers.

"I'll see you later then," Lindsay said.

"Wear shorts," Amelia said. She waited until Lindsay was out of sight before she quickly finished feeding the animals and headed to the main barn for a fast and furious date setup. Like Zoey said, it was always a home run.

Amelia tried hard to play it cool at Lindsay's reaction, but it was nearly impossible. She had outdone herself. She designed the hayloft like a drive-in movie theater. A giant painter's cloth hung on the back wall and an iPhone projector rested on a small table several feet away. She had hay molded as seats under soft blankets that could easily be converted into something flatter if things went according to plan. She ran a mosquito net across the loft doors and turned on the ceiling fans to offer some relief from the heat. Flameless aroma candles were placed nearby to help disguise the earthiness of the barn. Tiny white lights hung low across the space above them. The ambiance was romantic in a rustic, midwestern way.

Lindsay clapped her hands. "This is wonderful. I love it. What movie are we watching?"

"We have several to choose from. Personal favorites include *Chicken Run, Field of Dreams, Babe, Charlotte's Web*." Amelia listed movies until Lindsay laughed.

"Stop. Those are all farm movies. Don't you have any other movies?" Lindsay asked.

Amelia showed her the list on her phone. "Tons. Pick one. Do you have a favorite?"

"Do you? I think it would be more fun if we watched something you liked."

"How much of it are we really going to watch?" Amelia put the iPhone on the projector and playfully pulled Lindsay down on the hay with her. "Let's just start whatever and if it's bad, we'll find something else to do." She loved how lately Lindsay found reasons to touch her. Sometimes she tucked Amelia's hair behind her ear, other times she ran her thumb across the back of Amelia's hand when their fingers linked. They were simple gestures, but they meant so much to Amelia.

"Let's watch something fun. How about *Wallace and Gromit: The Curse of the Were-Rabbit*? Nothing says date night like Claymation," Lindsay said.

Amelia placed her hand over her heart. "It's a favorite of mine, but it's also scary. I mean, were-rabbit."

Lindsay curled up on the hay while Amelia queued up the movie. "This is such a great place for a date night. I love the lights and it's cute to hear the animals down below."

Amelia adjusted the volume and curled up next to Lindsay. "They're a bit smelly but they are sweet."

Lindsay rested her head on Amelia's shoulder. "Who knew this would be my life?" She sat up quickly. "I mean in the interim. I went from rubbing elbows with Hollywood's elite to rubbing snouts of Missouri cows."

Amelia kissed Lindsay before laughter bubbled up from her lips. She pulled Lindsay into the crook of her arm. "Okay, that's cute. Muzzles. Not snouts. Pigs have snouts."

"Whatever. You know what I mean. It's been kind of a culture shock. But in a cool way," Lindsay said.

"I'm sure you've learned more about farm life this last month than you ever thought you would," Amelia said. She tried hard not to overthink the reasons why Lindsay was still at Mizzou Moos. She appreciated every day Lindsay stayed, but her anxiety was ramping up knowing that any day Lindsay was going back to her California life. Amelia had to try harder to learn and be social media savvy so Lindsay could have her life back. But tonight, she could be greedy.

"I have a new appreciation for farm life and people who take care of animals," Lindsay said.

"That's sweet for you to say. But nights aren't about work, they are about play." Amelia held Lindsay's hand on her lap and tried focusing on the movie but it was hard when she just touched and tasted Lindsay earlier today. That memory was still fresh and her body wanted more.

Chapter Twenty-two

L indsay didn't care what a were-rabbit was and didn't care if the movie was in focus or not. She only cared that she was here, next to Amelia, sharing this special moment in a place she never thought could be romantic. "Thank you for doing this for me." She kissed Amelia softly and snuggled closer. She knew so much weighed on Amelia's mind.

"You're welcome. I'm not going to lie. I had an ulterior motive," Amelia said.

"Oh, yeah?" Lindsay pulled herself away from Amelia's embrace to carefully straddle her on the makeshift hay seat. She was going for sexy but ended up toppling them over into a heap. She giggled and tried to untangle herself from Amelia's long legs and arms but Amelia wasn't letting her go. "I'm so sorry. I didn't mean to ruin the moment."

Amelia flipped her so she was on her back. "You didn't ruin it at all. As a matter of fact, this speeds things up." Lindsay reached up to pull a few strands of straw from Amelia's hair.

"You have such pretty hair. And I love that it's wavy and has natural highlights," Lindsay said. She smiled. "I can't believe people mix you guys up. You could never fool me."

Amelia tapped her nose gently. "Not anymore. You mean to say not anymore."

"True. You fooled me at first." Lindsay shifted her body so Amelia was beside her. She leaned up on her elbow. "You have to admit, the way we met is unique. As adorable as Becks and Robbie's story is, it doesn't compare to ours. Twins? Trading places? Come on. That's movie-worthy," Lindsay said.

"Speaking of movies, are we giving up on the were-rabbit?" Amelia pointed to the screen.

"Was it ever really about the were-rabbit?" Lindsay asked. She rolled so her body was pressed flush against Amelia's. She closed her eyes when Amelia slid her hands under her shirt and stroked her back. "That feels wonderful."

When Amelia's lips touched hers, she forgot about everything. Amelia's lips were soft but demanding. A heat that came from within spread throughout her body igniting sensitive spots. Her nipples hardened and her clit throbbed with need. She draped one leg over Amelia's thighs giving her full access.

"I'm glad you wore shorts," Amelia said.

"My girlfriend told me to." Lindsay's eyes widened at the bomb she just dropped. They hadn't defined their relationship. Hell, she didn't even know what was going to happen tomorrow. What if she got the job offer and they wanted her back in Hollywood immediately? Instead of pushing the conversation, Lindsay did what she always did and side-stepped. "It's too hot to wear anything but shorts." Could Amelia hear Lindsay's suddenly rapid heart? Could she feel the sweat that popped up on her skin or see the flicker of fear in her eyes?

"Hmm. Interesting," Amelia said. She ran her hands under the hem of Lindsay's shorts. "There's always a skirt or a summer dress."

"My wardrobe is severely limited here. I probably should've packed more than a week's worth of clothes. It's been almost a month," Lindsay said. She didn't want to have a weird conversation right now, but she didn't want to obsess about the word girlfriend.

"Has it really?" Amelia sounded surprised.

"More like three and a half weeks. And why are we even talking about this?" Lindsay said. She kissed Amelia again and moaned when Amelia's hand moved up to cup her ass.

The kiss felt different. It felt heavier and more meaningful. She wanted to taste Amelia again and again, but when Amelia tugged on her shorts to pull them down, Lindsay didn't stop her. She was desperate for Amelia's hands and mouth all over her body. She kicked her shorts off to the side and flung her T-shirt somewhere behind her. The other night happened so fast and ended too soon.

Amelia ran her fingertips over the swell of Lindsay's breasts. "You're so soft and beautiful," she said.

Remembering to take her time and enjoy Amelia's touch, Lindsay relaxed and watched as Amelia's palms skimmed her breasts and the curves at her waist. When Amelia's touch lowered, Lindsay spread her legs apart. She wasn't shy about it. She wanted everything. Her hips lifted every time Amelia stroked the soft skin of her inner thighs. The lacy underwear was starting to restrict her swollen pussy and the pressure against the textured material gave Lindsay the friction she wanted. Before she had a chance to enjoy it, Amelia slid them off.

"You're so wet. And you're all mine," Amelia said.

The sincerity and softness of her voice made Lindsay weak. A flash of heat worked its way through her body and settled between her legs as the words took root. She was hers. At least for tonight. Amelia's low, raspy voice sent chills over Lindsay's body. Lindsay swallowed the lump of words in her throat that she refused to say out loud and nodded instead. She moaned when Amelia settled between her legs. She liked feeling Amelia's long, strong body pressed against hers. Lindsay captured Amelia's mouth in a hungry kiss and rolled her hips searching for friction. She dug her heels into the hay and smiled thinking how a roll in the hay really meant something now. Amelia broke the kiss and moved her mouth lower down Lindsay's body.

"I'm so happy we have room and a blanket this time," Amelia said.

Lindsay's laugh sounded hoarse and somewhat pained. Amelia's hot breath and strong fingers near her pussy made her squirm. She grabbed the blanket and moaned her approval when

Amelia's fingers stroked her pussy and lightly brushed her clit. Lindsay selfishly raised her hips wanting more pressure, more warmth, and penetration.

"Please," she whispered. As much as she told herself to enjoy the attention, she needed release. Her skin tingled and burned under Amelia's fingertips and she gasped with pleasure when Amelia finally entered her. She lifted her hips and met each thrust hard. Amelia sped up and Lindsay was able to concentrate solely on reaching the orgasm she so desperately and selfishly wanted. The first one was for her. The second one she would take her time, but right now she could only think about the pleasure that filled every atom in her body. A kaleidoscope of warm colors exploded behind her eyelids when she closed her eyes as Amelia helped her race toward her release. Lindsay climbed higher and higher and didn't slow down until she crested the peak of her orgasm and cried out with complete satisfaction. Her body shook as ripples of pleasure worked their way out of her body. She gasped for air. She couldn't remember the last time she came that hard or that fast and she didn't regret it one bit.

When she felt Amelia's tongue flick across her sensitive folds, she bucked but knew she still had another orgasm left. She opened her eyes and took a deep breath. The tiny lights that hung across the barn looked like stars. Even though the movie was still being cast on the makeshift screen, the loft was dark and romantic. She rested her hand on Amelia's head. Her mouth was doing delicious things to Lindsay's body and she didn't want this feeling to stop. As much as she wanted this night to last forever and as weak as her body felt, she couldn't stop the second wave of pleasure as it washed over her. She was spent. Her body went limp and she whimpered when Amelia slid up her body and gently settled between her legs. Amelia softly peppered Lindsay's face with soft kisses.

"That was amazing." Lindsay found enough energy to make room beside her so Amelia could comfortably fit in the small space between the two small mounds of hay. "Also, I'm sorry we destroyed the makeshift couch you probably took a long time making. I'm just thankful you brought a blanket this time." She felt the rumble of quiet laughter bubble up in Amelia's chest before she heard it.

"I'm glad you like my attempt at wooing you up here. And you learned from the other night that hay isn't as soft as it looks. It's prickly," Amelia said.

"But perfect." Lindsay wrapped her arms around Amelia and held her close. She smiled when she looked at the wall and saw the were-rabbit bounding across the screen. It was a silly movie, but one she would never forget. "Except for the fact that I'm naked and you're still dressed."

Amelia leaned her head up and looked Lindsay in the eye. Even though it was dark, enough light filtered in for Lindsay to see unguarded emotions swirl in Amelia's eyes. This wasn't a quick roll in the hay. This meant something to her too.

"Let's remedy that," Amelia said.

Within seconds, Amelia's naked body was pressed against Lindsay's. "We could always go back to the house, but that would require a lot of effort, and I'd rather expel it here."

Energy came roaring back at the thought of touching and kissing Amelia all over. Lindsay ran her hands up and down Amelia's warm skin anxious to give her pleasure again. Slowing down and appreciating every touch, hearing every sharp intake of breath when Lindsay did something she liked, and watching Amelia's body respond so perfectly was an incredible aphrodisiac. It was well after midnight before they got dressed and headed back into the house. Lindsay slid into bed beside Amelia and fell asleep before Amelia shut off the light.

Lindsay wasn't surprised that Amelia was gone when she woke up. She remembered Amelia placing a soft kiss on her lips and disappearing quickly. Running Mizzou Moos was a twenty-four hour seven days a week job and the animals kept Amelia on a tight schedule. Selfishly, she snuggled under the covers and tried to get an extra hour of sleep but guilt made her open her eyes and stretch awake. On autopilot, she grabbed her phone to check the socials like she did every morning.

"Holy shit!" She quickly sat up and looked at the tip jar amount and followed the link to the GoFundMe. Combined, they had over five thousand dollars in just a few hours. She shook her head in disbelief. She got out of the site and jumped back in it to rule out any glitches. It was trending. What happened since yesterday? With unsteady hands, she pulled up the account and saw two of the pinned videos' views had soared. Why? She popped over to YouTube and the amount of subscribers had quadrupled. Lindsay quickly scrambled out of bed and threw clothes on. She brushed her teeth, her hair, then rushed downstairs. She slipped on boots in the mud room that were far too big for her, but finding Amelia was top on her list. If they had that much money after just three weeks, what would happen by the end of the year? She marched out to the barn desperate to find Amelia and sending texts in case she wasn't there.

Hey, where are you? She kept the message light because she didn't want to scare Amelia. She was stressed enough.

In the field fixing a fence along the property line. Why? What's up?

Lindsay warned herself not to get too excited. This was probably an anomaly rather than the norm. *I just wanted to show you something.*

I'll be back soon. Need to pick up different tools. Looks like somebody cut the wire so the cows could get loose. Joke's on them. They'd just go over to Beck's place and she'd round them up and send them back over. Amelia followed her message with laughing emojis.

Alarm bells went off in Lindsay's head. Too many coincidences were happening. Maybe this was typical farm life, but it all sounded suspicious. *That sucks! I'm sorry. I'll meet you at the big barn in a bit. I think Tater and Tot would like the sprinkler system on for a few minutes. It's a hot one today. I'll shoot a few videos of them while we wait.*

Lindsay marched over to the small barn and turned on the sprinklers. Tater loved the water and pranced happily through the fanning droplets. He snorted when the water tickled his muzzle, made adorable faces while trying to bite at the water, and neighed his excitement when Lindsay turned the hose on him.

"He really likes you." Amelia startled Lindsay by sneaking up on the video shoot and put her hand on Lindsay's hip.

"He's so sweet. I'm so glad you saved him."

"He's turning into quite the ham. What's going on? Is everything okay?" Amelia asked.

Lindsay switched from video to one of the socials. She handed Amelia the phone without saying a word.

"What am I looking at?" Amelia asked. Confused, her eyes bounced all over screen until they finally landed on what Lindsay wanted her to see.

"Holy shit!" Amelia exclaimed.

"I said the exact same thing!"

CHAPTER TWENTY-THREE

I just got your message. Is everything okay?" Zoey called Amelia ten minutes after Amelia sent a text that said they needed to talk but that everything was okay and she shouldn't panic.

"I told you everything was fine. Everything is great. Two of our videos went viral last night. Like really viral. I thought they were popular before, but that was nothing compared to this. We don't know how or why but suddenly people are donating to our tip jar and the GoFundMe and I just don't know what to do," Amelia said. She was overwhelmed with gratitude and happiness.

"That's great! But I think I might know why. Alec Montgomery shared on his socials and he has millions of followers," Zoey said. Her excitement was infectious.

"What? That's amazing. What happened? How did Mizzou Moos even come up?" Amelia asked.

"Last night we were sitting around the fire just talking and I told them about Mizzou Moos and what happened in Vegas and Alec looked at our videos and blasted them out on his socials. How cool is that? I didn't even ask. He just did it. He barely knows me. And then Gracie did it and now we're blowing up," Zoey said.

"That's amazing. You'll have to thank them from us. We have so many new followers and the GoFundMe for the barn has reached its goal in like one day," Amelia said.

"Alec said when we're done shooting he wants an invitation to visit Mizzou Moos," Zoey said.

"Well, if you don't invite him, I will." Amelia couldn't believe how something that only took them a few seconds to share changed everything for the rescue. It was unbelievable.

"Look, I know you don't want to hear this, but everybody here thought that what we did in Vegas was brilliant."

"I wouldn't say brilliant." Amelia snorted. "It was stressful and I'm sure I have an ulcer over it. But it was very nice for your co-workers to share." She decided to turn the tables on Zoey. "Alec is very handsome. Is he single?" Zoey cleared her throat—a sign that she was nervous and Amelia pounced. "Ha ha. You have a crush." She felt guilty for teasing her sister after the good that she was responsible for. "I say if he's available and it doesn't get in the way of your work, go for it."

"No. We learned the hard way not to date people we work with," Zoey said pointedly.

Amelia put her forefinger on her lip. "Did we though? Because I'm still waking up next to a certain ginger who is in the business."

"Ha. But you're not in the biz. And he's just being nice and I'm starstruck. He's the biggest star right now and I'm on set with him. It's incredible. He's a great mentor and has already taught me so much," Zoey said.

Amelia wisely left that conversation alone. Zoey was an adult. She didn't need her sister giving her dating advice. "Well, I like him because he did a great thing for us and we have a cushion now. Lindsay's going to pull a chunk of the money from the tip jar to order more merch for the store." Amelia put her hand on her stomach and took a deep breath. "This is happening so fast. I'm grateful, but it feels like Vegas was last week and you were here yesterday. What has happened to my life?"

"Some pretty incredible things," Zoey said.

"Without a doubt. Tell me all about South America. What's it like? How's the weather? Tell me everything." Amelia missed her sister terribly but was happy Zoey finally caught her big break.

"I'll call you when we wind down tonight. I just wanted to check in to make sure everything was okay," Zoey said.

"It's more than fine. Everything is great," Amelia said. She didn't want to bring up the fence being cut because the cattle were accounted for and there wasn't a need to worry her sister who was twenty-seven hundred miles away and couldn't do anything anyway. She had played it off with Lindsay too, but it worried her. "Go have fun. Check in when you can. I'll keep you posted on everything that happens here."

"I love you," Zoey said.

It always melted Amelia's heart when her sister said it. "I love you, too. Go win the Oscar."

"Or just get the job done," Zoey said.

"Or that." Amelia disconnected the call and greeted Becks who rolled up in the driveway ready to start the day. She leaned her hip against Becks's Chevy truck and pretended to study her nails until Becks humored her.

"Okay, I'll bite. What's up?" Becks crossed her arms and stood in front of Amelia. She toed the gravel next to her truck's tire and waited.

Amelia handed her the phone and stood silently while Becks digested the information. She wasn't disappointed.

"Wait. Wait a minute. Is this right?" Becks pointed to the phone.

Amelia grinned and nodded. "Apparently so. I just chatted with Zoey and she told me that Alec and Gracie both shared our videos and channels and told people about what we do here and bam. We woke up to a lot of money."

Becks jumped up and down. "That's amazing!"

Amelia thumbed behind her. "Lindsay's inside ordering stock for the store so we can expand our inventory." She counted out on her hand. "We're ordering T-shirts, mugs, tote bags, and keychains to start off. We don't know if it's going to take off or not so we're starting small." Amelia pointed at Becks. "And do not cry because if you start, I'll start and we have tours in like thirty minutes."

Becks flapped her hands quickly—a thing she did to keep from crying. "I'm trying not to."

"We have a long way to go, but this is a solid start," Amelia said. She checked the time. "Okay, I have to go fix the fence, but I should be back in time to help feed the goats."

"What happened to the fence?"

Amelia shrugged. "It looks like somebody cut it. I called Sam about it. He's coming out later to take a look at it." She waved Becks off. "Really, it's not a big deal. Go inside and grab fresh coffee. Lindsay's in there somewhere. She can answer more questions about everything that's happened in the last twenty-four hours." Amelia hopped on the four-wheeler with the tools and wire she needed and drove off. She stopped when she saw Sam was calling. "Hey, Sam. What's going on?" She didn't know if she could emotionally handle any more news—good or bad.

"I wanted to let you know that we might have a lead on that Brian guy. Obviously, he's not a reporter, but somebody a few counties over thought they saw him on their trail cameras breaking into a cabin. They're going to send me the footage. If it's the same guy, we can arrest him on sight. Then maybe we can squeeze some answers out of him about what his interest is with you and Zoey."

"Fuck. I hope he's not a stalker. We don't need that here," Amelia said. Zoey changed her last name to Stark because it was a strong name and it afforded Amelia and their family and friends' privacy. It kept Hollywood out of their lives. It kept fans away until now. Amelia always knew Zoey would hit it big. She didn't know the extremes fans would go through to get to her. Being a twin was scary. What if they thought she was Zoey?

"If it is, we'll get him. But I do want you to take this seriously. I don't like that someone cut your fence. Vandals will sometimes do that, but they tend to hit multiple farms and I haven't gotten any other reports," Sam said.

"What happens now? Do you think we should hire somebody to patrol the farm a few times at night? What if somebody was on our property?"

"Hiring a few guys can't hurt. I know a few young deputies who could use the extra money and would do a good job. At least until we figure out what's going on around here," he said.

It wasn't the way Amelia wanted to spend the precious dollars she just received, but the thought of somebody trying to hurt her or Lindsay or the animals made her stomach turn. "Send me their numbers. I can't be too careful right now."

Amelia wasn't going to check with anyone. The sooner they got help, the better. She went from extreme high to extreme low in the span of a minute. She disconnected the call and looked around. This was her piece of heaven. Did somebody want her farm? Have a grudge against her family? Was obsessed with Zoey? It was the unknown that was scary. Were people watching her now? She scanned the horizon but only saw cows, the tops of trees swaying in the strong breeze, and a few turkey vultures circling off in the distance. Nothing seemed off, but she couldn't stop the feeling that somebody somewhere was watching her.

❖

"No, ma'am. I don't have a problem staying awake."

Amelia was only three years older than Randy but felt a lot older. He nervously twirled his deputy hat in his hand as they walked along the property lines. "It's not very big but it's good, flat land. There aren't many holes or ruts or drop offs." She gave him the gate code and told him she'd see him tomorrow night. Becks joined her as they watched him drive off.

"I think this is a great idea. I've always worried about you alone over here," she said.

Amelia turned to her and smiled. "But I'm not alone. I have Lindsay and Wally and Tigger. God help whoever runs into either of them late at night."

"This is all happening so fast. Just this morning we were celebrating thousands of dollars and buying inventory and now we have to hire cops," Becks said.

"It won't be forever. It's just until they find this guy. Honestly, I don't think we'll see him again. It's been a while. Whatever he was doing, he's moved on," Amelia said. She wished she believed her own words. She gave Becks a firm nod. "Okay, go home. We've got this."

"Be safe. Don't forget. Dinner tomorrow. We have a lot to celebrate. Robbie has a new recipe she wants to try out," Becks said.

Amelia ensured the gate was locked before heading inside. Lindsay gave her an incredulous look when she walked into the kitchen. "What?"

"You're almost to twenty thousand," she said.

Amelia felt weak and had to sit. "No. Really?"

Lindsay turned her laptop around. "Numbers don't lie. And I've been working on the latest video of Tater and Tot. Tab over to watch it." Amelia studied the numbers across all platforms. It was amazing how fast they grew from followers to subscribers to donations. Lindsay was right. It was the perfect time to start growing Mizzou Moos.

"When will the new merch get here?" Amelia asked.

"Everything should ship out next week," she said. Amelia tapped her fingers on the wooden table until she felt Lindsay's warm hand stop her. "It's going to be fine. If we run out of stock, we'll order more. Point Press can mass produce. We might have to say something like 'please be patient while we fill your orders. Mimsey chewed up the printer and we're running a bit behind' or something cutesy like that. People will eat it up."

"Oh, I like that. I boxed up the books in the library. It's climate-controlled because it's inside the house and the shelves are deep enough for stacks of clothing and other merch," Amelia said. It was hard to not fantasize about the what-ifs, but every once in a while, Amelia allowed herself the luxury of pretending Mizzou Moos was thriving. She hated turning down so many rescues over the last few months because she didn't have enough money for more stables and corrals.

A rescue in Kansas needed to rehome four teacup mini cows and had reached out to Amelia earlier today. She desperately wanted to say yes, but building another barn cost money and now that was a possibility. She could integrate Tater and Tot into the medium-sized barn and keep them in with the goats and give the small barn to the teacups in the interim. This was also an opportunity to help another rescue. First, she needed to make sure the donkeys were going to work well with the goats.

"Where'd you go?" Lindsay asked. Amelia didn't respond until she felt Lindsay's touch. The zaps of electricity brought her back to reality.

"I'm sorry. I'm trying to figure out if I have room for four teacup cows and where I can put them," Amelia said.

"I'm sorry, what? What are teacup cows? Like Pippin and Patches?" Lindsay asked.

"Oh, no. These are super adorable and smaller and don't have pointy horns. After the mad rush of everyone wanting Highlands, the teacup cows were bred. Cuter, smaller, without horns and are about the size of a large lap dog or Wally," Amelia said.

Lindsay grabbed her hands. "You're telling me there are cuter animals than what you have already? When do we get them?" Her enthusiasm was infectious. It made Amelia want to load up the animal trailer and hightail it to Chanute, Kansas.

"They are probably already rescued by now. And full disclosure, rescue animals aren't perfect when they get here. They need a lot of love, patience, and medical attention. It takes a bit of time for them to warm up, if they do at all, so they won't be introduced to the public until I clear them after the vet clears them. I need to ensure they don't hurt anybody or themselves."

"I'm going to pull them up right now to see how cute they are," she said.

Amelia put her hand on Lindsay's phone. "I don't recommend this. Because you have a bleeding heart and you'll want to leave right now and I already know they need a lot of work. It will be a while before they cuddle with you." She held up her hand. "Plus this all depends on Tater and Tot and the goats."

Lindsay brushed her off. "Oh, the goats are totally sweet, right?"

"You've not met them on a bad day, which is almost every day. Tomorrow, we'll give it a try, but I make you no promises," Amelia said.

Lindsay crossed her heart. "Why can't we try now? Tot is super harmless. And non-threatening. His personality doesn't scream 'I want attention' like Tater's does." She pouted and blinked at Amelia knowing full well Amelia had a hard time saying no to her.

Amelia rolled her eyes and gave in. "Fine. We can try now even though Tot is wet and is going to be incredibly smelly and the goats are going to like him even less," Amelia said.

"Right. Goats are going to be offended by the smell of a donkey. Sure." Lindsay shook her head and headed outside. When they got to the corral, she grabbed the halter from the peg outside and handed it to Amelia. It was such a natural and easy move that it didn't dawn on her how fast she integrated herself into this place until that very moment. A month ago, she didn't know what a halter was or even that mini donkeys existed. Now she was ready to lead one into a pen with pygmy goats. She couldn't help but smile at herself. The other day she broke a nail while helping Becks unload feed and didn't think twice about it. It would have been an emergency a month ago. She simply clipped and filed her nails down and finished the day with shorter nails.

"Okay, buddy. Let's go meet your new besties," Amelia said. She led him over to the gate and let the goats meet him through the fence. They were curious about him, but not enough to startle him. He eyed them warily but didn't stomp his hoof or make any sudden movements.

Lindsay held her breath when Amelia led him inside. She smiled when they took to him immediately. She put her hands on her hips and smiled smugly. "Told you."

"Okay, Farmer Lindsay. But he's the easy one. We still have to deal with Tater," Amelia said. Lindsay held up a finger.

"Hang on. I'll go get him," she said. Another thing she didn't picture herself doing. She found these simple things rewarding. And Tater loved her. He trotted over to her, let her put on the halter and lead him over to the pen where Tot and the goats were kicking up dirt and running up and down the fence line.

"We'll have to give them more space," Amelia said.

"Is there enough money for a new fence somewhere?" Lindsay asked.

Amelia pointed to an open space between two shade trees. "I'd like to build a lean-to for shelter and make a nice area for them over there, but it's so far away from the rest of the sanctuary. It's going to make for weird tours."

Lindsay hooked her thumb in the belt loop of Amelia's jeans. "Don't overthink it. You can bring them up to the barn on tour days."

Amelia kissed the tip of her nose. "And that's why I love you. For your mind and smart ideas." Everything stopped when those words slipped passed her lips. She felt her blood rush and flood her senses. It pushed against her skin and pounded in her ears. Love wasn't a word she took lightly or heard often. Her life wasn't complicated by sticky, emotional entanglements. It wasn't that she didn't want it, she didn't know she needed it until she said those words out loud. It scared the shit out of her.

CHAPTER TWENTY-FOUR

Lindsay immediately knew it was a slip up. Amelia's eyes widened with panic. Her mouth opened and closed several times as though she was trying to figure out a way to get the words back. Lindsay wasn't sure how long they stared at one another, but she knew she was going to have to be the one to say something. Amelia looked scared as hell.

Lindsay tried to drop a nonchalant chuckle, but it came out more like a cackle. "That's why I get paid the big bucks." She tapped the side of her temple. "For my ideas." It was corny and ridiculous and when her phone rang, she answered it quickly instead of ignoring it. "This is Lindsay."

"Lindsay, it's Simon Barkley. Do you have a moment?"

Why did she have to answer her phone? It was stupid. She mouthed the word "sorry" and walked away from Amelia. "Yes, what can I do for you?"

"Sarah and I would like to have a follow-up interview so you can meet members of our production team. Are you up for it?" he asked.

It was the last thing on her mind. "Of course. When are you thinking?"

"If you're still out of town, we can send a Zoom invite tomorrow. How does your afternoon look?" he asked.

They had an early dinner planned with Becks and Robbie and she had some samples from Press Print arriving before noon, but the rest of the day was going to be spent working on videos and posting online. She quickly calculated the time difference. "I'm open until three."

"Great. I'll send you an invite," he said.

"Sounds great. Thank you," Lindsay said. She heard the call disconnect but kept the phone up to her ear. She was nervous to turn around and face Amelia. Was this a fair conversation to have? They both knew that this was temporary, right? She took a deep breath and slid her phone in her pocket before she turned to face Amelia.

Amelia was across the pen picking alfalfa from the feeder and scratching the heads of curious goats. They could talk about it, or Lindsay could go inside, start dinner, and they could have a mature, intelligent conversation about the relationship over food. If either of them could stomach it.

She called out, "I'm going to clean up and throw together a salad for dinner. Do you need help with Tater and Tot? Are they staying here?"

"I'll put them back. Baby steps." Amelia winked. Lindsay wasn't sure if that was directed at their relationship or Tater and Tot.

"I'll see you in twenty," Lindsay said.

All the way to the house, she replayed Amelia's words over and over. The word love flowed so easily from Amelia's lips and the terrified look on her face made it clear to Lindsay that she wasn't expecting to say it either. Now what? She had an interview tomorrow for a job that could take her away from Amelia and Mizzou Moos. They hadn't identified their relationship so what was keeping her here? But also why wasn't she in a hurry to leave? She looked at the clock. She had seventeen minutes to figure it out. She didn't remember cutting the tomatoes or chopping the lettuce. She sliced too many peppers and radishes but added them anyway. When she heard Amelia open the mudroom door, panic fluttered in her chest. She turned left, then quickly right, not knowing where to be or what to do. She decided to stay put and appear to be cool, calm, and collected.

"How'd they end up doing?" Her heart leapt in her throat when Amelia entered the room. Amelia's smile made her knees weak.

"They didn't want to leave the goats. I'm going to have to figure out how to increase that space if we get the minis," Amelia said. Lindsay watched Amelia wash her hands and loosen her hair from the braid. The color had lightened over the last three weeks to a dark honey. "But also I want to make sure we can afford them. I'm afraid of overcommitting. I don't know if this just a spike or if we're going to grow."

Lindsay brought the salad to the table and walked over to Amelia. "I haven't checked the numbers, but with Alec Montgomery reposting and sharing, everything is growing. The beautiful thing about him is that he has a ton of fans who analyze his posts so they'll share with other fans. And guess who they're talking about?" Lindsay nodded. "Yep. Mizzou Moos." She held up her phone. "Should we look at numbers? I think the tip jar and GoFundMe will keep things moving until the other platforms start paying off." She reached up and pressed her fingers against Amelia's furrowed brow. "Trust the process."

"I'm trying. It's just all so new," Amelia said.

Lindsay pointed at the table. "Have a seat. Let's eat." She sat across from Amelia wondering who was going to start the conversation first. Amelia kept her eyes averted. Okay, it was going to have to be her. "Can we talk about what happened back there?"

Amelia's shoulders sagged. "It was a slip. It was an exciting moment. I just let my emotions get in the way." Her voice was quiet and laced with embarrassment.

Lindsay touched Amelia's hand. "I didn't mind that you said that. It's very flattering."

Amelia groaned and dropped her head into her hands. "This is so embarrassing."

"Don't be. We've grown so close since Las Vegas." Lindsay didn't want to say the words because saying them entangled her and Amelia together and her life wasn't here. A long-distance relationship at their age wasn't sustainable. Amelia couldn't leave the sanctuary for more than a day or two and if Lindsay was offered the Barkley Swan job, she would have long days and terrible nights getting a new show off the ground. "Being here has been the best thing for me on so many levels." Lindsay shook her head. It sounded too clinical. "What I mean is that I came here to help but also to spend time with you." She knew she was being selfish sleeping with Amelia knowing it couldn't lead to anything. Lindsay was hoping for a happy for now relationship, but Amelia wasn't that kind of person.

"I know you have to get back to California and find a job. I'm not trying to do or say anything to make you stay. Back there was just an emotional slip-up. I can't tell you what a buffer you've given us. We lost important funding. It's been very stressful so I just blurted out my happiness," Amelia said.

"I'm happy to help and I'm glad it's a nice cushion. I know I sound like a broken record, but this marketing plan is a slam dunk. We should celebrate." Lindsay walked over to the small wine rack on the counter and grabbed a Pinot Grigio. She held it up for Amelia's approval. At her nod, she expertly opened the bottle and poured two glasses. "Here's to expanding and rescuing all the sweet animals who need saving." Amelia's smile seemed forced, and Lindsay tried to ignore the guilt in her heart.

"I'm ready for more babies around here," Amelia said.

"Have you heard back from the place in Kansas?" Lindsay asked. She hated that their conversation had deviated from heavy emotions, but she had to stay strong.

"Not yet. Was that Simon who called?" Amelia asked.

"Yes. They want to have another chat tomorrow. Sounds like they are getting close to deciding." This was not the night Lindsay wanted to have with Amelia. With the end coming sooner than either of them wanted or expected, time together was important.

She wanted to hold hands and walk around the sanctuary and pet the sweet animals she already loved. She gave a small smile when she thought of that word. What a raw, bring-you-to-your-knees word. When was the last time she said it to another person? When was the last time she heard it from somebody who meant it?

"Is your meeting tomorrow afternoon? I'd like to try to do a video from start to finish and see how I do. I can edit during your meeting. I think I learned a lot. I need to figure it out sooner than later," Amelia said.

"Sure. What do you have in mind?" Lindsay asked.

"Maybe just another overall video or see how Pippin feels. We've been giving so much attention to Tater and Tot that I think he's feeling left out." Amelia pushed her plate away and moved her wine glass closer. Lindsay did the same. Neither of them was hungry. There was too much between them that remained unsaid.

"What do you want to do tonight?" Lindsay asked. She'd been sleeping in Amelia's bed all week, but tonight felt like maybe they needed space. "Do you want to go into town and catch a movie or grab an ice cream cone?" It seemed like a sweet gesture, and they needed a change of scenery. They hadn't left the farm in several days and as much as Lindsay enjoyed the peace, she needed to be around people, too.

"That sounds like fun. I could use a break," Amelia said. She looked at the time. "Do you want to go now? The ice cream place closes at eight."

Lindsay scooted back in her chair. "Let's go. I understand Lincolnville has the best soda shop in the area." She always smiled when she read their sign whenever they drove through town to pick up feed and other supplies.

"My first job was there. Well, besides working the farm."

Lindsay pulled Amelia close to her. "You were a Frostie girl?"

Amelia smiled. "I'm pretty sure every kid who worked on a farm worked at Fritz's. We didn't have too many options. I wasn't strong enough to work at the feed store so it was either Fritz's or the grocery store."

"Aw. That makes tonight even sweeter. I get to see where you worked," Lindsay said.

"It's a small shop that's been around forever, but they do have the best ice cream." Amelia automatically linked her fingers with Lindsay's. It was something that always gave Lindsay a little jolt and put a smile on her face. Even though they were quiet on the five-minute drive into town, they never stopped holding hands. Lindsay knew Amelia was going to pull back emotionally, but she selfishly hoped the physical connection would continue. It made Lindsay feel safe. She stopped at feeling anything more than safe. They strolled into Fritz's and stopped in front of the display of over thirty flavors.

"What do you recommend?" Lindsay asked. Ice cream wasn't her favorite dessert, but this was such a cute moment for them that she was going to eat whatever Amelia suggested.

"I love anything with cookie dough or peanut butter," she said.

"Girl after my own heart." Lindsay immediately regretted those words after feeling Amelia stiffen next to her. It was too soon. It was too raw. She hurried to elaborate. "Nothing beats cookie dough and how did you know peanut butter is my favorite cookie?" It wasn't true but anything to get them off the mushy words that kept falling out of their mouths. "What was the most popular when you worked here?"

Lindsay kept her attention on the ice cream flavors in front of her, but she was very aware of Amelia's nearness and how heat radiated from her body. It was so hard not to lean into her and absorb everything about her. Her quiet strength, the soft, floral scent of her lotion, the sweet smile that seemed only reserved for her. If Lindsay's feet weren't firmly planted on the floor, she would float away. She shook her head. Just a minute ago, she was trying to keep a wall up between them so that nobody slipped any more. Feelings were starting to stick around longer. Lindsay had to make some hard choices soon.

"Chocolate chip. I don't understand it, but it was always the most popular," Amelia said.

Lindsay wrinkled her nose. "That's boring."

"What's boring is that one of my favorite flavors is vanilla. Sure, strawberry is nice in the summer, but nothing beats the simplicity of a classic like good old vanilla," Amelia said.

Lindsay ordered two vanilla cones and paid before Amelia could dig in her pockets for cash. Lincolnville ran on cash and credit cards. Apple Pay and Venmo were nonexistent out here. Lindsay felt it would be several years before everything was upgraded to contactless payment. She grabbed napkins and followed Amelia out. It was the perfect evening for ice cream and a walk around the town square. She licked the cone and moaned. "You're right. Vanilla is underrated. This is delicious."

"Everything in small towns taste better," Amelia said.

"I can't argue with that," Lindsay said. Her flirtatious wink made Amelia smile. It felt nice that they were slowly coming back together after today's word bomb. She checked her watch. "What time is Dusty reporting for duty?"

"He's working eleven to five in the morning. We're trying to figure out the best time though." Amelia shrugged. "All of this is new to us."

"I wish we knew what that guy wanted," Lindsay said. It was unnerving not knowing if the mystery man would return or why he was there in the first place. She hated not knowing for Amelia's sake and safety. "Not that I want to keep bringing this up, but I don't like this at all. Everyone here seems so nice and you grew up with these people."

"I'm happy Sam's out there trying to figure it out," Amelia said.

"Let's go home. I'd feel better if we were there. Just in case, you know?" Lindsay asked. She didn't even care that she called it home. They finished their cones and drove back to the farm in silence. It was a heavy night, but it was far from over.

"I'm going to check on the animals. I'll be upstairs in a little bit," Amelia said.

"Do you want me to go with you?" Lindsay asked.

Amelia kissed Lindsay's forehead. "No, thank you. I'll be up in a bit."

Lindsay watched her head toward the barn and decided a warm shower might erase the heaviness of the evening. She didn't want to go to bed feeling melancholy. She wanted to fall asleep in Amelia's arms after a solid hour of touching, but she wasn't sure if Amelia wanted that, too. She showered quickly and crawled into Amelia's bed. The pressure in her chest when Amelia entered the room was almost unbearable. She watched Amelia stripped down and grab a T-shirt and boxers before heading into the bathroom. Waiting was the hard part. Two minutes after the shower stopped, Amelia came out with wet hair and crawled into bed. She slipped under the sheets and pulled Lindsay into her arms. She was tender and sweet and very quiet. Too quiet. Lindsay was dying to ask her what was on her mind, but she knew. Instead, she placed her hand on Amelia's bare stomach. Her skin was soft and smooth and warm. She smiled wondering if Amelia ran hot in the winter, too.

"Am I too hot for you?"

"Not at all. You feel nice against me." Amelia's voice was low and sexy.

Lindsay gently ran her fingertips along back and forth across Amelia's bare stomach with nothing in mind other than touching her. How many nights would she have like this? A heavy day didn't mean the night had to end the same way. "Thank you for today. I've learned so much about myself by being with you." In the past, Lindsay never gave a thought to people who lived in small towns between the coasts. Her job was in California with small stints in large cities like Las Vegas or Chicago or New York. In the last month, she learned about animals and the hardships farmers and people who worked with animals faced daily. Places like Lincolnville, Missouri were what she saw on television shows set in small towns. Nice people, everyone knew everyone, and there was always at least one nosy person who meddled. She smiled thinking of some of her interactions.

"I can feel you smiling," Amelia said. That only made Lindsay smile harder.

"I was just thinking about the people here," Lindsay said.

"Here at the farm or here in town?"

"Well, both. I can't get over how sheltered my life has been. This is such a different vibe than I'm used to," Lindsay said. Amelia's fingers stopped playing with her hair.

"Is that good or bad?" Amelia asked.

"It's definitely good," Lindsay said. She stroked Amelia's skin above the waistline of her boxers enjoying the barely audible inhales and exhales so close to her ear.

"Tell me how good?"

Amelia's words shifted everything inside Lindsay. Her heart swelled with feelings she chose to ignore and instead focused on how Amelia's body was responding to her touch. She moved her hand down Amelia's hip and slipped her fingers underneath the material that hugged her thighs. Amelia tilted her hips to grant Lindsay better access. "The vibe here is sexy and fun." She brushed Amelia's pussy with her fingertips and felt a slight buck when she touched Amelia's clit. She bit her bottom lip when she felt how wet Amelia was. It took all her willpower to not rip Amelia's boxers off and fuck her hard and fast. She wanted to give her an orgasm that bubbled up before Lindsay's deeper emotions did.

"Only sexy and fun?" Amelia hissed out between clenched teeth.

"Oh, the vibe covers so much more." Lindsay slid one finger inside and moaned with Amelia. "It's hard work, good times, rewarding…" Her voice trailed off as Amelia's hips began thrusting against her hand. Words were forgotten. The need to pleasure her took over.

Lindsay pulled down Amelia's boxers the best she could with one hand until it became obvious they were going to have to stop for a brief moment to get clothes off. Lindsay was pleasantly surprised when Amelia climbed over her so they were face-to-face and her knees were on either side of Lindsay's thighs. She didn't hesitate. She ran one hand down Amelia's body and slid two fingers inside. The other hand held the back of Amelia's neck. Even though Amelia's wet hair fanned their faces, Lindsay could see a passionate flush spread up across Amelia's cheeks.

"You're so beautiful," she said. Amelia kissed her passionately and moved her hips against Lindsay's hand. Lindsay shifted down to suck one of Amelia's nipples while she continued fucking her. She felt Amelia's pussy tighten against her fingers. "Don't come yet," she said. She slowly pulled out and continued shifting down the bed until her mouth was right below Amelia's pussy. She placed her hands on Amelia's hips and slowly brought her down onto her mouth.

"Oh my. I've never—" Amelia didn't finish her thought.

If this was a new experience for Amelia, Lindsay was going to make damn sure it was enjoyable. She carefully sucked Amelia's clit and the soft flesh around it into her mouth and gently flattened her tongue against as much as she could. Amelia's moans and soft cries empowered her. She dug her fingers into Amelia's hips and kept her body tight against her mouth. Amelia's nails scratched the sheets beside Lindsay's head. This was how she wanted Amelia to come. Actually, it would feel a lot better if Amelia sat up instead of hunching over her. Lindsay tilted Amelia's hips so she was forced to sit up more.

"Oh, yes. This. This is—" Amelia paused as words escaped her. "Wonderful." She rocked her hips back and forth against Lindsay's face.

Lindsay almost came on the spot when she watched Amelia squeeze her breasts and pinch her nipples. Everything about Amelia was intoxicating. How she loved, how she gave herself pleasure, and how beautifully she came. Lindsay had to lift Amelia's hips up a fraction so she could still move her tongue. Amelia threw her head back and shouted when the orgasm hit. Lindsay watched as Amelia threw her arms around her shoulders and tried to keep her body balanced as the aftershocks wracked her body. When she rolled over on her back gasping for air, Lindsay followed.

"I'm not done," Lindsay said. She slipped two fingers inside Amelia's quivering pussy and swiftly moved in and out until another orgasm burst from Amelia's body. She stopped only to roll Amelia onto her stomach.

"I don't know if I can handle another one." Amelia's voice sounded pained.

Lindsay crawled on top of her and whispered in her ear, "Do you want me to stop?"

Amelia continued panting but shook her head. Lindsay spread Amelia's legs apart with her knees and slipped her hand between their bodies. This was her favorite angle. Amelia was so wet and accepting that she was able to slide three fingers inside with little resistance. If she had her strap-on, she would've fucked her so fully and completely, but she only had her hand to work with. Amelia groaned her disappointment when Lindsay slipped out of her.

"Oh, don't worry. I'm not done." She almost slipped and called her love. Instead, she bit her lip to keep from saying anything too revealing and pulled Amelia's hips so she was again on her knees, only this time Lindsay was behind her. "You want me," Lindsay said.

"Yes." Amelia's voice was shaky but strong.

Lindsay scraped her teeth over Amelia's ass and bit softly. "Do you have a dildo or vibrator?" Amelia looked over her shoulder and nodded. "Can I use it on you?" Another nod. This time Amelia pointed to the bottom drawer of the nightstand. Lindsay quickly jumped off the bed and opened the bottom drawer where she found two purple dildos. One was average size, but the other was thicker and longer and thinking about using it on Amelia made her legs go weak. "Which one do you want me to use?"

Amelia was silent for three very long seconds. Lindsay thought maybe she didn't hear her and was about to ask again when Amelia answered. "The big one."

Lindsay's pulse pounded in her ears as she carefully got it and a bottle of lube out. "I'll be right back. Don't move." It hurt to walk. Her pussy was swollen and her knees felt raw. She quickly washed the dildo, grabbed a hand towel and returned. Amelia was flat on the bed. "You moved."

"I was resting," Amelia said. She wiggled back onto her knees and looked at Lindsay. "Is this better?"

Fuck, who was this woman and why did it take Lindsay so long to find her? "That's perfect." She generously lubed the dildo and returned to her spot behind Amelia. She started with her fingers until Amelia asked for more. Lindsay rubbed the dildo up and down Amelia's slit until Amelia reached between her legs and guided the dildo inside her. They both gasped. Lindsay watched the dildo slide inside Amelia. It was such a sexy moment.

Once she had a slow rhythm going, she moved so she was on her knees behind Amelia. She kept the dildo in place by leaning her pussy against it. She grabbed Amelia's hips and let her move at the pace she wanted. Amelia was slow at first. When she pushed her hips back, the dildo hit Lindsay's clit. Lindsay moaned and rolled her hips to keep the pressure off. She didn't want to come this soon. Beads of sweat popped up on her body. Her nipples were painfully hard.

"Faster," Amelia said.

It was hard to control the motion without a harness of any kind, but Lindsay obliged. She moved closer so their thighs touched and wrapped her arm around Amelia's waist. This was the only way she could pump hard without slipping out. When Amelia pussy was at the right height and her body was writhing for friction, Lindsay started moving her hips fast and hard. She never wanted to please anyone this much before in her life.

Amelia moaned and yelled words like "yes, harder, fuck me, yes" until her entire body stiffened and she cried out with wild abandonment. Only then did Lindsay allowed herself her own orgasm. A kaleidoscope of colors and feelings and moans poured out of her. She thought sweat was in her eyes, but the burning sensation in her sinuses alerted her that she was crying. She released her hold on Amelia's waist and carefully removed the dildo. Amelia sank onto the mattress. Lindsay wrapped the dildo and lube in the towel and dropped it on the side of the bed before falling next to Amelia. Her heartbeat was pounding fiercely against her skin and even though she just had the most amazing orgasm in a long time, her body wasn't done. She spread her legs apart and slipped a finger inside, moving it quickly in and out.

"Let me," Amelia said.

Lindsay stopped and leaned up on her elbows to watch Amelia fuck her. "Don't go slow."

Amelia's eyebrow quirked. She sat up and slipped two fingers in and moved them so fast and so hard that Lindsay couldn't form words or even make a sound. Her mouth opened and she threw her head back once she felt the orgasm drive straight down to her pussy and explode. She drenched the sheets and Amelia's hand.

"Oh, my God." Amelia said.

Lindsay gave a pained laughed and fell back against the cool sheets. "Well, I wasn't expecting that."

"I'm never going to be the same again," Amelia said.

Lindsay moved over to the other side of the bed with Amelia and collapsed in her arms. She was never going to be the same again either, but those were words better left unsaid.

CHAPTER TWENTY-FIVE

Pippin's cry made Amelia sit up straight in bed. He never cried unless he was under duress. She threw back the covers and bolted. Something bad was happening. An orange glow illuminated the night. She knew immediately the barn was on fire. The loud shrilling fire alarms kicked in a moment later and only intensified her anxiety. She grabbed a pair of shorts, threw on a T-shirt, and took the stairs two at a time. She heard Lindsay close behind her.

"Call 9-1-1!" Amelia couldn't tell if she yelled or whispered it but knew Lindsay knew what to do. She raced to the barn cutting her feet on the sharp gravel but felt nothing. She flung the door open and stumbled back. The smoke that billowed out burned her eyes and lungs. She coughed but pushed forward. "I'm coming!"

Their cries got louder either because they heard her or the flames were getting closer. She bent low and felt her way until she reached their pens. There was no way to get them out the front of the barn. She had to push them out the back into the corral and assume they would stay away from the flames.

Amelia unlocked the back door that led to the small corral, held her arms out and moved toward the frightened boys. Once Pippin made his way out the door, the rest of the boys followed him. She quickly closed the stall and crawled into the next pen. The girls were quick to bolt out the second she opened their door.

The flames were getting closer and louder but Amelia didn't care. The animals came first. Her muscles were strained and she gulped for fresh air but didn't stop until all the minis were out.

"Amelia! Where are you?" Lindsay's voice cut through the hissing pops and crashing of a rafter as the barn slowly started falling apart.

Amelia could see Lindsay standing twenty feet from the barn's entrance. Amelia's heart dropped when she thought about Lindsay getting hurt. She waved to get Lindsay's attention. "Stay there!" Amelia prayed Lindsay could see her through the thick, black smoke that surrounded them. "I'm coming out."

She hoped Lindsay wasn't going to rush into the burning barn looking for her. It groaned and leaned to one side with flames that licked higher than the walls. The stored hay and alfalfa was only fueling the fire. It was a muffled bark that made her stop.

"Tigger! Where are you?" Amelia dropped to her knees and called out again. "Tigger!" She heard a low whine and knew he was stuck somewhere. "Shit!" She grabbed a rag hanging near the entrance and covered her mouth and nose and rushed back into the billowing smoke. "Tigger!"

His whines intensified. She was getting closer. She moved her free hand around until her fingers came in contact with fur.

"Oh, Tigger!" She dropped the rag and felt around his body to figure out why he couldn't move. Barbed wire had twisted around his back leg. She felt the blood on her fingertips and told herself to remain calm. "Stay. Stay." She hoped her voice calmed him even though she knew she didn't have long to save both of them. "It's okay, buddy. I'm going to get you out."

The wire had tightened as he fought to free himself. If she had wire cutters, two snips and they would have been free. But the tools were too far away and she knew that if she left, Tigger would only hurt himself more trying to chase after her.

"You're being such a good boy," she said as calmly as possible. She coughed as the acrid smoke stole the oxygen around her. The wire tore into her flesh but she wasn't leaving without him. Amelia pulled hard at the wire at source, the barbs biting into her fingers, until it finally loosened its grip on Tigger's leg. He instinctively pulled free, but didn't leave her side. She picked him up with strength borne of adrenaline and carried him out of the barn. Lindsay raced to them and guided them away from the flames and away from the firetrucks racing up the gravel driveway.

"You're bleeding! You're both bleeding," she cried. She opened the tailgate of the truck so Amelia could set Tigger down, but seemed at a loss of what to do next.

Amelia knew she was going to need stitches in her hand and wrist, but she was more concerned with Tigger losing his leg. "I'll be fine. I need to check Tigger." Amelia applied slight pressure up and down his leg until she found several puncture wounds. "There's a first aid kit inside the truck. Can you get it for me? And there should be a blanket in there, too."

Lindsay quickly returned and opened the kit. She dropped a stack of T-shirts next to it. "I didn't see a blanket, but these are okay, right?"

"Yes, that's perfect." Amelia grabbed a T-shirt and held it to Tigger's wounds. He leaned up and kissed her cheek as she carefully tended to his leg.

"I can't believe this. I can't believe this." Lindsay shook her head in disbelief.

"Love, I need you to apply pressure to his leg. I'm going to talk to the firefighters." Amelia put Lindsay's hands against his leg and wrapped her own hand in a T-shirt to stop the bleeding. She stumbled to the captain on the scene.

He held her up by the shoulders. "I'm sorry, but we can't save it." He pointed behind the barn and called to the firefighters at the pumper truck, "Do what you can to keep it from spreading but be careful. There are animals in the back."

It took a moment for Amelia to realize Peter Watkins, the guy she went to high school with and who now was a captain for the Columbia Fire Department, was the one barking out orders.

"Thanks, Pete." She steadied herself and clutched her throbbing hand. She hissed out a breath. "I need to get to the minis over to the small barn. They're so scared." She swallowed a sob knowing she needed to stay strong.

"You need to see a medic before you do anything." He insisted and marched her over to the ambulance where they quickly inspected her hands and burned forearm. She hadn't even noticed the burn.

"Just bandage me up for now." She tried hard not to focus on the pain.

"You're going to need stitches," the EMT said.

"I'll get them as soon as I move the cows," Amelia said. The EMT muttered their disapproval, but wrapped her forearm and hand in gauze. Amelia strained to see if all six Highlands were safe in the back of the corral. They were still too close to the fire.

"I wrapped Tigger's leg and closed him off in the mud room. We'll have to take him to get stitches when things calm down. Are you okay? Tell me you're okay." The desperation in Lindsay's voice was hard to miss.

"I'll be fine." Amelia stepped away from the EMT. "I'll be back. Thanks for wrapping me up." She turned to Lindsay. "We need to move the minis. They're still in danger that close to the barn."

"I know. I grabbed everything I could find in the garage to help move them," Lindsay said. She held up a handful of leads, a small bag of alfalfa, and a pair of boots for Amelia.

Amelia pointed at the back of the corral. "We're going to have to knock down some of the fence and walk them over to the small barn." She kept her arm and hand stiff to minimize further damage and followed Lindsay to the cluster of Highlands huddled in the back of the corral. She climbed the fence and softly put leads on the spooked animals.

Lindsay moved the top two wooden beams giving the minis a low enough height for them to be able to leave the corral. Cramming six Highland cows in a corral meant for two donkeys was tight, but they were safe and that was all Amelia cared about.

"Now let's get go back to the EMTs and let them finish working on you," Lindsay said.

Amelia nodded and gritted her teeth to keep them from chattering. The adrenaline was leaving her body and anger was quick to slip into its place. She couldn't handle losing anything else at Mizzou Moos.

"Are you okay? We raced here as soon as the alarms went off." Becks started to hug Amelia and recoiled when she saw her bandages. "What the hell happened?"

Amelia had never seen Becks crack before. She was always the level-headed one. There was something about her voice and how she gutted she sounded that broke Amelia. She couldn't stop the tears.

"Somebody tried to burn down the barn. I'm going to need stitches and so will Tigger, but we're okay. I don't understand who would want to do this to us." She covered her face, hoping the sounds of the fire and the firefighters working drowned her sobs. Lindsay put her arms around her and she leaned into her strength. Becks joined in on the hug careful to not press against Amelia's arm.

They stood there and watched the barn fall under the strength of the fire and the weight of the water. Ten firefighters were raking the ground around the barn to keep the flames from jumping to another building.

What if the alarms failed and the Highlands got hurt or worse? She wiped away tears and scolded herself for letting her imagination take over. Her anger returned when she saw Dusty's cruiser fishtail on the gravel road racing toward the barn. Where the hell had he been?

"I'm going to talk to him." She headed straight for the cruiser ready to unload on him, when she saw a figure crouched in the back seat holding a bloody towel against his face. Her body burned when she realized it was Brian, or whatever his name was. His face was bloodied and one of his eyes was swollen shut. Amelia could hear him moaning in pain. She wanted to bump his pain level up a notch or two.

"Whoa. Whoa. Hang on. Let's wait until Sam gets here before you beat him to a pulp." Dusty came out of nowhere to stand between her and his car. Blood from a gash above his eyebrow had trailed down his cheek and dripped onto his brown shirt. Dirt stains covered his mouth and nose. He looked wrecked.

Amelia turned her attention to him. "We have to get that cut cleaned up."

He brushed her off. "I'm fine. Besides, help is coming up the driveway now." He pointed at the two sheriff cars with flashing lights that were racing up the driveway. "We'll figure out why this asshole did what he did."

"Who opened the gate?" Amelia asked.

"I did when I came in." Dusty moved his jaw from side to side as though checking to see if anything was broken. He wiped the blood from his forehead with his sleeve. "I was making my rounds and saw a figure run across driveway and hide behind the trees near the entrance, so I followed him. I'm so sorry, Amelia. I didn't know he set the barn on fire or I would've let him go and helped get the animals out."

Amelia threw her arms around his neck. "Thank you for being here. The animals are safe and you caught whoever this asshole is. Had you not been here, that guy would've been long gone and God only knows what else he would've done." She looked up at the sky as though her parents or some higher power was looking out for Mizzou Moos.

Sam's car skidded to a halt ten feet from them. Sam greeted Amelia with a concerned hug. "This is terrible, Amelia. I'm so sorry." Sam shook Dusty's hand. "Good job on catching him, Dusty." He shook his head and looked at the barn that had crumbled into an unsalvageable heap. "Are the animals okay?" He turned Amelia so she faced him. "Are you okay?" He carefully held her arm away from him after he noticed the bandages.

"I'll be okay. The animals are scared but they're okay. We got them out in time." She was already coming up with a plan to install automatic gates that would open whenever the smoke alarm was triggered.

"That's good. Now, I need to talk to Dusty before I interrogate that guy, but I need you to stay put. I know you want at him, but we're going to do this by the book. You're going to have to let me handle him," Sam said.

Amelia wanted to break every bone in that man's body. She wanted the Highlands to trample him and Wally to have a shot, too. Oh, fuck. Where was Wally? Her body grew weak again.

Sam steadied her. "Hey, let's get you inside. You need to sit down," he said.

"No, I need to stay right here. Wally's missing." She hoped Brian hadn't hurt him. She whistled sharply, hoping he would come galloping toward them.

"Let's get you sitting down. Then I'll go look for him," Lindsay said.

Amelia couldn't wait that long. She waved Becks and Robbie over. "Can you look for Wally? He's not out here," Amelia said.

"I'll check the house," Robbie said. She carefully squeezed Amelia's shoulder reassuringly. "I'm sure he's fine."

"Honey, check the garage, too. You know how sometimes the doggie door gets stuck. Don't worry. We'll find him," Becks said.

"What do you want me to do?" Lindsay asked.

There were so many things she wanted to say. So many feelings rushed to the front of her mind and pounded in her heart but she kept it cool. "Staying right here by my side helps me more than you know." She smiled when she felt Lindsay's arm snake around her waist.

"I'm so angry at that man right now. Why isn't Sam finding out why he did this?" Lindsay asked.

"He said they are doing everything by the book. If they mess up, he could go free." Amelia knew that even if he did walk, it wouldn't be until after everyone questioned him thoroughly. And maybe turned off a few cameras in the process. Sam was a great guy and good sheriff, but small-town rules weren't as messy as big cities with big lawyers.

Amelia knew the cameras in the barn caught most of the action unless Brian figured out a way to disable them. There were also the trail cameras near the front that probably picked him up. She pulled out her phone to look at the video feed before the fire burned the cameras but was interrupted when Zoey called. Amelia rejected the call. She would deal with Zoey later.

She pulled up the app and found all but one camera was disabled. That motherfucker really was surveying the property. They should've never pointed out the cameras to him during their encounter. Thankfully, he didn't find the one in the corner under the loft. It clearly picked up his face and the dangerous smile when he threw a gas can toward Pippin. Amelia stifled a sob when she heard Pippin cry out in the video. He ignited the flare and raced out of the barn. The camera in the office caught him running down the driveway. Amelia quickly downloaded the video to her phone thinking that if she didn't, somehow it would be erased. Zoey called back and again Amelia declined the call. *Not now, Zoey.*

"Hey, Zoey," Lindsay said. *Shit.* Amelia should've answered. Now Lindsay was caught in the middle and she knew Lindsay wouldn't know to keep her emotions in check. "No, she's right here. I'll let you talk to her." Lindsay handed Amelia her phone.

"What is going on? I'm getting notifications that the smoke alarm is going off, but I can't pull up the feed," Zoey said.

Amelia sighed. She forgot Zoey was on the account, too. Her sister deserved to know the truth but she didn't want to upset her while she was so far away. "Don't get upset. We're fine. The animals are fine."

Zoey's panic was unmistakable. "What happened?"

"That guy, Brian Jones, came back and burned down the barn. Dusty caught him. Everything is fine here, so please don't stress." It was a condensed version of what happened but she needed to make sure Zoey didn't freak out.

"What!" Zoey yelled.

"Sam's got him in the back of the car. The fire department put out the fire, but the barn is gone. Lindsay and I moved the Highlands to the small barn. Needless to say we'll cancel tours for this week and figure out how to fix things," Amelia said. She wasn't going to tell her about the injuries on her arm or that Tigger was going to need stitches because it would only make her worry more. "Let me call you back later, okay? Everything's fine. I promise."

Headlights from behind got everyone's attention. Becks stopped the car from getting too close. Amelia rolled her eyes at whoever drove all the way up the driveway just to rubberneck. She shook her head when she saw it was her neighbor, Bob Teeter. Of course. His wife probably sent him over to get the story before everyone else in town. Or he was going to insult her with another offer on the farm. She could practically hear him tell her about how this was the reason it wasn't safe for a woman to be alone on a property this large. Becks made sure her body was directly between Amelia and Bob. Nobody had the energy to deal with him right now.

"What's going on? Is everyone okay?" he asked. He craned his neck around Becks and spoke loud enough for everyone to hear.

Amelia turned her back on him and kept her focus on Zoey's call. "Give me thirty minutes to clear everyone out and I promise to call you back. Bob Teeter just showed up."

"I love you. Please be careful and call me back when you can," Zoey said.

Amelia pocketed her phone and walked over to Mr. Teeter. "Hey, Bob."

"Amelia. Are you okay? I heard the sirens and thought I'd come over to see if you needed help," Bob said.

It wasn't that she didn't appreciate Bob's concern. He just never cared before. He only talked to her when it benefitted him. "Oh, we're fine, Bob. Just a little arson." She thumbed behind her. "Dusty caught the guy."

Bob pursed his lips and nodded. "Well, I'm glad you're okay. Mary sent me over to make sure. You know how she is," he said gruffly.

"Where is she?" Amelia figured she was laid up somewhere because no way would Mary not be the first person here getting the scoop.

"She's a bit under the weather but was very concerned for you. Up here all alone and all," he said.

"Tell her thank you."

He nodded and pointed at Sam's car. "Is that the guy?" he asked.

Amelia didn't bother answering the obvious. "Have you seen him before?"

He shook his head and shoved his hands in his pockets. "He's not from around here." He rocked back and forth on the balls of his feet. "Well, I guess since you're fine, I'll head home. Call me if you need anything."

"Thanks, Bob," Amelia said. It was normal for neighbors to show up during trying times, but Becks and Robbie were already here. She didn't need the Teeters hanging around.

She heard Wally before she saw him. He barked and raced toward them. "Wally! You're okay." Amelia braced herself as he jumped on her and licked her face. "Where have you been?"

"He was in the garage. That guy put a board across the doggy door," Becks said. She jogged over to them and petted his head while she caught her breath. "He scratched up the inside of the door trying to get out, but he's not hurt."

Wally shifted his attention from them to the person in the patrol car.

"No, big boy. You stay here," Amelia said. She turned to the group. "Actually, I'm going to take him into the house and check on Tigger. I'll be right back." She patted her leg and he fell in step beside her.

Once she was in the safety of the house, she sat at the kitchen table and processed the night. The what-ifs were too big to think about. She was so fortunate. The alarms did their jobs. Dusty went above and beyond. The animals were physically fine. She brushed away the first few tears with the swipe of her hand. The rest she couldn't stop. She put her face in her hands and sobbed. It was too much to keep inside. Wally lay at her feet concerned and ready to protect.

She looked up when she felt a warm hand on her shoulder. Lindsay stood next to her and pulled her close. Amelia wrapped her arms around Lindsay's waist and let the tears fall. She needed Lindsay's strength. She cried because of everything that happened tonight, sobbed at her misfortunes at only twenty-eight years old, and broke down because the comfort she sought in Lindsay was coming to an end.

CHAPTER TWENTY-SIX

"Thank you for the generous offer. I'll have an answer for you tomorrow." Lindsay disconnected the call with Simon Barkley and stood in the middle of the room not knowing how to feel. She was excited about the opportunity with a fledgling company with solid shows under its belt, but so much was up in the air here with Amelia. The fire was four days ago and the animals were finally settling down.

She tapped the phone gently against her forehead while she mentally made a list of the pros and cons of taking the job. Professionally, starting the marketing effort for Mizzou Moos was refreshing. She learned so much in the past month about social media and ways people could make money. Amelia made a little over two thousand dollars in the first month from her YouTube channel alone and that number would multiply tenfold. That number also didn't include other platforms, the tip jar, and GoFundMe that exploded after their subscribers and fans found out about the fire. The video she posted yesterday had more comments than any other video on their socials.

Lindsay knew people loved the animals at Mizzou Moos, but so many of them were distraught over Pippin's brush with death. They showed concern by donating to the GoFundMe that was now at a staggering two hundred and eight thousand dollars. Lindsay was sure Amelia didn't know. She had accomplished exactly what she wanted and now it was time for her to focus on herself, but damn, it was hard. She heard the door to the mud room open and shut.

"Lindsay? Are you here?" Amelia's voice held a note of panic.

Lindsay called out. "I'm in here. What's going on?" Lindsay's heart always hammered when Amelia walked into a room. Today she was wearing jeans, a white tank top, and a light blue denim shirt with the sleeves rolled up. It was the boots that sealed the deal. Amelia was sexy as hell and Lindsay was going to miss seeing her and touching her every day.

"Sam just called. You're not going to believe this." Amelia started pacing. "I can't even believe it myself." She put her hands on her hips and stared at Lindsay. "Guess who Brian Jones is?" She didn't give Lindsay time to answer. "His real name is Wes Zims and my fucking neighbor hired him."

Lindsay stood. "What? Which neighbor? Why?"

"Bob. It was Bob because he was trying to run me off my land," she said.

"Bob the man who came over here because his wife Mary was worried? That Bob? But why?" Lindsay asked.

"Because he needs twenty acres of our land for some solar panel farm," Amelia said. "Apparently, there's a two-hundred-acre minimum for this deal he signed and he's twenty short. He figured out a way to get it approved without the town's blessing. Something about the way his property is zoned." She chugged a glass of cold water and licked her lips when she was done. Lindsay scolded herself. Amelia was finally getting answers to all the bad shit that had happened and all Lindsay could think about was Amelia's full lips and how, just a few short hours ago, they traveled down her body and woke her up when she was on the precipice of an orgasm. It was an amazing way to start the day.

"Sit down, babe. Tell me more." Lindsay put her hand on Amelia's thigh while she listened to an in-depth explanation of what the police told Amelia.

"Here's the deal. Had I known about this agreement he signed, I could've worked out a deal where I would give him the stretch of land behind the barns and he could pay rent. But he's a greedy fuck. He figured our social media plan would tank because of the scandal. That's why he hired that Wes guy and the other one who was asking about Zoey. He thought he could make us think the community didn't support us."

"Well, he really underestimated you. You don't give up that easy." Lindsay rubbed small, comforting circles on Amelia's back to soothe her.

"I probably would have if you hadn't shown up. And then when we started making money on the socials, he decided to burn things to scare us off."

"That son of a bitch. How long did it take for that guy to spill his guts? When will you find out more?" Lindsay asked. She wondered why it took them four days to get this information. Amelia and the farm were still vulnerable while this was unresolved.

"Sam said that after they listed all the charges being brought against him—arson, trespassing, harassment, beating the crap out of a deputy—he sang like a bird. They wanted to get all the information gathered first before arresting Bob. There was also another guy, the one who kept calling us asking for Zoey. Sam said his job was to make it look like a stalker was after her to throw off the scent," Amelia said.

"Did they catch him, too?"

"Yes, but that one's tougher. His only crime was harassment," Amelia said.

"This is bonkers. I'm in total shock." Great. Lindsay was getting ready to leave and Amelia was still dealing with this crime.

"Me, too," Amelia said.

Lindsay kissed Amelia softly. "I'm glad they figured out who and why. Do you think anyone else is going to come around and try to sabotage Mizzou Moos again?" She knew Amelia hired a contractor to add a sprinkler system to the two existing barns. It was an expense that was never on anyone's radar until after the fire.

"Everyone seems to think it's all over. That doesn't mean I'm going to relax around here. With so much online exposure, the last thing I need is a copycat," Amelia said.

Lindsay gave her a soft smile. "It's good that you're aware, but I'm sure you have more people out there on your side wanting the best for you and this place. I don't think you need to worry anymore." She pointed at the baskets and flowers and food trays that neighbors dropped off. "You're loved around here. Not just this stuff, but all the farm supplies they donated." In the last four days they'd had deliveries of hay, feed, harnesses and tack, buckets, and so much more.

Amelia stood and started pacing again. "They really came through. I'm still going to have to install more cameras, more motion detectors, and whatever other safety measures there are available. I can't stand the thought of the animals getting hurt."

"Will you keep Dusty and Randy on for a bit longer?"

Amelia nodded. "At least another month or until all repairs and systems are installed. I know the guy who quoted me the project, but I also knew Bob so knowing somebody doesn't mean it's safe anymore." She blew out a deep breath and returned to the table. "Tell me how your phone call went."

Her words cut right through Lindsay's chest and exposed her heart. She felt the sting of tears and quickly thought about something happy to stop them from falling. This wasn't the conversation she wanted to have right now, but it wasn't fair to wait any longer. "Well, they offered me a job."

Amelia's smile faltered but remained in place. "That's great. Now that everything here is taking off, thanks one hundred percent to you, you can finally get back to Hollywood and kill it on another show," she said.

Lindsay looked for any signs of distress on Amelia's face but saw only encouragement and something that could only be described as unconditional love. She remembered Amelia telling the story of when Zoey left for Hollywood and how she had to let her go so that Zoey could live out her dream. It was happening to Amelia again. "They gave me twenty-four hours to get back to them."

Amelia looked confused. "Why would you need time? I took great notes on how to edit videos and splice them together and I'm not afraid of telling the story here. You did that for me. You gave me the strength I needed to believe in myself. Now it's my time to give you yours."

She was being entirely too understanding and, truthfully, it broke Lindsay's heart. She wanted Amelia to fight a little bit harder for her but also understood that Amelia was the most selfless person she knew, and no way would she put any pressure on Lindsay to stay. "I just wanted to make sure you were in a good place. With everything that's happened, I'm nervous to leave you." *Just tell her the truth.*

Amelia squeezed Lindsay hands. "It's okay. I have enough people around here who will check on me. Sam's already going to patrol the road more, but nobody thinks I'm in danger anymore. You need to take care of you. I can't thank you enough for everything you've done for us here. Not to mention how wonderful it's been having you in my life, sharing my world. Thank you."

Fuck. Lindsay blinked back tears and looked away. She wasn't an overly emotional person. But truthfully, she hadn't put herself in emotional situations on purpose. It was always about work and getting ahead. It was never about her heart. "I'd say I'm sorry about the scandal, but I'm not. It worked out for everyone. I mean, you had to go through some totally unnecessary shit, but look at you and Mizzou Moos now. And look at Zoey. She's out there killing it on set."

Amelia interrupted. "And now it's your turn. You supported us and now we're going to support you."

Lindsay knew that Amelia added Zoey to the conversation to keep it from getting too personal. She was going to have to respect that. It made no sense to try to push Amelia to reveal her true feelings, get Lindsay to reveal what was in her heart, and then leave. The wall between them was doing a good job of keeping emotions on either side and it was for the best for them. Correction. The best for Lindsay. "Thank you. I still want to give it twenty-four hours. Once I accept, I have to be back in Hollywood right away."

"Then we should celebrate tonight. Let's invite Becks and Robbie and grill out," Amelia said. Since tours were canceled this week, Amelia didn't have the added stress of getting people off the property. Lindsay nodded even though she wanted tonight to just be about them.

"I can go into town and pick up some groceries," Lindsay said.

"I'd go with you, but I'm afraid too many people will ask a lot of nosy questions and I don't want to answer them," Amelia said.

"Then it's settled." Lindsay smacked her hand on the table. "I'll go. I'll call Robbie and see if she wants to go, too. I can't imagine she wouldn't want to make five billion different salads or desserts."

The first genuine smile since she sat popped up on Amelia's face. "She would love that. Becks said she's going bonkers trying to figure out what to do with her time. This would be the perfect distraction."

Lindsay stood when Amelia did and walked into her outstretched arms for a hug. It felt like more than a hug though. Amelia held her tighter and longer than normal. Lindsay dropped her arms first and grabbed her purse that hung from the corner of the chair. "I'm going to swing by and see if she's up for it." She needed time away from Amelia and the animals to think through everything.

"Call me if you need me. I guess I'll get back to painting. I don't know what's worse: Smoke smell, fire retardant toxins, or paint fumes. Either way, the Highlands are loving being in the open field with the cows. It's going to be hard to wrangle them up when we're done." Lindsay watched Amelia stroll to the barn after they said goodbye at her car. They didn't have a lot of time left and she felt guilty for agreeing to dinner with friends. She punched in Robbie's number.

"Is everything okay?" Robbie's voice sounded breathless on the other end. Lindsay didn't blame her. The last few phone calls they shared were high anxiety.

Lindsay suppressed a small giggle. "Everything's fine. I'm calling to officially invite you and Becks over for dinner tonight. I'm on my way into town to pick up a few things and wanted to see if wanted to go with me," Lindsay said. She drove slowly down the driveway waiting for Robbie's answer to let her know if she needed to turn left into town or right to pick her up.

"That sounds nice. Yes. Come on by. I'm doing absolutely nothing," Robbie said.

"Be there in five." Lindsay disconnected the call. Amelia made Robbie take the week off. Becks hung around to help feed and take care of the animals, but Robbie had personal paperwork to catch up on so she stayed home.

"You're a lifesaver," Robbie said when Lindsay parked in front of their house. She was waiting for Lindsay with reusable shopping bags in one hand, and her purse in the other.

"Thanks for coming. I don't know what to expect in town today so I need the backup," Lindsay said. She'd been around long enough that most people knew she was staying at the farm with Amelia. Maybe they didn't know the nature of their relationship, but knew they were somehow linked.

"How's Amelia doing? Becks just called and told me everything. I can't believe Bob did that. I've known that man for twenty years." Robbie shook her head. "He could've just asked. Since they'll be in jail for a long spell, maybe we'll buy his farm, put the panels up, and make the millions he expected to make."

"Millions?" Lindsay asked.

Robbie turned to face Lindsay. Her voice low as though she was whispering it. "Millions. Millions of dollars."

"So was Amelia's family approached by these companies?" Lindsay asked.

Robbie nodded. "A lot of farmers were. But now, Amelia doesn't have enough land. There's a minimum amount of acres you need for these large deals. Midwestern farmers like what they do. They like knowing they are feeding communities all over the world. Money isn't everything here. Becks and I were on board, but when it got voted down, we just shrugged and moved on."

Lindsay had always been driven by money. Money got her nice things. She understood Bob's greed, but after spending time with incredibly selfless people like Amelia, Becks, and Robbie, her vision was skewed. "Speaking of money, the GoFundMe is over two hundred thousand. I'm not sure Amelia has even seen it." The squeal that slipped out of Robbie's mouth scared Lindsay so hard that she jerked the wheel.

"Two hundred thousand? Thousand? Oh, my God. That's amazing. That's going to help her so much," Robbie said. She squeezed Lindsay's forearm with excitement. "I am so thankful you came out here to change Amelia's life. Having you here has been a blessing."

It was time to let Robbie know, too. "I'm so glad that this marketing plan worked. I think Amelia won't have to worry about money hopefully ever again." She looked at Robbie out of the corner of her eye to gauge her reaction. "And I got offered my dream job in Hollywood so I'm probably going to go back home soon." Robbie looked crushed. She started talking and stopped several times before she found words she could share. Lindsay was afraid she was going to lay into her, but she didn't and a part of her felt disappointed.

"I'm sorry to hear that you're going to be leaving. I kind of liked having you around," she said.

"I've really enjoyed the time I've spent with you and Becks."

"And what about Amelia? It seems like you got pretty close over the last month," Robbie said.

Lindsay took a moment to answer. She pulled into a parking spot at the small grocery store and put the car in park. "I think she's wonderful and I'm going to miss her, but we have two different lives." She could tell Robbie was holding back and trying to be respectful. A part of her wished Robbie would push harder, but she simply grabbed her bags and opened the car door.

"I'm thinking of making a watermelon gelato. And maybe something with lemons. Do you have a favorite lemon dessert? I know it's just the four of us, but I tend to over-bake when I'm stressed." Robbie grabbed a cart and pushed it over to the produce. Lindsay looked around to see if anyone was paying attention to them, but nobody approached them. There weren't a lot of people shopping. Lindsay didn't think she had it in her to be polite or explain anything to anybody. It wasn't their business anyway.

"I think most foods go well with a barbecue," Lindsay said. She grabbed a pack of boneless chicken breasts and her new favorite barbecue sauce. "Also, hats off to Missouri. This sauce is delicious. You might have to send me some after I run out."

Robbie held up her finger. "Or, hear me out, you can come back and get some. I can't imagine you aren't going to visit from time to time." She looked at Lindsay who quickly looked away and focused on a pork rub she wasn't going to buy but read the packaging like it was her job.

"I'm sure I will, too, but this new job will keep me busy for several months." Lindsay knew people didn't understand what went into running a successful television show. Farmers worked long hours, but so did producers and production assistants. Their job was seasonal just like farmers.

"Well, try not to be a stranger," Robbie said. She dropped a canister of baking powder in the cart. "We like having you around and you've been good for Amelia."

Her words hit Lindsay right in the chest. "I know I'll be back." She wasn't sure in what capacity, but she knew she couldn't walk away from Mizzou Moos or Amelia. Even if it was a trip here and there just to check in and maybe show Amelia and Zoey updates or new things that were always popping up on social media.

"I haven't seen Amelia this happy in a long time. No pressure, but I think you are perfect for each other. I should know because I'm with my soul mate," Robbie said.

Gah. Now that it would be only a matter of days before she left, she was trying to keep emotions at a controllable level. Robbie dropping powerful words wasn't helping. "You're very lucky. I adore both of you," Lindsay said.

"Are you ready? I don't like how Eloise Gardner is eyeing us. I don't think the word about Bob has spread yet so let's get out of here before she corners us." Robbie pointed at Lindsay. "And I know that you're too nice to push back. Let's go."

❖

It was almost midnight. Lindsay and Amelia were sitting in the dark, on the porch swing, looking up at the stars. The bullfrogs and cicadas were loud, but the noise didn't bother Lindsay anymore. It was peaceful out here. Amelia had her arm around Lindsay's shoulders and was absently twirling a strand of hair. Lindsay leaned into Amelia and rested her hand on Amelia's thigh.

"When are you leaving?" Amelia asked.

It was pointless to pretend the future wasn't going to happen and that she wasn't going to leave. The job was everything she wanted. The money and benefits were incredibly generous and they were willing to give her a creative license she didn't have at Meador Entertainment. Saying no would be career suicide.

"Saturday. I'll book my flight in the morning. I need at least a day to acclimate back into my California life." There was dry cleaning she had to pick up and a refrigerator she was scared to open. She was sure her plants were dead. She forgot to extend the housesitting service for the last two weeks so what she was going home to was going to be a surprise.

"I can't thank you enough for everything," Amelia said.

Lindsay looked at her. "I'm just so glad I could help. I wasn't sure if it was going to take off or not but I'm so thankful it did." Becks told Amelia where the GoFundMe was at during dinner tonight and everyone started crying. Even Lindsay who already knew the amount cried. Her tears were for more than just the money, but it was an appropriate time and she was able to cry for everything she was going to lose.

"I can't believe how much money we have. And the tours are full for the next three months. I won't have to worry about money for a long time," Amelia said.

"I can't believe I'm going to miss the mini cows," Lindsay said. Amelia had worked out transporting them to Mizzou Moos, but they were still in quarantine until next week.

"Be sure to check the socials. I promise to post lots of videos there," Amelia said. Lindsay elbowed her in the ribs and smirked at Amelia's grunt.

"You're going to have send me photos before any videos go live," Lindsay said. She felt Amelia's lips on the top of her head.

"You know I will. We should probably go to bed since Tater will want his breakfast at six a.m. sharp." Amelia stood and pulled Lindsay up and into her arms. They stood there for at least a minute holding one another. Saying goodbye was going to be hard.

Lindsay stifled a yawn. "The adrenaline rush of tonight finally left and I'm so tired."

"Let's go."

Lindsay stripped off her clothes and curled up naked next to Amelia in bed. They were both too tired for anything other than lying in one another's arms. Lindsay fell asleep before Amelia turned off the lights.

❖

A ringing phone made Lindsay jump up in bed and groggily look around. Where was she? She smacked the nightstand until her fingers found her phone. Simon Barkley was calling. What time was it? She rejected the call. It was nine thirty! Why did Amelia let her sleep so long? She jumped out of bed, threw on a T-shirt, and went to her room. She wasn't ready to have a conversation with Simon. That would make it final. Plus, she was still fuzzy from sleep. She grabbed a quick shower, checked her emails on her phone and after working up enough nerve, dialed Simon's number.

"Mr. Barkley, I'm sorry I missed your call earlier."

"Ms. Brooks, thank you for calling me back. We're excited to find out if you're ready to join our team."

Lindsay covered her face with her hand. This was the moment of truth. She couldn't hide out at Mizzou Moos anymore. It was time to go home. "I'm ready."

"That's great news. The start date is still Monday. I'll have all your credentials at the front desk. Joey Stillwater, my assistant, will meet you. Just call if you need anything. We're glad to have you on our team."

"I'm looking forward to it. I'll see you Monday," she said. She stared at her phone before shoving it in her back pocket. She needed to find Amelia. She jogged down the stairs and looked in the barn. Becks was busy cleaning water out of the troughs. "Have you seen Amelia?"

"She's fixing the chicken coop." Becks pointed behind her. "Tell her Robbie made her favorite sandwiches for lunch."

Lindsay waved. "Will do." She followed the path down to the chicken coop. Seeing Amelia working on the wire quietly chatting with the chicken tugged at her heart. She couldn't stop the tears from falling. She was leaving this little paradise and going back to her life. Amelia's expression went from happiness at seeing her to concern. Lindsay walked until Amelia's arms were around her. She sobbed when she felt the safety of Amelia's embrace. It was over. Lindsay had made her choice. A selfish, cruel choice that was going to impact the one person she never wanted to hurt in this world.

CHAPTER TWENTY-SEVEN

The minis are hella cute," Becks said.

"What?" Amelia turned when Becks elbowed her side.

"The new rescues. I thought it was going to take longer for them to warm up to us. Look at them. They're frolicking. Have you taken videos of them yet? I haven't seen anything posted on the socials lately," Becks said.

She hadn't posted anything new in almost three days. She told Zoey she was busy taking videos of the four minis, but she just needed to take a step back. Running the socials was emotional, but she knew she had to keep the momentum going. She sent uplifting messages and photos to Lindsay of the new moo crew, but sparingly. She didn't want to be a bother since Lindsay was starting a new job. At least that's the lie she told herself. It hurt to reach out. It hurt when Lindsay didn't respond immediately.

"Okay, how about we do a few videos before the tours start?"

"I love it! I promise to do a good job. I've seen enough of Lindsay's videos to know what angles work and what to capture," Becks said.

"Great. Watch your step." Amelia gave a soft whistle and waited. Three of the four minis jogged out from the barn curious at the noise. It was something she was working on with them. "Hello, girls. Where's Moodonna?" Moodonna was Amelia's favorite. She was white with soft, black hair around her ears and hooves. She had the longest lashes and was the most photogenic of the new rescues. "Moo Moo? Where are you?" A tiny snort came from inside the barn. Amelia peeked inside at the same time Moodonna was coming out and they ended up scaring one another. "There you are! Come on. We're going to introduce you to the internet today." She sat in the rustic chair she built for videos and waited until one of them came close. "Ready?" she asked Becks.

Becks gave her a thumbs up and Lindsay started talking to the camera. She introduced each mini and explained how they came to be at Mizzou Moos. The star was Moodonna who tried to climb into her lap during her introduction. Amelia threw back her head and laughed. Moodonna was the size of Wally. Her sharp hooves were painful, but somehow she made it on the chair with Amelia. "I'm going to have bruises after this, but look at how well these girls are adapting to their new home." She scratched Moodonna's chin and rubbed her ears.

"You won't have much editing to do. This is great," Becks said. She took still photos, too, and AirDropped them to Amelia.

Amelia laughed at Becks. "Look at her. How am I going to get her off my lap?"

"Looks like you have a new best friend. Okay, work on the video. Tours are starting soon. I'll see you down here for goat feeding." Becks walked away even though Amelia was still laughing for help.

"What am I going to do with you, Moo Moo? You're so adorable. Lindsay would fall in love with you." The moment she said Lindsay's name, a sadness washed over her. "Okay, ladies, I have to go now, but I'll be back after lunch." She groaned as Moodonna shifted to climb off her and pinched her thigh in the process. She rubbed her leg. "So many bruises."

She gave each mini a piece of apple before she left. She still accepted the grocery store throw outs, but now she could afford fresh fruit and vegetables. She closed out the GoFundMe since they had enough for two new barns. Amelia didn't want to appear greedy. The tip jar was still open and people were exceedingly generous. Amelia grabbed a water and sat at the laptop to work on the new video. Becks was right. The videos she took were good and Amelia's narrative informative. The new minis were going to be a hit. They were cuddlier than the Highlands and didn't have sharp horns. The video took her two hours to cut and splice and she was pleased with the result. It was foreign to see herself smile and laugh. She added a heartfelt caption with appropriate hashtags and uploaded it. She knew Lindsay would see it right away. If she wasn't buried with work. When her phone dinged she quickly pulled it out of her pocket, hoping it was Lindsay. She was slightly deflated. It was Zoey.

I love the new minis. Please tell them I'm sweet and to not attack me like Mimsey.

Amelia laughed. *I wonder what they will do when they meet you. It'll confuse them, I'm sure.* She waited a few seconds. *How's the movie. Aren't you done yet?*

Zoey sent laughing emojis. *I've only been on set two months. I'm hoping to be home at Christmas. Too bad you can't come for a visit.*

Tears sprang in Amelia's eyes. Being away from her sister this long was brutal. FaceTime was nice, but it was still hard. And with Lindsay gone, Amelia was lonely. *I know. But I'm nervous to leave the farm after everything that's happened.* When Amelia told Zoey about Bob, Zoey was ready to catch the next plane home. It took her, Becks, Robbie, and Sam to convince her to stay on set.

You have enough money to hire people to fill in for you. You know Becks won't let anything happen to the rescue. There are plenty of people who want to work there. You're not super woman.

Amelia scoffed. It was easier to stay busy to keep her mind off the pain she felt. She wasn't a stranger to loss, but she was tired of it. *I know and I will. The university reached out already for internships. Oh, get this. Full circle. Mary wants to know if I want to buy their land. Somehow she got out of that mess and is moving to Philadelphia to live with her sister.*

Zoey responded in all caps. *SHUT UP!* She followed up with several angry emojis. *Did you tell her to fuck the fuck right off?*

Amelia laughed out loud. *Except I want the land back now that I can afford it. Becks, Robbie, and I are working out a deal.* Before she could finish her text to Zoey, a message from Lindsay bannered across her phone.

You did a great job on the video. She dropped several heart emojis and a cow face.

Amelia's heart twirled in her chest. She waited fifteen seconds before answering. She didn't want to appear desperate. *Thanks. Becks figured it was time to get their sweet faces out there in the world.* She hit send and stared at her phone hating how much time she wasted waiting for a morsel of attention from Lindsay. They never established what their relationship was when Lindsay left. Deep down, Amelia knew long distance wasn't going to work. Best-case scenario they would be friends for as long as they both made the effort. Amelia always tried to be friends with her ex-girlfriends. It didn't make sense to hate them after sharing intimacy of being lovers.

Well, I'm impressed. How are renovations going? Do T and T love their new space?

Amelia was too excited to wait several seconds. *They're about to get a little brother. But, yes, they love it.* She almost dropped her phone when it buzzed with a call instead of alerting her to another text. She took a deep breath before answering. "Hi."

"You couldn't get these cute animals while I was still there? I'm sad," Lindsay said.

Amelia wanted to tell her that she would just have to visit, but that was a situation she didn't want to put Lindsay in. It wasn't fair. "I know and I'm sorry. They have to be quarantined before I can even bring them on the farm."

"Tell me about this new little brother," she said.

It was wonderful to hear Lindsay's voice again. Amelia stressed every time they talked on the phone, though, wondering if this was their last conversation. She tried not to obsess about it, but reality was a tough pill. "Snowball is a mini horse from Excelsior Springs which is about an hour and a half away. He's almost two years old and he needs to be rehomed because the little girl who wanted him didn't want to take care of him. Her parents reached out last weekend."

"That's terribly sad, but at least they're doing something about it. Have you met him? Is he nice?" Lindsay asked.

"I've only seen videos. He's spunky so I think he and Tot are going to be besties." Amelia was too nervous to sit. "How's the job? Are you loving it?" She wanted to hear that Lindsay hated it and was miserable, but that was a shitty thing to wish for somebody she loved.

"It's a lot of hard work, but they are giving me a lot of leeway and so far, they like my ideas," she said.

"I know a food show wasn't what you wanted, but are you warming up to it? Was it a good thing that we watched all those *Top Chef* episodes?" Amelia tried to sound lighthearted. Lindsay didn't need to know Amelia struggled daily without her.

"It's not my favorite genre, but all the things I'm learning are invaluable. What I've learned here in less than a month is more than I ever learned at Meador Entertainment. Working for a smaller company has perks I wasn't expecting," Lindsay said. Amelia checked out Barkley Swan and all the shows it produced. It was the fastest growing entertainment company in Hollywood. Lindsay was lucky to get in.

"That's great. How are the people? Are they nice?" Amelia knew Lindsay was worried about fitting in and if anyone knew about her hasty departure from Meador.

"I really like Sarah Dutton. She's taken me under her wing," Lindsay said. Amelia tried not to bristle because she wasn't the jealous type, but she saw Sarah's professional photo on their website and couldn't help but feel inferior. She was striking with a butterfly haircut and bright blue eyes. She had a power look that gave off strong boss vibes.

"Is she your direct boss?" Amelia asked.

"No. We all work directly for Simon. At least for now," Lindsay said.

"I like that concept better than the crap you dealt with at Meador," Amelia said. She didn't know why she kept talking about Lindsay's work, but anything to keep the conversation moving.

"You still have the best employees, hands down," Lindsay said.

"You're forgetting about how they don't listen to direction, they go to the bathroom wherever they want, they chew with their mouths open, and their hygiene is questionable." Amelia loved hearing Lindsay laugh. She missed how it made her stomach clench and brought a smile to her face.

"Ah, hell. They're calling for me. Please send me a photo of Snowball. And if you're thinking about it, maybe one of you, too. Your hair looks so light," Lindsay said.

"I know I need to do a better job of wearing hats. I've been out setting up for our Fall Festival that starts after Labor Day and runs until Halloween. But you need to go. I'll send pics but you have to promise to send me some, too." Amelia hated that their conversation was cut short, but it was a nice surprise that Lindsay called at all. "Go. Do all the things. Get your experience and knock 'em dead. Or whatever the production person says."

"You're adorable and I miss you so much," Lindsay said.

Amelia told herself to keep cool and not to cry. "I miss you, too. Try to get some sleep and take care of yourself." She disconnected the call with mixed emotions. She loved hearing from Lindsay, but it always sent her spiraling down a path of what-ifs.

She joined Becks at the goat feeding station and went through the motions like always but was getting weird looks from Becks. Amelia was terrible at hiding her emotions, especially from somebody who knew her well.

"Let me guess. You heard from Lindsay today," Becks said after the tour cleared. It was just them with dozens of empty bottles and pygmy goats with full bellies.

"I did. How'd you know?" Amelia asked.

Becks made a circle motion in front of Amelia's face with her forefinger. "It's written all over your face. When are you going to confess your undying love and win her back?"

Amelia pffted. "Yeah, right. And then have her hate me forever for keeping her from her dream job? No, thank you. I don't need that." The grand gesture scenario that was in every romantic movie and romance novel played out in her head several times several different ways, but it wasn't an option in the real world.

"That whole saying about setting something free and see if it comes back to you is dumb. Whoever came up with that was never in love," Becks said. She kicked a rock out of the pen.

"You're almost taking this harder than I am." Amelia was joking but Becks was clearly upset about Lindsay leaving, too.

"I hate seeing something so perfect fall apart because of a stupid job. People always talk about how on their deathbed they don't ever say how proud they are of their job. They talk about their loved ones and how they made all the difference."

Amelia held up her index finger. "First of all, no one's dying here. Secondly, it's only been like a month. And we don't even know if she loves me."

Becks scoffed. "Stop it. Y'all were so close that my marriage seemed boring compared to your little spicy relationship. And my marriage is far from boring."

Amelia's shoulders slumped. "Becks, I really don't want to be the one to keep somebody from their dreams. You know this. People fall in love all the time but can't make it work because of distance. I don't want to put that unnecessary stress on Lindsay. She has enough going on. Plus, we only spent like six weeks together. You can't give up everything after barely a month."

Becks put her hands on her hips. "Have you heard of lesbians before? And, to be fair, even some straights. But back to lesbians. We have the U-Haul joke for a reason. Because it's true."

"I'm sure Lindsay feels the same way about her job. I would never want to leave Mizzou Moos. This is my home, my heart, my job. These animals need help and I can help them. I will do this for as long as I can. I would never give this up. Not even for love." Amelia looked up so that the tears wouldn't fall.

Becks squeezed her hand. "You've sacrificed a lot in your life. I know it's rewarding, but I want you to find the perfect person who understands this about you and accepts you for who you are and all that you do. I still think that person is Lindsay. She knows it, she just hasn't realized it yet."

Chapter Twenty-eight

L indsay wasn't bored, she just wasn't feeling the success or gratification she thought she would at her new job. She was learning so much, but everything felt off. Simon praised her daily to the point where she felt uncomfortable when she saw him approaching. It was nice to be appreciated, but it was almost too much. How did they have such successful shows if people weren't doing at least bare minimum? Or maybe he praised everybody all the time. She wasn't used to it and didn't need that much affirmation.

"How's the budget?" Sarah asked. Upper management was having their weekly meeting about the shows currently in production. *Bake Off Battle* was just getting started. They were still vetting the contestants.

"We're under for at least the first episode," Lindsay said.

Everyone looked at her. "Really?" Sarah asked.

Panic fluttered in her chest. Was she wrong? Lindsay flipped to the budget folder on her tablet and quickly reviewed the spreadsheet hoping she hadn't missed anything. She scanned it twice while all eyes were focused on her. She looked up. "Really. Right now I show us twelve percent. Subject to change of course." She hit the ground running on her first day at Barkley Swan calling everyone she knew letting them know she was back in the business. People wanted to work with her, especially since Barkley Swan was the fastest growing entertainment company in Hollywood.

Simon smacked his palm on the table. "Excellent news." He turned to Joey. "Check my schedule. I want to get the writers together tomorrow and discuss future shows."

Lindsay couldn't help herself. "What kind of future shows?"

"Do you have some ideas? We'd love to hear them. Joey, make sure Lindsay's included in the meeting." He stood. "Are we done here?" Everyone nodded. "Good work, everyone."

He and Joey left immediately, but nobody else seemed to be in a hurry. Being a part of a team within a team was a different experience. Roger Pitts would never think of inviting her to a meeting about potential future shows. Well, maybe call her in to order them all lunch. She snorted to herself at how laughable working for him was.

"What's so funny?" Sarah asked.

"Oh, nothing. I was just thinking about my old boss and how ridiculous and sexist he was. Simon's tough but fair and I really like it here," Lindsay said. Getting back to a routine was hard after a month of making videos at random times, learning about animals, and keeping up with the ever-growing social media platforms. Her schedule was flexible at Mizzou Moos. And was it really a job? It was fun and flirty and she had an amazing time with an amazing woman. She refused payment when Amelia tried to compensate her once the money started rolling in. Taking it didn't feel right. She was there to help the cause, not pilfer from it.

"Simon's great. He poached me from Ace Productions. It sounds like you and I experienced the same bullshit at our old jobs," Sarah said.

"Even though we had a human resources department, the boss was untouchable. Do you know Roger Pitts?" Amelia asked. Sarah rolled her eyes and made a disapproving noise.

"He's terrible. I'm glad you're out of there. Meador's gone downhill in the last few years," Sarah said.

"It's too bad because they have pretty good shows. They just need a hard reset." Lindsay grabbed her bag and waved bye when Sarah answered her phone. Her office wasn't far from the conference room. The stark walls and boring gray furniture reminded her she needed to decorate. Maybe she could blow up some Mizzou Moos photos. No, that was too weird. Plus, she was trying to untangle herself from the Midwest. It was hard.

She knew she shouldn't call Amelia so much, but that video she posted tugged at her heartstrings so hard. Amelia was beautiful and carefree, and her love for the animals came through. That video already had hundreds of comments—some of which made Lindsay jealous—and thousands of likes. The world was watching Mizzou Moos and falling in love with Amelia and the animals just like she had. Shit. It was the first time she admitted to herself that she was in love with Amelia. Whenever that word tried to wiggle its way into her brain, she squashed it. When it tried to sneak into her heart, she quickly diverted it back out. She didn't have time to love or be loved. She thought being away from Amelia would make the feelings fade, not make her heart grow fonder.

She sat at her desk and pulled up Mizzou Moos's website and was surprised to see photos of the Moo Crew. Damn she missed that place. Amelia was doing a great job of journaling every few days keeping subscribers and visitors up to date on the happenings at the farm. She was so proud of her. She grabbed her phone to send her a congratulatory text message and stopped. No, she had work to do and knew that Amelia was busy finishing up the final tour of the day. Lindsay put her phone down and checked her emails instead. Work was always the answer when her heart hurt or when she couldn't stop thinking of Amelia.

"How late are you staying?" Sarah popped her head into Lindsay's office at the end of the day.

Lindsay looked at her watch surprised to see it was almost seven. She stood and turned off her monitor. "Leaving now."

"Great. We can walk out together. Some of us are going to Cashmere bar if you're interested," she said.

"Thanks for the offer, but I have a bunch of paperwork to do. And thanks for waiting for me." Lindsay didn't like to be alone in the office late at night.

"No problem. The garage can be a little creepy. I know it's safe, but still. You can never be too careful," Sarah said.

"Tell me something. Have you ever pitched an idea to Simon?" Lindsay asked. She fell into step beside Sarah after adjusting her bag over her shoulder.

"All the time. He's very open but the pitch has to be stellar because we don't have a lot of free money to throw at it," Sarah said. She hit the button to go down to the garage. "Why? Do you have something?"

"Not yet, but maybe. I don't want him or you to think I don't like working on the show because I do. I'm just appreciative that he's willing to listen to ideas." Lindsay learned a long time ago not to share her ideas unless it was in front of the person who could make it happen. It wasn't that she didn't trust Sarah. She didn't trust anybody.

"Well, don't work too hard tonight," Sarah said. She slipped into her sleek Mercedes sedan and waved as she drove by. Lindsay shoved her bag into the passenger seat and sat behind the wheel for a solid minute before she turned the ignition. She had several ideas for shows but did any of them fit Barkley Swan's image?

The morning came sooner than Lindsay wanted. Her eyes felt scratchy from lack of sleep and there was only so much makeup she could wear to hide the dark circles under her eyes. She was crabby, spilled her coffee all over the passenger seat of her car, and barely made it to work on time. Everyone at Barkley Swan looked refreshed sitting around the large conference room table. Maybe today wasn't the day to share her idea. The pitches were mostly boring and only a few got Simon's attention to where he asked more questions. She pulled out her phone and saw Amelia had posted another video of the Moo Crew. How many videos did they have now? She scrolled through their page and smiled at how many there were. The two pinned videos had millions of views. Lindsay sat up straight and caught Simon's eye.

"Lindsay. It looks like you have something to say or something to pitch."

She smiled. "It's another reality show, and I think you're going to love it."

❖

Lindsay knew it wasn't fair to show up unannounced, but she wanted to surprise Amelia. She called Becks to get the code to the new reinforced gate, promising to call her later and tell her everything. She drove slowly up the driveway and parked in front of the house. Wally met her at the car wiggling his butt with happiness and licked her hand several times. She climbed out of the car and patted his head affectionately.

"Where's your mommy, big boy? Huh? Where is she? Go find her. Show me where she is." As though he understood, he trotted off toward the small barn. Lindsay took a deep breath and took in the sights. Oh, how she missed this place. She closed the car door and followed Wally. She smiled when she heard Amelia greet Wally.

"You're in a good mood tonight, buddy." Amelia gave him a slice of apple.

Lindsay could watch Amelia all day every day just be herself. She wanted to pull up a chair and watch her, but she also couldn't wait to touch her again. "He's not the only one in a good mood."

Amelia whirled around and stared at Lindsay. Her face was stoic and for a fraction of a second, Lindsay thought she'd made a mistake, but the smile that blossomed on Amelia's face almost made her heart explode. This was exactly where she needed to be. And Amelia's reaction told her she did the right thing. She finally let love in. She didn't toss it aside or tamp it down. She embraced it.

"Oh, my God. What? Why? I mean, hi." Amelia stumbled over the gate and raced to Lindsay, pulling her into a tight hug. She released her only to kiss her passionately. Lindsay couldn't get close enough. She threw her arms around Amelia's neck and moaned at how wonderful this moment was. The warm body in her arms, the full lips against hers, and the reciprocation of what she knew in her heart was true love. She didn't know if she wanted to cry or laugh or fall to the floor and do both.

"I love you," Lindsay said. Three little words that packed the biggest punch in the English language and Lindsay didn't think they were good enough for what she was feeling.

"I love you, too. I have since Vegas." Amelia looked deep into her eyes and kissed her softly. "I know that sounds ridiculous but it's true."

"I've been lying to myself. I hated that I left you. That I didn't say anything back when I should have. I was just scared and stupid, really. I've never felt this way before and I handled it poorly. Will you forgive me?" Lindsay asked.

"Are you kidding me right now? One hundred percent forgiven." Amelia touched Lindsay's face as though she couldn't believe it was her. She stroked her hair and touched her neck and kissed her again. "Are you really here? And for how long?"

Lindsay laughed. "I'm really here and for how long depends on you."

"Forever. Or for however long you need or want to," Amelia said.

"I have something I want to talk to you about. Can we go inside?" Lindsay asked.

"Uh-oh. It must be serious if you want to walk away from all this cuteness without wanting a proper introduction." Amelia pointed at the mini cows who stared at Lindsay curiously.

Lindsay sensed Amelia's nervousness. "It's not serious. It's all good but I want to give you all my attention first and then I want to love on these babies after. Deal?"

Amelia grabbed her hand. "Let's go to the house. Are you hungry? Thirsty? Can I get you anything at all?"

Lindsay leaned into Amelia when she felt Amelia's arm around her shoulders. She missed feeling this safe and loved. "I just need you."

"You got me. Without a doubt," Amelia said.

SCANDALOUS

Lindsay opened the door and stopped when she stood in the middle of the kitchen. She was flooded with the most comforting memories. This felt like home. She turned and pulled Amelia into her arms. "So, I'm here for both personal and professional reasons."

Amelia quirked her brow and frowned. "Am I doing a terrible job on social media? Because I can try harder."

Lindsay put her finger on Amelia's lips. "No, love, you're doing an amazing job. Part of what I do is pitch ideas to my company, and a few weeks ago we were bouncing around ideas. So, I pitched the idea of have a Saturday morning reality show about Mizzou Moos where people learn about this wonderful place and about each animal. You can teach them how big of a responsibility it is and mistakes people make and how to fix them. I just feel like this would be a great opportunity."

Amelia's eyes widened. "They said yes to your idea? So, we'd have a film crew here all the time?"

"Just on certain days. And honestly, we can film several thirty-minute episodes in a condensed time frame. That way we aren't interfering in the tours and we would be staying out of everybody's way." Lindsay could tell Amelia was warming up to the idea. "Here's the kicker. They are willing to pay you fifteen thousand per episode. I pitched six episodes to start off with and if it takes off, great. And if it doesn't, then you'll still be richer and a lot of people will know more about this wonderful place."

"What happens if it doesn't take off? Do you go back, too?" Amelia asked.

Lindsay knew this would come up and she knew her answer before Amelia asked the question. "My place is here with you. I learned that the hard way. I don't want to leave. I like my job, but I love you and I just know that I can have both here. Simon says I can work on development from anywhere, even here. And if it doesn't work, then I can still run the socials."

Amelia covered her face with her hands and started crying. Lindsay rubbed her back and kissed her temple. "Don't cry, babe.

I'm sorry I hurt you, but I plan on making it up to you. And to Tater and Tot and Pippin and Patches and all the animals."

Amelia sniffled and brushed her tears away. "I can't believe this. I'm so freaking happy. These are happy tears. I can't wait to tell everyone that you're back." Amelia stopped. "Wait. So, I'm going to be on television, too?" She laughed. "I can't wait to tell Zoey. She's going to flip."

"Send her a message and see if she can FaceTime," Lindsay said.

Amelia did and in less than five minutes, Zoey called. "Why are you crying? What's going on?" Amelia handed the phone to Lindsay. She waved.

"I'm back."

Zoey squealed. "You're back? For good?"

Lindsay nodded. "And we have news."

Amelia tilted the phone back to her. "Guess who's getting their own television show? I mean it's not like a blockbuster movie, but it's something that's going to generate enough money to keep Mizzou Moos going for a long time." They gave Zoey a quick rundown of the show's concept and how Amelia was going to be in front of the camera most of the time. The narration was still up in the air.

"Look at us. Twinning in life. Mom and Dad would be so proud of you," Zoey said. "And welcome to the family, Lindsay."

"I feel like they are super proud of both of us." She kissed Lindsay. "Our story is certainly an interesting one."

"Just think, if it wasn't for a tiny, little scandal, none of this would've happened. You can thank me for that," Zoey said.

Amelia grunted. "Yeah, no more scandals, no more trading places."

"Congratulations, sis. I have to go, but this is amazing news." Zoey ended the call and Amelia sat there holding the phone.

"I can't believe this," Amelia said again.

"It's really happening. Now that you know why I'm here, I think it's time you introduce me to the rest of your family," Lindsay said.

"They're going to love you," Amelia said.

Lindsay kissed her. The kiss started off softly but turned into an inferno within seconds. They broke apart gasping for air. Lindsay was tempted to pull Amelia upstairs into the bedroom and make up for lost time, but she knew it was important to Amelia that she meet the new babies. They held hands as they walked over to the new corral and lean-to shed Amelia built between the large elm trees.

Lindsay laughed delightedly at the mini horse who was half the size of Tater but stomping around like he owned the place. "Are you going to stick with the name Snowball? It doesn't fit him." Lindsay reached out to rub his soft muzzle and was surprised that he let her. "He's so tiny."

"He's keeping these guys on their toes. Come on. I want you to meet the real diva of this place." Amelia lowered her voice. "She might be my favorite."

"Moodonna? I loved the video you posted. Honestly, that was the video that made me face my feelings for you. You looked so beautiful and happy," Lindsay said.

"Then she's my favorite for sure if it brought you back to me," Amelia said.

"I love you," Lindsay said. A peace settled over her after finally telling Amelia her feelings. Love. It was new, exciting, scary, but she was ready to face it, hand-in-hand, hearts entwined, with the woman who made her feel it for the first time.

EPILOGUE

Amelia checked Zoey's location on her phone. She was east of town and would be pulling into Mizzou Moos's parking lot in five minutes. It was hard not to want to race down to the end of the driveway and wait for her there. Instead, Amelia stared out the window and waited for Zoey's rental car to pull up in front of the house.

"Would you like another cup of coffee while you not so anxiously wait?" Lindsay asked.

Amelia turned and smiled at Lindsay. "I'm good for now. Thanks, love." Lindsay showed up four months ago to record a six-episode feature on Mizzou Moos and never left. Amelia didn't want her to. Thankfully, Barkley Swan stuck to their agreement of allowing Lindsay to work remotely as long as she continued to pitch viable programs.

"The next few weeks are going to be bonkers," Lindsay said.

"In the best possible way. I hope the show is a hit," Amelia said. The rescue was the hottest farm on social media. They had millions of followers and enough money to grow, but Amelia was being overcautious. Mizzou Moos grew another fifty acres when she and Becks purchased the Teeters' farm. They divided the plot into four sections, each keeping one part and selling off the remaining half.

"The commercials and people emailing Barkley about the upcoming show seem very positive. You did such an amazing job. Even Simon agreed and he fought me the hardest," Lindsay said.

Amelia felt her cheeks flush with embarrassment. "Stop. That was hard for me to do."

Lindsay closed the space between them and wrapped her arms around Amelia's neck. "You are a natural at explaining how difficult and rewarding it is rescuing animals. Most people don't realize the mental care. These animals have to trust again, or for the first time, and you have the most patience. I'm so proud of you."

Amelia dropped a small kiss on Lindsay's mouth. "All of this is because of you. Had you not come here to show us the potential, Mizzou Moos wouldn't have survived."

Lindsay put her forefinger on Amelia's lips. "You and Zoey would've come up with something. You are too passionate about this place to let it go."

"I do love these little creatures. I hope the show boosts awareness and people don't rush out and buy mini cows or mini donkeys just because they are so cute," Amelia said. She just got back from Alabama with another teacup cow that somebody got bored with and had tied it up in their yard. It took a lot to get him into the trailer and out once they arrived back at the farm. Momo was finally starting to come out of the small barn she designed specifically for animals that needed rehabilitation in a safe, smaller space.

Lindsay pointed outside. "I think somebody is coming up the driveway. Go say hi. I know you miss her. I have an email I need to send and then I'll be out."

Production on *Meet Mizzou Moos* had wrapped up in October and was set to launch the first of the year. Lindsay was working remotely on two other educational programs not related to Mizzou Moos. Even though she had to fly back to Los Angeles once a month, Lindsay assured Amelia she was okay with the travel.

Amelia squealed and kissed Lindsay quickly before bounding down the steps to greet her sister. She opened her arms and crushed Zoey in her embrace. "I'm so happy you're home."

"It's so good to be back," Zoey said. She turned around and pointed out all the new things. "The big barn looks amazing. Everything does. So much has happened around here."

"Now all the barns have sprinkler systems. And all the animals have chutes that will take them outside if the fire alarm triggers. We did some massive upgrades. I can't wait to show you," Amelia said.

"I want to meet Momo and the other teacups. Every time I think one animal is going to be the star, a new one pops up and I fall in love all over again," Zoey said.

"You and everyone else, thank goodness," Amelia said. She grabbed Zoey's bags and followed her into the house.

"You're home!" Lindsay hugged Zoey affectionately.

"It's so good to be back. So much has changed since the summer," Zoey said.

"I know! We even built an addition onto the store. The merch is flying off the shelves," Lindsay said. She patted Amelia's arm softly. "Why don't you show Zoey all the changes. I have work to do. We can get caught up tonight."

"You're the best, babe," Amelia said. She grabbed coats and hats from the mudroom and handed one of each to Zoey. "We're in the middle of a cold snap. And I have a lot to show you so you're going to be walking."

Zoey tugged the cap on her head and slipped on the charcoal puffer coat that hit at her knees. It took her a second to realize they were wearing the exact same thing. "Are we shooting a video?" she asked.

Amelia laughed. "I didn't even think of that, but I guess we could if you're up for it."

She wasn't afraid of being in front of the cameras anymore. Shooting a television show for the last several months made her more comfortable with all eyes on her. She didn't want to be a star like her sister but didn't mind educating the world about Mizzou Moos. Posting videos was easier and the animals were fine with a camera crew around. Amelia swore they knew when a camera was on them. They either acted exactly how she wanted them to or did the exact opposite. Either way, the results were hilarious.

Zoey rested her head on Amelia's shoulder. "I'm so proud of you. Less than a year ago, you were struggling to keep this place afloat and now look at it. Our animals have the best of everything. And you have two full-time employees besides Becks and Robbie. That means you'll be able to take vacations longer than a few days. I'm still sad you didn't come to South America."

"I know but there were too many people here rebuilding and the animals were skittish with all the banging and sawing. I needed to be here," Amelia said.

"Well, maybe you can find a long weekend to visit me in Colorado this spring," Zoey said. The light, teasing lilt in her voice made Amelia pause.

"Why? What's happening this spring?" she asked.

Zoey shrugged. "Oh, just a little movie I'm shooting."

Amelia playfully pushed her sister. "Shut up. Why didn't tell me sooner? What is it?"

"It's a romantic comedy and I'm playing the lead character, Maven Reeves, who goes back home after a failed marriage and falls back in love with her high school sweetheart," Zoey said.

"That's sounds more like a Hallmark movie."

"Except the high school sweetheart is Zeller Erikson." She mimicked dropping the mic and turned to face her. "And it's being produced by a massive studio."

Amelia's jaw dropped. "That's incredible! Zeller's the kid from the football movie, right? How old is he?"

"He's twenty-nine." Zoey showed Amelia his TikTok account. "And he is in the top ten list of most followers."

"How does Alec feel about this?" Amelia asked. Even though their relationship was still private, Amelia knew they were dating and couldn't be happier for her sister.

"About the same way I feel about him making out with co-stars. It's hard, but it's the nature of the business."

Amelia was always going to worry about her sister, but she liked the way Alec treated her. "Speaking of Alec, is he still coming after Christmas?"

"He'll be here. He's been wanting to visit Mizzou Moos ever since this summer."

Amelia laughed. "I can't wait to see Eloise's face when she runs into him in town. It'll be priceless. I mean, that's if you want people to know he's here."

"I'm sure it'll come out. We know how people can't resist juicy gossip," Zoey said. The look she gave Amelia made them both double over with laughter.

"Gossip worked out for us. Mizzou Moos is thriving all because a few people couldn't wait to rat us out," Amelia said. She threw her arm around Zoey's shoulders. "Although it could've gone either way."

"I'm happy this is best-case scenario. The rescue is doing well, Lindsay moved in with you, and you have a lot of money socked away for growth," Zoey said.

Amelia shook her head slowly. "I still can't believe it. Everything I ever dreamed of is coming true. We're not struggling, you just finished filming a blockbuster and got your first lead, and we're both with people who love and respect us."

"Mom and Dad would be so proud of you," Zoey said. She had been saying that a lot lately to Amelia.

Amelia always corrected her. "Of us. Proud of us. I wish they could see us now."

"I'm sure they're watching us at this very moment," Zoey said.

"I miss them so much," Amelia said. She pulled her sister closer. Life didn't turn out the way their family expected. Tragedy struck twice. Seven months ago, she had no idea if the rescue would survive, but thanks to a what she now considered a small indiscretion, she was able to save the rescue. She met the love of her life, Lindsay, and her sister's career was booming. Their paths had changed, but the outcome was still the same. "Are you happy?"

"I don't like being away from you and Mizzou Moos for long stretches, but I'm happy. I love my job and Alec and I have something special. What about you?"

Amelia nodded. "I'm happy, but I miss you."

"Now you can come see me on sets. You have four employees who can fill in for you when you want to get away. You have the top-of-the-line security system and the animals love Becks and Robbie. Plus, you and Lindsay need to get away so you can celebrate you."

"I think that if we go somewhere, she's going to be suspicious. It's best that I just do it here." Amelia heard her own nervousness and felt Zoey's hand squeeze hers.

"It's too bad the animals are unpredictable or somehow they could help," Zoey said.

Amelia fished in her pocket until she found their mother's simple round cut solitaire diamond engagement ring. It was an heirloom and simple enough that she knew Lindsay would like it. Zoey insisted Amelia keep it for when she got engaged. "Do you think she'll like it? It's not big or flashy."

"If she doesn't like it, you can wear it. But she knows how important Mom was to us. I'm sure she would feel honored," Zoey said.

Amelia slipped the diamond back in her pocket and patted her fingers on her thigh to feel it through the denim. "I think so, too."

"When are you thinking of popping the question? Soon, I hope soon since you just happen to have it in your pocket." Zoey ducked hoping her words didn't carry into the house from where they were standing.

Amelia whispered, "When the time is right. Maybe we'll go for a walk tonight. The winds are supposed to die down so a winter night walk under the moon sounds romantic." Amelia's brain had been working overtime trying to figure out the right time and place.

She even tried to figure out a way one of the animals could help but feared something would go awry and they would accidentally eat it. A quiet walk sounded better.

"Whatever you do, don't do it in front of a bunch of people. Like at Christmas," Zoey said.

It was only going to be the five of them, but Zoey was right. "I would never do that. I'm too nervous already."

"If you need help, let me know," Zoey said. She grabbed Amelia's arm. "Oh, maybe we could do a twin thing."

Amelia shut her down quick. "No. That's what got us into trouble in the first place with Lindsay."

Zoey laughed. "But were you really in trouble? I'm pretty sure that ended up being the best thing ever."

"You're not wrong, but no more twinning." Amelia thought about another barn loft date, but it was too predictable. She wanted to do something special and smiled when an idea popped into her mind. "I'm thinking about the first time we kissed."

Zoey frowned. "You want to take her to Vegas? That's gross." She scowled at Amelia.

"No. She thought she was kissing you. I mean me. When she knew she was kissing me. I'm going to take her to bale of hay out in the pasture and propose to her under the Missouri night sky. I'll have to do it on a clear night. The stars have to be out and twinkling and some even shooting."

"Small ask." Zoey rolled her eyes.

"There are a few good things about winters in Missouri. Fun snow, beautiful sunrises, and clear, crisp nights," Amelia said.

Zoey clapped her hands. "I can help set it up. I can put a blanket down and have a bottle of wine and some glasses nearby. Or a thermos of hot chocolate and have a small fire pit ready to go. I don't think you should have it lit because then she would be suspicious," Zoey said.

"If she sees anything out of the ordinary, she's going to know something is up." Amelia's palms started sweating even though she was wearing gloves and it was a not so balmy twenty-eight degrees. "I could probably get away with the blanket on the hay bale because that's just something we do now. She won't be suspicious then."

"Done. If it's not cloudy tonight, I'll slip out and get things set up. Trust me," Zoey said.

Amelia side-eyed her. "Mm-hm. Sure."

Zoey bumped her shoulder. "No, seriously. You're only going to do this once and I want it to be perfect and a complete surprise. I'll hide things if I have to."

Amelia took a deep breath. "Okay. Let's see what happens tonight. Meanwhile, you should meet the new family members. You're going to love Moodonna."

It was the perfect night. Thousands of stars twinkled overhead. She held Lindsay's hand as they strolled along the footpath to the pasture.

"I can't believe you talked me into a night walk, but also, I'll never get tired of how many stars we can see out here," Lindsay said.

Amelia told herself over and over again to be calm, say boring things, and pretend this was any other night. That this wasn't the night that was going to change her life. "The four seasons are real out here, but I'm happy you haven't complained about anything. Of course, you haven't met a Missouri February yet." She pulled Lindsay close and kissed her softly before continuing their trek to the hay bale. "We'll talk again then. They're terrible. Brace yourself."

"I'm not scared," Lindsay said.

Her voice held conviction that Amelia knew would be challenged in six weeks. "Good because I'd hate to lose you during the cold months. I need your warm body beside me."

"You're the one who runs hot. I'll need you more than you'll need me," Lindsay said.

"We'll both need each other." Amelia liked their cute, nonsensical arguments and what-ifs.

By the time they reached the hay bale, Amelia was mush. She'd overthought the evening so every part of her was exhausted. A surge of adrenaline flamed through her body when she saw the blanket on top spread out and ready for them.

"Oh, what's this? Did you make this?" Lindsay pointed at a circle of large rocks about two feet wide and a foot tall. Amelia waved her off.

"Zoey did that. She was worried we'd get cold on our night walks and made this. Honestly, I think she did it for when Alec gets here." Amelia clamped her teeth together to keep them from chattering. She climbed up the hay bale, unfolded one of the two blankets Zoey left for them and used it as a cushion. She helped Lindsay up the side of the hay bale and used the other blanket to cover them.

"Is it okay that I don't want a fire? I'm still a little nervous, especially after what happened with the barn," Lindsay said.

Amelia tucked the blanket around them. "I totally get it. We'll leave the pit to Zoey and Alec." She breathed a sigh of relief that Lindsay hadn't caught on. She lay back and tucked her arm under her head for a cushion and looked up at the stars with Lindsay.

"Will we see any shooting stars?" Lindsay asked. She scooted closer and put her head on Amelia's shoulder. "I know we see more in the summer, but I kind of hope we see some so we can make a wish again." She leaned up on one elbow and looked at Amelia. "I remember what happened the first time you brought me here. I made a wish."

"I did, too, and my wish came true," Amelia said. She could stare at Lindsay for hours.

"Oh, look! Our first one of the night." Lindsay pointed off in the distance to a meteor that streaked along the horizon for a few seconds. "I guess we need to look more in that direction because of the time of year."

"Good point." Amelia propped up on her elbows so she could see the same thing Lindsay saw.

Lindsay pointed again. "Another one. Wait, is there a shower tonight? Huh. Usually, I'm better at knowing when they're coming. My Meteor Tracker app didn't tell me about any."

"Maybe it's an alien."

Lindsay playfully kicked Amelia's shoe. "Don't say that. You're going to creep me out because this is the perfect place for that very thing to happen. Middle America. Cow pasture. Late at night." She shivered and scooched closer.

"Don't worry. I know all the hiding places around here." Amelia laughed. Lindsay had more of an imagination than Zoey.

"Oh, look. What's that bright thing?" Lindsay asked.

Amelia looked in the direction Lindsay was pointing. "Where? I don't see it."

"Follow my finger," she said.

Amelia moved her gaze to Lindsay's delicate hand and followed her pointer finger. At the end was a bright, shiny object that wasn't moving in the sky. She couldn't process what she was seeing until Lindsay moved her hand closer and held the ring between their bodies.

"I wanted to do this before life got hectic before the holidays." Lindsay cleared her throat and looked into Amelia's eyes. "I love you. I love who you are, what you do for Mizzou Moos. I love how big your heart is and how much you've sacrificed for everyone else's happiness. You, Amelia Roberts, are one hell of a person. You've shown me unconditional love and I can't imagine the rest of my life without you."

Tears sprang to Amelia's eyes. What was happening right now? Did she find out that Amelia was going to propose? "Lindsay."

"No, wait. I need to finish," she said with conviction.

"Hold that thought, love." Amelia reached into her pocket and pulled out her mother's ring. Lindsay covered her mouth in surprise. "You've shown me unconditional love and I can't imagine the rest of my life without you."

"Are you kidding me right now? Did we both come up with the perfect proposal on the perfect night?" Lindsay asked.

Amelia pulled Lindsay close and held her face with her hands. "I'm so lucky. Of course, I will marry you. It would be my honor." She slipped the ring on Lindsay's finger. "This was my mother's ring. If you want a different setting, we can have it modified to whatever you like."

Lindsay held up her hand. "It's beautiful, Amelia. I'd love to wear her ring. I love you. Yes, I'll marry you."

Amelia's hand shook when Lindsay put a beautiful princess cut diamond on her ring finger. "I love it." She pulled Lindsay close and kissed her soundly. She would never get tired of Lindsay's lips, how sweet she tasted, and how perfect she felt in her arms. Life took a tragic turn years ago, one she and Zoey weren't prepared for, but something beautiful and pure came from that twist of fate. True love.

About the Author

Multi-award winning author Kris Bryant was born in Tacoma, WA, but has lived all over the world and now considers Kansas City her home. She received her BA in English from the University of Missouri and spends a lot of her time buried in books. She enjoys kayaking, photography, football (not soccer), and spending time with her family and friends.

Her first novel, *Jolt*, was a Lambda Literary Award Finalist. *Forget-Me-Not* was selected by the American Library Association's 2018 Over the Rainbow book list and was a Golden Crown Finalist for Contemporary Romance. *Breakthrough* won a 2019 Goldie for Contemporary Romance, *Listen* won a 2020 Goldie for Contemporary Romance, and *Temptation* won a 2021 Goldie for Contemporary Romance. *Catch* was a Lambda Literary Award Finalist and *Cherish* won a 2024 Goldie for Contemporary Romance.

Books Available from Bold Strokes Books

Chasing Her Scent by MJ Williamz. When Sheridan Rousseau walks into Lisette Mouton's charming little bookstore in Quebec City, she unknowingly holds the key to a mysterious box hidden in a secret room. (978-1-63679-900-1)

Heart's Run by D. Jackson Leigh. Hoping to recover an escaped racing mare, stock transporter Tobie Mason locks horns with local wild horse advocate Maggie Wilkes. (978-1-63679-825-7)

Scandalous by Kris Bryant. When a Hollywood actress trades places with her twin sister, everyone's in an uproar about getting duped, but Lindsay's more concerned about finding out which twin she made out with. (978-1-63679-874-5)

The Art of Love by Ali Vali. When Mimi and Bianca both set their sights on Jolly, sparks fly, loyalties are tested, and hearts collide as they navigate the unpredictable nature of their hearts (978-1-63679-719-9)

The Other Side of Forever by Kel McCord. Will Kenzie and Rachel be able to make love work when Rachel's cozy suburban dream feels like Kenzie's worst nightmare? (978-1-63679-812-7)

The Secrets of Rhydian Hill by Ronica Black. A doctor in need of a new start. A woman running from a killer. A love story that could end in tragedy. (978-1-63679-880-6)

Feeling Lucky by Krystina Rivers. What happens when, despite suddenly having enough money to buy almost anything, Lucy and Tanner start to discover that maybe all they need is each other? (978-1-63679-876-9)

Iceberg by Gun Brooke. When Lady Arabella hires Zandra, she never expects to find love, especially not as a disaster looms on the horizon. (978-1-63679-908-7)

It Happened One Semester by Aurora Rey. After a Pride night hookup, can eager new Assistant Professor Hudson Greene and Dean of Advising Callie Shaw overcome the odds and ace falling in love? (978-1-63679-814-1)

It's Kind of a Bad Idea by Sarah G. Levine. What happens when an emotionally unavailable serial dater meets the one woman she can't help but fall for—who happens to be the one woman who told her not to? (978-1-63679-920-9)

Thankful for You by Tagan Shepard. Everyone deserves to find their person, maybe Karen has finally found hers? (978-1-63679-884-4)

What Happens on Location by Nan Campbell. How can Helen produce a successful movie when its director is the woman responsible for the demise of her marriage? (978-1-63679-904-9)

When Love Comes Around by Radclyffe and Ronica Black. Can Maya Sanchez and Nolan Wright trust each other enough to build something real, or will the past tear them apart? (978-1-63679-930-8)

Anywhere with You by Margo Glynn. On a road trip through the Great American Southwest, two friends discover nature, hope, and each other. (978-1-63679-907-0)

Burning Bridges by Lesley Davis. Can Clancy and Jude crack the case of eight missing women—and the secrets of their own hearts? (978-1-63679-872-1)

Dreams Entangled by Sophia Kell Hagin. Amid self-doubt, secrets, a pandemic, fear of attack and attempted murder, Pirin and Gracie's attraction turns to love and their lives will never be the same. (978-1-63679-892-9)

Echoes of Love by Catherine Lane. As Hazel's and Jo's paths intertwine, they're swept up in a whirlwind of long-buried secrets, sizzling chemistry, and memories that won't be denied. (978-1-63679-835-6)

Moonlight Obsession by Sheri Lewis Wohl. All it takes to stop a clever killer is moonlight, love, and a silver bullet. (978-1-63679-831-8)

My Boyfriend's Wife by Joy Argento. Amid betrayal and heartbreak, can two women discover a love that could heal their pasts and rewrite their futures? (978-1-63679-866-0)

Tapout by Nicole Disney. A struggling MMA fighter finds her edge in an underground ring, but as she falls for the magnetic and ambitious promoter behind the matches, their dangerous world threatens to destroy everything they've fought to rebuild. (978-1-63679-924-7)

The Fame Game by Ronica Black. Wild child Hollywood actress Luna Kirkman begins dating Hollywood's leading man, only to fall for his straitlaced sister instead. (978-1-63679-858-5)

An Extraordinary Passion by Kit Meredith. An autistic podcaster must decide whether to take a chance on her polyamorous guest and indulge their shared passion, despite her history. (978-1-63679-679-6)

That's Amore! by Georgia Beers. The romantic city of Rome should inspire Lily's passion for writing, if she can look away from Marina Troiani, her witty, smart, and unassumingly beautiful Italian tour guide. (978-1-63679-841-7)

The Unexpected Heiress by Cassidy Crane. When a cynical opportunist meets a shy but spirited heiress, the last thing she plans is for her heart to get involved. (978-1-63679-833-2)

Through Sky and Stars by Tessa Croft. Can Val and Nicole's love cross space and time to change the fate of humanity? (978-1-63679-862-2)

Uncomplicate It by Kel McCord. When an office attraction threatens her career, Hollis Reed's carefully laid plans demand revision. (978-1-63679-864-6)

Vanguard by Gun Brooke. Beth Wild, Subterranean freedom fighter, is in the crosshairs when she fights for her people and risks her heart for loving the exacting Celestial dissident leader, LaSierra Delmonte. (978-1-63679-818-9)

Wild Night Rising by Barbara Ann Wright. Riding Harleys instead of horses, the Wild Hunt of myth is once again unleashed upon the world. Their ousted leader and a fey cop must join forces to rein in the ride of terror. (978-1-63679-749-6)